A PATCHWORK HEART

Also by Elinor Kapp

Tales from Turnaround Cottage:
Fairy Stories for the Older Generation
Diadem Books, 2017
ISBN 978-0-2446253-1-3

Rigmaroles and Ragamuffins,
words we derive from Textiles.
Published by Elinor Kapp, Cardiff UK.
Distributed by Oxbow books, 10, Hythe Bridge Street, Oxford,
CX1 2EW
and Casemate Academic, PO Box 511, Oakvile CT 06779 Utah,
US
ISBN 978-0-9574759-0-8 paperback
ISBN 978-0-9574759-1-5 epub

Ruffians and Loose Women.
More words derived from Textiles.
Published by Elinor Kapp 2016.
Distributed by Oxbow books, 10, Hythe Bridge Street, Oxford,
CX1 2EW
and Casemate Academic, PO Box 511, Oakvile CT 06779 Utah,
USA
ISBN 978-0-9574759-2-2 paperback
ISBN 978-0-9574759-3-9 epub

A PATCHWORK HEART

Some memories from my Life

by

Elinor Kapp

DIADEM BOOKS

A Patchwork Heart
Copyright © 2022 **Elinor Kapp**

Published by Diadem Books
www.diadembooks.com

ISBN: 9798442259575

*These memoirs are dedicated to
my very much-loved family,
in particular to my children
and their own families,
with my love and blessing:*

*Amanda Foster BA
Rupert Rawnsley PhD
and also to the memory of their father,
Kenneth Rawnsley CBE.*

INTRODUCTION

WHERE DO YOU START when you make a patchwork quilt? How do you try to patch up a failing heart? And why should you want to do either? We're not talking about buying lots of expensive fabric in wonderful colours to make an art quilt, though there is nothing wrong with doing that. We're talking about a traditional quilt, collecting old clothes and rags, cutting up every piece you can lay your hands on, and piecing them together. Let's call that a Heart Quilt.

You can add bits and pieces from friends and lovers, strangers and enemies, pieces found in a cupboard or in a gutter, fabrics kept greedily for years or blown in casually by the wind. You will shake them out and turn them, lay them out and relay them, putting them just so!... just there! Every scrap will have a history, signs of wear and tear, and each may be cherished and chosen for its memories or for its colour or even for some random, unfathomable reason. Then you will sew them all together. The secret of that kind of quilt is that it is made of whatever is available and the result is always beautiful.

Our own hearts are full of thrown together fabric; bits and pieces of ideas, thoughts, memories and dreams. Whenever life tears into your heart and opens it, you quickly patch it up again to prevent all those memories pushing their way through and blowing away.

Just occasionally in life, things happen that are so bad your heart feels as if it has been cut to pieces. All you can do then is try to patch it up with memories of kindness, of better times, of love – and that's exactly how you make your patchwork quilt.

Why do we do this? Why do we make patchwork quilts? Why do we patch up the heart when we've been hurt? Because life is infinitely precious and we want to live. Real living, being properly alive, is to be aware that we exist contained and containing love. Being alive is to be safely made up of memories just like a quilt – even, paradoxically, when memory has gone, temporarily or permanently.

I know this because in May 2009, my physical heart was found to be failing. I was admitted to hospital as an emergency. After much preparation my chest was opened with the amazing skills of a whole team of people and my heart and aorta were patched up with a mixture of organic porcine tissue – pig to you and me – teflon mesh, finest silk threads and catgut, plus several pints of blood, donated by unknown benefactors.

Everything was sewn up again and returned to me, in order that my life could continue for a while longer. All this having been freely given to me, thanks to the kindness of so many strangers who loved life too.

1

SURGERY OF THE OPEN HEART

S O, LET'S ALLOW THE MEMORIES to come alive. It is May 2009, I am in the University Hospital of Wales, Ward C6 in the main building, Cardiac Surgery, to which I have been admitted as an emergency.

My aorta – the large artery that carries the blood on the start of its journey around the body – has doubled in size, like some great big playground bully. My heart can no longer cope, but only protest silently in wheezy, tearful breathing, like any other poor little victim.

The technical description is that I am to have open heart surgery for a repair of an aortic aneurysm and replacement of the aortic valves to my heart; the reality is that I am totally at the mercy of professional strangers, albeit ones from my own 'tribe' of the medical profession.

I've had a couple of weeks of tests. It's been very restful with lots of concerned and kind visitors; now the operation is scheduled for tomorrow. It's almost exam time for the students. How well I remember that, though it is over 40 years ago!

I counted 22 young people who have sidled through my door over the fortnight and asked, very nicely, if they could examine me before my interesting medical signs vanish. What fun! I become an expert in my own case, showing them exactly how to place their fingers at my wrist to detect the collapsing 'water hammer' pulse, and telling them bits of my personal history.

This place is full of bittersweet memories. My husband, Ken Rawnsley, was Professor of Psychiatry here. When I started work as an SHO in his department in the early 1970s I had no idea that we would be together for 20 years and have two children, nor that a new Psychiatric Unit, built in the grounds, would be named for him after his death in 1992.

Lying passive and patient, my heart is full of memories of myself as a young doctor. "If I walk out of this ward and down two flights of stairs and turn left, I will be on A4 where I am a lecturer in Ken's department," I say quietly to myself, willing it to be so. But of course, I can't do that. The ward is now something else, and the Rawnsley Unit is out across the grounds.

I cry quietly in the night and fall asleep listening to the iPod on random shuffle, that Rupert and Amanda, my children, in their care for me have filled. A Bach chorale. Elvis singing 'Heartbreak Hotel'. Elgar. Jazz. Bryn Terfel's voice: 'If I should ever leave you.' Little snippets of my favourite bits of the Goon Show and 'Under Milkwood'. Sometimes you need surgery of the open heart if it is to heal fully.

In my dreams I take that walk down the stairs to Ward A4, catching repeated glimpses of myself in the dark windows. A young woman in all the absurd glory of 1970s clothes. Knee-high boots and a green minidress, crisp as a lettuce. A baker-boy hat over a ruffled shirt and black leather waistcoat. A wide sleeved blouse in an angular pattern of turquoise, lime and orange. My, don't I look good!

2

A POEM: WRITTEN FROM THE HEART

The heart is a pump
they told us at the school of medicine
back when I was young
it has four chambers
each with its own and separate task
to circulate the blood
all eight pints or more of viscous fluid
then there's all the tubes
they said
they are containers too
it would all get very messy
if that red blood were not contained!
It's only a pump they said
we boys and girls
for we were little more
eyed one another up
ignoring the lecturer
our glances boxing
with gentleness and skill
touch of a hand
pressure of foot
fluttering heartbeat
a smile a proposition
expecting the answer no
it was another world then
when I was young.
It's only a pump they said
a set of boxes
keeping the body going
we knew they lied
and we contained the lie, professionally,

and held it close throughout our lives.
It's only a pump the surgeon told me
before he opened its container
and cut respectfully
into the boxes of my heart
I have been glad of that
glad that in my six-hour sleeping death
my blood was still busily
going round and round
circulated by pumps outside the box
and the lung cavities were
filled and emptied by machines.
My frozen heart gave up its secrets
to the surgeon's skill
then it sighed
and obediently returned to life
to everyone's relief
it's only a pump
the surgeon said
no trouble at all
we both knew he lied
and oh how grateful I am to him for that!
it was all put back into the box
sorted and tidied mended healed restored
after all it's only a pump the heart
Except that out of it has poured
in all its redness
seventy years of dreams
exposure is complete
my heart is now open to all
and nothing will ever be the same
you can't expect somehow to return
the sighs desires conspiracies and fires
of seventy years into a box
and hope they'll circulate again discreetly
contained and hidden,
can you now?
the lie's exposed

spilling its bright message everywhere…
No! No! hold it in and spell it out
say after me –
the **Heart** is **Only** a **Pump**

3

THE KINDNESS OF STRANGERS

I **THOUGHT OF CALLING THIS** – in the style of old-fashioned writings – "In which I have a breakdown and fail my Final Examinations", but that sounds a little sad. My memories of medical school were mostly happy – even happy-go-lucky. Blood? Yes – plenty of that, both actual and metaphorical. It seems to be the first thing people talk to you about when you go up to med school.

Being in hospital in 2009, with the tables turned on that young medical student who was me, I can see the importance of blood in all its symbolic glory and of the relationships, connections and links it represents. Above all though it represents the kindness of strangers; those who gave me their blood literally during my operation, and those who, years earlier, made it possible for me to become a doctor myself, when I could so easily have failed and taken another path.

The summer of 1963 was indeed a very unhappy time for me. After three years on the wards at the Middlesex Hospital, I came up to my final medical exams. I suppose one likes to feel one has had some sort of excuse for having a nervous breakdown. My mother was seriously ill and I had just got married to another student, so I felt hugely conflicted. I had begun to hate medicine and medical school. I knew I had to finish and this would require passing the exams, and doing a year as a House Officer before I could give it all up, as the internship was needed to complete the degree.

I remember weeping at a bus stop from the cold, with Roger my husband massaging my gloveless hands as we made the long trip to Croydon to see my mother. I felt guilty at seeing her so little and even more guilty when I went, losing the hours of study and being even more incapacitated when I returned, having seen how hard it was for my father, virtually on his own and over 80.

Of course, my predicted crash happened. In retrospect, a breakdown can be the best and most necessary response to bad things happening. It allows others to be kind and care for you and for you to learn first-hand that this is the most important thing you can do for others.

The most important rule for doctors is said to be, rightly, "First do no harm." The second rule should be a recognition that we are all vulnerable, all would have a breaking point, all deserve and need as much respect, if not more than the seemingly well and mentally strong. Several times I tried to get some help with the revision, talking to the tutors and consultants on the firms about my fear that I was going to fail the exams and that I wasn't coping. Always I was patted down with platitudes like: "You'll be fine," "Everybody feels that way." "So, your mother is ill, but we all have to learn to cope."

So, why have I actually called this chapter The Kindness of Strangers, when it seemed to me at the time that nobody around Roger and I even noticed a need for kindness? Because I met this kindness at the time of greatest need from people outside the medical school itself. They would have been astonished to know the immense effect they had; I'm sure they felt they were only doing their job, but they did it with care and compassion.

I went into the examination halls on the afternoon of the first exam in a fog of denial, sleeplessness and despair. All the final examinations in the University of London took place in a central building devoted to nothing else. Big rooms with rows of desks, an usher, administrators and supervisors. You filed into this impersonal emporium, sat at a desk, turned over the exam paper when you were told to and wrote away for three hours, or however long it was. Then you repeated the whole thing until all six papers were done, before the clinicals and vivas.

I sat down in this fogged and blank state and turned the paper over. I could not read it. I had completely lost the ability to make sense of these strange black marks on white paper. I remember the enormous relief of that moment, as I sat for a while studying this incomprehensible sheet, and the reasoning in my head went, "You can't read, so you can't do the exams. No problem."

It was a classic example of what was called in those days 'hysterical', but would now be called – less pejoratively – a 'dissociative' phenomenon. Sometimes when the human psyche is put under too much stress it simply tunes out, blocks cognitive processes and blocks certain abilities. For example, I could have had a paralysis of my writing arm, or a sudden psychogenic blindness with the same effect; being unable to sit my exam. This defence mechanism, dissociation, though sometimes extreme, actually works very well in its own way. It not only reduces the unbearable anxiety, but goes even further – it abolishes it. I will never forget the amazing calm of what is called the 'belle indifférence' [beautiful unawareness] of that moment and the pseudo-rational ideation of, "I can no longer read so I can go home."

When I got up, very calmly, and walked out at the back, I was stopped by a quiet middle-aged man, the usher. Very gently and deferentially he told me I should stop and talk to the woman in the office, close by. I argued a bit, but I was basically lamblike with calm and agreed to go and sit with her and explain. Under her equally gentle and kindly questioning, she conveyed back to me that I was undergoing some sort of breakdown, that this was very common in the circumstances. I didn't need to feel bad about it, but maybe I needed help? That was easy to accept, but it was harder for her to get me to go back and sit through the exam, even without doing anything at all. "If you don't go back you can't sit any of the exams," she said, and I felt that was a marvellous solution as I didn't want to sit any of them.

She shifted tack, took me to the nurse in another office, who made me a cup of tea, and between them they persuaded me to keep my options open and go back in for the rest of that exam and again the next morning. An arrangement was made for the coming days. I sat in a daze on my own at the back with my cup of tea, until we were released. I slipped out, saw the nurse again, who gave me an appointment later that day with a local GP.

Talking to that doctor was a luminous experience for me, and very helpful in terms of a role model. He did not take refuge in a sphinx-like silence as was the prevailing orthodoxy but showed and expressed sympathy and understanding, He explained the dissociative experience as an understandable response to the extreme pressures I had been under, prescribed a mild sedative and returned me to my worried husband, Roger, to be cosseted. We cried a lot and comforted each other.

Every day of those exams the nurse and the administrator looked out for me. I was seated at the back, near the door so I didn't feel claustrophobic. Halfway through each three-hour exam, the nurse came in and took me out for a ten-minute break and a cup of tea. The GP managed to arrange some counselling.

To my astonishment, although I predictably failed the other three subjects, I passed Surgery, and therefore had one less to sit in the next six months. I had come to my senses and truly wanted to qualify and become a doctor. I haunted the path labs and the tutors, informally, and made up for all the missed bits, passing the Pathology exam respectably a short time later.

I passed the Midwifery and Gynae papers later on, but failed the Clinical, probably because I had done my 'midder' in Dublin, a wonderful experience, but that's another story. I passed without any trouble the next time around, qualifying as a doctor a year later than I should have, but much more knowledgeable and far wiser than if I had got through the first time on cramming.

Belatedly, the medical school arranged for a Senior House Officer to tutor me in clinical practice. Though rather bored and superior, making it clear he was not at all pleased to be given this extra burden, he conscientiously stuck with it twice a week.

I had always found hearing heart murmurs difficult on ward rounds, so – for example – after trying to make out the differing 'lub-dups' and 'lub-didups' in the past I would give up and pretend I'd heard it [I'm not the only one to confess to this, years after!], too aware of the impatience of the other six students and the stoicism of the patient.

Now, with the benefits of a one to one, I would refuse to leave the bedside till I truly understood the heart condition. When I sat the final exams again I was told, unofficially, that I had achieved a standard equivalent to distinction in the general medicine papers. I'm not sure who was more astonished, me or the Registrar. He attributed it, mostly correctly, to his expert tutoring. I can't even remember his name, but here was another person just doing the job he was told to do by spending time and trouble with me, not particularly kind, but I am so grateful to him. I hope he had a stellar career and a happy life.

I have only one regret. The resits were done elsewhere, and in my recovery and the hectic pace of medical studies and my family problems – which of course did not go away – it never, I'm afraid, occurred to me to go back to the examination halls and thank the staff or acknowledge I probably owe my career to them. If they had not done their job properly, I would almost certainly have left medicine and done something else. If I have ever shown consideration for admin and support staff it is probably no more than a small repayment on the roundabout of Kindness to Strangers.

4

A DREAM OF THE UNIVERSE

I **DREAMED** the other night of a country which stood as a
symbol for the whole Universe, a common enough picture.
Imagine, if you will, the most beautiful landscape you know. Mine
might have been the Yorkshire Dales, or maybe the green hills of
the borderlands between England and Powys. I was standing in the
exact middle of this saucer of natural loveliness, and it stretched to
the horizon in each direction.

In front of me was a cage, made of closely crossing metal wires,
about 7 feet high by 4 feet wide like a fruit cage, with a small open
door facing me. In the outstretched palm of my hand lay a small
bedraggled bird. The story was clear in the image. An accidental
opening. A foolhardy bird longing to explore. One does not need
details of a narrow escape from a predator, rain and wind, terrors
of lightning and of darkness.

The little sparrow lay on its side, panting, its brown, dusty feathers
stuck out at angles, its wings half spread, matted with mud. Tufts
of the downy undercoat were missing, exposing wrinkly yellow-
spotted skin. Each panicky beat of the heart seemed to press the
skin further into my fingertips and suck itself round them. Too
terrified to open its eyes, the bird could not see that it was safe,
could not see that it was near home and in the gentle hand of a
Preserver. My heart was filled with the greatest tenderness and
love; all of my longing at that moment was to reassure and save it
from pain. But I could do nothing to calm the sparrow and the
increasingly frantic beating of its heart was putting it in real danger
of death.

I did the only thing possible. Very gently I laid the tiny creature on a branch within the cage and closed the door. Then I waited, watching over it. The bird rested, its breathing easing as the familiar feel of the twigs and leaves slowly brought it back into calm. It would survive. I woke in that calm, feeling the familiar pillows and sheets, instantly and completely understanding my dream.

The dreaming 'I' was God. The fugitive rescued bird was myself, Elinor. The protective cage was made of the imprisoning senses of my own body; all that keeps us from recognising our place, held within the Hand of God in this beautiful Universe. The cage keeps only the body within its confines. All the scents, breezes, sunshine, showers, sights and sounds of the Universe permeate the mesh, both coming in and going out freely. The dream message had to cast God as the dreamer, for Elinor, the terrified sparrow, cannot open her eyes and see how safe she is, how precious and how much loved.

5

YOU MUST WEAR A HAT,
MY MOTHER SAID

S O, LET'S PROGRESS BACKWARDS and see what had brought me to studying medicine in the first place. I had always wanted to become a doctor, like my mother, preferably a psychiatrist too, which I thought was like her also, though there are considerable differences between the path of general psychiatry and the extreme specialism of psychoanalysis. First of all, of course, you have to study at medical school if you want to become a doctor of medicine (psychoanalysts can do this or not, as they wish).

In those days, the criteria for getting into medical school were laughable, compared with more recent times; I'd never make it now. Put simply, you had to fulfil the basic criteria for getting into a university and then persuade a particular medical school to take you on. For London University that was, if I remember rightly, something like half a dozen O-levels, including Maths and Latin, and two A-levels in any subjects; mine were French and English. It was a brief window of opportunity in the 50s, closed not many years later. There had been a lot of public fuss at the time about the narrowness of doctors' education, and encouragement for those in the arts to come in and this possibility was wonderful for people like me.

Acceptance by a medical school was equally laughable in those days – it rested on a simple interview with the Dean of any medical school to which you cared to apply and who would accept you on a whim. Or, in my case, traditional nepotism. My mother was a doctor and my father was a Governor of the Middlesex Hospital Medical School.

"You must wear a hat," said my mother, not trusting nepotism unadorned.

We bought a small hat-shaped object in green felt with a bow. I remember it as resembling nothing so much as a dead bird. With matching gloves and this unfortunate budgerigar look-alike perched on the back of my head, I took the train to London.

The Dean of the Middlesex Hospital Medical School interviewed me in his office. He luckily left his own specialism or any other scientific subject entirely out of the discussion. Since this was all long before John Cleese and the deceased parrot sketch, we didn't refer to the hat either.
In fact, we hardly talked about anything.

He mumbled something like, "Why do you think you want to be a doctor?" and I mumbled something in return.

He then shook my hand and congratulated me on being accepted, very relieved to not have to talk to me anymore. Like so many doctors he was socially shy; this was definitely a social rather than a medical occasion.

With my future secured, I could relax and look forward to a whole summer of amazing freedom. What fun things could I do? How could I make the most of it now that I had my place to study medicine for October?

6

MY GLORIOUS CAREER IN MEDICINE
IN WHICH I GET DOWN AND DIRTY
WITH THE BEDBUGS

"**W**HY DON'T WE SPEND THE SUMMER** working as Butlins Redcoats?" said a school friend in Walthamstow Hall, as we discussed this pressing question of how to spend our months of freedom from boarding school.

"Lovely," I responded enthusiastically.

So how on earth did I find myself on my own in a hospital kitchen, at 5.30am on a July morning, cooking up piles of greasy eggs and bacon, and serving them to sleepy nurses, no older than myself and very puzzled by my classy accent?

My friend's mother had felt that it was not appropriate for her daughter to go away to a Butlins holiday camp. She obtained for us both employment as domestics at the Shrewsbury County Hospital. I looked forward to it, nevertheless. My friend, Sally, was legendary at school for her charisma, sophistication and wonderful social life, so I expected a few weeks of light domestic duties interspersed with tea parties, dances, and above all – young men.

It didn't quite work out like that. For some reason I have never been able to fathom, my friend's mother decided I couldn't stay with them, but would have to board in the hospital. I was quite hurt, as I had thought she liked me.

Sally said, "I'd have been quite happy to share my room with you, but…"

Consequently, not only did the hospital claw back most of my meagre wage in return for my board, but I was put on split shifts all the time. This timing, working mornings 5.30am till midday, off in the afternoon, working again from 6-10 in the evening, was death to any social life. My friend worked the normal day shift. We hardly ever met.

Of course, I was upset for a few days, but I soon began to realise that this, my first taste of adult freedom, would be a wonderful training for medical school in the autumn. I was fit and young; quite able to cope with cooking breakfasts for the nurses and even the backbreaking scrubbing of floors. I was a constant source of interest to the patients and they to me. When I was supposed to be cleaning I was more likely to be chatting by someone's bed, leaning on my broom in true music hall style, gossiping about lumps and bumps and life-threatening operations. I felt I was experiencing True Life at last!

The Ward Sisters were a tough bunch. They were hard on the nurses and particularly horrible to the auxiliaries – the ones who had the light duties I had imagined my own; dusting lockers, arranging flowers, wiping bums and carrying bedpans to and fro. Thank goodness I hadn't got that sort of job! We domestics were not directly under the medical hierarchy. Apart from a written rota saying where and what we were to do each day, nobody seemed to notice us. When the Sister on Surgical 3 found me eating food from the ward fridge, she turned a blind eye. When a pair of pinstriped legs trod up my newly washed corridor I slopped the bucket over the shiny shoes of a Consultant Physician. I glanced up at the angry pout under the moustache and dried off the shoes with my dirty rag, saying a perfunctory and hypocritical "sorry."

In a few months, such Consultants and Sisters would hold my professional life in their hands and regard me as lower than the dust I left under the beds. For now, I was immune, and wow! Wasn't that a gas! Best of all, I spent a lot of my time with the older domestic cleaners. I didn't have much in common with the girls of my own age, who probably thought me toffee-nosed because of my accent. The middle-aged women saw it differently. They evidently felt it was up to them to educate this naïve middle-class girl.

"Coming for a cuppa?" Mrs Bird would wheeze, fag dangling from her mouth.

Her 'mate', Mrs Bathhurst – did they even have first names? I'd never have presumed to use them – would make tea. The heavy white cups were always full to the brim with an evil dung-coloured brew, so thick I swear it clunked on the table as it spilt. Then they would be off; giving me the low down on marryings and buryings, sexual shenanigans, child-care, husband-care, leavings and homecomings. They would reminisce about their – invariably horrendous – birth experiences and the vital organs cut out of long-dead relatives.

No self-pity. No quarter given. Births, deaths and hospital tea. All I needed to become a Doctor!

7

MEDICAL STUDIES:
PRE-MED, MY FIRST YEAR

MY FIRST THREE YEARS at medical school were good fun. We were not so different from any other students; long holidays, and plenty of time for larking about and socialising. Of course, I had to do a lot more science, by an extra year at the beginning, for 'Pre-med' or 'First MB', before Medicine proper, so I knew I would have three years 'Pre-clinical', then another three years 'on the wards'.

I started in the autumn, having spent that exciting summer as a skivvy in the Shrewsbury Royal Infirmary. We were quite a rum lot in the First MB group. Some slightly older Arts graduates, a professional Organist who didn't last long, and some eager young ignoramuses like me. For half a dozen out of the 30 students, our scientific knowledge could only be described as pre-pre-pre-basics.

It quickly became apparent that more had to be done for such a mathematically challenged bunch and we six were given extra tuition from a tutor we called The Cherub. This was due both to his plump, rosy cheeks and his angelic temperament. His tutoring went earlier and earlier as he uncovered deeper and deeper layers of our ignorance. Finally, he found our level:

"Now," I remember him saying, "you have a group of five sheep in one field and six goats in another."

At last I began to understand a few simple arithmetical concepts and never looked back. Kind man. I also found that it would really,

really make sense to learn my times tables, a message that a wartime education had somehow not got across to me. No wonder I barely scraped my O-level Maths. It had been hard to do all that counting on my fingers and toes in a three-hour exam. I duly learnt all my tables by heart, chanting them in the bath and while dressing.

Overall, I did so well that I was given a first-year prize for the student who had worked best to overcome their difficulties, though I don't think the authorities suspected that I was still a bit shaky on my 8-times. I still am, come to that.

8

FRENCH LEAVE

THIS STRANGE LITTLE ADVENTURE, my very own Brief Encounter, probably belongs to my 20th year. I was a little low in spirits as the train whistled and clanked out of the Gare du Lyon that summer day. I had cried all the way to Folkestone after an argument with my parents. A chat in French to an old lady on the autocar had cheered me up a little. At the station, an officer in the French Army saw me struggling with the train door and helped me in, gazing into my eyes with the automatic admiration of a Frenchman to anyone in a skirt. He closed the door carefully and saluted as the train drew away.

The corridor smelt of smoke and grime, of garlic and urine. The dirty toilet shocked me, a naive English girl travelling on my own, but the tiny incident had thrilled me. 'What an adventure I'm on,' I thought, 'What a romantic adventure!'

The train was full of French soldiers. They looked so young; younger even than me. Did they have National Service like us, I wondered? I don't even recall what the argument with Mummy and Daddy had been about. I remember I wiped my eyes and turned resolutely to look out of the window. Perhaps my tears had been noted; perhaps it was a common opening gambit. One of the young soldiers was addressing me.

"You are sad, Mademoiselle?" he queried in French.

I looked at him. Soulful brown eyes, olive complexion, short black hair. About my own height, or a little more. "No, not really," I said, also in French, and smiled, "I'm alright, thank you."

Of course, we continued to talk; it was a successful gambit. As the hours passed, we chatted endlessly, sharing biscuits and mugs of weak Belgian beer. It occurred to me that my schoolgirl French was more than adequate. He was a simple country boy and we would not be discussing Sartre and the French Impressionists.

I didn't care. Live for the moment would be my guide. '*Vive le moment!*' No, of course that would translate back as 'Long live the moment!' Well, perhaps that was even better. For a while we slept, heads on each other's shoulders, my hair across his cheek. It was a very trusting thing, and as we woke I smiled at him and he kissed me, briefly, awkwardly. The train was coming into the Gare du Marseilles.

"I'm going back to camp," he told me, "It's at Frejus, not very far from here."

"I'm going to stay with my… what do you call it? My *Parain*, my Godfather. He lives nearby too," I replied.

I had hardly ever met my Godfather, Cyril, and his wife Margaret before. Cyril had been a British Consul and they had lived mostly abroad. They had recently retired to live on the Riviera and it was wonderful to be invited to stay for a fortnight of my summer holidays.

My soldier boy was Jean-Paul. I can no longer recall anything else about him, not even his surname.

"Please, please," he insisted as we parted in the clattering smoke of Marseilles station. "Here is my address and number. Please come and see me. I love you!"

Well, against all expectations, I visited him. Where my parents would have called caution and envisaged horrid things relating to the white slave trade – that is, after all, the role and responsibility of parents – my Godfather just laughed and looked up the bus times. So, one hot, lavender-scented afternoon I went down to Frejus. When I found the camp, I realised what an impossible, ridiculous thing I was doing. There was a gate and a guardhouse but the place was huge and inside the fence, I could see rows and rows of huts stretching into the distance and hordes of indistinguishable young soldiers. I learned later that there were 3,000 of them in the camp.

I had my piece of paper with Jean Paul's name and army number, but there was no way, no possible way in all the world, that I could go up to that guardhouse and ask for him.

Defeated, I turned away. Coming past me, towards the camp, was a young soldier. "Excuse me," I said to him, "I have come to see this man." I showed him the paper.

"Jean-Paul?" he said. "He's a friend of mine; in my group. I'll get him for you."

An astonished and ecstatic Jean-Paul turned up within the half-hour. What young man would not be thrilled at such a romantic gesture? All that sun-drenched afternoon we wandered the dunes hand-in-hand. For years, I could not smell pines without being swept by the dreamy eroticism of young romance. No, we did not carry it through to anything more than tender youthful kisses. Those were more innocent times and I suspect he was as virginal as myself. We were both in love, not with each other, but with our dreams and ourselves. He returned to camp after seeing me gallantly onto my bus and buying the ticket.

For a few months we corresponded, but it flickered out fairly soon. Jean-Paul told me that on his return to camp he was in huge trouble as he was supposed to have been on duty. He didn't say whether our stolen, golden time was worth his spell in the camp lock-up.

But maybe, just maybe, at this very minute, far away a portly French gentleman is putting a little footnote in his memoirs. He is recalling a young English girl who sought him out one pine-smelling, sunflower-glorious summer afternoon. He is heaving a sentimental sigh and forgetting the punishment for taking French Leave.*

=====================

I find that not everyone now is familiar with the colloquial use of the term French Leave: it was the custom (in the 18th century prevalent in France and sometimes imitated in England) of going away from a reception, etc. without taking leave of the host or hostess. Hence, jocularly, to take French Leave is to go away, or do anything, without permission or notice.

9

WRITING UP MY MEMORIES

I **NEVER FELT** I wanted to write a straightforward autobiography. I think it would be impossible to be detached enough to be really honest, and if I wasn't honest, it would feel unsatisfying. Anyway, I guess I embarrass my children enough without that. My style is better suited to memoirs – which I regard as short pieces, almost more like 'essays', a genre that is long gone, I believe. They satisfy my frequent wish to record my life experiences in some form.

So for a good many years I tried writing some reminiscences, mostly for the family, but also anyone else who might be interested. My paternal grandfather did that, and it was wonderful – I never knew him, as he died in the 1920s. My grandmother, who I also never knew, kept the manuscript and never even gave it to my father. She was apparently a secretive and paranoid woman, or at least became so after her husband died. She also lost her younger son, Norman Kapp, my father's brother shortly after the First World War. Apparently he had been her favourite. She went to live in Italy, refusing to see her son – my father – or anyone else except her faithful Italian maid, Edvige Dagostin. This lady kept all her papers, so it was only after her death in the 1970s that the local priest packed up the contents of her desk. He traced me through the Public Trustee.

I remember reading the manuscript on a grey November evening, when the children were very young, but I don't recall exactly when. It was so moving – a grandfather unknown and long dead, who had written: "I hope that my future family may be interested in these notes." I began to cry; it was as if he spoke directly to me from beyond the grave, his hand on my shoulder. I suppose that is in itself rather an interesting story. Sometimes you don't realise it yourself until you come to record these things.

So – let's look again at our quilt. A quilt is often made by sewing a line or cluster of smaller pieces together into groups, partly for ease of working. Later these can be put together in larger groups to make a pattern. Occasionally, uttering imprecations, they can be unpicked and re-membered. So, on the 27th of December 2008, the day after Boxing Day, I finally sat down to start a few scrappy memoirs; a sort of commonplace book of my life. No real reason to start then and I only know the date because I – unusually – wrote it down precisely on my notes. Not a good night to choose, somehow. It is often a low time, just after Christmas day, but before a New Year with its promise. The fag end of the year, even for a non-smoker!

Really, I was preparing to remember things for the family tree. We had discussed it as a family over the holiday and agreed it should be more than just a record of dates; it should have little snippets of memories, descriptions, stories handed down orally, research of the social history and other memorabilia. Even so, it did also need to include dates. Rupert my son set me up for computer recording and asked me a simple and obvious question: "What was the date and place of your mother's death?"

A complete blank. I absolutely could not remember the date or place of my mother's death. How odd.

No, not odd. Even as I stammered and changed the subject, I knew that it was opening a very terrible part of my life. A part often visited, particularly in therapy, never wholly healed but a part of tremendous value. Too important to be a small bit of another task. A piece it would be good to write about for my children.

Not everyone looks forward to celebratory times, such as Birthdays, or the Christmas period, with the unalloyed joy and excitement of all those sparkling, feel-good adverts that we are supposed to believe in! Christmas and birthdays have mostly been happy times for me and I know I'm lucky in that. But I also have had quite a lot of bad years and I sympathise with those who dislike, even hate, the 'Festive Season', or, like me, found it hard to celebrate my birthday for many years. So – if you wish – you, the reader, can share the next few pieces – memory snippets – or skip them, as suits you.

10

PIECE 1: MY FAMILY UNRAVELS

S O, HERE IS WHERE, perhaps, my memoirs will really start. Another key point, a nodal point, late in 1964, with me aged 27, married and expecting my first baby. Increasingly worried about balancing the needs of a sick mother, recently diagnosed with dementia, an elderly father and a husband with a drinking problem.

The death of my parents came at a difficult and troubled time of my life, quite apart from the sadness of losing them. It was also the prelude to the worst time of all, less than two years later: the death of little Andrew Walter Tudway, my firstborn, in 1965. I am happy to talk about him – indeed to share him – now. He is still a very precious part of myself even though he is gone from this life. Please don't be afraid to read about him, but also don't feel bad if you want to skip parts of my memoirs, that's alright too.

But if you're still with me, let's get these things over, face the darkest time so far. I think people are divided into those who, when woken in the night by a scary sound, either sit bolt upright, eyes straining, or hide under the blankets. Basic fight or flight. Neither of them is better or worse or more or less useful than the others. On the whole, I'm the former. I need to know what's coming to get me, not feel something creeping up and pawing away my defences. Of course, there's also the freeze option for later; eyes wide, mouth shut, maybe frozen for years.

My mother's illnesses started in about 1960 – when she would have been 62 – and I was in my early twenties and a medical student. I remember her taking me for a walk in the park behind our house and telling me she had been diagnosed with Parkinson's disease. I think I was completely inadequate to support or help her; I didn't know what to say. I hope I hugged her at least, but I can't remember much about it.

She was treated in a ward of 'our' own hospital, the Middlesex, by an eminent neurologist with no interpersonal skills whatever. Being told that she had it mildly did nothing for her. She knew it would get worse and it just added more guilt to the "I'm a therapist, of course I can cope" syndrome. In fact, the tremor was not particularly evident, but I understand from other patients that the stiffness, the 'locked-in' feeling is worse than anything on the outside.

About four years later she was diagnosed also with bowel cancer. Treatment in those times was fairly brutal and she had to have a permanent colostomy. She took it very badly, becoming deeply distressed and depressed. She found the hygienic aspect terribly upsetting and her increasing tremor made the management difficult. It drew up many feelings from her early childhood, perhaps especially from her upbringing in India, of being rejected, somehow 'dirty' and unacceptable. To this was added the professional therapist's humiliation at being unable to heal herself. Negative aspects of early religious teaching on the need to rise above disaster probably surfaced too.

Of course, it is only with hindsight I can see these underlying strands. Particularly now I'm old myself and have had a lot more life packed into me, whether I wanted it or not. We can face old age and the gradual loss of our faculties with defiance and bravado initially. Or we can try hiding from it in denial – and all shades in between. Let's face it. 'Life's a bummer and then you die' about sums it up for the period of time, long or short, that one needs in order to become reconciled and accepting of the Final Things. I'm not quite there yet, but I'm working on it. It's a bit like a seesaw. Sometimes I'm OK with the idea that I will die, at other times I want to wail like a banshee, "No... NO... NO!!!"

I do try not to use any religious platitudes either. However we deal with such miseries, there aren't usually any easy short cuts. I have found that insights and life-enhancing changes have as often come to me from secular, even anti-religious sources and especially from conversations with friends of all sorts, religious, atheist, or spiritual of all shades and of none.

My religious beliefs and the wonderful Mystical experiences I have been given are a tremendous help to me and I am truly grateful for them. They give me a wonderful sense of order and Love governing the universe. I believe they come from 'God' and are God – but they don't exempt me from sharing periods of doubt and despair, as experienced by most people I know. I don't expect others to necessarily believe in my 'Truth' just because I say so – it's my deeds, not my words, that will count at the end.

11

PIECE 2: LEAVING THE PAST BEHIND

MY **FIRST HUSBAND**, Roger Tudway, didn't get on well with my father, who was worried, rightly, about his drinking, but Roger adored my mother. He had been instrumental in having her come to stay with us when we were doing our house officer year in Hereford so that we could get her seen by my boss, an extremely kind and caring general physician. At that time her dementia was probably very early and was not diagnosed, but he reviewed her medication and her care for the colostomy. Most of all, he talked to her as a fellow doctor and with respect and sympathy. His approach was holistic, suggesting various things that she found helpful.

From 1964 everything began to unravel, though that is not how one sees it at the time. Roger and I had been living for some time in his parents' garden, in a caravan. Although I loved his parents, who were always kind to me, I hated the set-up there. I didn't think that Roger would ever break from them and deal with his drinking and depression while he was there. I was struggling with these huge problems in my marriage, though I wouldn't have put it like that at the time, so I was very pleased that Roger had been offered a job as SHO in radiotherapy at The Red Cross Memorial Hospital in Taplow, Buckinghamshire.

I wasn't too sure that radiotherapy was a good idea; it was his highly successful father's field and smacked too much of identification and competition to me. However, I was pregnant by this time and happy to give up work, with no particular plans about resuming my career. We moved into a small flat, right by the hospital, which went with the job.

Just before Christmas, my mother came to stay. She had suffered a sudden panic attack when taken out in a car by some friends, becoming apparently lost and confused, screaming and crying until brought back to the familiarity of home. This seemed to me to be a classic 'Goldstein catastrophic reaction' requiring proper investigation, but she wasn't getting any specialist care.

I was eight months pregnant, with no medical connections anymore, unsure this time how to get her help, but the decision was taken for me. By this time my mother was very unsteady and she had a fall in our flat, cutting her head. I dialled 999 and sat with her head on my lap until the ambulance came, as I couldn't lift her. In the Casualty Department, Roger and I persuaded the House Officer of the need for admission and full assessment. This resulted in a proper referral to the Middlesex Hospital, overriding her GP.

Dr Janet Michael, her GP, was a lifelong friend and colleague of my mother and had been too close to see what in retrospect became obvious; my mother was suffering from dementia, probably arteriosclerotic and which had probably started at the same time and been the cause of her Parkinsonism. Much more recently, I have realised she probably had Lewy-Body Dementia (from which later on my cousin David Wilkins died) which was unknown all those years ago. My mother had concealed it very well and we had concealed it from ourselves. As there was no cure this was very possibly a good thing, but I think my father then felt bad about the times he had got very cross with her for forgetting and losing things. He loved her so much and was so frightened at losing her that he had found this period of their relationship very hard.

12

PIECE 3: THE LAST CHRISTMAS

I **REGRETTED** in retrospect that Roger and I did not see my family that Christmas; of course, we did not know it would be the last for both my parents. Because my mother was still in hospital in London, my father went to stay with Auntie Mary. She was his cousin and only living relative. Auntie Doria, as we called her partner, was her companion in their house in St John's wood and as much an 'aunt' to our family as Mary herself.

My brother John, with his wife Janet and six-month-old Annabel, went too, and my mother was allowed to join them for the day. Roger and I had decided we couldn't cope with any more family, on either side, and just wanted to be together. It was not well received by either set of parents, so Roger volunteered to do some On-Call – usually done by the non-Christian Indian doctors – and clinched it. So Christmas was a calm time, waiting for our baby in our own little flat.

It had already become obvious that my mother could no longer stay at home in Croydon. My father had the sad job of seeking out a permanent nursing home place for her. He also began the huge task of clearing and selling Gardole, our childhood home in Croydon, with my brother John's help. He made arrangements, in his usual stoical way, to move into a Residential Hotel. They also had the task of clearing out the house and its attic, stuffed full of clutter.

I was unable to do anything to help. I was grateful that they were doing it, but also upset and mourning the knowledge that so much was being thrown out without me having any chance to check it out. They did make every effort to keep things for me, especially my childhood books, but of course couldn't really second guess what I would have kept myself.

My father initially found a nursing home very near the hospital in Buckinghamshire, making it a long journey for him. I seem to remember the idea was that I would be able to see her a lot, with the baby, and that later a place might be sought nearer Croydon. As it turned out, I never did visit the nursing home. Just after Christmas, she was re-admitted to the Red Cross Memorial Hospital as an emergency, with an infection. She was delirious and seriously ill. We were warned she would probably not survive the night, and my father came to stay with us.

That night, as a result of stress and alcohol withdrawal, Roger became agitated, psychotic and paranoid. He talked wildly, believing my father's presence would somehow harm the baby. When I tried to use the telephone – being pretty panic-stricken myself – he pulled the cord from the wall. That did it! I insisted we walk round to the hospital.

They really didn't know what to do with us. I was checked over and kept in the Gynae ward for a couple of days, being almost at term with the pregnancy. Roger was locked in a side room of his own ward until the psychiatrist came and told them not to be so silly.

So the medical authorities had three of us in different wards until the psychiatrist sorted us all out and started some ongoing therapy for Roger. I was allowed home to the flat and my brother and Auntie Joyce, my mother's sister, came and supported my father and I.

My mother survived the night and I sat with her in the hospital ward each day before my baby's birth. She lived for another six weeks and although she didn't really know where she was or what was happening, she seemed much more at peace.

Often, she talked as if she was on a ship; sometimes a holiday cruise ship such as we had taken down the Rhine when I was in my teens, or sometimes it seemed more like earlier memories of her own life, of her returning from India. She often became anxious, particularly as to whether I would be able to get off before the boat sailed. I would hold her hand and try to reassure her. We could not let ourselves fully acknowledge that we were facing a deeper separation and a longer voyage than anything either of us had experienced before.

13

ABOO LOST

NOTE: *this is a true story, although I've changed the names. It was originally experienced and written in September 2012. My baby was born, safe and well, on* **January 7th 1965 – Andrew Walter Tudway.** *Instead of continuing with that part of my life, and the death of my parents, I have inserted a later piece of the Quilt – a little incident, which happened many years later in Cardiff. I hope any readers can see how it fits in, as a preparation for the tragedy recounted ahead.*

September 2012 – I walked home from Evening Service the other week; it's not far. On the corner of a road near home, I saw a couple looking at a little girl. They were white and she looked to be Asian, between 2 and 3 years old. I was intrigued, or maybe 'nosy' might be a better word. I slowed down.

"Do you know this little girl?" the woman asked, eagerly. Her partner stood back, fearful of being involved, as a man often is in these suspicious times.

"I'm afraid I don't," I said, joining them in studying the child, who looked back at us impassively.

She was dressed in a candy-coloured fleece, with turquoise trousers and a white and yellow striped t-shirt. On her feet were pink jelly crocs. Lost! How had she got there? Had she come from one of the houses? Had she been brought by children who then left her?

"What is your name?" we coaxed, kneeling down to her level.

"Yasmin," she replied. But when we asked where she lived she waved a regal hand first one way, then the other. She looked across the empty street and suddenly called, imperiously, "Aboo!" and again, after a pause "Aboo!"

"I think that's 'Daddy,' I said. Yasmin looked at us. "Aboo lost!" she declared.

The woman and I spoke quietly together. We certainly couldn't leave her and we didn't know where to start with the rows of houses. It began, softly, to rain.

"We'll have to ring the police," I said, and the woman agreed.

The female officer on the 999 desk took the details quickly and efficiently. As I put back my phone, Yasmin, suddenly tiring of us and of this adventure, turned and ran off down the road. We adults puffed along behind and saw her run up the path of a house just before the main road. A few confusing moments followed, with a surprised mother hugging Yasmin and asking us where she had been. It seemed that she had followed her father and older sister out to the chip shop, both parents assuming she was with the other, but her father hadn't noticed and had driven away.

All was well. We agreed the first couple should continue on their way and I would call the police desk again to tell them. I was a little embarrassed as I explained, but the operator exclaimed warmly: "Ah, every mother's worst nightmare!" and I knew I had been right to phone.

Yasmin's mother came back out and invited me in, distressed and relieved at one and the same time. Fuller explanations were exchanged. Yasmin's mother identified herself as Shamina and made cups of tea. The father and the older girl appeared, having been summoned. They all talked rapidly and agitatedly, then father vanished once more on the aborted mission to get a chicken and chips supper.

As we relaxed together, I told Shamina how good Yasmin had been. "She stayed on the pavement," I said. "She didn't go near the road and she found her own way back. What a clever girl!"

Yasmin stared at me solemnly and ate chocolate biscuits. Her mother tried to say, "Wait and have your supper," but her heart was not in it and the little girl made the most of her chance, munching through the plateful.

We drank tea and became friends, finding we knew some of the same people at the local school. There was a ring at the door and Shamina and Yasmin went out. I heard the unmistakable sound of two pairs of policemen's boots in the hall and the officer saying:

"A busybody phoned up."

I was not offended; it was obvious from his words and tone that he had summed up the situation correctly and wanted to reassure them that this was a friendly, non-judgemental call. All the same, I couldn't resist putting my head round the door:

"I'm the busybody," I said. "I'm having a cup of tea!"

The officers seemed just like every pair on the telly, one older and tougher, the other ["he's got kids himself"] younger and smiley.

I walked home with tears running down my cheeks, but they were tears of astonished happiness. This little incident happened on the evening of the 16th September 2012. Each year, the 17th of September is a tragically significant date for me. 45 years before, my 20-month-old toddler son, Andrew Walter Tudway, had done the same thing on that date, slipping out of the house momentarily unnoticed, straight out into the main road, to be killed instantly by a car.

I have long since made my peace with the memories of that night, but one never forgets. It is a time when I remember all the other parents who lose children, in whatever circumstances. What a wonderful tiny domestic miracle to be given to me on the eve of the anniversary of losing baby Andrew! What a message of forgiveness and love! I could almost hear the words that God was saying to me, to all of us:

"Look, my darling, these things are happening all the time and if they are anyone's fault, they are Mine and I have already put it right! You were allowed to put it right for someone else, so that one of my best beloved little ones was not even frightened, but praised and loved. What's more, tonight, ten people were left feeling better connected and relieved. You and two other strangers became good Samaritans and went home feeling better about yourselves. You connected with a police phone operator and allowed her to feel human. Yasmin, her two parents and an older sister were helped, before they even knew there was a problem, and they were grateful for it. Two policemen dealt with a case in which no bad things happened nor ill words were spoken. They went off knowing they had a valuable job, which they could do well. But, even more important, no-one was lost. No-one is ever lost. Yasmin's earthly father may have been a little absent-minded, but he wasn't lost, nor was my little Yasmin and nor is my little angel, Andrew."

As I walked on home, I reflected that our Heavenly Aboo is never lost either. We children may think he is. "God is dead. God doesn't exist," say the philosophers. We call out in desolation with the Psalmists, asking why He has deserted His people. Most poignantly, even Christ cried out on the cross, as the weight of all the world crushed him, "My God, my God. Why hast Thou forsaken me?" but that was not his last word, either.

Maybe, when we think God is lost, it's just we ourselves who have mislaid Him. He is busy preparing the Great Feast, to which we are all invited. Chicken and chips and chocolate biscuits in Heaven! That'll just about do me. What about you?

14

REFLECTIONS ON A CELTIC POEM

T HIS POEM was written in 6th Century Ireland, probably by Íte, who was an important church-woman. The poem is to be found in the commentary on Félire Óengusso, translated by Gerald Murphy. It is a wonderful poem and doesn't really need any comment, but at the end are my thoughts on it anyway!

It is little Jesus
who is nursed by me in my little hermitage.
Though a cleric have great wealth,
it is all deceitful save Jesukin.
The nursing done by me in my house
is no nursing of a base churl:
Jesus with Heaven's inhabitants
is against my heart every night.
Little youthful Jesus is my lasting good:
he never fails to give.
Not to have entreated the King who rules all
will be a cause of sorrow.
It is noble angelic Jesus
and no common cleric
who is nursed by me in my little hermitage –
Jesus son of the Hebrew woman.
Though princes' sons and kings' sons
come into my countryside –
not from them do I expect profit:
I love little Jesus better.
Sing a choir-song, maidens,
for Him to whom your tribute is due.

Though little Jesus be in my bosom,
He is in his mansion above.

We can only partly relate to the culture in which the poem is set, in which the sons of the great are fostered out for paid nurture by countrywomen, but the poet's tenderness and sense of being privileged can still move us greatly: "It is little Jesus who is nursed by me in my little hermitage." This speaks firstly of the love possible for a baby not your own. Somewhere in the back of our minds, we know that a foster mother's breastfeeding is made possible by her own pregnancy and birthing, but we are given no hint as to the fate of this woman's own child. We are left to identify with a human foster mother, simply and lovingly doing her job. Maybe we are being reminded momentarily of those darker things, left in the shadowed corners of the room, as the next line hints: "It is all deceitful save Jesukin," but immediately, for contrast, she has used a pet name sweeter and more personal than any we are used to. 'Kin' is not only a tender diminutive, it reminds us of kinship and the way we are all – laywoman, cleric, churl, prince and king – connected and related. She is also reminding us that this baby will become the man who teaches us to call God 'Abba': "My Daddy."

Towards the end her joy begins to spill over, it can't be expressed only by her. She cries out to the maidens, whoever they are, to "Sing a choir-song, maidens, for Him to whom your tribute is due." This is where we can truly join this woman who, for whatever reason is nursing babies not born of her body. This tells us that anyone, male or female, child or adult, fertile or barren, can give nurturing love to the Christ child by generosity of heart to the poor and helpless, anywhere, anytime. Even more, it is a due tribute – "You owe it to him!" we might exclaim in today's idiom.

Finally, she resolves the paradox that the Son of the Living God is both her Lord and her nursling by taking us to another level of being altogether. "Though little Jesus be in my bosom, He is in His mansion above." Her joy is complete, as the heart within her and the heart of the Universe are shown to be One.

15

ANDREW'S BIRTH AND AFTER

T HE BABY I have been writing about, my first child, was born safe and well on January 7th 1965 – Andrew Walter Tudway. Early on the morning of the 5th I seemed to start in labour and was admitted to the maternity unit. There, I was prepared, known in those days as being 'given an OBE' – Oil, Bath and Enema! At that point, the labour process promptly stopped and I was sent home again. This is apparently quite common, but I was devastated and cried all afternoon. So did Roger.

Two days later, on the 7th of January 1965, we did the whole thing again, OBE and all. Andrew Walter Tudway was born that afternoon after a long but normal labour, with a thatch of strawberry blond hair and big purple feet. Nothing else seemed to matter at all. Clean wiped. A new start. I remember Aunty Joyce and my father creeping in to see me; later on, my brother John, then Bob and Winifred Tudway, my in-laws.

The very next morning, the nurse encouraged me to wrap the baby up warmly and take him to see my mother, which involved wheeling him outside for a short way through the hospital grounds. Mummy was lucid and took great pleasure in seeing us. I also have a lovely memory of my elderly father sitting the baby on his knee and showing me how to burp him, his hands very gentle and his pride in this, his second grandchild, very evident.

I was kept in hospital for nearly two weeks; the normal practice for those times, now long discontinued. I had visitors but it was all curiously muted. Most of our young colleagues didn't really know what to say – should they be happy for us with a new baby, in the circumstances? Was my husband a nutcase? What could they say about my mother, who none of them knew as a person but knew to be probably dying on another ward? Much easier not to come, or to call in and out very quickly.

I didn't understand this at the time. A baby trumps everything else and the hormones ensure that the mother's attention is totally focused on the joy of having the baby at last. I was quite hurt and upset at the time. I had kind of expected lots of flowers and presents and there was hardly anything tangible. Still, I had Andrew and was in a happy bubble for a while, only marred by having difficulty breastfeeding and having to give bottle supplements.

Going home was another matter. I found the weeks after that very difficult. I hadn't a clue about baby care, stayed glued to Dr Spock and found my own hormonal variations totally impossible to cope with. New parents are also very, very tired all the time; living in a twilight state even worse than that of the average house officer. I tried to visit my mother, knowing her time might not be long, but almost unable to let it affect me. That time is all very blurred. I can't even remember how long she stayed in the hospital, or whether she went back to the nursing home.

Her death was expected, occurring six weeks after Andrew's birth. We were phoned up at the flat and told in the early morning that she had gone. After a while, I slept fitfully again.

I dreamt that I was in my parent's bedroom in Gardole, the house in Croydon and the room in which I had been born, my childhood home. I could see the worn carpet with its plum and ochre pattern very clearly, and my father's writing desk and battered typewriter. My mother came towards me looking beautiful and well, in her old blue dressing gown. She held me in her arms and we were the same height, so we rested our cheeks against each other. I remembered what it had been like when she held me as a little child, how warm and protective she had been, the safest place in the universe. I remembered how in her long illness she had been reduced;

shrunken, fragile, fearful and shaking, and how I would hold her gingerly, overwhelmed with grief and panic myself; no use to her. Now she was healed and strong, I had no more fear or revulsion of her, nor of myself and we were equals.

My mother said to me, in that dream, "You know I can never come out of this room anymore, but I will always be in here. If you ever need me, you can come to me."

When I woke I knew I had been given a very good dream, predicting a relationship of maturity within my true self, though not to be realised fully for many decades.

Indeed, we were to need all the comfort we could get. Two days before my mother's funeral my father had a heart attack and died. My brother had been with him and taken him to hospital, but there had been no time for anything else. At our mother's funeral, therefore, it was my brother John's sad task to announce our father's sudden and unexpected death and the probable date of his funeral.

For me, both funerals were a blur. For the first one, I held my six-week-old baby firmly cradled in my arms the whole time, letting everything wash over me, helped by Aunty Joyce, my mother's younger sister. She was a wonderful stabiliser in this sad situation.

She came early to the flat to take me to the church. I had no suitable dark mourning clothes, all mine were brightly coloured. Anyway, I remember crying afresh at the very idea of surrounding my lovely, magical little boy with anything dark and threatening - I wanted to wear my everyday bright yellow duster coat.

My wonderful aunt said simply, "You and John are the chief mourners. It is up to you what you wear, for there's no-one else who can be offended."

43

Years later, when I talked to older relatives who remembered the funerals they told me that the sight of the tiny baby, held within a circle of bright yellow, shining in the front row of the dark, gloomy church, for the first funeral was the most moving thing about that day, and remained always in their memories of my mother – Dorothy Mary Kapp, nee Wilkins, Rest in Peace. Also my dear, dear father, Reginald Otto Kapp, Rest in Peace, both united together in Love and in Death as they were in life.

16

THE DEATH OF ANDREW

I **THINK IT IS TIME**, in my patchwork, to come to the death of Andrew, a short jump in time, when my parents had only been dead themselves for less than two years. The loss of a young child – and at that time he was my only child – is hard for other people to cope with too. Because I am by nature sociable and outgoing, I found myself often in the years after he died, having to cope with comforting other people when they learnt of my loss. At least I myself had learnt, eventually, that one can survive and come through to live well and with happiness. Indeed, I was lucky to have two more wonderful children, now grown up, by my second marriage some years later.

After the death of my parents I stopped work and concentrated on bringing up the baby, while Roger struggled with a career in medicine. His hours were long and he also had to be a resident House Officer for the first few months. He was drinking heavily and eventually accepted help, as an inpatient in the Maudsley Hospital, in London. It was a terrible time to look back on, but very purifying professionally. You can hardly go lower in the social scale than that of a family with serious mental health issues and I met, on an equal level, so many good and wonderful patients and their families struggling in a hostile and – often – contemptuous world. There indeed 'but for the Grace of God go I' – or rather, have been there.

In that time I relied greatly on my aunt, Joyce Wilkins, who became even more close in our joint grieving for my mother, Dorothy Kapp, her older sister, but I had really nowhere to live. For some time before Andrew was born we had lived in a caravan in the garden of Roger's parents, in Bristol, but it seemed better for me to move to Sussex and live for a while near Auntie Joyce, while keeping my independence and a car with which to get to the station and visit Roger every few days, with the baby.

I found, for a peppercorn rent, a very broken-down old caravan in a field belonging to an artist friend of my Aunt. There was a camping style toilet at the far end of the field, plus a tap, from which to get the only water supply. The caravan had a wood-burning stove and holes in the joints through which the wind whistled at night. I and baby Andrew wrapped up tight and thrived on the healthy outdoor life. The two of us lived there for about ten months, the happiest and healthiest time in many years. I no longer had the burden of anxiety about Roger, and I was near enough to Aunty Joyce to have some meals with her, good healthy walks and washing little Andrew in her sink when he got old enough to tip over the washing up bowl that had served as a makeshift bath for him! I felt that all would be well.

I still had the car Roger had favoured – a large, very old Mercedes; it looked odd in the field, where it seemed nearly as large as the caravan! We made long term plans to stay in Sussex, for when Roger would come out of hospital and we bought, with my parents' legacy, a small but lovely bungalow in Punnetts Town, also near Auntie Joyce in Heathfield. It was on the side of the Sussex Downs, a few miles from the sea. In a good light you could see the coast of France as a thin gold line on the horizon.

We were just waiting to move into it when the fateful decision was made to visit friends of Roger's in Belgium, in the time before we could do so. He had very happy memories of a long summer spent with them going caving, just before I got to know him. His hobby of speleology was not mine, but I had bravely followed him down some of the easier Mendip caves during our courtship! I get very claustrophobic and it just shows what love will do, but at this time we simply wanted to have somewhere to rest and recuperate, with our little toddler.

So, for us to spend the time waiting by staying on a Belgian farm with this good-hearted family seemed to be an excellent idea and we duly packed and travelled there by ferry and train. I have blamed myself too long for our inadvertent carelessness that allowed the tragedy to happen. Small toddlers are adventurous and sometimes too many people are looking after them, so it's easy for no one to do so for a few tragic minutes. Other parents have told me of situations like that which could have led to disaster, but luckily didn't.

We were with the family and a large group of children after supper, just before twilight. Roger and I each thought the other was looking after our lively 20-month-old toddler. A small child came up to me and said, in French - "the door is open and the little one has gone out."

I was up and out in an instant, through the open back door, seeing the old grandfather loading his car. I was only a few paces behind Andrew as he came out of the back door but he did not stop. I think he was attracted to the bright lights across the darkening road and ran on forward. I heard the impact of the car which hit him, the screech of brakes - and then I was holding his body and screaming unstoppably while people came running and surrounded us.

The night was a blur, first at the hospital, then back in the Berthaud's house. The Gendarme who came to interview us the next morning was in tears himself as I suddenly realised the significance of the date. This had happened on the 17th of September 1967, the evening before my 30th birthday. It was at least 20 years before I could celebrate my natal day in any way.

I am glad of this chance to share this terrible experience, the nightmare of every parent and the source of an unending feeling of guilt and remorse for what happened, but I particularly want to add the beauty of the experience a few days on and the many ways in which I was held and comforted by others. There were beautiful things about his funeral too, as well as sorrow.

The day before the funeral, the local pastor came to see us to talk about it. He was the minister of the small minority Protestant church. The Berthaud family, with whom we were still staying, must have said we were Protestant; they were Catholic. The Pastor had a kind face, full of deep sympathy, and a gentle voice. I don't remember anything he said, but afterwards he read the 23rd psalm. He spoke French with a Belgian accent and the familiar words, yet unfamiliar, swept me into a state like a guided meditation, almost lucid dreaming. I was out of my body, in another place, but was still aware of my surroundings; two scenes superimposed.

I was walking through the 'Valley of the Shadow of Death'. I somehow knew that was what it was, though it was so dark I could see nothing. At first, it seemed terrible, but to my surprise, I gradually realised it was the natural darkness of great pine trees in a deep, rocky gorge. I could smell and feel the needles under my feet and make out the shapes against the sky but see nothing ahead or around. In spite of that, I trod firmly over rough, hard stones without stumbling – somehow I knew I was safe. Suddenly I stopped, the dark walls fell away on each side as I reached open land. Ahead was a beautiful pastoral country. It was full of fields and tiny trickling streamlets, trees and wildflowers. The evening shadows were long on the grass and away over by a hedge my little Andrew was playing, totally absorbed in the stones he was picking up, as I had so often watched him in our Sussex home.

I stood very still. I knew I could not go nearer, he could not see me, nor could I stay long, but I had a very pure sense of peace and safety. I knew nothing could harm him, not even the streams, which were the 'living waters' of paradise. Very soon, a safe 'someone' would come to find him before the cold dark of nightfall. Andrew would look up with trust and recognition and take the hand held out to him, to be led home to a safe house, loved and cared for beyond my imagining.

The scene faded, leaving only the scent of fresh water and a faint sound; the murmur of the approaching someone and Andrew's response. I was fully back in the room in Belgium. My son was gone. The pastor was just drawing the words of the 23rd psalm to a close.

The experience was profound and lasting. I cannot say it was a comfort for there is none for the loss of a child, but I think it saved me from a complete breakdown. Was it a 'true' vision, if there is such a thing? Does the unconscious, in its role of cushioning the person and making sense of experience, the balancing act that protects the psyche by feedback loops, provide us with something so profoundly healing even in extremis? If these more rational-sounding explanations are true psychologically, I believe it is only because we are designed that way. I do not know if there is an afterlife in any way that we can recognise as like this life – in that sense I am still agnostic about it. Do I believe in a loving creator God, who wants good for us? Yes indeed, and never in any doubt about it.

God gives us what we need to survive and grow, individually and communally. The pictures, visions and stories are metaphors and rationalisations but part of our clever design, evolved to cope not only with the 'nasty, brutish and short' aspect of life but with the 'man as little lower than the angels.'

Roger's parents and brothers came, as did my brother and family and Aunty Joyce. Others made all the arrangements, I was unable to take anything in, but sat by Andrew's body as long as possible. Neighbours came in, unknown, but caring – they cried with me. They brought little practical gifts, clothing and a child's bonnet, often choking with sobs, permitting mine to be heard.

The funeral was beautiful. Because there was only a small Protestant church, permission was given for it to take place as a joint service in the Catholic church, with joint pastors. Many strings had to be pulled, faraway Bishop's permission given. Such a thing had never happened in all of Belgium before, we were told, and had only been made possible by the Second Vatican Council of Pope John 23rd in 1962, a man I have always loved and admired.

The death of a child is a unifying, purifying tragedy that can bring a community together, however briefly. The Protestant congregation supported us entirely, as a historic occasion. Similarly, the Catholics came in large numbers, the nuns and the school children lined the path. I do not remember anything about the service, but the church was full to overflowing and the whole of that part was certainly a comfort. There is real human meaning and necessity in the rites of passage societies follow. Andrew's brief life could be said to have counted for little in the wider world, but in death he had done something healing for people in the community and towards unification of the whole Christian church.

Andrew's little coffin was laid in the family vault of the Berthaud's, where it remains; a great kindness. I did not know it but the normal practice was to put bodies for two years in a common vault and then the bones would be buried unmarked and coffinless. In fact, this would not have troubled me greatly. In the months and years after his death, I faced the knowledge of what was happening to his body and felt no revulsion nor horror. How could I not love him still and everything about him? I lost any distress at 'mortal corruption' then and forever. Nor did I feel a need to have his body returned to my own country; he is forever in my heart. If I prefer cremation for myself, as indeed I later did for Ken, my second husband, it is more because we have nothing tying us irrevocably to a particular part of the land. In an overcrowded world, I do not feel entitled to take up six feet of it permanently.

More than five decades have passed now, since these events. All my feelings and thoughts have gone through many processes, so that some of the grief of course remains, but some has been distilled into elegiac dignity.

Lullaby For the Mother of a Dead Child

Oh cradle the child as if he were sleeping.
Lullaby mother, and hushed be your weeping.
The tears are not his, nor the pain and the sorrow,
For he is awake in a golden tomorrow.

It is you who are sent to a darkness unending.
Whipped for no fault, you lie, uncomprehending
Oh desolate child, you must wait for the dawning,
But your son is awake on a bright summer morning.

Strong hands hold him up and he chuckles with laughter,
Grasping at stars and the Angels laugh, after.
Then, petted and kissed, from their knees he is springing
To search the green fields where the children are singing.

17

'JUST DON'T MENTION THE WAR' AND A TRIBUTE TO MY MOTHER

Just Don't Mention the War

THE BIG TRAUMAS IN LIFE can be managed, for better or for worse, according to the experiences one has had earlier, even from the times before memory and how other people dealt with the little, dependent child. My early experience of separation was when I was little more than three years old. It was felt brutally and suppressed for years, but inevitably coloured my life. It was also followed by restoration, an equally important part of the whole experience, granting a measure of optimism and resilience that has helped me time and again.

So – is it now time to visit those early days? "Just don't mention the war!" But of course, I have to. I was just two years old when it began and therefore seven when it finished, most of it just about within my memory span. .

My mother said: "We sent you to Sawley Grange in Derbyshire to my cousin's farm for the summer. It was so hot that you ran around in the fields all day in pants. There weren't any air raids after all, so we brought you home. It was called the 'phoney war.'"

Of course, I must have missed my parents, but I have no memory of this time. My mother added: "Everyone around then remembers listening to the radio and Chamberlain saying we were at war with Germany." I was born in September 1937 and this was September 1939. My father was a Professor of Electrical Engineering at

University College in London. My brother John said to me recently: "Everyone was saying it would be over quickly, but Daddy didn't believe that. He had everything in the department in packing cases. When the order came to evacuate the faculty to Swansea, all he had to do was nail down the lids."

After the phoney war, Swansea, with its docks, coal and factories, was a prime target for bombing. The local children had to be evacuated out again, this time without our families, I think in 1940. My brother John, at 4 years old, was about to attend Bryn Mill primary school when the war started. He thinks we were evacuated out about two years later. When I was older, my mother used to show us the family photo album.

"The whole school was evacuated to Pumpsaint, near Lampeter in mid-Wales," she told us. "John was already at school, but you were too young. They took you as a favour, Elinor. Look – here are pictures of you with two of the teachers, Miss Dunsford and Miss Dodds. You loved them, they were so kind to you." My poor mother! Poor children! She tried to make the best of it, but it was a terrible separation and she knew it.

A Tribute to my Mother

I ALWAYS KNEW my mother, in particular, loved me. That is the most vital ingredient for the healthy growth of a child: to know that your parents, or at least someone, loves you no matter what. My mother was a gentle, quiet person, but with a great sense of humour and of the ridiculous – a fun person to be with. She was the oldest child, born in 1898, with two younger sisters and a brother. In her own childhood, she had to take on a lot of responsibility for the family when her parents went away as missionaries to India and she eventually had to stay behind, in the care of relatives.

In her teens in boarding school, she became fascinated with the work of Sigmund Freud, whose writings were just coming out in

English and she determined early on to qualify in medicine and then become a psychoanalyst. What an amazing ambition for a young woman of that time – there was only one medical school in England then, the Royal Free in London, which admitted women at all and psychoanalysis was barely thought of as a respectable career!

She struggled through the years of study by applying for grants and teaching surface anatomy to the life drawing art students at Bedford College when she started her medical studies. She never knew, each year of her six-year course, whether she would be able to find a grant to continue, and in the later years, she also had to become guardian at times to her sisters as they returned to the UK. I have only patchy memories of her telling me about the years after qualification and meeting my father. I will just say that she married comparatively late, and had first my brother John in 1935, then myself in 1937. I was born on her 39th birthday and she used to joke that it was very tactful of me, as the focus shifted to me and no-one bothered about her age after that.

When the Second World War broke out, our family moved to Swansea, as my father was a Professor at the University of London and the faculties were all moved out to other University towns around the country. My mother was already working as a psychoanalyst, but her sense of duty compelled her to offer herself as a GP in place of a man who had been called up. My father and she argued for a while, as he wanted us to be sent to Canada for safety in case Britain went down. Maybe his schooling in Germany and experiences in the First World War gave him a greater fear of the might of the German war machine. I'm glad my mother prevailed, though any of these places might as well have been the moon to a toddler.

For years I felt I had to avoid the subject or comfort her when it came up, but we were able to talk a little when I grew up about how much it hurt her, with her greater understanding than most of her generation of the effects of early separation because of her psychoanalytic training, as well as her maternal instinct. My mother also eventually told me it also brought up much of her own early experiences as the daughter of missionary parents, and it seemed to her a dreadful thing to be repeating it with me and my brother. Neither she nor I could explore it together very much, even then. It was so painful. It took me many years and much therapy later on, as an adult, to recover from this, but I now understand and empathise with her dilemma. I also repeated it in a very diluted form by being a working mother. In the profession we call that 'repetition compulsion', to make it feel better.

I can't really imagine what it must have been like to be living through not just one but a second World War, as both she and my father had to do. I am sure she was a good GP, but she hated it. She had to take great responsibility and had difficulty getting advice and support. She must have worried constantly about the safety of her husband and children, her own competence and the fate of the country, particularly in the early years of the war. It's different looking back now, knowing the outcome.

She never knew what she would find when she was called out and drove miles with only a torch strapped to the front of the car instead of proper lights because of blackout regulations. She told me, with a laugh, that once she was called out at night to a 'pit accident' and drove miles across the wild Welsh hills with this ramshackle lighting, imagining a major disaster. She found the mine, with just one man who had gashed his arm, needing a stitch.

On another occasion, she was driving through a Valleys village and a small child dashed out almost under her wheels. She stopped and rushed to pick him up, sure that she hadn't hit him, but as she picked him up he crackled. "My God!" she thought, "I've broken every bone in his body!" The child was untouched and bawling loudly. He crackled because he had been sewn into several layers of newspaper under his combies to keep him warm for the winter!

A satisfying epilogue to her work in Aberdare came to my brother John and I after my mother's funeral, in a letter from the daughter of the GP she had replaced. Unfortunately, we didn't keep it and I don't remember the name. Apparently my mother's last task in the practice had been to deliver the baby of the GP and his wife. This baby, now a young woman, wrote to say she had herself just qualified in medicine.

I also took pleasure in 1997 in speaking at my own retirement party about my mother's work. I read a letter about "Dr Kapp, appointed by Swansea council during the war, to work some sessions with children with mental health needs". I guess this probably made her the first child psychiatrist to work in Wales. I read out the references for her, which were good, before telling the audience that it was a different 'Dr Kapp.' It was from such a childhood that I was able to fully engage – later – with the experiences of anxiety and loss that marked my education at primary level, and then boarding school, finally influencing me to go on to study medicine.

18

A PLACE OF FIVE SAINTS, GOLD AND A MURDER

MY OWN EARLIEST MEMORIES come from the place to which the children of Bryn Mill school and their teachers were evacuated. Pumsaint is a village, now in Powys, named for 'Five Saints'.

"Gold has been dug up here since Roman times," they will tell you in the village shop, with its tourist attraction posters. The place we had been sent to was a mansion, Dolacauthi Hall, no longer standing. I found out later that it was remembered locally for being the place of a notorious murder, where a servant savagely hacked his master to death in the mid-Nineteenth Century.

When I went back there with Ken, my husband, in the early 1980s, I looked across the garden at an apple tree and said confidently: "There's a swing on that tree". When I examined the tree, I found deep grooves from long ago where the ropes had cut into the bark. It had not been easy to find the place. We had driven up from Swansea after a meeting and spent some time searching the area. Eventually, we went down a drive into parkland and the land began to feel familiar, albeit like a place seen in a dream.

I found a modern house. The owner was friendly, perhaps used to the occasional historian or tourist. She told me that her house had indeed been built on the site of Dolaucothi Hall, pulled down sometime after the war and I was welcome to wander around the garden.

As I walked around, trying to see where the Hall had been and which way it had faced, I felt myself as a very small child with two or three others, giggling and whispering, daring each other to approach the glass porch of the house. "Snakessss, there are snakessss in there," whispered the older children. I remember being a terrified half-believer, yet somehow aware that I was enjoying a pretence.

I remembered sitting in the corner of a huge bay window, my brother at the far end, both howling dismally for what seemed like hours. There were shrubs outside and the light made squares on the wooden floor. It seemed a very big place, smelling strange and old. My brother told me, after we were grown up, that he remembers it too; it was the day our parents left us there.

I remember being very small and looking out through the bars of a cot, probably the cot sides of a child's bed, playing with the stripy shadows of the bars. Another time, I am in the same cot lying with my cheek on a wet pillow. I am aware that I have just been having a most almighty outburst of rage. High over my head in a vast dark room, I can hear shocked whispers about me from the grown-ups, but I am drowsy, spent, it seems to have no relation to me anymore, it's gone and I feel better.

The Gold in the Shadow

When I went on that visit in the 1980s, walking in the garden of the modern house that had replaced the great Hall, I looked out across the parkland beyond. I could see in the middle distance a huge, beautiful tree, an oak I think, just coming into leaf. Suddenly, now in my forties, I was overwhelmed with my first memory of God, what I 'knew' had been my first experience of the mystical.

I was no longer on the ground but looking out of a great window on the first floor at that very tree. I knew it was very early morning, barely light. I could see the milky mist coiling around the trunk and the crown, in full leaf. I am as sure as one can be that it was a true memory, but there is no proof.

The wooden floor under my feet feels cold and slippery. The glass seems to radiate cold at me. I know it is naughty to be out of my dormitory before getting-up time with no-one around, but my misery is too much for me. I cannot put my sorrow into words but my whole world has been taken away and I am sick with the loss of my mummy and daddy.

I look at the tree and it speaks to me, not with words to the ear but something directly in the heart: "I am TREE. I was here long before your father and mother and I will be here long after you are all gone."

I am far too young to understand what it is saying, but somehow I know in a way beyond any four year old's understanding that it is saying "I am GOD"; the words tree and God are the same because GOD has chosen to show me the real essence of being through a tree. I remain standing there open-mouthed, my feet squirming in the cold and eventually make my way back to bed, the experience folded small and tucked away in my memory only to be woken by this visit. Was it real? Was it a true memory? How can I say? Time does not exist in a mystical experience and this was a re-experiencing.

I do know that it must have been the source of something of which I have been consciously aware all through my childhood and adult life – a knowledge of the existence of God. I have never been without a sense that, although we live in a marvellous scientifically-ordered universe, at the heart of it is a great mystery of personal love beating down on us, evoking a response. Both within us and around us. As I grew up, that sense seemed to match up, near enough, with what other people called God, so I used the term. It never seemed to fit, though, with the caricature judgemental man with a long white beard.

One thing seems to me to give it a hallmark of authentic 'otherness'. If I was going to hallucinate or project something, even in memory, to a child that would comfort her in the desolation I experienced at the loss of my parents, even now I would be unable to resist making it obviously comforting. It would have to be a warm glow, a sense of being hugged, a visit by an angelic being. I was a very physical child, well used to cuddles. This experience was almost harsh in its sparseness but somehow it gave me something more valuable than comfort; a lifelong sense that there was order and love in the universe beyond anything we can imagine.

Today I still only know those three things about Pumsaint, all of them very valuable. And I found not just five saints, but the massed ranks of heaven and something more precious than gold.

19

THE RETURN

MY PARENTS CAME BACK. How lucky I was! How very grateful I am, when I remember to be, that I was not one of those whose father or mother, or both, were killed in the war. I believe it was not all that long, a matter of months perhaps, before the children who had been evacuated to Pumsaint were returned to Swansea, including of course myself and my older brother John. I never thought to record it or enquire during my parents' lifetime. John thought it might have been about six months. But any time is an eternity to a small child.

I think I carry a fair measure of 'survivor's guilt' within me. Along with 300 years of nonconformist ancestors and schooling that emphasised service to others, I suppose I was always likely to choose a caring profession. I do think that one source of my naturally optimistic state – glass half full, not half empty – was this Restoration. I remember the moment Mummy and Daddy first came back to Dolaucothi Hall to visit us, though they left again.

I am in the great big hall where we have our meals, sitting with lots of other children at a long table. I become aware that all the children at the table are whispering and giggling. It's about me, but it's nice. Some great happy secret. I am very puzzled, but then look up and find that my parents have arrived and they appear in the doorway.

The emotion is so great that I have no picture at all of them in my memory! Burnt into my mind by joy instead is the picture of what is in front of me on the table: a white bowl with deep red plums and yellow custard. Never have plums been more plum-coloured, custard more golden or china more white. I can see them still. During my art degree, many years later after I retired and was over 60 years old, I tried to paint the scene. My drawing skills are still negligible, but it was therapeutic to paint those plums and custard pudding. I spent a lot of time on it. Almost in a trance, I then outlined two figures against yellow light in the doorway and painted them black. Intriguingly, the angular shapes of the figures have a real feel of drawings of the 40s, no doubt seen in advertisements, dredged from unknown memories.

When I studied my picture after finishing it, I began to cry. It showed me two truths: one artistic, one psychological. If you paint in black against a light colour, you are painting a hole, not a substance. Even after so many years, what I painted there was the absence of my parents – a parent-shaped hole in my life.

So. What were my parents really like? How were the early years with them? It's time to set a little of it down. A happy childhood, in spite of the separation and the war.

20

I LEARN TO READ & OTHER GAMES

I **SUPPOSE** my joined-up memories really begin in about 1942, well after we had come back to live with our parents in Swansea. The worst of the bombing was over – maybe the docks were unusable by that time. I remember this time like somewhere seen in a dream. The little up-and-down streets and the bombed houses; the rubble-filled gardens already turning to coarse grass and fireweed.

We had lots of games to play in the streets in those middle days of the war. We would spend hours picking the urban wildflowers and making shops with brick dust 'lemonade' and weeds. There was hardly any traffic and lots of other children around.

John could go much further afield on his own than I could of course; he would regularly go and swim off the beach. I could only go with the grown-ups. We could walk out along the sewer pipe into deepish water, but at certain times you might find yourself among toilet paper and turds and have to scramble for shore. I don't remember any of us getting ill from it. Perhaps the bugs were frightened of Hitler too and kept away!

John remembers on one of his expeditions seeing the whole of Swansea Bay crammed with ships: yachts and dinghies, coasters and steamships of all sorts. They were preparing for the D-Day landing, but of course, he didn't know that till much later.

Behind the house, Number 9 St Albans Road, was a very small garden with a square of muddy grass and sweet-smelling pinks edging the concrete path in summer. A steep flight of stone steps led down to a wooden door opening onto the lane. I spent hours playing with that door, creaking it to and fro, picking at the blisters in the green paint to reveal a blue layer beneath.

Going fast up or down those slippery steps was often hazardous. I recall an experimental moment when I skinned my knee at the bottom. I opened my mouth and started crying, intending to go up and seek my mother. Then I remembered something. If you waited, the pain went away. I waited. The pain went away. I stopped crying and went back to my games, rather thoughtful. My first scientific experiment in the field of psychology: creating a hypothesis, testing and verifying it!

I know when I learned to read, the exact moment, because I have the book and the memory. We didn't have many books in my early years because paper for publishers was rationed and in short supply. Most children's books were pre-war. We did have a series called 'Pere Castor's Wild Animal Books' by 'Lida', translated by Rose Fyleman "with that delicate gaiety which shows they come from the French". They were illustrated with lithographs, mostly black and white, but a few in a limited range of colours. I re-found the series in the attic after my parents died. I seem to recall *Quipic the Hedgehog* and a brightly coloured Kingfisher, but the one with which I learned to read was *Bourru the Brown Bear* and I still have it.

Written on the flyleaf is 'To John and Elinor with love from Mummy and Daddy, Christmas 1942', so I was a little over five years old. I used to look at the pictures while my mother read aloud, no doubt over and over again. I remember that suddenly a magic thing happened! The picture was a dull one, just a dark hole in a bank in muddy colours. But the black marks beside it were suddenly much more interesting, shifting and moving, telling me the story.

From then on I was hooked on anything in print and have always been one of those people who read the labels on marmalade and pickle jars if there is nothing else. My mother confirmed that I had suddenly taken over reading, though she put it a little earlier, when I was four. When I re-found *Bourru* in the attic, after she died, my heart beat faster as I turned the pages. Sure enough, page 18 had the dull little hollow and the blocks of print and a sudden brief sensation swept over me; the thrill of discovery.

21

THE WAR AGAINST FEAR

T HE SUNSHINE of most of those previously discussed memories obscures the fact that our playgrounds were bombsites. Under the grass and flowers, behind the façades of the little streets, there was suffering, bereavement, poverty, war work and graves. And fear. A lot of fear. The adults were very calm on the surface, but children are not always fooled by the stiff upper lip; they smell the fear leaking from every pore. A child breathes it in and can be poisoned by it, because the grown-ups are the sturdy earth beneath their feet and if that rocks, nothing is safe.

But because I was a child, I could live in the moment and breathe in the sunshine as well as the fear. There were still raids and alerts when we came back to Swansea. I learned from adult talk over my head that it was all because of a nasty man called Hitler. At night, especially when I had been naughty, I would stare out across the wrinkly sea to the opening of the bay and imagine Hitler was coming.

I do remember one night standing shivering in the bedroom of our little house, 9 St Alban's Road. I had dreamed I saw Hitler swim across the bay and I knew he was going to walk up the hill, straight past the Patti Pavilion towards our house and I was convinced it was really happening. I remember my father coming in and kneeling beside me, with his arm around me, as I sobbed out what I had seen and him telling me it must have been a nightmare.

"Look at that little tiny light," he said pointing out to the centre of Swansea Bay. "That's the Lightship. It's full of brave soldiers. You know, however hard he tries, Hitler can't get past that; they'll stop him. Look, it's your very own little star!" After that, if I woke in the night, I would watch the little light until sleep would float me back into dreams.

Sometimes my father would go out on blackout duties and sometimes my doctor mother would go out for a mysterious thing called 'on-call'. At those times, I would have to go to 'Auntie' next door after school for a while, or the cleaning lady would stay on. Auntie was not a blood relative; grown-ups who were a bit special were always 'aunties' and 'uncles' then. I don't remember if we used her name as well, or what it was. She was in a wheelchair and therefore was home all the time, but I would only be there for short periods. I think someone – a maid, a relative – looked after her, but that is shadowy.

I think I was rather a sickly child, though with nothing serious. I remember having mumps, very, very painfully in my right cheek, and waking one morning to find the other side swollen up too. "Mummy," I shouted, totally outraged by the unfairness of it all, "now it's gone TO THE OTHER SIDE. Boo hoo hoo!" Probably I had no more illnesses than most children, but my mother was especially close and caring if we were ill and didn't seem to go out so much. My father was not very tolerant of unwellness; he got irritable and frightened, so it was sometimes like a little secret between my mother and I.

Mind you, my father had great tolerance at times. I remember many occasions when I was very small, after we came back from Dolacauthi, when I wouldn't eat. My daddy would sit with me on his knee doing the time-honoured: "This is a car, *brrmm brrmm brrmm*, open your mouth... this is an aeroplane, *wocka wocka wocka*... this is a bicycle, *brring brring brring*..." and down it would go, spoonful by spoonful.

Our kitchen was the place where we spent most time, as did most families. It was practically filled with a Morrison shelter. I wonder how many people remember having one of those? The fully bomb-proof Anderson shelters were built underground, in gardens and you could almost live in them, but many homes just had a big reinforced metal table, named after the Minister for Security, Herbert Morrison. All the family was supposed to climb under it if the siren went off. It was designed to keep you safe when the house caved in. You'd have to wait to be dug out, I suppose. It took up most of the space and I hated it because the day after I was given a lovely doll for Christmas, I turned round suddenly. Crash! The china head broke into irreconcilable pieces against the horrid metal corner.

22

A LONG LONG TRAIL A-WINDING

THIS IS A STORY I wrote in 2006 when I heard a radio report about the pardoning of the soldiers, mostly very young, unjustly shot for cowardice in the First World War. I sat in the twilight, crying because of the tragedy of the young lives lost – and the plot of this story unravelled backwards in my mind, almost like a ghost story told to me by those lost young people. I want to emphasise, though, that this story is entirely fiction, but it was enhanced by my use of the memories I had of Swansea. I wrote and rewrote it many times, doing a lot of research, as any writer should.

* * *

Listen! Oh listen! A little girl is sitting on the knee of her Auntie Gwladys, who is singing to keep the bombs away. "There's a long long trail a-winding," Auntie sings,
"into the land of my dreams."

You have to concentrate on my story, for it covers two lifetimes, two World Wars and 60 years of peace since the second of them. It takes me right up to 2006, when that announcement in the paper brought it all back. That's why I'm telling it to you. I think Gwladys would like to have it told, now; a secret can eat into your life and leave it full of wormholes.

* * *

I was two years old when the Second World War broke out, but my memories really start when we lived in Swansea; oh I suppose it would be about 1943. I remember little up and down streets and bombed-out houses, already softening under rough grass and fireweed. There were still occasional raids and alerts, all due to a nasty man called Hitler. One night I called for my father,

"Daddy, daddy, I saw Hitler swimming across the bay. He's coming to get us!"

My father held me tight and said, "Shh, darling. It was just a dream. Look at the little light there – that's the lightship. It's full of brave sailors. Hitler will never get past."

After that, I would lie in bed and watch the star on the horizon until the twinkling closed my eyes in sleep.

I told Auntie Gwladys about the little star. "Auntie Gwladys. Do you know about Hitler?"

"Yes dear, I do."

"He's a Very Bad Man, you know, but you don't need to be frightened 'cause he can't come here. The lightship won't let him get past, ever, Daddy says!"

"Yes dear, I'm sure your daddy's right. Now would you like a cup of tea?"

I stayed with her some nights, while my father was out fire-watching and my doctor mother was 'on-call'. Auntie Gwladys wasn't a blood relative, just a neighbour, but we called most adults Auntie and Uncle in those days. I loved being offered tea like a proper grown-up lady. It was only 'milk with a splash,' but I drank it from a china teacup with rosebuds. I loved that teacup, almost as much as I loved the silver teaspoon with which I ate a real egg, instead of nasty dried stuff. I loved the frozen piece of rainbow, which Auntie said was a tropical shell, the red strawberry pincushion and the tiny hussive with thimble, needles and bodkin, tucked like a secret into an ivory umbrella, just the size of my hand.

I wasn't so sure about washing in the echoey bathroom, or the big spare bed. The headboard was like a dark, frowning face over me.

"Sing to me, Auntie, like Mummy does," I demanded the first time I stayed there. Auntie Gwladys flushed awkwardly and tried to say 'no' but I insisted as only a child can.

Hesitantly, clearing her throat, she said, "I can only remember the one song now. I'm not sure... I can't remember the beginning," then she began to hum a tune, eventually breaking into words:

> "Old remembrances are thronging
> Thro' my memory
> Till it seems the world is full of dreams
> Just to call you back to me..."

She seemed to break down in tears for a moment and I watched her in wonder. Then she hugged me – I remember that because it was the first time – smiled and sang more confidently,

> "There's a long, long trail a-winding
> ... to the land of my dreams.
> Where the nightingales are singing
> And a white moon beams..."

My eyes were closing. I held her finger and drifted off, comforted. When my parents were putting me to bed the next night, I told my mother about it.

"She sang to me, Mummy, like you do, but a bit different."

My mother seemed to stiffen. She and my father spoke to each other, not to me:

"Surely not? She's not sung a note for many years!"

I insisted: "Yes she did mummy, it was about a road winding away into the nightingales and the moon and the dreams."

My mother sang:

>"Where the nightingales are singing
>…and a white moon beams."

Then she said to my father: "Yes Reggie, that's one she used to sing. It was his favourite, but she told me she could never sing it without breaking down,"

My mother sang again: "'Nights are growing very lonely, Days are very long…' Poor Gwladys!"

My father sat down beside me and said, gently, "It's a sad story, Ellie, and a grown-up one. Auntie Gwladys had a sweetheart when she was young, but he went to be a soldier in the war before this one; the one we call the 'First World War'. He was killed in action and she never married. They used to sing duets. She had a lovely voice. She used to sing in chapel and festivals, but she couldn't sing after he died."

My mother said, "I'm glad she could sing for you, Ellie, but don't pester her if she doesn't want to." To my father she added, "I think Ellie's a comfort to her; perhaps like the little girl she never had." Smiling at my father she sang again: "…I forget that you're not with me yet
When I think I see you smile…"

But I was already almost asleep.

After that, it became a little ritual when I stayed with Auntie Gwladys that I would sing 'Baa baa, black sheep' and other rhymes and she would sing children's songs, some in Welsh. Always she would finish, because I asked her, with 'the one about the nightingales', and always her voice would be different, tearful even. She never refused and I would hold her finger and go to sleep. Her sorrow somehow eased for me the atmosphere of fear, never spoken of, that clouded our lives in those days.

Time passed. Before the end of the war we went back to Croydon, but we used to visit Wales most summers, going on holiday to the Gower. We would call on Auntie Gwladys for tea. She always gave me the same china cup with the rosebuds, but we never sang.

I married and moved several times and Auntie Gwladys became hardly even a memory. In the 1960s my parents died, within a week of each other, and Auntie Gwladys wrote me a particularly moving letter about how much my mother had meant to her, so after that, we exchanged a few words in a card each year. I sent her my address when I moved to Cardiff in the early 70s, promising to visit sometime, but you know how it is; I never did.

Then, in the late 70s, I had a phone call out of the blue. "Hello," said an unknown woman. "You don't know me, and this may seem a little strange, but – could I ask – was your mother's name 'Dorothy'... I mean, are you Dorothy's daughter?"

When I said yes she introduced herself as Sister Phyllis, a nursing nun in charge of a hospice.
"We are looking after Gwladys Jones. I'm sorry to tell you that she is seriously ill."

"She's my Auntie Gwladys," I said, "not a relative; a family friend."

"The thing is," continued Sister Phyllis, "she has no relatives or visitors at all. Since she realised she wouldn't get better, she's become very troubled; she has something on her mind. 'I should have told Dorothy,' she keeps saying. 'I must tell the truth. Dorothy's daughter will know what to do' – and then she cries a lot. We looked in her address book and found your number with 'Dorothy's daughter' beside it. Would it be possible – is it too much to ask – could you visit?"

Sister Phyllis let me in. I thought I was prepared for the changes of illness and age, but I was shocked. I couldn't recognise Gwladys in this shrunken wraith in the bed, but she knew me. Or did she?

"Dorothy, Dorothy!" she said, "Oh thank you for coming!"

"I'm so pleased to be here," I said gently, "But I'm not Dorothy you know; I'm her daughter, Elinor. Ellie, you used to call me."

Gwladys took no notice. "I must talk to you, Dorothy," she continued, "I should have told you. I so often wanted to tell you, but I couldn't. I couldn't tell anyone. You were so kind to me; you and Reggie. I couldn't bear for anyone to know…"

The words were tumbling out and I sat down and took her hand in both mine. I suddenly remembered the fragility of the needlecase umbrella and the shell and the rosebud cup. It seemed for a moment as if I held her life and my childhood in my hands too; how we are all so breakable and yet so tough.

"What is it, Gwladys?" I said gently. "It's fine to tell me anything you want now."

Gwladys was sobbing. "It was Jonnie… my fiancé… I never told anyone. It killed his parents. It would have killed mine. Nobody must ever know. Forgive me, Dorothy. You were my doctor; you did so much for me, but nobody must ever know."

A strange thing happened. As I sat stroking her hand I heard the distant boom of heavy guns. The sound swelled around me, but I knew it was inside my head.

A man was shouting. "I've got him, Sarge. Bleeding coward. He's in the chicken coop." I heard the absurd clucking of disturbed poultry and a terrified young voice, almost that of a boy rising hysterically, not funny at all. "No, no, no, no, no, no, no, no… I can't… I can't go back!"

The first voice said gruffly, "You'll have something to scream about in the morning!"

Then the young man again: "Oh God, no. Oh God, no, no, no, no!"

I held my hands to my head, so terrifying was the experience, but I couldn't stop it. There was the sound of boots marching and a cultured voice gabbling a prayer. I spoke quickly then to block out the click of rifles being cocked and took her hand again.

"It's all right, Gwladys. It's all over now."

"Will it ever be alright?" Gwladys sobbed, "My Jonnie, my lovely Jonnie; he let his country down. What would anyone have thought of me if they'd known? He… he wasn't killed in action. Shot at dawn, they said, a disgrace to his country, they said!"

Somehow I understood the story even before Gwladys poured it out. They had both been so young. Her sweetheart Jonnie, a farm boy from the Swansea Valley who had lied about his age to enlist. Like so many, he had no idea what he was letting himself in for and cracked very quickly under the strain. So many boys, so much courage, so much bravado, such an unmentionable obscenity of waste and grief and shame. Such poison for the whole of someone's life.

I held Gwladys until she quietened. "Please sing to me," she said and the song flowed between us effortlessly as I sang:

> "All night long I hear you calling,
> Calling sweet and low;
> Seem to hear your footsteps falling,
> Everywhere I go."

Gwladys was asleep, holding my hand like the trusting child I had once been to her. I stayed long enough to be sure she would sleep for a while, then went to find Sister Phyllis. I told her what had happened but not the details.

"I'm just a bit worried, though," I said. "She desperately wanted to tell me her story, but she thought I was my mother. She couldn't seem to understand that I wasn't. Was I right to let her tell me, even so?"

Sister Phyllis gave my question the dignity of reflection, rather than instant reassurance. Then she said, "I'm sure you were right. Gwladys has been very, very troubled by whatever her secret was. These things are seldom as bad as they seem when they come out. She needed to tell someone."

Two days after I got home the phone rang. Sister Phyllis's voice: "I promised I'd tell you when… Gwladys passed away last night."

"Oh, oh yes. Thank you for letting me know," I said.

She added, "I thought you'd like to know how much your visit helped her. After you left she was very peaceful. She just faded away gently. Oh, and I thought – because of what you asked – that you'd like to know that yesterday morning when I went into her room she said, 'Dorothy's daughter came to see me. She's a doctor, just like her mother.' I thought you'd like to know that she was aware of who you were in the end."

I sat for a while, crying quietly for Gwladys and Jonnie and other lives destroyed and damaged by all the wars. I cried a little for the loss of my parents and for myself and for life generally. Then I put it all behind me again and went on living.

* * *

Many years have gone by and I almost forgot about it till now. Till that piece on the radio. Till you asked me why I was sitting in the dark, holding a newspaper.

So now I've told you and I'm going to show you the paper. August 16th, 2006. 'Soldiers shot for cowardice in First World War pardoned,' says the headline. They knew that youngsters like Jonnie should never have been shot, even in war, but it's taken 88 years to say it. Much, much too late for Gwladys and her Jonnie.

How strange! I can hear a voice singing:

> "Though the road between us stretches
> Many a weary mile…"

Listen! Is it a radio?… No; it's Gwladys. Can't you hear her? The voice is joyful, but it's definitely her.

> "There's a long, long night of waiting
> Till my dreams all come true…"

Now there's another voice joining hers. A tenor with a valley's accent, sweet and true:

> "Till the day when I'll be going down
> That long, long trail with you."

….Listen! Oh listen!….

23

ROBERT RABBIT, THE GORSEINON SWEETIE COLLECTIVE, A RESCUE, FIRST LOVE & OTHER MARVELS

"**W**OULD YOU LIKE** this footballer rabbit? He's called Robert," said Mummy, showing me a knitting pattern. Rhetorical question. Of course I would; we had very few toys. Little Cubby, so miraculously rescued at Dolaucothi Hall, belonged to my brother John. This was during the last summer we spent in Swansea before our return to Croydon.

Anyway, although I had no interest in knitting myself, nor indeed in football, I longed for Robert. I watched fascinated as he grew on knitting needles. Robert was 'dressed' in yellow and blue football stripes and black knitted football boots. Miraculously, one morning, long before I thought he could be finished, there he was on my pillow when I woke. I was miserable and ill with chickenpox and my mother must have stayed up half the night to finish him. I kept him for years and years, till eventually the moths got him and I had to send him to the great football pitch in the sky. I must have been in my twenties by then!

A little time before we came back to Croydon I developed eczema of the scalp. It itched and oozed and made me miserable. It began to spread until it covered my whole head. My mother was always very deferential to doctors, even though she herself was one. The medical powers decided that it was so bad I must be admitted to hospital. I have terrible, if farcical memories of the Gulag which was Gorseinon Hospital. Don't forget that this was about 1944. Attitudes to children in hospital were still stuck in 19th-century mode. In addition, most of the younger nurses and doctors had been called up or were doing war work. Terrifying elderly ogresses had been conjured up to look after the little victims. That makes it sound as if I was beaten or starved. Of course not – but I remember the insensitivity and – once again – the sense that even my parents were powerless in this alien, angry world at war.

Nobody explained anything. My hair was roughly and painfully cut off, right down to my scalp. Conversations went on in loud voices over my sore, medicated head.

For days, I didn't dare have a poo because there was no toilet paper. When, in pain, I conjured up the courage to say, "Is there any toilet paper?" The nurse gave me some paper, laughing and saying, "What a goose you are!" Of course I was, but it hardly helped.

I didn't want to eat but there was no kind daddy to spoon it in, they just scolded me and took the tray away again. Or said the world's most hateful phrase: 'Many a poor child would be glad of that.' I remember the boisterous older children, who teased me unchecked, the busy rush of the nurses passing by. If I did pluck up the courage to ask for something it was no use – they'd gone before my timid words had reached my trembling lips.

I also vividly remember being woken up in what seemed for me to be the middle of the night and all the bandages being stripped off my head for a mysterious visit by a 'specialist'. After he went, the nurse forgot to come back to replace the coverings. I was terrified of getting into trouble if I fell asleep and soiled the pillows with my nasty head and I tried desperately for what seemed hours to stay awake. Unsuccessfully of course, and no one mentioned it next morning.

I remember, worst of all, that when we were sent sweets from home they were instantly taken into common use, locked away in a big tin in a cupboard and distributed to all the children once a week, after lunch. The sweets themselves didn't matter so much, for I was a very well-brought-up child who would have handed mine round without complaint. What hurt was that we never knew which sweets would have been ours: one tiny, direct contact of love from my parents, withheld.

I know, I know, the nurses were much too busy to label packets of sweets, sugar is bad for you, what about the poor children who didn't have any, 'from each according to his ability, to each according to his need,' blah di blah. Try convincing a homesick five-year-old that communism is a just and humane system! What with Hitler trying to take over Swansea and the ogresses of the Gorseinon Sweetie Collective, I suppose I had the advantage of being inoculated against both fascism and communism at an early age!

My mother to the rescue!

These things may seem a little trivial when written down, but of course, they are the whole of the child's world, particularly when separated from home, in my case, for the second time. The real trauma was that my parents were not allowed to visit. It really was believed in those days that a child wouldn't miss its parents if they were excluded and that 'spoiling the child' by allowing visits would be disastrous. I was supposed to be left alone for the full six weeks I was there. To my mother, who as a psychoanalyst knew what it was doing to me, particularly after my time as an evacuee, this was torture, for her as well as me. She pushed her way into the ward every Sunday afternoon, claiming medical privilege. I remember quite a big fuss, raised voices and a ripple of disapproval at the ward entrance the first time. Then my mother appeared at my bedside, flushed but smiling.

I know now what an effort it must have been for her. Deferential by nature, gentle of temperament and lacking confidence, my mother's action was truly a mouse confronting lion in defence of her mouslet. Lions are afraid of mice, but mice don't necessarily know this, certainly not the first time.

After I had been there six weeks, with my scalp getting more repulsively covered in oozing sores by the day, she had the necessary courage to sign me out against medical advice and take me home. She took off all the bandages, abandoned the ointments, put me to bed in front of an open window for the healing sea breezes of Swansea Bay to get to my head and spoiled me rotten with tender care and nourishment. The eczema went, defeated by her love.

The morning my mother came for me in Gorseinon Hospital, I remember one of the ogresses in a very grumpy mood dressing me, saying snappily, "Your mother's coming for you." I certainly picked up the disapproval and hardly dared believe I was going home till Mummy walked in.

It was one of the happiest days of my life. She had knitted two little pixie hoods in a red and black plaid so that I could always have a clean one to wear when we went out and not get cold, nor look strange, because of my lack of hair. I remember holding Mummy's hand and skipping in joy as we walked out of the dark hall, then tiptoeing along the narrow stone edging between lawn and drive, bursting with relief and happiness. Even my mother's choice of wool was a sign of her sensitivity and secret ability to buck the system. Little girls at that time were invariably dressed in pastel colours, which didn't suit me nearly as well as the dramatic black and red she had chosen.

It was in 1952 that the influential film, *A Two-Year-Old Goes to Hospital* was brought out. It beautifully and heartbreakingly showed a child left in hospital for a week, charting her progress from grief and rage to despair. Eventually, she becomes apathetic and passive; the 'good child' who has 'settled in' of the institutional myth. The film gradually changed the practice of paediatrics forever. I saw it as a medical student some 15 years later, when it had become a classic, and found it extraordinarily moving and therapeutic.

As a little coda: It had been good of my mother to try and shield me from teasing but, alas, nothing could save me when I recovered and started at a new school before my hair had grown. "You're a boy, you're a boy. You shouldn't be in our school!" sang some of the girls to my grief and mortification. "I'm not a boy, I'm a GIRL!" I shouted back.

Never mind. Some 65 years later my hair became very short, stuck up in hedgehog spikes and was bright purple and maroon in stripes, remaining like that until I was well into my 70s. I wonder how that happened?

24

MY VERY FIRST LOVE.
HUW, WHERE DID YOU GO?

I DO REMEMBER one briefly lovely time during my hospital stay in Gorseinon Cottage Hospital. There was a boy in the next bed to me for a while who had been in hospitals on and off all his life. His legs seemed to be twisted, rigid in plaster and were pulled right up by a pulley and wires. He must have had a lot of pain or at least discomfort, but he never complained. Looking back, I think he must have had congenital dislocated hips or possibly bone tuberculosis – TB was very common in Swansea.

We chatted for hours, a refuge for both of us. Did he even have parents? I don't think he talked about them. He seemed at one and the same time very grown-up and yet very naive, as children often are when they have suffered much pain and spent time in hospitals. We talked a lot about the Fairies and although he must have been all of seven years old to my six, he still believed totally in them. I already knew that Fairies were imaginary beings who didn't 'really' exist and I was filled with great tenderness and sorrow for him. Not for anything would I have disillusioned him; it was a protective, almost maternal love.

I don't think he was in the ward long, and as happens in hospital, he simply vanished. Did he go for another operation, or to another hospital? Did he die? Was he discharged? I will never know, but I still occasionally think of him. His name was Hugh, presumably spelled 'Huw', and I know he was my first true love.

Huw: Gorseinon Hospital 1943

Did you die,
Or did they just take you away
To another ward?
Boy in the next bed,
Plaster legs high on a gallows
Where your small body hung.
You smiled at me
With all your seven years,
And I, a year younger,
Fell in love with you, there and then and
Always and forever.
Huw, Huw, Huw: the cooing of a dove.
For hours we talked about the Fairy Folk
I knew they were a story,
You did not. Shy, hospital-bound child,
Older and younger than your years.
Not for the world
Would I have disillusioned you.
I would have held your ears
In my child-small hands.
I would have given all I had
To save you from that truth.
Neither, for all the world
Would I have let you go.
Did the Fairy Folk take you?
Did you die?
Or did they just take you away
To another ward?

25

MORE ABOUT MY PARENTS

MY PARENTS MET as a result of both of them having an interest in the Freudian Analytic movement. In fact, they were part of it at a very early stage. My mother, as a young doctor, was very impressed by this new therapy and during her work in a psychiatric hospital near London she managed to arrange to have weekly Psychoanalysis from a distinguished Analyst, who was himself an analysand of Anna Freud, Sigmund Freud's daughter. This was for the purpose of training in this new technique as well as for therapy – indeed both were always regarded as complementary. It is still essential to have a training analysis before being allowed to practice in the Freudian mode (which I never did).

At the same time, a slightly older Engineer, Reginald Kapp, was also attending sessions with this doctor. He had been a homosexual for the greater part of his life, but longed to be able to marry and have children. I knew nothing of this until many years after his death, as my parents of course never spoke of it to me – homosexual actions were still illegal and socially abhorrent in those days. I knew my parents to be socially tolerant and broadminded about such things and grew up with complete acceptance of them – but I think that would have been very different to them telling me, all those years ago.

I learnt of it from my Godmother, Dr Doreen Firmin, many years later and it unfolded gradually in my mind in a very relieved and healing way after that.

I also learnt from her that they had not only been introduced to each other by the Psychoanalyst, but he realised that they would be a good match for each other, brought them together and took them, in a group holiday, to Morocco.

Many, many years later I had the wonderful privilege of meeting Anna Freud, when my husband Ken was President of the Royal College of Psychiatrists. As Lady President it was my job to look after her and I shared my story with her. She was charming and talked readily about the way the movement had developed. It was commonplace for groups of patients and Analysts to go on day picnics and even weekend or overseas trips in those early years. She remembered her own trainees well, including their Analyst and shared other interesting insights with me. I am not sure of the year, but it was not very long before she died in 1982

My final reconciliation with my mother

This is one of the strange, mystical events that have happened to me on many occasions – very few of which I have shared. It happened in 2011. One weekday I had felt low and, as I quite often did, went to see if there was a Service at the local Catholic Church. Though disliking much of their theology and practice, I recognise the goodness of many of the members and priests of that church.

When I went for the 12.15pm weekday Mass I found myself desperate to get there, for there to be a service. It almost felt like the urge to be sick and get to a basin before disaster happened! I experienced tears of relief and a great longing for God as I went in and knelt at the back, begging him to heal me. "Lord Jesus Christ, Son of God, Saviour, have mercy on me a sinner."

At 10.45am I came back from Mass at St Marys in a quiet mood and put my head down to have a rest. I was swept by the realisation that what I gave my mother was always pure, unconditional love, and that was what she always gave me. In that moment I knew that

I forgave and was forgiven in a relationship with her of total love, in which we are both one and separate.

That was the meaning and memory of my dream when she came to me just after she died. I knew then that, somehow, I had to grow into it. It has taken me 45 years to understand and take hold of it fully. Yet all that 'time' it has been there, in my eternity within. In the Divine Perfection within me.

"Forgive us our trespasses as we forgive those who trespass against us." That 'as' means 'Now', 'Both at the same time,' 'In the Eternal Instant.' This related to my late teenage and 20s, when she was deeply depressed, suffering from Parkinson's, then bowel cancer, then dementia. We never really connected again till the terrible events surrounding her death, and I was always in conflict about my duty.

I was also realising that we did indeed connect both ways, at times and with tenderness, but I was always burdened by guilt and could not gain from the knowledge. I visited her when I could, had her to stay with us in Taplow, cradled her head, when she fell in the flat when I was nearly 9 months pregnant. I fought (as did Roger) for her to be properly assessed in hospital then, discussed with my father and John what to do, brought baby Andrew to see her in the ward, sat with her reassuringly when she thought she was going on a cruise ship as she was dying.

What wonderful healing can take place, if we allow ourselves to receive it, even many years later on, in our earthly lives!

26

HOMEGOING

W E WENT BACK to Croydon, our home, the place where I was born, sometime before the end of the war. I think it must have been in late 1943 or 44. I remember everything about the house feeling strange and yet familiar – I had no real memories, only a sense of familiarity, of *déjà vu*, if you like, as of course I had been there for my earliest years.

I also remember that there was no room in the kitchen for the Morrison shelter and it was kept in the garage. In theory, we were supposed to go out and crawl under its iron roof whenever the siren sounded, but in practice we never did. The space underneath it gradually filled up with garden tools and onions and dusty dahlia bulbs throughout that last year of the war. For daytime air raids, my parents would take us to a bit of the house that my father said was structurally the strongest, a small area between the kitchen and the hall. Since he was an engineer and had commissioned and supervised every girder and brick of the house, he was probably right.

My parents had moved into it with John, my brother, while the workmen were finishing it and just in time for me to be born there in September 1937. Now, we had returned. My parents probably had little choice. We had gone to Swansea because my father was Professor of Electrical Engineering at London University and his faculty had been transferred to Swansea. Now it had been moved back.

When the siren sounded its dreadful wail at night, Mummy and Daddy would take us into their own bed. I hated this because their breath smelt. I think it was the fear again. There was an irregular mark on the ceiling that looked like a porcupine with a human head and a top hat. I hated it too. I thought it would come down and get me in my sleep.

The air raids were very frequent. I imagine my parents had decided, fatalistically, that it was impossible to traipse up and downstairs all the time and felt that what mattered most was that we would all go together. Croydon Airport had been a prime target earlier, but now the bombs were mostly dropped by German aircraft being chased from London and lightening their load. Right over Croydon. I believed that they probably knew that Daddy had fought them in the First World War and were getting their own back. When the V1 rockets came, we did not go downstairs, even at night. You heard the whining, droning, metal sound get nearer and nearer then cut out in unbearable silence until you heard the impact. One fell less than a mile away and the house shook, but it was alright because the tension went when you heard the blast; you knew you were still alive.

I just knew that smelling my parents' fear was still worse than anything I could fear myself. The rise of the 'All Clear' siren should have been a relief but it was as horrible to me as the Air Raid Warning one. In old age, all these years on, I still feel physically sick when I hear either of them.

27

GROWING UP:
STANHOPE ROAD, CROYDON

THOSE WERE THE DAYS when there were still two postal deliveries a day; my parents complaining about their reduction from three. Bread was delivered twice daily too, in the baker's own blue van. Milk came in a horse-drawn cart, which we looked out for in school holidays. Sandra, my dearest and closest friend, adored horses. We were allowed to stroke the patient creature and offer him carrots correctly on an open palm. Just occasionally if no one was around and the milkman was in a particularly good mood he would say, "Come on up, girls!" and we would ride on the shaft of the cart up Stanhope Road, sniffing luxuriously at the horse's steamy farts.

Our house was, of course, the centre of the world. Stanhope Road was 'unadopted', a phrase we did not understand but gathered that this explained why it did not have neat tarmac and stone pavements but was much nicer, covered in yellow-brown gravel with weeds growing at the edges. Three doors down from us the orphan road became even more unadopted and had a bumpy brown surface of mud, packed hard. There was no pavement, but each side of the road trees grew thickly, their roots sticking through the dirt like knees and elbows. We called it 'Leafy Lane', but I learned later that to the locals it was 'Lovers Lane'.

Sandra and Lueen lived in the last house before the lane and came to live there with their grandparents shortly after the end of the war. Sandra and I were the same age and between 7 and 11 years old we were inseparable. Lueen, younger by several years, came tagging along, puffing to keep up with her elders, by turns tolerated, excluded or made use of. My brother John was off with his gang of boys most of the time but joined us when he felt like it, particularly for dangerous activities like tree-climbing or running homemade carts down the hill.

Incidentally, when I was a small child I was not really aware of who John was. When, at 3 years, I was evacuated to Pumsaint, as previously described, I apparently referred to him as 'John Kapp', as if I sort of knew he had some connection with me, but not what it was and for years afterwards I apparently always referred to him as 'John Kapp'. I thought he was wonderfully strong and clever. "I know what 'tricity is," I said, "John Kapp told me." I was also told by our parents that we wore them out with our constant bickering, arguing and one-upmanship. With only 17 months between us, I was determined to catch up and he was determined to keep the lead.

28

SCHOOL DAYS

I SHOULD SAY SOMETHING about my schooling after the war, on our return to Croydon – still in wartime. I was first enrolled into Croydon High School, Girls' Private Day School Trust, chosen by my parents, an all-girls private primary. It was near enough for me to walk to in about half an hour, at first with a parent, then later on my own. I must have been there for 3 years, from 8 years old to nearly 11. My father was usually the one to take me, on his way to the station at East Croydon, as he had returned to his job as Professor of the Faculty of Electrical Engineering at London University. The path from our house led through a couple of footpaths to one which ran high up above the railway – the mainline from the coast at Brighton into Charing Cross. I loved the trains – of course, all steam engines in those days. Halfway along that footpath was a prefab owned by a greengrocer, where we could occasionally get bananas, now that the war was over.

Many decades later I walked that route again – and the shop was a ruin. I had a strange startled reaction, that I don't remember ever having before. "Oh my goodness – it must have been bombed!" was my instant response, jolted into an anachronistic idea. It shows how deep the scars of war can run. I still occasionally dream of bombed-out buildings, rubble and ruins – but then, I suppose that's a common dream symbol.

My memories of school then are rather vague. I wasn't unhappy and I worked well. Apart from being very upset by being teased at first for my cropped head, I was not bullied – the teachers must have quietly seen to that. Photographs of the time show me as a happy little girl with an impish, mischievous look. My best friend, Sandra, was at a different school. She was the granddaughter of the local vicar and lived with her grandparents and mother in the vicarage, two doors down from us, so almost all my out of school time was spent with her and her younger sister, Lueen, or my slightly older brother John.

Leading up to our 11th birthday, we all had to sit the 11 plus exam to decide where we should go for secondary education. I was told by my parents that I had done well. Well enough to be offered a free place at a Grammar School a little way away in Selhurst; not quite well enough to have a free place in the Higher School where I was. My family was not particularly well-off among the middle classes, as academic salaries were notoriously low. My father was a professor and Head of Faculty of Electrical Engineering at London University. My mother's very small private practice in the new-fangled psychoanalysis was similarly very small. I, of course, had no idea of the sacrifices they must have made to put my brother and I through fee-paying schools, but they never complained or made me feel guilty. Indeed, they continued to pay for my lengthy training in medicine and my upkeep well into my mid-twenties.

My parents did something that must have been unprecedented then, possibly not common even now. Having no doubt assessed the pros and cons of both schools and approving of both, they actually asked me, an eleven-year-old, to make the choice! It was a momentous event in my life. I stared at my plate for a few intense moments – and I can describe the plate better than any memory of my feelings. It was cheap wartime china, part of a set, but with a pretty, brightly coloured design called 'Indian Tree'. I can see it now, though the last plate and teacup went the way of all things breakable many years ago.

Apparently what I actually said – and my father was so struck by this that he told people about it on a number of occasions – "I think I'd like to go to the new school. I like new worlds to explore."

Some 70 years later I think that characteristic is still recognisable in my life, though the 'worlds' have been interior ones of the mind and relationships rather than in exploring the physical world around us.

So, at a little over 11, there I was on my way to Selhurst Grammar, an excellent school educationally, with an amazing headmistress, six bus stops away, in one of the slummier and poorer districts of Greater London. I was labelled as 'posh' from the beginning, something I'd never thought about before. I wasn't bullied, but certainly regarded as a bit shocking, especially my accent and when I admitted we had a maid to do the cleaning and food preparation. I tried to explain that she had to let in the patients as my mother was a doctor. No good. I can still hear the note of slight scorn with which Barbara – I think that was her name – said "Huh! So what. My mother goes out to clean other people's houses and then comes back to clean our own."

What of course neither she nor I could have known was that these 'maids' were part of a very humane and beneficial social experiment to bring people out from the mental hospitals where so many had been inappropriately neglected and the general welfare of the 'insane', ignored for centuries. Few of the general public have any interest in the history of mental illness and I can't say I blame them for that. We are talking about the late 1940s. The mental health act of 1959, which allowed for patients with mental illness to have the vote or even be discharged and live in the community again, is many years off. Just as bad was the plight of those who were sent, often as children, to 'subnormality' hospitals, as learning disability was known.

My mother, as a psychiatrist trained in the 1920s, knew all about mental institutions. Her best friend at College, Dr Doreen Firmin, had become Medical Director of a very big Subnormality Hospital. (That really was the title in those days!) It was at St Laurence's in Caterham where she had already started all the moves, along with other pioneers, to change these patients' lives and status. One way was to train them, then allow them out 'on licence' to work as maids and gardeners, or other servants. This was still a time when quite a number of non-aristocratic households would have a maidservant or manservant, so it was not as demeaning as it may sound to modern ears, quite the contrary.

So down the years, we had a series of youngish – or even not so young – women, who would be trained further by my mother, in her inimitable gentle and understanding way to do this type of work. Most didn't stay very long, six months or a year at most, not because it didn't succeed, but because the women benefited greatly. They were given skills, treated with kindness and respect and instead of having to say that they had come out of a mental hospital they could reasonably talk about their last job as maid/housekeeper to an eminent doctor. They were certainly a colourful and interesting addition to my – mostly uncomprehending – everyday life, but I wouldn't have wished it any different. Indeed, I am quietly very proud of my mother and her colleagues.

29

SCHOOL DAZE

ALTHOUGH I HAD CHOSEN to go to Selhurst Grammar School and was doing well there, it was probably a good time for a change. The school was in a rough area, to which I had to travel, and it happened that I did not have any very close school friends there.

In the summer of 1950, aged 13 and three quarters, I remember being taken by my mother to a meeting of her Old School Association in Sevenoaks. My grandparents had served in the Baptist Missionary Society for many years in Orissa, India. Indeed, my grandmother had been educated in the UK – Walthamstow Hall, School for the Daughters of Missionaries – and her own stepmother had actually been one of the original little girls when the school was founded in Walthamstow, London in 1838, before being moved to Sevenoaks, hence the name. My mother's schooling had been entirely at this school, since her parents had to take her- and later each of her sisters – back to England at a very early age, as India was not a physically healthy place to bring up children. Nor of course could she ever go out there for holidays, a six-week voyage by ship each way, each time! So, as the oldest child, she was farmed out to various relatives for holidays and often stayed at school, with a small number of similar boarders for the brief half-term holidays. The girls eventually also had to look after their much younger brother, Eric, who went to the 'brother' school, Eltham College in London.

The call to work as nonconformist church ministers and missionaries was a major feature in 200 years of my maternal line.

Truly, as my Aunt Joyce used to quote, with a slight and understandable edge to her voice: "The grown-ups heard the call and the children paid the price." A hard childhood for the three Wilkins girls, I'm afraid. However, in other ways they were happy and settled at the school, all three sisters making lifelong friendships. At the time my mother took me to the open day, the headmistress was Miss Emmeline Blackburn, a close friend of my Aunt Phyllis since schooldays.

As for me, I remember the school in Selhurst with some affection, but I didn't find it as easy to make friends as I had hoped, partly I think simply due to the distance, so my friendships were still mostly with local children. Sandra had moved away, though we still wrote to each other – and our friendship lasted the rest of her life. In this summer of 1950, I think I may have been ready for another move. I was an avid reader by now, indeed always had been. I loved all the old-fashioned girl's stories about boarding school: Enid Blyton, Angela Brazil, among others.

The day of the reunion was warm and summery. I was put in the care of a girl my own age and taken on a whistle-stop tour of the boarding part, plus the wonderful grounds, plus a very good tea with lots of homemade cake. What's not to like?

I remember going back to the headmistress, Miss Blackburn, and saying to her politely – we were very well brought up to be polite in public situations – "I think this is a very nice school. Can I come to it?"

I remember Miss Blackburn saying equally politely, "Perhaps we had better ask your mother?" and taking me to find her.

So I started the very next term, the autumn I turned 14. It took many decades when, one day it dawned on me that it had almost certainly been a set-up! Never mind! If it was, it was a benign conspiracy that worked overall very well! Initially, however, I was desperately homesick almost the whole time for the first term, and I know – from later – that my parents missed me terribly too. But both educationally and emotionally, it was definitely the best place for me. Nowadays I would agree that single-sex schools are not at all a good thing in general, but in the 50s it was in some ways a boon to live out one's troubled adolescence, with crushes and sexual secrecy and experimentation, in a safe, female environment.

I know too that the homesickness didn't last and I did not suffer from it again to any extent. The recurring theme of exchanging home for school and school for home for four years of regular holidays meant that at least six times a year, including the half-term holidays, I must have relived the traumatic 'separation and restoration' that was my early childhood evacuation experience until its edge was blunted. I was able to come to terms with it because – most importantly – it was my own decision to go to the school. I was in charge, if you like.

This is a mental mechanism known in psychology as 'Repetition Compulsion,' when we obsessively follow a line of behaviour over and over again to 'make it come right'. It is mostly used by ourselves unconsciously and often does not work, or is counterproductive, such as when – at the extremes – people marry consecutive abusive or unfaithful partners. But in many cases, it is a helpful and indeed essential inner device, used in minor ways without even thinking about it – because flexibly trying and retrying can indeed work and is the basis of our self-education.

Walthamstow Hall gave me a very good grounding in some subjects, mostly the ones I enjoyed, like English Literature and French, plus fulfilling my previously dormant yearning to act. I was in all the school and class plays, draped in sheets and spouting Shakespeare at the least excuse.
Many rules would be regarded as very petty today, but the benefit of such a system was that quite small acts of rebellion could be acted out most satisfyingly with a sense of being a really dangerous rebel – such as never quite being properly respectful to school uniform rules. I found many ingenious ways to disrespect my hated frumpy school hat without quite going to extremes that could merit punishment. The staff didn't like it when, in my final summer term,

I used the winter hat as a bedside lampshade, with me pointing out that there was no rule that you couldn't sew a beaded fringe on it plus other colourful adornments and use it in this way. Being fair-minded, they grudgingly conceded this one.

Wandering around the school after lights out, skilfully avoiding the patrolling staff, was another adventure that always made me feel like the dangerous heroine of a spy thriller or an escapee from a concentration camp. The only time I was ever caught doing this, there was just a relatively harmless scolding and I was more careful after. School then wasn't at all like the fictional genre of the Enid Blyton type stories – and yet in some ways, it was! To tell the truth, from things told to me years later by these amazing teachers, I think they actually enjoyed the spirited girls like me who tried colourful, but harmless ways to flout the rules and probably mostly had a laugh about it in the staff room. I shudder to think what you have to do today to earn the title of 'The Naughtiest Girl in the Lower Fourth'. Run a crack den or a brothel in the attic?

So I could express the naughty side of me against tough but wily grown-ups and – mostly – spare my mother from my teenage rebellion, though I did throw a few major tantrums at home too, I seem to remember. Anyway, I had four years of a most interesting and satisfying education, made many lasting friends, had many ups and downs, but it was never dull, and I emerged from it – eventually – with the ability to scrape into medical school as previously described.

30

THE ANIMAL KINGDOM

IT WAS WARTIME. We kept chickens. We had cats. The chickens inhabited a wire mesh enclosure taking up a large part of the vegetable garden. The cats would sit and stare at the chickens through the mesh, slinking gradually closer. The chickens would begin to assemble at that place. When a cat reached the wire the whole flock would be there squawking and flapping and shrieking and the cats would slink away. This little drama would be repeated at intervals throughout the day. The chickens provided us with eggs all through the war and ate food leavings, doubly helping the war effort. The cats were simply themselves – that's the function of cats.

My mother loved all animals, even human ones. Growing up, she must often have been lonely at school and moving around different relatives, but there were always animals. Walthamstow Hall boarding school had a 'young farmers union' for many years and my mother thrived there in her free time as a girl. We always had cats, mostly pedigree Siamese seal point, and she began to breed them after the war as a hobby. While I was away at boarding school, the numbers rose and my father eventually built her a special cattery at the bottom of the garden; I remember counting 15 cats at one time, but that included two litters of adorable tiny kittens.

Oh, and we also had, at various times, budgerigars in cages (semi-tame), fish in small aquaria (non-tamed), and even for a time, hamsters. These did not mix very well with the cats and there were occasional tragedies. The cats also sometimes brought in trophies of wild birds, which I would take away from them, screaming. Me screaming, I mean – not the birds. All this gave my friend Sandra and I many opportunities to have burial services. As the granddaughter of a vicar and with a taste for exotic drama, Sandra would devise the rituals. A strange liturgy of a wholly individual nature would be followed by a solemn procession, usually including Sandra's younger sister Lueen and sometimes my mother, at these tearful burials of small creatures, wrapped up tenderly in purloined hankies.

I loved the cats too, but had no illusions about them. Coquette, my favourite, was very loving and adopted me when my mother was not available. One of her sons, Tito, remained with us. A big, neutered male, he would sit on my lap while my mother was frying a full English breakfast. I would cut up my food, chatting to my mother. The slightest distraction from my plate and there would be an almost invisible flash of paw and I would find the bacon inexplicably gone, with Tito purring lovingly and looking innocent. One of our Tito's litter brothers was given to Dr Doreen Firmin, my mother's friend, head of the 'Special Hospital' in Caterham. We would see him there on our visits, as he lived to the ripe old age of 25, monarch of all he surveyed.

But the dogs – ah! The dogs were different. My parents gave me a little Pekingese puppy when I was about 10, I think, and she was my constant companion at home from then on, cats or not. At about the same time Sandra had a slightly larger 'lovable mutt' – a black and white mongrel called Sooty. My mother looked after Ping, as we called her, in the term-time when I went to boarding school, but all through the holidays Sandra and I would have our doggy companions and explore the world on long walks, up and down 'Leafy Lane,' or round the recreation ground, to Addington parkland and the Shirley Hills, all countryside then, with few people around except other dog walkers.

One of these walkers was a woman who told us to call her 'Margery', and who sometimes had two or three other dogs in addition to her own two, presumably a 'dog walker'. Sandra, who had been taught to call her mother 'Audrey' and her grandparents 'mummy and daddy', probably didn't find it strange. But for me – like most of my age group – it was revolutionary! The closest you got to first names with adults always had the prefix Uncle or Auntie. So Margery was special from the first – and if anything I held her more in awe, not less, for this informality.

I can't really guess how old she was – adults often just seem 'old' at that stage, but I guess now as probably no more than early 40s, if that. She invited us back to her house, a little bungalow on the edge of some woodlands, and we met her husband, who she asked us to call 'Uncle Ulick' because, she said, he was a lot older than her. I remember a benign smiling man, always seated in a big chair at the far end of the room, who greeted us but never joined in conversation.

My little dog Ping should have had flowing silky hair, but it never seemed to grow like that. I didn't mind. I had no wish to show her off and didn't want to brush her hair a lot, any more than brushing my own short bob of straight fine hair. Sandra and I did go through a phase of dressing our dogs up in silly ways and laughing at them. Without openly criticising, Margery somehow got us to see that our dogs put up with it because they loved us, but were not really at all happy, so we gradually let them be dogs in their own way. I have never really wanted to dress up animals to be funny since then, although I do admit the pictures are very cute.

Margery taught us a great deal else, without ever seeming to. She would pick grass stems and leaves and get us to study them closely, finding similarities and differences, but with a sense of joy and wonder, not of learning lessons or names. She would often take out a magnifying glass, and look even closer. Then she showed us how you could shine the sun's rays onto a dry leaf and write words on it, as it charred, moving quickly. I realise that she was very responsible, in all this. She taught us never to shine it on our skin, or dried grass which might burst into flame and never, ever to look through the glass at the sun or any other light.

She gradually shared what I can only call her religion with us, though it was never overt. Margery pointed out that God was Dog spelled backwards and indeed there was a sense that both she and Sandra shared an almost worshipful attitude to their dogs. As we grew a little older, she introduced to us the idea of spelling out these words by burning them into a dried leaf. You had to be very quiet and still – difficult for me, who was a fidgety wriggler at most times – but gradually, under the longing to do this, I held my hand steady and made many quiet 'prayers' in this way. Indeed, she also taught us that another name for God was OM, which we inscribed on many leaves and incorporated into Sandra's religious rituals, with no understanding of where it came from – and none necessary!

Life changes and moves on. Even before I went to boarding school, Sandra's grandfather retired and later on the whole family moved to the country near Guildford. Sandra and I wrote to each other, even visited a few times, but of course, it was never quite the same. Gone were the days of long walks and seeing Margery, by a natural change of our holiday ways. I don't even remember if we ever said goodbye to her at the time, though each of us, separately, paid a sort of courtesy call many years later and found her and Uncle Ulick much the same, smiling, friendly and accepting.

My mother looked after Ping during my terms away at Walthamstow Hall and by now my little dog was old and breathless, more than content to sit curled up on my lap in the holidays, or snoring at my feet while I read about magic castles and beautiful princesses and dreamed of travelling the world. She died while I was away at school and I mourned her, but without the extreme grief that would have attended me earlier on.

Years later, reading about other cultures and religions, I realised that Margery had probably been a practising Buddhist, well before the Beatles and the whole Eastern hippy movement, and what she had shown us was undoubtedly a form of mindfulness.

It also meant that when, at 16 years old I joyfully decided to be baptised and become a practising Christian, I was very open to the whole idea of mindfulness prayer, meditation and the works of mystical saints to which my teachers at boarding school introduced me, without ever realising that Margery herself, this quiet unassuming woman, whose last name I can't even remember, had been another of the best influences in my life. I knew she had loved Sandra and me, Sooty and Ping, with an unassuming and steadfast love, which asked nothing but gave so much, making no complaint when our company was lost to her.

31

HOMAGE TO MY TEACHERS

A T THIS POINT I find that I do not want, necessarily, to write of the girls I was at school with. Most of the memories are happy and the friendships certainly have lasted many years, unless sadly cut short in a few instances. Having worked with the mentally ill and with difficult children and their families, I count myself extremely lucky with the people who became my closest friends at boarding school. The occasional snide remarks and teenage quarrelling are mild by comparison with my later professional experience. Rest easy, Maggie, Mary, Barbara, Anna, Joan, Hester, Philippa – and so many others – my memories of you are all so good as to be boring to a reader, and that is how it should be.

The teachers were all, looking back, remarkable women. Like my mother, they may have grown up with expectations of marrying conventionally and having children as well as a career. The First World War put an end to that for so many of the 'five million superfluous women', as my Aunty Joyce used to say, though I gather the number was at least nine million active servicemen lost. We mourn with respect – and rightly – for the men who died, but what about the women left behind who never had any choice, but often made such positive goodness of their lives?

Miss Hackman, plain, small and lively, who shook her head sadly at my mangling of the Latin language, but brightened up when she gave us little classical plays in the language to act. "Your Latin is dreadful!" she exclaimed, and then her face brightened into the loveliest of smiles. "But!" she cried, "You can ACT!!" and I was involved for the rest of my time with the delight of school and house plays. I loved her very much, though never realised till after I left. I did keep in touch with her, though.

Mrs Moore and Miss Third, the teachers who did my happiest subject, English Literature. Miss White, French teacher, who shook her head sadly at my struggles with the grammar, but was never less than gentle and kind and got us all quickly into French romantic and avant-garde poetry.

Miss Mitchell, an awe-inspiring disciplinarian, but a profoundly thinking Quaker and an excellent General Science teacher. Even the other Science teacher, who we mocked, was kind and gentle and I apologise to her in my heart. Miss Deed, who tried unsuccessfully to teach me needlework – I wish I could have shown her my BA in Textile Art so many decades later! And Miss Emmeline Blackburn, Headmistress, keeping a close discipline and definitely a careful eye on me. Any fondness for me, as the daughter and niece of her dear school friends, was not in evidence until my calmer, more mature sixth form days when we older girls shared collective time with her at weekends. She did her best to curb my wayward undisciplined spirit with strictness and no favouritism, but fairness with it. It dawned on me, after I left, that she had almost certainly loved me very much. She and Miss Mitchell and Miss Deed retired together to Littlehaven in Pembrokeshire, West Wales, and were always happy to see 'Old Girls' and their families, so when I was living in Cardiff I was able to go there on occasion.

I think this care and interest they took in us is shown by an incident just after my darling husband Ken died, in 1992. They were by this time very elderly indeed, and they had a little separate cottage which they let out as a small source of income, often cheaply. I must have contacted them during Ken's prolonged last illness.

The morning after a funeral is often one of the worst times. All purpose, meaning and business have gone out of your life. I woke up on that Saturday morning the 2nd May, desperately wanting, needing, to get away. Anywhere! Anyhow!

In my morning post was a letter from Miss Blackburn, offering me the cottage free for this very week. It was all decided within the hour: Rupert opted to stay in Cardiff and field any letters and enquiries, and Amanda and I phoned the ladies, threw some things into a suitcase and were paddling in the Bay by teatime! We found the cottage tactfully deserted but with all immediate necessaries in place and a salad supper and dessert waiting for us! Amanda, at 14, had stood bravely with her father and I throughout his last weeks. This peaceful holiday was magic, kicking up sand, building castles, exploring rock pools – and reconnecting with each other, mother and daughter, in the loveliest possible way. That is the sort of kindness that is beyond price, and never to be forgotten.

A good deal later, remembering that time and all my teachers, official or not, I wrote a prose poem, which I print here:

Homage to my teachers

When I was young we mocked the science teacher
Because she was gentle and fat
And looked, we said, like a bus.
The young are sharp and bright like hunting knives
And clot together in packs,
Against the dark of the centuries.
In the dawn time of my civilisation
Compassion stirred for her, and was stifled
Lest I too be thrust from the tribe.
Others we loved and held up as totems,
But secretly knew we chose other paths.
Warm salty ways of fantasy and desire,
Despising the sunlit spinster way they trod.
Manless and barren, they had no children,
We thought, in our ignorance and conceit.
Oh surely, as Job said, we were the people!
Wisdom and knowledge would perish with us!

The promise of life crowded our loins.
Now at the end of life, so-called maturity,
Learning at last – with Blake – t o bear the beams of love,
How changed is the historical perspective!
Knowing the best that I can hope for
On my deathbed, tomorrow or at ninety two,
That someone will say, "This promising piece of dust."
I look back and I see the riches poured by you
On a stone-age tribe, who hardly knew how to begin,
Yet grew the centuries in a few short years.
I look back too at the secret paths, and the sunlit road,
Looking perhaps to find what makes a mother?
Now a mother myself, of two grown children
And one small grave, and a great many other people
Who each share a piece of the maternal love
And fury and indifference – now I can answer that!
You who did more than teach, forgive me, I was blind.
Oh mothers of my soul, my heart, my mind!

32

JUST DON'T MENTION THE WARDS

S O! WE'VE FINISHED with school and covered my starting at university, with my inadequate science background safely behind me. Middlesex Hospital Medical School – an ambition achieved! As they say, 'Be careful what you wish for!' However, I enjoyed the first year very much. As before mentioned, I had to do a full year of what was known as 'First MB'—now abolished, as I and about 20 other students had not done science at A-Level so we all had to do a crash course year on Chemistry, Physics, Biology and Physiology. Then there was another two years of preclinical study, before the last three years 'on the wards' doing the clinical course in many different firms and specialties.

I very much enjoyed my student life out of the hospital and even, much of the time, on the course. However, all the time I looked forward to this clinical three years as being the 'real medicine', as in a way, it was. On the course itself in those years, there was much that I, a rather lively but oversensitive, very naive young woman in the 60s, found extremely challenging.

When life occasionally became intolerable – such as when the patronising scorn of some of the tutors became too much to be borne – I would creep off and find my new cronies, who were the cleaners for the medical school, just like it had been in my holiday job. Dear ladies, I spent many happy hours when I should have been studying, tucked in your tiny broom cupboard, out of the supervisor's line of sight. I might choke in the constant cigarette smoke, but I knew you accepted me – and my gifts of chocolate –

as, even though I had no clear idea myself of who that

.ıll, when I started working 'on the wards', I found it
.ng and a great disappointment. I had enjoyed my pre-clinical
ıts of ways, but always waiting for the true, the real, the WORK
w.th patients. The sick people were fine. What I hated was the
attitude of the staff: to me, to the patients, to each other. The nurses
(all female in those days) hated the female medical students
because they saw us as competition for their designs on the doctors.
The male medical students were testosterone-filled rugby playing
bulldozers, in competition with each other and everyone else in the
world. The senior doctors were unsympathetic, they didn't see why
they should be nice to anyone; they'd had it tough, so should we.
The House Officers (first level junior doctors) were just exhausted
all the time.

The patients knew their place, which was at the bottom of the pile.
Most seemed creepily dependent and demoralised. Stroppy
patients had a bad time.

Of course, all this was only very partial truth. Many of the young
male medical students were as scared and subdued as I was. Not
everyone hated me, nor did I hate everyone. Nevertheless, the
London teaching hospitals at that time had a bad attitude. I had been
brought up in an old-fashioned way, to respect everyone of any age
or class. I was used to speaking politely and being spoken to
politely. Those brought up nowadays, in the rough and tumble of
comprehensive schooling, must be much more able to deal with
sneering, sarcasm, scornful sexist remarks and a general belittling
of one's abilities and intelligence. Even so – was there really any
excuse for the way we were taught? I was bewildered to be scoffed
at for ignorance from day one on the Clinical Ward rounds, before
having had a chance to learn anything.

I dealt with it badly, withdrawing inwardly and spending as little
time as possible in the company of those who treated me like this.
So, I didn't shine, particularly in certain 'Firms' and did well in
only a few. I felt more comfortable with old-fashioned courteous

consultants, who simply ignored you politely if you didn't conform to the norm. Since the norm was male, rugby-playing, ambitiously desperate to come top, I didn't really stand a chance to conform to it anyway.

So, it was hardly surprising that I tended to spend a lot of time doing things other than those I was supposed to. I hated the morning rounds. We were expected to be standing in a group by the door of the ward for when the Consultant in his white coat swept in, no matter how late he was (they were virtually all male).

I was bolshie enough to believe my time was as valuable as his and just about tactful enough not to say that, but to ask the Ward Sister if I couldn't go and get on with talking to the patients. They would never let us. It was the last remnants of the old way and it was slower to go at the Middlesex than at most of the other hospitals. The Middlesex, I found when I delved into its history, had been the last teaching hospital to admit female students. It did so, grudgingly, only when compelled by law and still took the absolute minimum required. It also had the 'proud' distinction of having refused to receive Florence Nightingale, the heroine of nursing in the Crimea!

I did love talking to the patients on the wards and in the outpatient clinics, but alas, this was not so much for their fascinating cardiac complications and abdominal diseases but for their conversation and their life stories at a time when they were raw and open and vulnerable.

I already knew I wanted to practice psychiatry, though my ideas on it were vague and mostly wrong. If I could have realised that what I was doing was both a humane approach and a valuable base for my career, I would have been happy. I only knew I was constantly crossing invisible boundaries in my sitting with patients, always neglecting what I was supposed to be learning, losing confidence in myself more and more.

It took me a long time to recognise fully that I did not need to avoid the skills and knowledge of being a doctor in order to treat people as individuals and I needed all that knowledge and skill as well as a respect for my patients. More importantly, that outside the rarefied and artificial confines of the London teaching hospitals there were plenty of doctors and nurses too busy to play competitive games and too caring to ignore so completely the humanity of their patients as in the big London teaching hospitals, even if the pressure meant that patients often did get poorer care than they should have.

33

YOU'LL NEVER ADAM & EVE* THIS!

T HE OLD MAN in the garden says, "I made mistakes. What's done can't be undone. I'll try again someday, but just now I'm tired and bored with them. Should I just squash the clay and start again?"

The New Man says, "It's the Woman's fault. She talks too much and doesn't stop to think enough. Why can't she just get the idea that I'm hungry and get me something to eat?"

The New Woman says, "That Man! Never talks to me unless he's demanding something to eat, or making me make all the decisions. So – I make them and then they turn out wrong and he blames me! So, I got it wrong. Am I supposed to be wise already?"

The New Child says, "Why have I got a Dad who doesn't talk and a Mum who talks too much? How am I going to grow up knowing anything? They're going to die someday and leave me all alone, so what about me? Who am I going to play with? How am I going to learn? Where am I going to find a girl to marry? Hey you – Old Man – it's your fault, isn't it? You made my Mum and Dad, so it's got to be your fault! What are you going to do about it?"

So, the Old Man took the Child by the hand and they walked through the garden, the Old Man bending over the Child, heads together, pointing out bright new things to each other. They looked at all the flowers and fruit and tasted some of them. They danced together under the trees and out by the edge of the river and the Child fell in, but the Old Man fished him out again. They danced some more until they were both dry and breathless. Above all, they laughed and joked and laughed again like nothing you've ever heard on earth.

That is why Mums and Dads can safely be left to argue and bicker and run the world in whatever way they want to, while the Grandparents can safely be left to teach the Grandchildren that looking and laughing and dancing, pulling each other out of minor scrapes and having fun are the really important things in life.

=======================

For anyone who doesn't know, the title is Cockney rhyming slang for 'you'll never believe this'.

34

ON PROBATION

THE MEDICAL SCHOOL itself being a mixed time emotionally, I engineered other 'escapes'. We are talking the mid to late 50s here, not the 60s. Coffee bars in Soho, rather than binge drinking and drugs. I was a very temperate and rather inhibited young woman, I guess, even for the time.

So, when I wanted to try and get more experience outside the narrowness of the medical school by doing some voluntary work, I didn't know how or where to start, but did the best thing – I asked my mother. She, as usual, understood well and suggested some form of voluntary social work. However, this within medicine was still very rudimentary, with almost unseen 'Lady Almoners' in hospitals to help the poorer patients financially: a hangover from pre-NHS days.

My mother said, "Why not find the local probation service; they'll probably have some ideas."

Good thinking. The following week, I skived a boring pathology lecture and visited Bow Street Magistrates Court, telling myself, remarkably accurately, that they were likely to know what a probation officer was and introduce me to it. The various court officials looked at me a little oddly and directed me to a maze of shabby corridors in an adjacent building. The staff there looked at me a little oddly too and suggested I waited and spoke to the Chief Probation Officer.

When she came, Miss Mary Hamilton didn't look at me oddly at all but roared with laughter. In our friendly conversation over a cup of tea, I gathered that it was most unusual for anyone to seek out probation officers of their own accord and I wasn't at all like the usual clients of the department. At that time, these were obviously working-class, obviously villainous and few of them spoke at all like me. Nowadays, of course, it's different. Crime and antisocial behaviour are much more egalitarian. Then, I stuck out like a sore thumb.

Mary was tickled pink at my approach and decided to undertake my education in crime and deprivation personally, by taking me on as an unpaid helper. All this was unofficial; no talk of health and safety, no vetting or paperwork. She often introduced me to colleagues in the pub – where I seem to remember we did a lot of our networking and case discussion – laughing even more. She told them that I was the only member of the public ever brave enough to come into the probation web of my own free will.

Mary was a tall, handsome woman in middle life, tweed suited, single, chain-smoking, with many years of experience in work with criminals. None of the villains, wide boys, thugs, layabouts, drunks and loafing no-goods she dealt with could put one over on her or fool her for an instant. She knew the worst of life and of people and had a strong moral compass. But she was also completely uncynical and one of the most compassionate and warm-hearted people I have ever known. It was a very unusual combination. I now realise, looking back, that she had a huge influence on me and I loved her very much. I hope she sensed it.

Totally ignoring my Thursday daytime medical studies at the Middlesex Hospital, I thereafter spent every Thursday at Bow Street Magistrates Court or on its business, as well as other odd times out of hours. I was to get my comeuppance a couple of years later when I failed my finals and had to retake them, but it proved a far better basis for my later career in psychiatry than the missing bits of pathology and other essential, but boring (to me), things I had to painstakingly fill in later.

At first, I would sit in Court for the morning while the magistrates dealt with a sad procession of drunks, prostitutes up for soliciting, unsuccessful petty criminals and other shabby characters. Mr Blundell was – rather as his name sounded – blunt, practical and swift. Sir Laurence Dunne was tall, thin, with an aristocratic profile, a cultured voice and a shrewd, all-seeing look. Under these and other magistrates, I learned the oddities of men who loitered around parks with holes cut in their trouser pockets.

"I could see, m' Lud," the stolid policeman would drone, "that he appeared to be handling his Person." And yet another minor perv would be named, disgraced and fined.

One Thursday morning, Mary had gone out for some reason, leaving me sitting on my own in the wooden pew, engrossed as usual in the dramas unfolding before me. Sir Laurence Dunne looked across the crowded courtroom and said, "I see Miss Hamilton is absent but her assistant is here. Can you give me a report on this case?" As they say, I could have died. I staggered to my feet and managed to make some promise of consultation on her return and was allowed to resume my seat. He looked at me thoughtfully.

A little while later, the Clerk of the Court took me aside at the end of a session and said, "Excuse me, Miss. Sir Laurence would be very grateful if you would take tea with him." I remember Sir Laurence's pale, long-fingered hands with the papery skin of old age as he poured the tea into bone china cups. He was a charming host. I still don't really know why he wanted to meet me, but he drew from me my hopes of becoming a psychiatrist and hence my interest in his Court. I don't think he had much of an opinion of psychiatrists, perhaps justifiably. He said, "I recommend that you do not become a psychiatrist. You will be able to do much more good by not being one."

It was another thing that made me think more about what I was doing and why, even though I did not take his advice. I have occasionally wondered whether he was right and what else I might have done – but remain glad I did indeed follow that path nonetheless.

Some of my work was to go on errands of mercy for Mary, to support elderly people who had shoplifted or helplessly fallen foul of the law in other ways. They were always poor and often a little mad. Most had symptoms of dementia, too early to qualify for care, but too developed to cope with life's demands. I would check how they looked, whether they appeared to have food in the cupboard, were eating, or were in any sort of distress and trouble. I would report back, saving a little of the team's time and learning valuable insights. I would take people occasionally to appointments, surgeries, or bring them in to report officially to the office if they couldn't cope with coming themselves. Once I took a lady back from leave to the Psychiatric Hospital at Virginia Water. I regarded that as a treat, but was a little disappointed not to be shown around, as an interested party.

One of the most striking cases was an elderly woman who had been put into a mental hospital under a Mental Health Order. Mary suspected it was because her son wanted to get his hands on her money. In those days, apparently, if someone was in hospital compulsorily but escaped and wasn't caught in over a month, they were automatically free. To be honest, I'm not sure if that was the law – I have never thought to check it out – but this old lady believed it to be so and had escaped from the Asylum in late spring, shortly before I met her.

She had lived rough in a little triangle of woodland between busy roads and close to shops in the Home Counties for well over a month, sleeping under a hedge in an old blanket and raiding dustbins nightly for food. When she was caught, she had frostbite on her feet and legs and one of my tasks on visits was to check that it was healing. She was a sweet, slightly confused but sane old lady and she had been established in a little bedsit, where she managed well enough, courtesy of the Probation Service.

This and other cases were excellent life lessons for a young girl like me, brought up in relative wealth and comfort. I don't even recall this lady's name, but I often remembered her when I came to work in psychiatry. She taught me the importance of accurate diagnosis and of respect for the individual. Also, how alert you should be not only to the ulterior motives of some relatives, but to the risks of unthinking collusion with them. As someone well-versed in the discomforts of camping, even with all the proper Girl Guide equipment, I was also much impressed by her example of how to survive in wild suburbia. I wasn't tempted to try it.

35

DWELLINGS OF MULTIPLE OCCUPATION

THAT'S ESTATE AGENT-SPEAK for student digs, flats, bedsits, studios and peasant hovels. Where and how you live as a student is a whole world of amusing – or horrifying – stories. Or you could turn the phrase around and say, 'My Occupation of Multiple Dwellings.' I once counted up every place I had moved in and out of for a minimum of a week, not counting holidays. By my 32nd year, it worked out as at least 35 dwelling places. I doubt I can even remember most of them now, but I have no reason to doubt the calculation. It included student digs so awful that we moved out within days and at least four sojourns in static caravans. Most probably best forgotten. I survived.

After being in med school for a year, I wanted to live in London with my friend and fellow-student, Dilys. I knew my father would prefer me to stay at home, but as a retired professor himself, he knew that it was good for young people to be a bit independent. My parents were financing me totally. My first impulse was to have a major teenage-type tantrum and insist on my own way, which would have got me nowhere.

I was rising 19 and had to some extent learned a little tact. I wrote him a long letter – remember I was actually living at home – setting out all my arguments, including some against in order to appear impartial. This was definitely the way to his heart and I was allowed to go into digs.

I seem to remember that Dilys found our flat. It was a semi-basement in a lovely prestigious square in Chelsea and was of the 'studio' type – a big room, with a lovely plaster frieze of cherubs, a little toilet off the hall and a bathroom/kitchen whose table could be let down over the bath when you wanted to cook; very ingenious, though I dare say no longer legal.

We loved our time at 19 Carlyle Square. The landlady was an amazing woman who wrote cookery books and thrillers. One day I was reading a paperback and I thought, 'that's good, I wonder what else the author has written?' I turned it over and saw a photo of my landlady, whose *nom de plume* was Barbara Worsley-Gough.

Barbara's kitchen was in the other half of the basement, separated only by a curtain. She was always experimenting with cookery and sending us plates of delicious things to try. Often these were brought through by her helper, Mr Kettley. Unlike Barbara herself, he never knocked or called out but would just come through, on occasions finding us in a state of semi-undress, probably by design. We never felt in the least threatened or offended by this. He was a tiny elderly Irishman, gnarled like an old tree root, with a smile as wide as the Irish Sea. We believed him to be a leprechaun.

Our landlady had a nephew, Alastair, who would quite often ring up. He had a swooningly strong Scottish accent and we were on tenterhooks hoping to be there when he paid a long-promised visit. One of the pleasures of living in a semi-basement is that you can see the legs of every visitor. One great day, a taxi stopped and there were a pair of strong well-turned calves under a Royal Stuart tartan. Undoubtedly, Alastair had arrived. Alas, we never really made contact, though at 2am one morning the fire alarm went off and Alastair and I had a brief encounter by candlelight in the shared hall, with him in a red tartan dressing gown. I forget what I wore, but I suspect Marks and Spencer pyjamas.

If this was a novel, it would have led to a romantic encounter, a murder mystery, or at least a philosophical and life-changing discussion. He held up his candle to look for the fuse box, we shared a few words, succeeded in stopping the raucous noise and went our separate ways, unintroduced. Ah, the great might-have-beens of youth! I rather think Dilys felt I had fluffed a great opportunity that she could have made more of. Probably true.

Later on, Dilys had to move back home for a while because her father was ill. I couldn't find anyone to share the Chelsea flat with, and anyway, it would not have been the same. I moved a couple of times within the area.

For a while I was 'fourth girl' in a little house around the corner in Oakley Gardens. It was a lovely place and the three young women got on very well, but it was a revelation both ways as to differing lifestyles. They all came from what I suppose one would call the Landed Gentry. We are supposed to be very class conscious and snobby in Britain, though for most of my lifetime, reverse snobbery seems to have been more of a problem. I am always interested in the nuances of social and personal behaviour; it is after all part of my job to observe these things. The people I met there were not particularly academic or intellectual, but so what? They were kind, accepting and cheerful. My time with them I remember as amusing and they were as bemusedly tolerant of my lifestyle, as I was of theirs.

The girls – we should call them 'young women' now, but we were always 'girls' in those days – worked as personal assistants, well-paid compared with a student allowance. They were out every evening on dates to fashion shows, cocktail parties, films; returning at weekends to the Home Counties for Hunt Balls and other social events reported in *Tatler*. They never deliberately excluded me but they were as astonished at my life as I was at theirs. I couldn't afford the time to go out with them locally – anyway my meagre allowance and my relatively unsophisticated clothes would have made it unsatisfying. On the odd occasions that I was included, they were always very nice, but I felt a bit of a fish out of water with their friends and did wonder a little if the people they knew were judging me.

I was working extremely hard, day and night by this time, in order to pass my exams, and this life as a student was totally incomprehensible to them. Gill, one of the girls, had a faithful beau called Bill who had courted her for many years. He had a square, ugly face with a snub nose and was quiet, very kind and solid. I think he was an officer in the army. He talked to me quite a lot when Gill was out with other people and he seemed to me a lovely man whose devotion to her was touching and deserved recognition. A year later, long after I had moved on, I was very happy to learn that his patient wooing eventually won her. I was invited to the wedding, which was a splendid County occasion. The whole brigade turned out with their swords and formed a guard of honour for the couple and there was champagne on an immaculate lawn. Way out of my league but very enjoyable.

One of the small pleasures I remember – I am very easily amused – was getting the bus back from college every day and saying, "A ticket to the World's End please." I was sorry to leave Chelsea, but fortunately, the situation of my next flat allowed me to say the regular line, "I want to go to the North Pole, please." Both pubs of course.

In all those large London houses divided up into ROOMS TO LET, you will be certain to have the following fellow tenants:

- Two gossipy old ladies on endless watch-out-and-report mode.
- A young man on an upper floor who comes out and stares but never speaks.
- Young couples, apparently very loving, but you wonder…
- An old man in the attic: can that really be Cupid he lets out of a cage at times?
- A dark cellar. Don't ever go down – your earliest childhood horror is waiting for you.
- A goldfish in its bowl, because that's what you are.

Dilys and I were sharing a flat again: a much less classy one in the seedy end of Bayswater. The area could be described as the "I-was-once-very-genteel-but-I'm-coming-down-in the-world-and-have-to-do-all-sorts-of-things-to pay-the-rent" part. The first time a car pulled up beside me, I thought the driver wanted directions to somewhere and, in my helpful Girl Guide way, went up and spoke to him. Be Prepared! The place he wanted to go to was not at all what I had in mind. We quickly learned to ignore the daily curb crawlers who swooped every time you left the house.

We moved in and found ourselves perched on the top floor of a terraced house. The railway ran just the other side of the road, to Royal Oak station. Whenever a train went past, the flat rocked like an Elvis tribute band ("Uhh Ohh, I'm all shook up!" for those not around at the time). Since it was the main line in and out of Paddington, this happened all the time. At first, we would practically leap in the air, but surprisingly quickly got so used to it we hardly noticed. We would look at our visitors in surprise as they shot in the air or fell off the sofa.

In the early hours, the main line trains stopped, but it was then time for the engines to come to life and spend the night going to and fro, crashing their buffers together in a manic game of Thomas the Tank Engine and Friends. I still thought of mechanical objects as having a secret life of their own. You also learn to sleep through anything as a student. You learn to sleep for five minutes at a tube station, three minutes while buttering toast, all the way through most pathology lectures and while leaning on someone at a party pretending to snog him.

The landlady lived downstairs in the basement. I suppose there were other people in between. In the true tradition of landladies, she was a bit of a tartar and very easily 'put out'. When 'put out', she would use her worst threat, the nuclear option of landlady threats. "Any more of this," she'd say, "and I'll send Billy up to talk to you!" He never did come up. We often imagined Billy, her small, timid husband, sitting for a while on the bend of the stairs and then going back down again, to boast, "I told them off, my dear, I told them off proper. There'll be no more trouble!"

Dilys had to leave again and I stayed on. After a while, I got thrown out, which is a rather dramatic way of saying that the landlady finally did worse than 'send Billy up', but gave me notice. Read the next memory snippet if you want to know the disgraceful reason why!

<h1 style="text-align:center">36</h1>

<h1 style="text-align:center">GOING DOWN IN THE WORLD
BETWEEN WORMWOOD SCRUBS
AND THE GASWORKS</h1>

SO, YOU WANT TO KNOW what crime I committed to get me thrown out of my student digs without notice? Read on!

What happened was an unexpected consequence of a decision to do some form of social work, as an out-of-hours volunteer, to learn more relevant – to me – skills than those I was supposed to be content with at Med School. Miss Hamilton, my friend and mentor from the Probation Office at Bow Street, had put me in touch with the North Kensington Community Centre. It was reasonably near the Bayswater flat and ran social welfare work for the elderly, for young mothers, for the unemployed and the sick. The locals were encouraged to run their own things by the very few paid staff and it attracted a few outside volunteers, of which I became one. This indeed was an area between Her Majesty's Prison, Wormwood Scrubs and the North Kensington Gasworks.

Wormwood Scrubs, as its name might suggest, was a largish area of public scrubland, not very appealing and dominated by the famous prison. Nearby was a Peabody Estate, built between the wars. This part of Kensington was by no means a slum, but a good old-fashioned working-class area of mostly council accommodation, and had its own community centre with funding from a charitable trust to run activities for the local inhabitants.

"I need someone to run an art class for the youngsters," Megan Etholan said.

In vain, I told her that I couldn't draw, had no idea about teaching and would be a lousy youth leader. "Nonsense," she said, "Anyone can teach these kids and we have all the stuff."

The 'stuff' was a collection of brushes, paper, paints and things, donated to the community centre by some well-wisher. So, I taught art to anyone who wanted to attend, once a week after college. I really and honestly had no skill in art at that time and it had never been even a hobby of mine. What irony that more than 30 years later I was suddenly overwhelmed with a need to become an artist embroiderer!

I couldn't complain. After all, coming to help had been my own idea. Megan Etholan, who ran the centre, was another tough, competent woman. She was divorced, after a very brief marriage. She admitted she knew it was a mistake on the morning of the wedding but hadn't the courage to run away. Later, she had spent some years in the army and was now in her forties. She became a true friend and another great influence on me.

It turned out to be great fun. My inability to draw was no worse than that of my pupils and what they really wanted, sometimes desperately, was a little adult attention. Of course, at first, a number of older teenagers slouched in and drew pornographic pictures. It was handy being a medical student; I pretended to take it very seriously and criticised their work from the anatomical point of view, adding gory tales from my dissecting room days. Most of them quickly slouched out again. Those who remained actually tried to draw and paint and retained a wary respect for me. "You really cut up DEAD PEOPLE? Ugh!"

Most of the class were younger and a small group of the 7- to 10-year-olds became very persistent about getting more of my time. I had never previously had much to do with young children. My parents were older than average and so most of their contemporaries were either childless or into the grandparent range. I was flattered and charmed by these strange beings. Some of them

– like 'my' twins, Billy and John Singleton and their friend Barry – were obviously very much loved and shown affection at home, but even so, life was hard on the Peabody estates; both parents worked and some of the other children were emotionally neglected. It wasn't long before I could not enter or leave the centre without a group of little ones crowding around and physically hanging on to every spare bit of my person, all talking at once. They always called me "Miss", no matter how often, in my egalitarian way, I tried to get them to say 'Elinor', and their conversation never stopped.

"Miss! Can I come to your place?" "Miss! Miss! Are you here tomorrow?" "Miss! I fell over in school/ knocked Billy down/ had a tooth out/ Kate got told off/ Barry hit me/ John lost his dinner money, today!" "Miss! Miss! My mum says can you come round to tea?" "Miss! Can you do sums?" "Miss! Look at this scab what I got."

They were desolated that they didn't see me at weekends. Saturdays I regarded as reserved for my own social life, but Sundays – well, Sunday afternoons in London everyone knows are designed by the devil as a foretaste of eternal boredom. I thought perhaps we could have a Sunday School. On Sunday mornings, I attended the thriving and lively Bloomsbury Central Baptist Church, but I couldn't see myself traipsing these little live wires through London every week. Anyway, my memories of occasional attendances at Sunday Schools were of rather dull, old fashioned activities and little homilies. I thought I could do better.

So, for a while, I went to the community centre on Sunday afternoons, collected up a little group of some 6 to 8 children and walked them back to the flat in Bayswater. There we sang all the noisiest and most thrilling hymns I knew, sandwiched with simple bible stories about their 'friend Jesus'. I finished each week by reading aloud short instalments from *The Lion the Witch and the Wardrobe* by C.S. Lewis. We also had simple prayers about everyday things. Prompted by the children, who were used of course to school assembly but much preferred being in charge, we prayed for Barry's wart and Kate's mum and the new baby and healing for Billy's scab and all the poor little children in the world who hadn't enough to eat. And thank you Jesus for everything, Amen.

It was not to be expected that my landlady would tolerate this for long. She contrived to indicate that these were the lowest sort of children, who might be expected to bring all sorts of nasty things in. We were much too noisy and her husband, Billy – officially unemployed – needed his rest after working so hard all week. I thought of telling her the children would pray for her Billy right after praying for the scab on our Billy's knee, but I held my tongue and just said I thought that the children deserved a little fun in a Sunday School but we'd keep the noise down. No good, she told me, either the Sunday School went or I did.

Even if I had wanted to stay, which I didn't, I got so much pleasure out of recounting this that it was worth the hassle.

"I got thrown out of my last digs," I used to say casually and watch my friends' eyes gleam and their lips glisten as they waited for salacious revelations. "Yes," I would continue, "I ran an illegal Sunday School there," and watch their faces fall.

The day I got so unceremoniously asked to leave by my Bayswater landlady was the Sunday evening, on my return from walking all the kids home and returning to the flat. The next day, Monday, I called round to the Centre after college and told Megan about my disgrace, which amused her very much. "You'd better move in here," she said. "There's a room on the first floor you can turn into a bedsit. Rent-free if you do another evening group." Done! We cleared and painted up the room and moved me in the next weekend. I bought exactly the colours I wanted: black, dark green, white and a silver ceiling. Very student.

By living in the Centre, I got drawn into all sorts of things, somewhat to the detriment of evenings of study. It was more fun to help Megan in a hundred and one little jobs, chat with the elderly or the young mums, and keep an ever-changing group of children amused and off the streets. My own little group, including the twins, Billy and John, plus Barry, were always around. I shouted at the older teenage louts when they rocked cars or graffitied walls in a way that would be unthinkable today. Now I would probably be knifed – then they looked shocked and moved off muttering apologies.

I took the children on occasional outings in London. Few of them had been for so much as a bus ride away, so Megan provided petty cash for the bus or tube and refreshments. I think they found the transport the most enjoyable thing each time. They were probably intimidated by the British Museum and Nelson's column and the things I felt we should visit. A trip to Richmond Park for a picnic started out wonderfully, but they took one look at the Round Pond, took off their shoes and socks and jumped straight in. It didn't occur to me we shouldn't do it, so it was probably lucky that the only person to step on a broken bottle was me; the pond was full of them.

"Cor! You're bleeding Miss! Look at that! Cor! Do you think you'll die?"

They all had to be bundled out and I had a trip to Casualty later that day for an anti-tetanus jab.

Probably the funniest trip was when I took my whole art group, mostly children and early teens, on a visit to the National Gallery. They were enormously shocked at the nudes, particularly those of them who had started off by drawing porn. "This place! All these dirty pictures!" The portraits didn't help either. "Ugh, they're so ugly!" they cried. I had to soothe them by finding some battle scenes, particularly ones at sea. Anything with guns and blood and a sad death scene cheered them up enormously. Fortunately, many of our famous artists, or their patrons, seem to have had small-boy tastes in gore and the visit was ultimately a success. It is hard to imagine this degree of naivety in today's children, who live in a world of explicit images and wide exposure to culture, but not only was this pre-television age, few of the younger ones had even been to a cinema.

Megan had to deal with officialdom a lot of the time. Most of those who visited to check up on the Centre seemed to have little idea of what we were doing or why, but were fairly easy to convince. In a non-heroic sort of way, we believed heartily in the welfare state, the essential goodness of people and that we were helping the young to better, richer lives. Real old-fashioned socialism. I no longer have any idea if any of these things are true, but I'm glad I followed them. I am a little depressed that the great improvements to people's lives that we believed to be around the corner still haven't happened.

My social life was still very good. Mind you, any young man who took me on a date was liable to be tested out by a visit to our Centre. If he did a bit of voluntary work, he was in. If not, he was quickly forgotten. Megan said I was very useful bait to get young male helpers, always the hardest to recruit. She wasn't bad at it herself and ended up marrying a grand chap with the unlikely first name of Bysshe – his mother had been a sort of admirer of the poet, Shelley – and they left not long after I myself had to move on. Their wedding took place in the Centre and was a real London community booze-up.

A couple of months before that, Megan's elderly father needed a placement and I was only too happy to yield my colourful room to him and share Megan's flat. I had begun to realise that I would have to move on sometime soon, if only to get back to serious study, but I had started to spend much of my spare time in her flat anyway. I loved the life we lived, she was a good cook and very hospitable, sharing haphazard but nourishing meals with anyone who happened to be around and in need of feeding. Another thing I learned then – and retained – was the pleasure of casual, take-potluck-and-join-the-family-when-you-wish entertaining, leading later on to shared roast Sunday lunches and Thursday evening potluck meals, as my preferred form of hospitality over formal dinner parties.

In the meantime, in the year I lived there, we got so many people involved, both locals and volunteers that we put on three musicals and some concerts for the old folk, with me as one of the lead singers, but lots of other talent. The art lessons got quietly dropped. Every morning, when it was time for me to catch the bus for Medical School, my group of faithful little followers, five or six of them, would wait outside to escort me to the bus stop around the corner. They would wait with me and when the bus came in sight would line up to be kissed on the cheek and wave till it was out of sight before going to school. The chances were high that no matter what time I got back one or two of them would be hanging around and spread the word.

You have to picture every activity in which I was involved as a sort of medieval or renaissance painting, in which my figure is surrounded by a group of extremely grubby cherubs.

37

HEREFORD: A YEAR OF HOUSE JOBS

W**E ARE STILL** in the medical training years, but things of course changed radically for me when I met Roger Tudway, my first husband. I met him in my penultimate year at medical school. I remember talking to this loud, smiling, crazy-looking student in the dinner queue and learning he was in the year behind mine. He had trained first in Cambridge, where at that time some students did their pre-clinical training before coming to London for the clinical years, so though he had only just come to London, he was in the group just a year behind me.

He had a strikingly mobile, handsome face. To my surprise, he seemed to pop up all the time after that. Roger later told me that he had lost no time in checking out my timetable and pursuing me relentlessly. He made me laugh, we could have long serious conversations, he was intelligent, we shared tastes in music and books and just hanging out together. Within days he sent me a Christmas card with verses from the Lord of the Rings – a clincher to a fan of Tolkien like me. In a few weeks we were deeply in love and completely committed to each other.

We married in October 1961, in London, thanks to the support – particularly the continuing financial support – of my parents. The medical school took a dim view of such an activity and when, as commonly happened, one or other of us had to spend a few weeks 'living in' or working in another hospital, no provision was ever made for a couple: indeed, it was actively disapproved of. Remember, by this time I was 24 years old!

Our wedding day was happy and full of hope, though much had to happen before any real stability was possible in our lives. In addition to the lengthy time for all medical students, mine was extended to some seven years by the 'catch-up' year of First MB and then an extra year at the end by my failing my finals. After that came the obligatory 'Houseman' year, as a Pre-registration Doctor, before being fully registered and able to start specialist training. In those days there were no set schemes, whereby you had a certainty of remaining in one place, so even if you could afford a mortgage, it was pointless until you became a Consultant, or at least a Senior Registrar with some security of tenure for three years.

So, we took a small flat in west London, though we both continued socialising in the Community Centre for a while until Megan Etholan and Bysshe got married and left. The next major change came when I – at last – successfully passed all my final exams and obtained a post, for a year, as a Prereg. House Officer in Hereford, with six months' surgery first at the County Hospital, then six months' general medicine at the General Hospital. Roger stayed in London, or at his parents' house in Bristol, with occasional weekend visits.

This ordeal was known as 'house jobs'. At that time, it was barely regulated or managed properly. You think I'm joking with the word 'ordeal'? Three of my young colleagues died during (or just after) this year of incredibly tough work – from a heart attack, suicide, and car accident when sleep deprived. I knew of several more who had severe mental health problems after, always hushed up of course.

The atrocious pressures and risks taken with our health and abilities in that time drove me, a few years later, into medical politics and Chairmanship of the Junior Hospital Doctor's Association to fight for the rights of these doctors. But that, as they say, is Another Story for Another Time, though recently several young doctors have written highly informative and witty accounts of their hospital times.

We junior doctors bonded well on the whole and helped each other out wherever possible. Another kindness, until the workload defeated it, was the good attitude of one of the Ward Sisters. She was in charge of the Uro-genital ward at the General Hospital and had seen countless first-year house officers come in green with ignorance and go out with, hopefully, the rudiments of surgical practice. She had no time for bumptious know-it-alls, but if you spoke to her with respect and asked her advice, she taught you everything you needed. She did it very tactfully too, particularly in public. "Dr X likes you to do such-and-such for his patients," she would say, as if it was a personal quirk you couldn't be expected to know and not some vital piece of basic practice!

So – those were the touching and good things. However, I can do no better for the bad side of this than describe the situation in my last month of that first six-month period, at the end of my surgical placement.

Basically, in those days your contract was to work all week, with one official 24 hours off, but the understanding was that the on-call rota would mean two or three other doctors sharing the out of hours work. In practice, if they became ill or left, you could find yourself as the sole frontline doctor for several wards and emergency-covering the rest. Older Consultants seemed to have no idea, either, of how much more complex the investigations and treatments were than in their day and expected you to carry on regardless. I was extremely conscientious, particularly over calculations, always my potential weak point.

There may well have been other near misses that I never found out about, but to illustrate the constant 'Disaster Waiting to Happen' of this way of 'managing' a medical service (if you can call it that), here is the true account from the last of my six months in that job. One day, the Consultant Surgeon suddenly discovered, in a side room, that a postoperative patient nominally in my care was so dehydrated that his blood was like tar. The nurses, who collected the daily 'fluid in and out' data, apparently never read it - the Ward Sister who would usually be a backstop for inadequate medical care was on holiday. There happened to be no Registrar cover either. The patient, rehydrated, fortunately made a full recovery so there was no official enquiry.

The Consultant questioned me and found that for the previous three weeks, the two other Surgical House Officers, who had only just started, were absent – they were a married couple and I think the father of one of them had died. I was doing the routine work of three junior doctors: single-handedly looking after two acute surgical wards, four orthopaedic wards, and the ENT ward, day and night. All I could do on my own was dash from crisis to crisis all the time, wherever I was called, to deal with collapsed patients, diagnose acute surgical crises, catheterise patients and put up drips. Whenever I explained and asked for help, I was regarded with indifferent disapproval and simply told to carry on.

Oh! And during this time I was also on-call for Accidents and Emergencies: the Casualty department as it was called then. The General Hospital in Hereford took all the surgery and most of the Accident and Emergency work for the whole area.

My opposite number was Harry, a kind, solid young man who went on eventually to become an army doctor. He was the only other doctor sleeping in the residency and covering all the general medical wards, also on his own. We shared the on-call for the Casualty department alternate shifts, day and night. There were some senior house officers second on-call. On paper, we were meant to have one night off a week. In practice, there was only a thin partition between Harry's room and my own. Every time one of us was telephoned, both were woken up.

Called to Casualty, one might find anything, from nose bleeds or choked-on fishbones to heart attacks and other life-threatening conditions. Because the General Hospital took in all the trauma cases for Herefordshire, we also had to deal with broken limbs and life-threatening injuries, usually victims of farm disasters or major traffic accidents. Of course, we called on the senior doctors, even the registrars and consultants, as soon as we had dealt with the life-threatening bit.

Normally all of this work was shared between at least five junior house officers, but by the time of these dreadful final weeks, there were only the two of us even for the first line Casualty Department. Six months earlier, I wouldn't even have had a clue how to cope. Now, Harry and I helped each other as much as we could and stopped complaining after being told off every time.

The extraordinary thing was that until we nearly lost that poor patient, no-one seemed to have noticed or taken responsibility for the situation. If I failed to respond quickly enough to a Casualty call, a more senior doctor would be there before me, very angry but oblivious to my explanation of dealing with a crisis elsewhere in the hospital. I was constantly the recipient of snarling fury from nurses waiting in Casualty, nurses waiting on wards, and Consultants angry because they had no junior to assist them in theatre anymore. In vain, I had tried to point out the problem. No-one listened.

I could hardly sleep for adrenaline, even if I wasn't called up. I had virtually stopped eating because the constant interruptions gave me indigestion. Over the six months, I had lost nearly three stone in weight. Talk about skeleton staff! I was living in a twilight state; a disaster waiting to happen.

The day they found that poor Mr X was almost dehydrated out of existence, his Consultant looked thoughtful and went off without a word. If I didn't get any sort of apology, I didn't get a reprimand either. The next day, a couple of locums turned up, one of whom dropped a tray full of instruments on the floor during an operation and gave three consecutive patients an infection. Soon after that, I finished my first six months and went on holiday with Roger for a fortnight, before my next house job. We went to a little B&B in the country, where I ate and slept most of the time.

I had somehow got through the surgical pre-registration six months not quite killing anyone, even the aforementioned Mr X, as far as I know. I didn't shine as a medical house officer either, in the second six months at the Hereford County Hospital, but I didn't want to. I was just grateful to have been so thoroughly 'blooded' that nothing was likely to throw me again. All I wanted was that I and my patients should survive and I wouldn't have to face the coroner or my consultant. My terror was much greater in relation to them than the slightly unreal idea of a patient dying as a result of my ineptitude, but I guess that was a form of denial that had allowed me to continue working in the previous job.

My second six months, with an acute medical team, was a good deal more civilised. It took place in the other hospital in Hereford, the County, about a mile away from the General. There were several more doctors and specific casualty SHOs during the day, though we were still on call at night. We were nominally responsible for emergencies out of hours in the children's ENT and paediatric wards, though thank goodness these were very rare and we were always backed up immediately, both there and with any minors in casualty, by the paediatric team. It was almost certainly safer to be a child than an adult!

There were also good things about it all. I remember that some of the patients and things that happened to them were at the time very funny, but not really in a repeatable way. The laughter was lavatorial, infantile, inappropriate and magnificently politically incorrect. Laughing into hiccupping hysterics, hopefully out of the patient's hearing, was a marvellous release from tension and the only stress-buster available most of the time.

I remember a patient who asked when meeting me the morning after a night admission, "But where's the night doctor?" In fact, a lot of them asked this and were absolutely incredulous at the hours we worked.

There were occasional small kindnesses here too. I remember one particular lady because when I said how much I loved the lily of the valley flowers on her locker, she described where they grew in her garden and promised me some when they finished flowering. Sure enough, a few weeks later, long after her discharge, I had a big parcel of roots. I don't remember what I did with them and I'm sure in my hectic life I didn't write and thank her. I lived in a very small single room in the hospital residency and of course, had no garden, but you don't forget a gesture like that. Wherever I have lived since I have bought and planted lily of the valley roots and thought of her.

Later on, when I became a lecturer in the Academic Department at the University Hospital of Wales, I remembered those first days as a junior house officer and used to tell my students to imagine the day they would start on the wards for real. "You'll find yourself standing by a bed with a collapsed, unconscious patient," I would tell them. "There's a team of people around the bed. You'll look around to see who is going to take control and you'll suddenly realise that they are all looking at you." The students would turn slightly green and become very thoughtful.

Another good thing about Hereford was that the drunks rarely caused violent problems, unlike most town drunks. The local cider seemed, for habitues, to induce a deep slumber, usually in the fields or on the grass verges of roads. The tougher men might wake and stagger into casualty with an almighty hangover, or the less tough be brought in after being run over by tractors, but there were not so many argumentative drunks on beer. The aggressive potential of pigs, drunk or sober, was another matter; we got a lot of nasty pig injuries. All sorts of wild and bloody accidents happen in the country, not surprisingly considering the murderously sci-fi nature of most farm machinery.

Roger joined me in Hereford for this second six months. He was doing the surgical job I had just finished. There was virtually no concession to married house officers in those days; you were not expected to be married and my room was tiny, with a single bed. After a lot of badgering, a second bed was put into a little flat opposite the General Hospital and Roger and I were allowed, as a special concession, to live there instead of in the tiny residency or apart. Another couple, both Sri Lankan, lived in the flat downstairs. There was no telephone in the building and the porters absolutely hated it because in the evenings and nights they had to come over, let themselves in, come to the bedroom and shout to wake us up. Not much fun for us either. Is it any surprise that when I became a committee member and then Chairman of the Trades Union, the Junior Hospital Doctors' Association, I spent a lot of my time shouting at administrators about junior doctor facilities?

The range of crises on the medical wards were fewer, or maybe more predictable. I do remember on one occasion diagnosing a rather rare heart condition and the astonishment of the registrar. "I'm not a total idiot, you know!" I said, a bit miffed. His expression said it all and I reverted to my usual submissive quietness. Heart conditions were what I had failed the first time around in my finals and I had overlearned them to the point of moderate expertise. What irony that one such ailment nearly carried me off, so many years later!

In the second term of pre-reg work we had fewer on-call shifts, though 'less' is a relative term. I was more likely to get my night off a week, as there were more of us around and we only covered the Casualty Department out of hours. There was even the very occasional trip into Hereford, to the pub of an evening or, in the day, to the Coroner's Office. Nothing to do with my faults you understand; we had a lot of geriatric patients who succumbed from natural causes.

I remember one real character. He was a Mr Smith, the head of a huge clan of local gypsies – 'Travellers,' we would call them now. He came in regularly with terrible chest infections and would be in an oxygen tent for a few days. You knew when he began to feel better because he would try to light up a fag in the tent. It was everyone's duty to look out for this and dive across beds and lockers to prevent the ward from being blown up.

I spent some time talking to his elderly wife, who took a bit of a shine to me. She told me one day how to cure a child's bedwetting. "You try the juice from dandelion stalks first," she said, "and if that don't work, take a mouse, skin it, boil it up and take out the bones. Sew them into a bundle in the skin." You were then supposed to put the little bundle under the child's pillow. "Never fails!" she ended emphatically. I never tried it as a Child Psychiatrist, though it ought to be a useful remedy. I guess a sensitive child would never sleep in the bed again on finding the gruesome thing, so it would be a sort of cure.

Mr Smith died one night and I was called over first thing. As I crossed the yard towards the ward, the whole clan, led by this matriarch, was just coming out. Seeing me, they changed direction and marched as one towards me. I had a moment of seriously wondering whether there was an old gypsy custom that involved massacring the responsible medical officer and if I should take flight. Fortunately, they only wanted to thank me, and all of them shook me by the hand and passed on. Phew!

Another slightly alarming incident occurred on one of my rare trips out of the hospital. I turned at a loud shout and saw a large group of youngsters on motorbikes chasing me. Before I could panic, I saw that the front guy was waving his hand in the air and grinning from ear to ear. He had come off his bike some weeks earlier and badly injured his hand. He just wanted to show me what a "lovely job" [his words], I had done on amputating the tip of one hopelessly crushed finger.

This takes me to the end of that incredibly tough year in Hereford. I can think of no better way to finish this account than with a tribute to the many kindnesses that we junior doctors exchanged under these incredibly hard conditions. This story is from those first six months – and it illustrates what helped most of us to survive.

On my very first evening at work in the County hospital, my first house job, there had been a 'patient collapsed' urgent call from the ward. I had got up, trying to conceal my panic. The outgoing doctor stretched casually. "My last night here," he said. "Nothing on telly. Do you mind if I come up too?" Tactful man! I had assured him that I had no objection to him amusing himself in this way and watched in admiration as he tipped the bed head down, checked the vital signs, prescribed, then allowed me to take over when the crisis was past, with no loss of face.

Six months later on my own last night, crisis over and replacement doctors in place. I was having a last evening in the residency with the new young man. A radiographer rang to say there was something really strange on an X-ray, like nothing she had seen before. Recognising the fear in his eyes, I pushed aside my plate and said, "Mm, that sounds interesting. Mind if I come along too?" and we went together. My experience told me that I wouldn't have a clue what was on the X-ray, but I would know something much more important – whether we should disturb the second on-call or wait till morning.

38

TRAVELLING HOPEFULLY

I THINK A BRIEF NOTE on my travelling experiences might be appropriate here. My family had strong links with the Continent. My father, though born in England, had been at school and later had worked for many years in Germany and Switzerland between the wars. He had many friends and connections all over Europe. After he retired officially from the university, he was very worried for a while about how he could keep a family, still quite young, on the small academic retirement pension. My mother earned very little in her psychoanalytic practice, with just a few patients, seen in our home. However, my father's expertise soon meant that he became involved as a Consultant for all sorts of electrical engineering projects and was paid a generous retainer by Kennedy and Donkin to attend conferences in Britain and the Continent. With his facility in languages and his liking for committee work, he thoroughly enjoyed this and we were much better off in those years.

I was largely shielded from these financial anxieties and their relief. I was used to a middle-class academic lifestyle that was comfortable but not flashy. I took it very much for granted, including the fact that I was completely supported financially until my medical training was over, in my mid-twenties. However, in casual enquiries I discovered that the amount my father supplied for me to live on was actually less than those of my friends on educational grants.

When I turned 16, my father opened an account in Barclays Bank for me and I stayed within my allowance for all personal expenditure. Soho coffee bars were cheap if you made one cup last, so were some of the new and exciting Chinese restaurants and my tastes were simple.

For most of my early childhood, our summer holidays were always to Wales, and they were magical. My parents had of course 'discovered' the West Wales coast during the war and were happy to take us there for our annual summer holiday, to a guest house in Rhossili on the Gower peninsula. We explored all the beaches, collected shells, made sandcastles – all the usual things. One unique pleasure though was to allow ourselves to be 'marooned' on the Worm's Head, which was mostly cut off from the mainland by the sea, but connected by a causeway at low tide. We children adored the frisson of adventure, from favourite books like *Treasure Island*. We loved the business of collecting wood, lighting a fire, cooking and eating our food and exploring, then coming back in the late afternoon-evening light, as the tide receded, to the surprised stares of the next batch of tourists, those lazy onlookers to whom we children could feel superior. My parents were very good-natured about it, as I think it may have been quite boring for them!

In spring 1951, aged 13, I had to have my tonsils and adenoids out. I felt very ill and miserable after it, and I was taken away on holiday by my Auntie Phyllis. She and Auntie Joyce were my mother's unmarried younger sisters, who I knew only from Christmas and other family reunion times. Phyllis Wilkins was another of those pioneering survivors of the First World War, who never married but made good use of the relaxation of (some of) the barriers to education and careers for women. She became an English literature teacher, then a Head Mistress, then an Inspector of Schools.

I had found her a little awe-inspiring, even intimidating, compared to her younger sister Joyce, but she turned out to be wonderful company. She was recovering from a major operation and we had an unforgettable fortnight in a coastal resort, going on gentle walks, playing with sand, eating ice creams and reading poetry together in the evenings. I think she introduced me to a lifetime favourite at this time – T.S. Eliot, by means of his humorous poetry. I devoured books in those days, especially poetry and fairy tales, and I thrived in her company. I spent some time with her later on in short visits to her flat in Newcastle upon Tyne, as well as at family gatherings. I am so glad I did, as she died a few years later of cancer and I would never have got to know her – whereas Auntie Joyce lived well into her 90s and in my adult life became my surrogate mother.

The first time my parents took us abroad as a family was when I was 9 and again when I was 11, the two mostly blurring into one. We travelled to many places, always by train, always staying in nice, friendly inns and meeting my father's old friends, many of whom were artists and musicians. My father had worked for the engineering firm Brown-Boveri in Switzerland and had been a close friend of the 'Brown' boys, sons of the founder.

On one trip I remember we visited the Swiss house of Mr Brown's widow. I remember a sweet, dignified old lady in an incredible, beautiful house. It was full of collector's items, including a room full of Canalettos, and many early works of the Impressionist painters, collected even before they became famous. I remember how kind and welcoming she was – also the delicious cakes for tea! Of course, I knew little or nothing about art at that time, but the original works by Renoir in her own private gallery also made a great impression on me. My father had told me that the Browns had started collecting works by these artists when they were young and not well off, mostly before the works were valuable and before they themselves became rich. I think that house did trigger in me a lifelong appreciation of art as something to live with for itself, not just its price.

Mind you, I'm as susceptible to bribery as anyone else. I suspect that it was after that visit that my father devised a fail-proof system for encouraging our cultural development – the offer of a nice tea with cake and ice cream if we consented to visit galleries and museums willingly and could pass a small quiz afterward. I continued to be a very willing participant in family holidays well into my early twenties, when my mother's declining health curtailed their own travel. The 'bribe' – bless them – was simply that they paid for the holiday, but it was a nice way of being with them in itself. Cake and ice cream are now optional, but – you never know – might still succeed easily as a persuader for me…

My parents certainly also brought us up to be independent. I was sent on holiday to the French Riviera on my own for the first time at the age of 14, rising 15 and just before going off to boarding school. I can't imagine letting a child do that quite so young now, but they arranged it very safely. I was met off the train in Paris by one of my father's old friends and spent the night at their family home, before being put on the train south, to be met there. It was a musical and cultural Summer School on the Riviera, again run by one of my father's old friends, mainly for French and American children and I certainly have quite magic memories of that too.

I felt that I was a seasoned traveller on the return trip and I remember chatting to a man on the train most of the way back to Paris. I had been brought up with good old-fashioned values for social exchanges. That is, to be courteous and friendly to everyone, whatever class or race, but without ever putting oneself forward or showing off. Behaving in a shy or awkward way in company was also not to be tolerated – since it should always be about putting the other person at ease, not about thinking of the impression oneself was giving.

So this very pleasant middle-aged man and I spent an agreeable journey talking about books and music and – more particularly – about painting. I found him to be full of interesting information about my favoured Impressionist artists, but also interested in my own, naive, views about them. At the Paris railway station, we parted and he shook my hand ceremoniously, handing me his card and thanking me for the pleasure of my company. My mentor collected me, and I told him about my pleasant journeying companion, giving him the card.

"Mon Dieu!" he exclaimed, startled. "Do you know who that was? Only the best art critic in all France – the Art Editor of *Le Figaro*!"

39

MY HAPPY VIENNA

HERE IS A LITTLE LIGHT-HEARTED adventure I was fortunate enough to experience during the later stage of my time in Medical School, in January 1961, at a time when I was still fancy free and enjoying life generally, and even had some holiday time.

First, though, a little background about our musical heritage and Continental connections. Our only living relative on my father's side of the family was my Auntie Mary – in actual fact his cousin, but they had grown up more as siblings. She was a large and very ebullient lady, who had been brought up in Italy. Her father was a scion of a quite famous aristocratic family – the Mildmays – whose ancestor Lord Mildmay was a bosom pal of the Prince Regent during the Regency, though my father was related to the Mildmays by marriage and not by blood. My father and she were united, as cousins, by their common grandmother, Luisa Kapp, whose stage name as a singer was Luisa Cappiani. In those days you had to have an Italian name to get anywhere in the musical world, but although trained to sing (as most fashionable girls were) it was only when she was left as an impoverished widow bringing up two children that she took it up professionally. Luisa became a famous singer in her day, in concerts and opera all over Europe and visiting America on tour. There are many family anecdotes about her – definitely a Diva and larger than life!

One of them I remember was about how she could sometimes embarrass my father when he was young. One afternoon, as a student, he was escorting 'Grandmama' as she was always called, over the bridge in Rome after leaving the La Scala Opera house. He had taken her to hear another star singing, and, timidly, he ventured a little compliment on the other diva.

Luisa drew herself up and said, "Yes, maybe – but she should have sung like this…" and drawing a great breath into her ample lungs she proceeded to treat the public to a famous aria, at top decibels, stopping the traffic and gaining a crowd of excited and applauding passers-by. Young Reggie cringed and didn't know what to do with himself. Calling all Grandmamas – admit it, wouldn't we all secretly love a double coup like that, if we had the talent? Stopping the traffic with a crowd of admirers and seriously embarrassing the grandchildren, all in one go!

We had other musical ancestors. One was in the Vienna Boys Choir as a child and was said to have been patted on the head by Beethoven one Sunday. His tutor is later listed as a pallbearer at Beethoven's funeral, so it may well be true. Another Krall ancestor was a founding member of the Music Society in Vienna, which built the beautiful Musikverein concert hall.

Mary Mildmay, my father's cousin, had been brought up in Italy, where her own father was British Consul in Milan. When I knew her she was living in St John's Wood in London, and teaching singing, Italian opera style, to singers, along with her lifelong companion Doria Grey as partner and piano accompanist. They were indeed highly regarded in their day, being part of an elite group of teachers who were regularly employed by festivals and opera theatres to coach and support the singers. They taught me to sing, during holidays, over several years, in what I realised later was Bel Canto style. I learnt the violin too and have always been very grateful for the lovely background understanding of classical music that comes from any learning attempts. My voice was tuneful and sweet, a Lyric Soprano if I had ever wanted to take it up professionally, best suited to lieder and folk songs, which indeed I love.

So, when we learnt from Auntie Mary that a previously unknown branch of the family had got in touch from Vienna, we were all very pleased and began some correspondence, carefully monitored and checked on by my aunt. These turned out to be fourth cousins, a young man a little above my own age, an engineering student, who spoke good English. His parents, who only spoke German, issued not only a general invitation to us, but an invitation personally to me to come and stay in January 1961, for a fortnight specifically to partner young Ernst to a Ball. What a wonderful once-in-a-lifetime opportunity! My aunt and parents facilitated it and off I flew.

My mother and my Auntie Joyce spent a lot of time helping me select and buy the clothes for this event. We had been told that there would be a lot of parties in the fortnight leading up to the Ball, at which I must wear a full-length white dress, so I went well prepared.

I was made very welcome by the family and had a wonderful time being shown round all the best sights in Vienna by Ernst and his parents. The second evening, he and I attended a cocktail party at which the business of the holiday started – a group of excited young people learning how to dance the Lancers, and other early Ballroom dances, to be followed at the Ball by a demonstration of the Viennese Waltz.

The latter dance was not the sedate 'poor relation' taught in England at that time, but a continuous whirl by the couple at high speed, of course to the music of Strauss – who else! Vienna was trying, at that time, to restore the glories of an earlier era and essentially this Ball was regarded as the equivalent of being a Debutante in England.

My dress for the cocktail party-cum-dance class was a strapless black number with tiers of short skirt, which stood out most flatteringly during the Waltz rehearsal. Unfortunately, my dress was more sophisticated than I was. I barely made it to the end of the dance before nausea took me on a mad dash for the hall leading to the garden, still spinning like a top on the way. As I checked my gyrations in front of a floor length mirror, I had an unforgettable view of the effect of black taffeta against a torso and face no longer flesh colour but grass green. I waltzed on out and was violently unwell into a convenient rose bush, before Ernst rescued me and took me home.

Undaunted, I practised rigorously several times each day, increasing the whirl by small increments, so that on the Big Day I not only performed the Lancers but Ernst and I, along with the other debutantes, accomplished an impeccable Viennese Waltz, ending with a deep curtsy before the President of Austria. To crown the pleasure I got from the whole experience, the Ball was being held in the very Musikverein of which my ancestor was a founding member.

After the slight drama of that first evening, the rest of the holiday was wonderful. Ernst and I didn't have a romantic liaison, in spite of the setting, but we remained really good friends and both families kept in touch over many years. His daughter, Dagmar, came and spent a summer with Ken and I and the children in Cardiff, and the family welcomed us when my husband, Ken, had to attend the World Psychiatric Society meeting in Vienna in 1983 – but that's another story. We continue to be good friends.

40

LIFE'S LESSIONS

SENDING MY MEMOIRS out first as a blog was very satisfying. I found that writing, and sharing, them in that form meant I received comments, both online and personally. Almost all were positive, but helped me to realise that I had given a wrong impression sometimes, and could take the opportunity to correct it, as the feedback made me see certain things I had said that might have been confusing.

So – regarding my writing about my time in Vienna, and my family history – I think they may have given an idea of a much more elegant lifestyle than we had, or that we moved in some exotic circles. Not really true, my childhood was not at all elegant and our house and lifestyle were mundane and practical, in the 'academic' tradition – 'plain living and high thinking'!

Although money was adequate, many of our family friends had more obviously luxurious surroundings. My father's salary as a Professor was not large until he 'retired' (when I was 16) and earned a great deal more as a Consultant in industry. Nor did my mother ever earn anything much by her small private practice as a Psychoanalyst, though both of them were highly respected as individuals. We certainly didn't ever move in aristocratic circles – I wouldn't even have wanted to be a 'debutante' in England. So the exotic lifestyle of my father's old friends and the events that came about on the trips abroad were all the more exciting.

Many of the things that have happened to me, that I have remembered and written about, can be seen as life's lessons. It is those – in bite-sized pieces – that I am concentrating on, with perhaps just a few words of explanation, or mentioning my age, to show that I am leaving out, or putting on hold, great chunks of my life.

* * *

I would like to recount here another couple of incidents from my time in med school, which have influenced me for the better throughout my life. The first one is funny, the second one very touching, both are, in my view, beautiful.

The first one was quite early in my time on the wards. Earlier still, at the beginning of my student life, I had been living at home. I would take the train from East Croydon up to London – Paddington Station – and walk to the medical school through Soho, even more colourful and exotic in its foreign shops and nightlife then than it is now. It would be early, around 8am, and often in fine weather small groups of 'ladies of the night', winding down for their sleep time, would be sitting on the nightclub doorsteps, smoking, gossiping and calling out saucy things to the passers-by. At first, I was embarrassed, but I quickly realised they were harmless and fun.

So when one day, a couple of years later, a Soho lady was brought in to Casualty at the Middlesex Hospital while I was doing a student stint there, I recognised the type, though not of course the individual. She had been severely beaten up by her boyfriend and her face and body were, frankly, quite a mess. The nurses and doctors cleaned her up and sutured some wounds, briskly and professionally with no judgement, as they would for anyone.

She was admitted for what was left of the night and I sat with her through it, for a long time. She held my hand and poured out her life story and her pain and frustration with her abuser. Luckily, I was too inexperienced even to make the classic mistake of asking why she didn't leave him. I just sat and listened, pained, helpless and absorbed, till she slept. Later the next morning I was with the other students, tagging behind the Important Consultant on his daily ward round. When he got to this lady, he checked with the nurse and told her she could go home and attend for wound dressing later.

She thanked him dramatically and then raised herself up in bed and cried: "But here is the wonderful young doctor who helped me. I owe her SO much!"

I found myself grabbed and pulled into the embrace of this large enthusiastic lady. My feet – literally – slipped from under me and I nose-dived into her huge scented cleavage. I hugged her back as best I could and extricated myself, to see the contained giggles of my co-students, swiftly suppressed by the icy look of the Boss, who harrumphed, glared at me and led a silenced group away.

Me in the wrong as usual, I felt. But, years later, she and her ilk became the models behind my 'Fat Goddess' series. My favourite is the applique cartoon these Soho women inspired, of a large night club lady, with the embroidered caption: "Even God gets fed up with religion sometimes. Otherwise why did He create topless go-go dancers?"

Notes on my Fat Goddess pictures

Here is a note on a series of my embroidered pieces. I call them my 'Fat Goddesses'. They only represent one side of the Feminine Divine and are meant to be to be regarded somewhat tongue-in-cheek. They represent the wonderfully loving, overwhelming, warm, sexy and expressive feminine power of the human body. Because they are archetypes they have no real heads or brains – not because women don't, but because an archetype only represents one aspect of anything. I hope they offend no-one. They were meant to be followed by a contrasting series of Skinny Saints, who represented the archetype of purely masculine emphasis on the head and brain, but only a couple of these got made.

Of course, no real life human being, male or female, is complete without the inner goddess and inner saint of feminine and masculine characteristics, intellect and sensuality, working together and nourishing the Whole – maybe under the guidance of what we might call Soul.

These little *jeu d'esprit* emerged after a period of mourning for one of my most loved relatives, my Auntie Joyce, who would have been very amused by them. I find that coming out of a period of grief, or any sort of blockage, often results in a time of growth and even of laughter and playfulness – sometimes almost disconcertingly so, if it has been a major bereavement. It's good to have such an experience and to rejoice in it, as a wonderful gift from the lost person, or from the Universe.

The picture is a cross stitch repeater pattern derived from the original inspiration for the Goddesses. That was a small newspaper paragraph and photo of a very fat ballerina – the daughter of the world-famous Russian dancer, Nijinsky! The joyous way this large woman was twirling, almost flying, on one toe was a delight! She is ignoring all the restrictive ideas of what a ballet dancer should look like and I found this both inspirational and funny at the same time. She became a decorative device and then further morphed into applique Goddesses with three-dimensional boobs made of thread-covered spiral wires, with outrageous accessories and saucy titles.

* * *

Towards the end of my time as a med student, I was taking my conventional medical learning much more seriously than earlier. But I had another lesson to learn. A small group of 5 or 6 students were assigned to each ward, mine at this time being Cardiology. One day I was taking a history from a man in his 40s with a very serious heart condition. Having done this, I handed over to the qualified medical team and had a brief chat with his wife. They were childless, Irish Catholics, and had in fact only been married for a couple of years. He was ill enough to be put in a side room on his own and I had no particular interaction with either until an emergency alert went up – he had collapsed. We students were expected to go there, of course, to observe and learn what to do in a crisis.

As I got to the door, I saw that his wife, looking stunned and shocked, was sitting outside. There was no way, no way in all the earth that I could walk past and leave her there alone. I knew my real duty was to go in with the other trainees, but I couldn't. As I sat down beside her, without saying a word, another awfulness hit me. I had – literally – no words to say, nor comfort to give. How could I, a young woman with no direct experience of marriage and loss, say anything? I was being a fool, for nothing. I should be in that room helping, but I couldn't, somehow, leave her. I sat there for many minutes, feeling stupider and stupider. I wasn't even thinking of her, poor woman, but self-immersed in my own uselessness – which still slightly shames me to admit! No role of inner prayer even. After about half an hour of complete silence, the door opened and she was beckoned in, while I slunk away.

Her husband survived for another week, but eventually, sadly, died. I was on another ward by then, a routine changeover. However, sometime later I had a card from the widow, with a photo of him and an invitation to tea the following Saturday. I went along to their little flat. The lady was warmly welcoming and we had a very nice tea. She gave me a small embroidered tray cloth, which I still have, and talked a lot about her late husband and her plans to return home to Ireland soon.

As I left, she held my hand and asked me if I remembered the day a week before he died, when he collapsed and I had sat outside the room with her – and I indicated that I did. She then said to me, with great certainty, in words I can still hear clearly: "I will never forget how you sat with me and the many wonderfully kind things you said to me."

We hugged and I went home, stunned. I knew I had not said one single word. Whose voice had she heard, comforting her so well, covering my inadequacy, yet picking up my good intention?

It remains a precious memory and a reminder that there is often no need for words and certainly no need to feel bad. The presence of another is often more than enough.

41

ON CALL

I HOPE THE PREVIOUS PIECES of my life story, though maybe seeming randomly chosen and placed, are beginning to form a pattern of how I, as a person, developed and – hopefully – matured and improved through years containing times of great joy, times of great sorrow. There were also times of mistakes and failures. In between, of course, have been many, many times of mundane living, and static boredom, which I'm mostly missing out, but which we all have, however we may pretend to our friends and even ourselves that we live in a constant state of excitement!

So, I will add in here a reflection on the 'on-call' system as experienced by many other professions, no doubt, but a nagging life-long affliction in the medical profession.

* * *

In Hereford circa the 1960s, the on-call system within the main hospital building was remarkably primitive, but at least it didn't involve an embarrassed porter having to come into our bedroom and shout, as they had to do out-of-hours in my first residency in Hereford.

In the main hospital building, there was a strip of three coloured lights above every door and in every corridor. Each light could flash or remain still, so every doctor, from pre-registration houseman to consultant, had a combination of one, two or three lights, still or flashing.

Does anyone remember those? Someone better than I at maths could work out how many possible combinations there were. It was cumbersome, inefficient and extremely tiresome to have to keep looking up at the lights no matter what you were doing, however urgent, then break off to go and find a ward phone – long before anything mobile.

Mine was a single, still, orange light, not flashing. I remember well that at the very end of my time on Surgical, when the locums had come, my colleague Harry and I were both replaced and found we had an evening off together, actually managing to leave the hospital for a couple of hours in the nearest pub. Awash with good Hereford cider, we walked back arm in arm. Harry looked up at the orange street lights. "Just look at that, Elinor!" he burbled, "Your light is on all over Hereford!" Well, it was funny at the time; a sort of revenge for being totally at the mercy of an electric light bulb.

Moving on, it was not so necessary in psychiatric hospitals, with few emergencies and where you tended to have to leave word of where you were likely to be and could be traced by bush telegraph from ward to ward. Later still, a wonderful state-of-the-art gadget called a BLEEP was invented and it could catch you out even on the loo, but didn't receive sounds – you still had to get off and go and find a phone.

This was a disadvantage remedied by the next invention, the fully mobile phone. The first of these were the size of bricks and wouldn't fit in a handbag or trouser pocket. It could of course find you wherever you were, which was much more convenient all round. The disadvantage was, it also picked up outside sounds and could therefore betray the conversation on the loo by the whooshing flush or alternatively by the pub sounds in the background, if you'd illicitly managed an escape from the hospital.

Now we are all, on-call medics or not, really at the mercy of our mobile phones day and night, with a whole lot of etiquette that you ignore at your peril. Somehow, one just can't win.

I ♥ Fishponds Asylum

In October 1964, after my year as a pre-registration house officer in Hereford, I was fully on the medical register, and I was free to follow my calling. I started a job as a senior house officer in a mental hospital on the outskirts of Bristol, just after my time in Hereford, so as to go straight into psychiatry, my specialty of choice. Roger joined me after he finished his second six-month stint as a house officer and then also of course went onto the medical register. So I was there on my own for six months, but free almost all weekends to go back to Hereford and join him.

The mental hospital was a large, imposing building in a suburb of Bristol. Once known as 'Fishponds Asylum', by my day it had become 'Glenside Hospital' and brought some way up to date. I truly loved my time there and felt quite at home from the very beginning – which probably says more about me than I care to think about.

I wasn't just standing and gossiping, I was sitting with people who were willing to reveal their deepest fears and secrets once I understood the key. This 'key' was an intensive, thorough and well-thought-through 'history and examination of the mental state', starting with the patient's own words about their concerns and only then leading to a formulation of their lives and problems. This could be carefully conveyed back to them, followed by a discussion of the treatment plan.

This was, of course, the ideal and used for outpatients and those newly diagnosed with severe illness, admitted to the acute wards for a period of treatment, after which they would go back into the community. It was certainly not always possible to follow with most of the long-term inpatients under my care who had been there for years. Some of these were either still psychotic and often unwilling to talk at all until they learned to trust you. The vast majority of our patients were 'chronic' ones who had been in for years, with little hope of leaving. No wonder people had a dread of 'going into Fishponds', as with all other mental institutions.

My first consultant was a meticulous Scot who taught me the basics well and to a high standard. I am grateful for the rigour of his approach, though he had a few unfortunate old-fashioned phrases. "Tell me, young man," he would ask blushing youths, "do yer abuse yerself?"

He expected – a vain thing normally – that the chronic patients would be fully assessed both for their physical and mental state at least annually. Blowing the dust off the files, metaphorically, it seemed that hardly any of them had been checked by anyone for years. Being, as I have said elsewhere, something of a goody-goody, I set myself to see all of those chronic patients in wards under my care during my six-month time there.

I am so glad I did! No textbook, nor indeed my training otherwise, could have been half so useful as this seemingly routine task, nor would I have tried so hard to make contact with later patients with anything like the same devotion. The files probably went on gathering dust unseen for many more years after that, but I took away a great deal from this six months' work. The stresses were nil and on-call work was a doddle compared with the previous year. My mind and my heart expanded accordingly.

I have always tried to see things from the patient's point of view (a discipline which I was not to find common in psychiatry until I got to the academic department run by Prof. Ken Rawnsley) but this was limited by my lack of training and life experience. Like most young doctors, there was for me at that time a clear line between me and the patients, not just in the appropriate sense of the Hippocratic Oath, but in a feeling which was really of superiority, unstated and unrecognised. One way of dealing with a fear of madness is to become an 'expert' in it, a carer, to offer a hostage to the gods to take others, not yourself.

Life itself, with all my experiences of my own fallibility and inadequacy, has levelled the playing field and I can honestly say that any feeling of superiority has dissolved, it is much more a case of "there but for the Grace of God – plus good genes and good luck – go I."

42

SUSSEX BY THE SEA

IN **1965,** I was very happy to give up work and move to Taplow in Berkshire, as I was pregnant with my eagerly awaited first baby. My husband, Roger Tudway, had obtained a post-registration job in general medicine at the Red Cross Memorial Hospital there. I made no particular plans, though I certainly hoped one day to continue in psychiatry. In chronological time, this piece should be followed by the events of 1966-1967, covering baby Andrew's birth, the loss of both my parents and our 20-months of joy in our little son, followed by the tragedy of his death – but I feel these have been adequately covered much earlier in these memoirs.

My husband Roger and I had just completed the process of buying a little house in Punnets Town, a Sussex village a couple of miles from Heathfield, when baby Andrew died. We moved into that house in September 1967 on our return to England after that tragic loss in Belgium. It was quite small, basically an extended bungalow with two bedrooms. We were still grieving terribly for our loss and for a while unable to make any plans.

We had bought it in order to have a place to either live in or rent out. In those days one had little certainty of staying in one place for further training, which could mean periods of only six months at a time before having to move on. I had the money from my parent's estate, so it had made sense to invest in a house near where my Auntie Joyce, my mother's younger sister, lived at the time. It was good to have our own place to move into, so near to my closest remaining relative.

Grief was an open wound that could not be bandaged nor concealed. At such a time, you feel an embarrassment to acquaintances and a burden to friends. Many people have difficulty dealing with others' bereavement. The death of a child is just too awful to contemplate. For a long time, some people would simply change the subject or turn away when it came up. I had to learn to comfort strangers or sometimes even friends for my own loss. Indeed, the price of being part of society was to learn to do just that – comfort others, keep on top of emotion just enough to function in a group and save the despair for times alone with Roger or Auntie Joyce.

As time moved on, it sometimes felt an unnecessary burden to explain what had happened whenever I was with new people and the question arose – as it always quickly did – "Have you any children?"

Just once, I suddenly felt I couldn't bear to go through it again and quickly answered, "No." Mistake. Doing so hurt me terribly, as if the words were a betrayal, so that I was never tempted to do it again.

Only many years later when, in my second marriage, I had Rupert and then Amanda, did it begin to feel appropriate to refer only to them and not talk about Andrew except in special circumstances.

At first, and not surprisingly as he was more depressed than ever, Roger still wasn't able to settle into any work. Given his drinking and his recurrent depressions, it would be necessary for me to earn a living and fast; my parent's money wouldn't last, and anyway I had a horror of using up savings. I easily found a job as a locum SHO in psychiatry at Hellingly Hospital in Sussex. I was liked by the Clinical Director, who was keen to secure my employment if a permanent post should become available. I was getting a lot of support from relatives, particularly Auntie Joyce, only a few miles up the road. I was also reasonably near my brother and sister-in-law and their first daughter, Annabel, of whom I was very fond.

Then Roger was offered a job as a trainee Senior House Officer in the radiotherapy department at Velindre Hospital in Cardiff. His father was a very noted radiotherapist in Bristol, one of the pioneers in the specialty, and he had pulled a few strings. Roger decided he wanted a career in radiotherapy, though I wasn't at all happy about the choice of specialty, considering the problems he already had following in his father's footsteps and the complicated family dynamics. We had no connection with Cardiff and I was also not at all happy about moving there. I'm not sure I was even consulted; it was automatically assumed in those days that the wife followed the husband's job, even if she had a career in her own right.

I didn't say to Roger I wouldn't come to Wales, but I felt that these issues all had to be talked through and sorted out. Roger couldn't cope and was distraught at the slightest mention of my thoughts on this. In the end, I suppose I just gave in. I don't think he ever really forgave me for shaking his certainty and questioning our future in any way. That was a shame because nothing could have been further from my mind at the time than ending our marriage; I just wanted to plan and negotiate our future a bit. He was too fragile to cope and both his mental state and our marriage deteriorated from then on.

So, I remember that time as very, very hard to be sure, but much cushioned by the wonderful love of Auntie Joyce and my other relatives and the many, many friends who wrote or visited when they heard the sad news. My unmarried aunt truly became my mother from this time and I became her daughter – both finding the loss of my mother, Dorothy, softened by the memories of her and the similarities to her that we found in each other. This bond endured right up to her death in 1997 at 96 years of age.

So, here is a good place to share the eventual fruit of my long links with Sussex, particularly the genesis of my book of modern fairy stories: *Tales from Turnaround Cottage*. Here is an excerpt, which shows these sources very clearly – and it is actually a true story. It is the first chapter of the book and will already be familiar to some lucky readers!

Tales From Turnaround Cottage – Chapter 1

This is my own story, the true one, of the first house I ever bought, nearly 50 years ago, on the southward slope of the Sussex Downs. My address really was: Flitterbrook Lane, Punnetts Town, Sussex. From the top windows, you could see the sea: the English Channel and all the coast between Newhaven and Hastings. In the right light, you could see a silver-white line on the horizon, which was the coast of France.

Kneeling in that garden, one overcast day, I buried my wedding dress among the country flowers and creeping weeds, shortly before leaving the house forever. The dress was white silk velvet, sewn to my own design: a sweetheart neckline and a full sweeping skirt with a bustle, trimmed with a single silk rose.

I bought herbs and bedding plants, pansies, wallflowers, winter jasmine and a blue clematis a few days before I went away, not expecting to go so soon. I spent my very last morning bedding them in, not caring where, maybe over where the dress was already starting its long decay. I was not thinking of that but of the green-fingered pleasure I was leaving for the new owners in a house full of hopes and dreams.

I have never been back, but I have wondered sometimes if my white velvet wedding dress, no longer white, ever rose from the bed, turned over from the soil by a stunned gardener or marauding fox. What shocks might it have evoked in the finders? A tale of murder perhaps, till no trace of a body was found? Thoughts of theft or tragedy or a ghost story?

Do you think I should go back to that village, to the pub in Punnetts Town or the neighbours – or even to the house itself – and ask? I dare not! But you – you who love stories, love mysteries and have a far better imagination than mine – couldn't you make up a story about the wedding dress buried in a country garden, or maybe a story about who found it and what effect that had on them?

43

"I TALK TO THE TREES BUT THEY DON'T LISTEN TO ME!"
WHITCHURCH HOSPITAL 1: 1969-1971

IN 1969 I followed Roger, my husband, to Cardiff where he was working in Velindre Hospital as a trainee in Radiotherapy. There was no psychiatric post for me to come to locally, not even as a locum, but I managed to get a temporary job, also as a Senior House Officer, in Velindre, the local hospital for cancer treatment. I was there for about six months and because it was not a trainee post I had only very basic general medical responsibility, at a level that I could easily cope with. Although it was quite a while since my days of acute medical work, the patients were in solely for cancer treatment and were very carefully supervised by the seniors on the medical teams, so I quite enjoyed it.

Indeed, I could be useful at times. One day I was asked by a frustrated Consultant if I could talk to a tetchy old man who was adamant in refusing the treatment he'd been brought in for. I did my usual thing of sitting with him and asking artless questions about his life. Bored and lonely, he was only too happy to talk and gave me quite a detailed rundown on his life, with all its ups and downs. At the end of half an hour – without my having said anything at all about his medical condition or why he was there – he finished and said abruptly, but in a friendly fashion: "Right. What do I need to get this treatment going then?" Job done! but of course, this approach takes much more time than can be allotted in the hectic schedules of an acute hospital.

After a time of Roger and I living uncomfortably in separate rooms in the hospital residency, a flat in the grounds became available for us, so I had a home again, of sorts. We rented out the house in Sussex and eventually sold it, without very much reluctance. It held too many sad memories and we had never lived there with baby Andrew. It remains in my heart though, as the origin of magical *Turnaround Cottage*.

Whitchurch Hospital, the psychiatric inpatient hospital, was in the same grounds as Velindre and our flat. I put in for the next two SHO jobs going there. I didn't get the first, which went to a local young doctor, but I got the second in competition with a couple of other hopefuls. I received several unpleasant comments over the next few weeks from staff and colleagues who were upset because the post had gone to me, an incomer, and not to a Welsh doctor. I was astounded by this. I had never experienced this attitude before, as of course I was indigenous English, whereas I guess many of the overseas doctors who staffed much of the psychiatric service had experience of such attitudes. It was also the brief era of Welsh Nationalists smashing up television studios and burning English-owned cottages. I soon met lots of them who believed in peaceful protest and were as upset as I was by the violent campaign. Since then, I have felt very welcome in Wales and have stayed here for 50 years!

I love mental hospitals, the buildings, I mean, not the way they were run. The ones built in the years around the turn of the 19th to 20th centuries are particularly fine. It was obviously a time of prosperity and philanthropic certainties. The asylums were little worlds of their own. They had farms and kitchen gardens, even their own orchestras and theatres where staff and patients could mix in a self-sufficient appearance of democracy. Outsiders often commented on how hard it was to tell the inmates and staff apart.

Sometimes caring for the insane was an inherited job: generations of nurses. I suppose that, as my mother was a psychiatrist, I also followed this pattern. In some ways, we all fitted too well into a very strange and abnormal environment. Whitchurch Hospital was a good example. My first impression was how closely it resembled most of those I had visited or worked in. A style you might call 'Palace of the Sun Emperor', as if the delusions of grandeur of some of the inmates were shared by the town planners. Or maybe a sort of patronising consolation for the contempt in which the 'mad' are all too often held. They have an imposing central block in fancy brick with a series of wings, holding two stories of long wards, fanning out halfway round.

They are set in well-planned parkland, like stately homes, and some even have a ha-ha: a fence hidden in a deep dip. The aristocrat had a ha-ha so as not to interfere with the view and his delusion of owning the whole world. The benevolent burghers of Cardiff wanted to soften the reality of incarceration for their charges. The buildings of the time show something of late Victorian and Edwardian ambivalence towards the mad. On the one hand, these palaces were light and airy, run with paternalistic care as hospitals rather than prisons. On the other hand, they were locked institutions, sited well away from city centres, both to protect the 'mad' from persecution and the 'normal' from contact with the underbelly of society. In most cases, the towns have crept up on them until they are now part of suburbia. Even so, they still hold a sense of aloofness and local children make jokes about what will happen if they take a shortcut through the grounds while their parents speak of the stereotypes of madness rather than the reality.

Coming into Whitchurch Hospital from the front is impressive. Laid out as the view from the windows were large green areas for cricket and bowls and a sense of luxury and space. Once inside, the luxurious area of mahogany and dusty opulence was confined to the boardroom and other official areas across the front of the imposing porch, to be instantly counteracted by the cream and green institution paint of the corridors and wards and the constant faint smell of boiling greens. The corridors were wider than many of our old institutions; the wards were no worse than others of their time.

In all the years I was there, or came back to visit after the unit moved to the UHW, I hardly ever used the front entrance. We always came in at the back, through the Hospital Residency. It was more convenient for Velindre Hospital, situated in the same grounds and nearer to my flat and the car parks. The residency was only locked at night. It had some reasonably comfortable sitting and dining rooms and a few bedrooms, used both for resident doctors and anyone on call who lived outside the campus.

We even had maids in those days, whose job it was to clean and to serve meals in the dining room. One of them, Millie, and I struck up a friendship during the time I was on my own there, before Roger joined me. We would chat over the inevitable cups of strong hospital tea and many a time when I was on call I would come back to my room to find that she had tucked a hot water bottle in my bed before she went off duty. Care of the staff is an important and often lost value. Anyone who lives or works in a big institution makes small alliances and learns how tiny acts of mutual kindness can make life bearable.

44

WHITCHURCH HOSPITAL:
AN EXCITING TIME TO WORK IN
PSYCHIATRY

I **ALWAYS DID A SLOW BURN** at how little the lives and welfare of the psychiatric patient counted for in our culture, but it was hard to see what real improvements one could make; a thorough change of attitude was needed first of all. I tended not to care too much about the presence or absence of luxury in my own surroundings at that time – having been brought up in the 'plain living and high thinking' academic tradition – but I felt that far more should be spent on treatments and research. The institutional nature of the buildings didn't trouble me as much as the feeling that the patients, particularly the chronic ones, counted for so little in the scheme of things.

Acutely mentally ill people in Whitchurch got reasonable management by the (low) standards of the time, considering our groping after knowledge and the early state of much of what we had to offer. Many staff on the acute wards were really caring and tried to give people who were extremely ill – sometimes wild, disinhibited and dangerous – a sense of dignity and selfhood. There were regular ward rounds, every day for the juniors, once or twice a week for the consultant. There was a constant watch for suicidal or self-destructive behaviour and planned care, at least in theory, was the norm.

That said, I didn't find Whitchurch Hospital particularly well equipped or forward-looking. The hospital housed the Academic Unit, which later moved to the newly built University Hospital of

Wales but was still very much part of the wider service. There had also been some sort of medical research unit within the hospital and a sense that the staff traded on past glories. Senior staff certainly seemed to feel they were superior and more advanced than other places and may have been partly so. I found Whitchurch to be in many ways rather insular and backward compared with the facilities and attitudes of some of the places in which I had been working or with which I had had close contact. I was tactful enough not to say this, but early on I recognised that it was vital to get one of the posts on East One, the Academic Unit, if I was serious about continuing my training, though at first I had virtually no contact with it.

I'm glad I held my peace about this because I had not been long in Whitchurch before the Ely Hospital scandal broke. Although the dreadful conditions in that 'subnormality hospital' (as they were then horribly designated) a mile or so from Whitchurch, were widespread, almost universal, it happened to be Cardiff that hit the headlines this time.

Of course, such public recognition was absolutely essential – and the conditions of such appalling care needed to be exposed country-wide. I did, though, feel sorry for Dr Jenkins, the Superintendent, who I knew only slightly. He had great support from the colleagues in Adult Psychiatry, rightly in my view, because it was unfair to make him the main scapegoat. He had been trying to bring the problems up with the health authorities for many years, perhaps not making enough fuss, but how do you change a whole culture? The disgusting conditions eventually exposed were, country – no, world-wide! Dr Jenkins was made a scapegoat to save the administrators and politicians.

There were many good researchers writing on the bad effects of institutionalisation at that time and many lessons were being learned. It was an exciting time to come into psychiatry. Maxwell Jones was bringing in a form of democratisation of the inpatient system. David Clark also brought fresh air into the debates in the psychiatric journals. Scandalous practises were no longer always being hushed up. I was an early convert to the idea that treatments should, as far as possible, be in the patient's own home or smaller, local units and that no-one should end up living in a large institution.

This brave idea is still only very partially realised. It's much more expensive, particularly needing teams of much better-trained staff. It is also due to the intransigent nature of chronic mental illness itself, particularly schizophrenia. It was becoming obvious in the 70s that not all the long-term symptoms – inertia, poverty of emotion and destruction of the thought processes – were due to the asylums; most could also occur as a result of the psychotic process.

Our early hopes for keeping patients in the community were high but did not produce the brave new world we had expected. The process of 'freeing' the patients was very slow, often hindered by poorly trained nursing staff, inadequate funding, entrenched public attitudes and the nature of their illnesses. Although much has improved, particularly for those with learning disabilities, the country has never invested the necessary amounts of cash and energy to give dignity of life to people with chronic mental health problems.

Of course we came across the work of Laing – you couldn't miss him as a young psychiatrist. He was a considerable influence and I appreciated his approach: that madness was simply an alternative form of creativity. The trouble was it didn't really fit with the sort of cases we had in the big wide world outside London. Schizophrenia, I still believe, is a heart-breaking deformation of the creative process and of the psyche. The disinhibiting effects of the illness can sometimes, at first, release useful strengths but, unless checked, the process can destroy the personality and the life.

Laing also seemed to me, in his psychoanalytic approach, to be confusing the content of the patients' delusions with the psychotic form of their thinking. The former could lend itself to explanation and at least a little psychotherapeutic help, the latter being intractable without medication. He also squandered the goodwill his early ideas created by his paranoid personality, heavy drinking and arrogance. A shame; he had a lot of influence outside the psychiatric field, with a whole generation of hippies and alternative therapists, and could have done much good.

Medication did indeed damp down the emotions and blunt the feelings. No wonder patients often hated taking their tablets and lapsed once at home. Unfortunately, their freedom to do so could conflict with the rights of others. An extreme example was one of our patients, a young man who lived with his elderly father. While in hospital, he would be medicated and sane. Each time he went home he stopped taking the drugs because he felt so much more alive and his symptoms were exciting and thrilling to him. Then his paranoid ideas would develop, mostly relating to his father and expressed in increasingly serious aggressive outbursts. The day he was luckily intercepted by a caller, chasing his father round and round the kitchen table with an axe, the old man at last consented to have him admitted under section for a lengthier period and stabilisation. He was supervised more carefully on discharge, with his father's heartfelt agreement.

One thing that really annoyed me in those days was that the Board of Governors met every month in Whitchurch Hospital. They heard a report from the Matron and Medical Superintendent and discussed policy. Now I had, and have, no quarrel with that. I am an unusual person in that I will freely admit to enjoying committee meetings, if well conducted. Even the less good ones afford a welcome change from being on one's feet and rushing around all the time. It's a good corrective for individual tyranny and can facilitate consensus management.

No, what I objected to was that they always had a very good lunch! Briefly, the smell of boiled cabbage would be replaced by more delicious odours at the front of the hospital wafting from the mahogany mausoleum.

"Why can't they have what the patients on the chronic wards are getting!" I would cry, to shocked uncomprehending looks. "It wouldn't hurt them to have a non-luxury lunch once a month. Why can't they at least have the bog-standard canteen food? How much does it cost to feed them all?"

Alas, no one was in the least interested in my French Revolutionary moments; a sort of reverse 'let them eat cake'.

45

ANNE'S STORY

"IT WAS AS IF A DOOR** in the ceiling opened and there was this old man staring down at us. His face sort of crumpled and he had tears in his eyes," said Anne. "I'd never seen a grown-up cry before!" Her voice was full of wonderment as she told me this over and over again down the years. I don't suppose the Meter reading man ever forgot that day either, when opening the door to the cellar on a routine visit, he found two frightened little girls, dressed in nothing but their underwear, staring up at him.

* * *

Anne was a 17-year-old girl when I first met her in 1967 in Whitchurch Hospital soon after I started to work there. She had been admitted from the casualty department of the CRI, out of hours, after an overdose of medication. I was 'on call' that evening, so it fell to me to assess her briefly and admit her to whichever ward was 'on take' that week. She was not under the consultant I was working for, so I thought no more of it at the time, nor expected to see her again – but Anne had other ideas about that and apparently picked me to be her psychiatrist in a unique connection!

Since we were a smallish group of trainee psychiatrists we often chatted about such cases, and I learnt from my colleague that Anne had settled in well, recovered fairly quickly and was discharged back into the community. This had been something of a pattern, not a particularly unusual one either. The overdoses, repeated at irregular intervals, were not necessarily regarded as serious. They were more 'cries for help' from a very young woman who had grown up almost entirely through the 'in care' system and was just out of a children's home, knowing she would have to move on into adult life, whether ready for it or not. All the social care ceased after a child left school – and in those days there was no planned after-support.

Believe me, it is never right to ignore or belittle such attempts. They are an indication that something is very wrong for that person. Surely even a 'cry for help' always needs to be heard by someone?

From then on Anne always asked for me, refusing to talk to anybody else, on the occasions, several months apart, when she turned up as a referral from the local casualty department. A mixed blessing as I wasn't always on call, but I always came anyway. I lived in the grounds and I had a soft spot for her from the first, which only increased as I learnt her history. So many of the people we saw, of any age, had been through terrible childhood experiences and not surprisingly were often unable to cope with the anxiety, depression and relationship problems caused by abuse in their early years. Abuse often taking place in the state Children's Homes of those times, including religious foundations, and under the noses of social workers.

Anne's life had been as bad as it gets but what I found different was her determination to bounce back. I began to see a pattern. Each time she came in, after a short time in the ward – which must have seemed like 'home' to an institutionalised child – she would go out and find some sort of job and a place to live. She would then keep herself going until the next disaster. Even though she had in a sense 'chosen' me, at first she had no internal mechanism whereby she could ask for help verbally, but fairly soon I was able to help her at least cut out the overdoses and accept outpatient appointments, phasing out the overdose routine, though it remained a risk for a long time. Even then, her ability to take initiatives, such as getting a job and finding accommodation for herself, was impressive, as it is often missing in 'cared for' children.

When I went to work in the academic unit, I made sure she was admitted under the professor for longer periods so that I could work with her intensively. I can say that I made most of my early mistakes in long-term psychotherapy with Anne! I certainly learnt a great deal and Anne herself became gradually able to take over her own life, so that later on, after I moved into child psychiatry in another county, I was able to befriend her at a personal level, no longer as a patient, with the knowledge and agreement of her GP.

Whenever we talked about her story, even years later, she always started by coming back to that one defining moment when she was nine years old and was rescued. Somehow, that memory, plus her repeating it over and over to me, became to her like a spell or mantra that kept her going.

"This big trapdoor at the top opened, and light poured in," she would say. The words varied slightly, but the facts were always the same. "This old man was staring down at us. His face all wrinkled up. He was crying!" Indeed, it was – quite literally – the moment that a light came into her life and she was lifted up, out of a prison of despair and into warmth, light and hope. She had been placed into care at an early age. Her memories of her childhood were blurred and mostly unhappy – children's homes, random staff and peer group cruelties, and always abuse in its many forms. She had a brief relief of foster care, along with a younger girl, Susan. This rapidly turned to horror as those foster parents became abusive and repeatedly flitted across county borders to stay out of the reach of nosy social workers for several years.

This moment she remembered so vividly she thinks that she was nine years old and, as happened daily, she and the younger girl were shut in the cellar of the house while Mr and Mrs Spencer went out to work. They would be there for hours, in dim light, wearing only their underwear so as not to 'spoil' their clothes, frozen in every sense. This was more frightening even than the beatings and sexual abuse she got from Mr Spencer.

She recalls that on that momentous day they were quickly taken out and looked after by concerned policewomen and other adults, warmed, fed and protected – it felt safe. The two girls were removed from the Spencer's care immediately, of course, and she doesn't know what happened to them. She had to face them in court and in her memory, she doesn't think they were sent to prison. Which, if true, is perhaps the most shocking thing of all. However, she never saw them again, nor the other foster child. She had one very good foster mother for two years, proper school attendance and was partially able to heal, on the surface at least, in spite of the random children's homes and other accommodation until she turned 16, when she was on her own. So that is her early story. At 16 she learnt about her mother, who was Welsh, and an older sister, but sadly just too late to see her mother who had died shortly before. In fact, she met her relatives for the first time at the funeral.

So, what happened next? I remember that a little later we met again. She thought she had found love, but eventually found herself deserted. So she asked me to be with her when her time came. By then she was doing well, thank goodness, living in a care home for expectant mothers. I was duly summoned to the hospital one early morning for the excitement of seeing the birth of a boy – to welcome lovely Rhys, a year younger than my own son, Rupert. It was such an honour to be his godmother as well.

The years moved on. Anne had two more boys and did whatever work she could, but her health could never quite recover from the deprivations and abuses of her childhood and – not surprisingly – things were at times extremely difficult for all the family. As a mother, however, she has certainly brought up three delightful boys and been a loving grandmother to their children.

Anne had spent some Christmas Days with my family earlier on, having no-one to go to. Just like my mother before me, I had a habit of inviting all sorts of people to join us occasionally for Sunday lunch, and always for Christmas Day – junior colleagues from abroad and on their own, single friends with no nearby family, a few of my ex-patients similarly placed. And just as my father had, my dear husband Ken accepted it and even brought a few to my attention. The growing Rahman boys were a great addition to these occasional Christmas and Sunday lunches. And they still remember and we talk fondly about these times. Indeed, Gareth even devised and performed a wonderful rap on it with his steel band! I think it relevant here to mention something about the richness of this family's genetic heritage – so typical of a seaport town like Cardiff and well accepted here. Anne's mother was Welsh and her father, who was not in her life, was from Bangladesh. The boys' father is from the Caribbean.

So, what happened to them all? How about a discreet peep, which is with their agreement?

- Rhys, my first godson, was very good at sport at school and had hopes of a professional career. A bad injury to his knee in his teens spoiled that hope and also his hope of becoming a fireman. In spite of these disappointments, he has a successful life, running his own taxi, and with a delightful wife, children, and now even a grandchild. I loved the jerk chicken post-Christmas lunch they made for me last year!

- Austen served his country in the armed forces and fought in Serbia. He became an excellent mechanic. Sadly, since I first wrote about him, things changed for the worse and with a tragic outcome. He died in 2021.

- Gareth developed musically from an early age. He even founded his own steel band, then studied music in Cardiff's College of Music and Drama, gaining a First-Class Honours Degree. He married a beautiful young woman from South Korea and the two of them went to join her family out there. They ended up working for seven years teaching, before coming back to Wales to live and work here, with a little boy of their own.

I couldn't be more proud of all of them, and of my friend, their mother (and grandmother) Anne Rahman.

46

FOR GWENT:
CHILD PSYCHIATRY, 1972 – 2005

WHATEVER ITS FLAWS as an institution, my time in Whitchurch Hospital was a good place to learn what should be done – and even more importantly not done – in mental health care. I joined the academic unit on Ward E1 and moved with it, as a lecturer in the School of Medicine, when the new ward on A4 was opened at the University Hospital of Wales. By this time, around 1972, my marriage to Roger had ended and I was working with Professor Ken Rawnsley, with whom I later had my two wonderful children. When our son Rupert was born in 1973, it became apparent that there was no way I could continue working for Ken in the academic department and would have to find another job.

I thought a lot about my mother's experiences as a psychoanalyst. My mother and I had not talked much about her work, something I greatly regretted as she had lived through interesting times and even worked for a while at the Maudsley Hospital in the late 1930s before WW2. From what I remembered, I felt that she had mixed her insights with a good deal of common sense and full medical knowledge as a doctor, unusual for those early times. Back then, the rift valley between the various (quarrelling) schools of psychoanalysis and the NHS 'working' psychiatrists was often impassable. Being under-confident, my mother never rated her eclectic, sensible approach as highly as she should have, being disowned by both sides.

To a minor extent, this happened to me too. Looking back to my time as a junior psychiatrist, before I met Ken, I realise that I should have been treated as something of a catch at work; bright, very interested in the specialty, caring of patients and extremely hardworking. Mind you, the standards overall were not high, but I know from Ken – though from nobody else – that I shone like a star. I don't remember any effort to keep me in the specialty and although sexism was far less obvious than in general medicine and surgery, I suspect it played a part. I never felt like a star!

Looking back, I also realise that it would have been difficult for me to give up work altogether, even though I always felt bad about leaving my children's care to others. I was still, of course, very sensitive about the loss of my firstborn. Going back to work and psychiatric training after his loss had not only filled a void but restored and healed me. I did not dare trust myself to look after him without being a smotheringly anxious mother. Thanks to a knowledgeable contact, I found a carer I could trust in Pam, later known as 'Mummy Pam', and I could relax at work in the day, then come back to collect Rupert after work.

Ken was – as he always proved to be – wonderfully supportive of whatever I wanted. "Why don't you go and see Andy Wills?" he suggested.

Andy was the Consultant in child and family psychiatry in Gwent, and Ken and he had been involved in some NHS problems a few years earlier. They thought highly of each other and I found that Andy and I got on famously. He enthusiastically wangled some funding to take me on as a Clinical Assistant for two days a week. I later also got two sessions as a Consultant child psychiatrist at the education department in Cardiff, working at the North Road Clinic and then one day a fortnight as a consultant to social services at Ty Mawr, a 'Special School for delinquents' near Abergavenny. Later on, I added another fortnightly day with a charity school for children with cerebral palsy, then known as the Spastics Society.

I was therefore regarded and paid as an 'expert' in child mental health in some of my posts, but really I knew little and had to hit the ground running. So in my time with Andy I was getting a speedy and marvellously useful apprenticeship type of training, although it was in a post in which I was not meant to have either training or expertise! Such were the oddities of the system in those days.

Andy Wills had been a GP in the Aberfan area during the terrible tragedy there and had changed to train in psychiatry afterwards, partly as a result of seeing the effects of the long-term trauma. I watched him work with the new and ragged team of nurses, occupational therapists, social workers, psychologists and others in trying to set up a completely new inpatient service for children and adolescents in the grounds of St Cadoc's Psychiatric Hospital in Caerleon. He had a facility for younger children in an old house called Pollards Well with a brand-new build, Ty Bryn, as a residential unit for the older age group, both with several full-time teachers as well as nursing and other staff.

This necessitated a huge cultural change of outlook for the adult services in St Cadocs, in which we were mostly lucky to have good support from our psychiatric colleagues, as well as some very enlightened nursing and management staff. But this was all against the huge inertia of the institutional attitudes of the majority at that time – often a nightmare to deal with.

In my sessions with Andy Wills, as his assistant, I was drinking in his tales of children and families he had worked with. I knew I was getting first-class training and a far more compassionate look at the world than even I had felt up till now. He involved me in building up the new adolescent unit from 1974. I was to stick with Caerleon, with short gaps after Amanda's birth and for my first year of retirement, for the next 30 years.

Two little anecdotes about Andy can best describe his approach. Very early on, just as we were developing the inpatient service, the agitated and upset staff told him that a boy who had run away from our unit had been picked up by the police and just returned to us. It was – I regret to say – then and for many years after, common for such children to be punished severely, and physically beaten if in social care. Andy sat back and drew on his pipe. "Has he had any breakfast?" he said. The nurse sputtered a negative. "Well, when you've fed him, perhaps you, Dr Kapp, would have a word with him and see what the problem is?" he said.

He knew he could rely on me to take a kindly approach and the nurses soon learnt. Those who didn't like it were gradually weeded out until we had a really good service. But I too needed lessons. Another early case was a young girl he had visited at her home. She had shut herself in the bathroom and wouldn't speak to him. I thought I was doing well when I persisted in visiting for three weeks running, sitting on the floor in the corridor and talking gently to the locked door before telling Andy Wills, my boss, that I was not getting anywhere.

He made no comment other than to tell me to leave it with him. Some months later I found that he had patiently gone back every week until eventually she had opened the door and listened to him, but with her hair down over her face, never saying a word. It took many more weeks before she – literally – began to show her face, to reply to him and then start attending our unit daily. She made a very good recovery.

"I gave up much too soon, didn't I?" I said, very chastened. He sucked on his pipe for a moment. "Maybe," was all he said, eyes twinkling. You never forget a lesson so slowly and kindly given.

Oh, how I envied that pipe smoking as a ploy! He was noted for quietly drawing at it in ward meetings, buying time, then coming out with something so deep and with such a kind understanding of the problems of troubled teenagers that his leadership was unquestionable.

Of course, I read the textbooks and followed the child psychiatry research in the journals. Most of all though, I learnt from each family who came into my orbit. My rather hit-and-miss collection of posts provided a very good range in practice.

The clinic in North Road, though paid for by the education department, was very traditional. Each of the three teams had a medically trained doctor/psychiatrist, a social worker and a psychologist. We would usually see two or three children in each session, with an hour each and some time for discussion; usually the social worker would see the parents while I did a play session with the child. The clinics were bright, spacious and very well equipped with toys, particularly sand and water. I learnt how to play and observe, something I missed when working in small NHS hospital clinics with no toys.

In Pollards Well, the children's unit in Caerleon, the nurses and occupational therapists did most of the hands-on playing, but at least I had the basis for discussing what they did and helping to train some of them. I cannot overestimate the amount you can learn from taking the most disturbed teenagers in your county into a psychiatric unit and running a full-time psychiatric residential and day service for them for a few years. You learn amazingly ingenious methods of avoidance, delinquency, disruption and a whole new vocabulary from these youngsters. Things that your own average teenage children could only gasp at.

Never a dull moment, I assure you – and if I didn't quite love every minute of it, I cannot think of anything that would have given me more job satisfaction or been more rewarding and team-building for us all.

Also, the pleasure many, many years later when the local staff say to you "remember so-and-so? I ran into him/her the other day" – and you hear that the troubled teenager is now educated, married, working, successful, happy or – at the very least – alive and functioning. Or maybe a smart young man fills your car with petrol or a smiling woman serves you in a posh shop, or someone with a car full of kids pulls up at the lights and they say "remember me?"

47

TY BRYN & POLLARDS WELL

THESE TWO BUILDINGS were the headquarters for the child and adolescent service for Gwent. They were in the very attractive park-like grounds of St Cadoc's Hospital in Caerleon. They had started with Pollards Well, built many years before as a private residence for the superintendent of the hospital. As a children's unit it was large, comfortable and not intimidatingly institutional. It made a good place for younger children.

Ty Bryn for the adolescent patients, age 11 to 16, was a new build at the time I started working there. It was a large, one-storey prefabricated building, a very basic place, covering offices of all kinds: outpatient waiting area, clinical offices and rooms for the nursing staff, along with a number of bedrooms for adolescents, a teaching wing with three classrooms and all other facilities for the needs of outpatient and day-and-inpatient children for Gwent. There was another identical building opened at exactly the same time in Cardiff covering South Glamorgan, later known as the Harvey Jones Unit.

Maybe it would be interesting to give a little more detail about the sort of work our team did – or at least give an idea of some of the youngsters we saw and the routine work with children and especially adolescents that I was doing throughout those years. Of course, much of it was quite low key and repetitive – but the individuals are always wonderfully varied.

After diagnosis and discussion, the nursing and other therapists in the unit, including the teachers, occupational and physiotherapists, did most of the long painstaking work with the youngsters. There would be a medical meeting with some of the nursing staff every day, including of course the community nurses, and all of the staff met every Friday afternoon. The Consultants also did a lot of clinics in other hospitals and home visiting and I often worked with the parents and sometimes larger family groups in 'family therapy'. We also trained junior doctors, on rotation in psychiatry, through each sub-specialty and hosted medical students at times. I loved the teaching side.

Let's meet some of the youngsters. I have changed their names and protected them by removing any overly identifying features. Remember, this is from the 80s and 90s. These notes were from a list I found recently but made in the late 80s when I spent a lot of (usually extra) time visiting GPs and nurses in health centres, residential and day facilities for social services, and all schools, etc. to try and tell them what we were doing and the sort of cases we could help them with – and what we couldn't. Just as an example, we were not in any way funded to treat learning disabled children, who came under a completely different team. Sad and irrational as this policy was, it was imposed from above by the authorities who funded us. We could therefore not treat these children – because children of course they were – without seriously affecting the standard of care for our group. We nonetheless communicated a lot with our colleagues on this and other boundaries.

Louise is 15. Her teachers and parents are angry with her for 'daydreaming', but the Educational Psychologist is not convinced it is a problem of behaviour and wisely sends her to us for urgent assessment. On her way to see us she apparently walks off the pavement almost under a car, which doesn't seem to me like daydreaming. Not long into the session, I observe an 'absence' accompanied by a complex series of finger movements like rolling a cigarette. An urgent request for an electro-encephalogram confirms her temporal lobe epilepsy and she has joint treatment from myself and the neurologist, with continuing work by the Ed Psych in the school.

Gavin is only 5. He is referred by the Paediatrician. He lives with his mother on the Ringland Estate (notorious!). Mum has been depressed since he was born and her latest boyfriend in a long series is a drug dealer. Gavin is completely confused by the unpredictable adult behaviour. Sometimes he's up watching violent videos all night, sometimes he is screamed at and sent to bed straight after nursery school. The debate is should he be taken into care? (known to be disastrous); or left where he is? (also known to be disastrous). He is excitable, hyperactive and almost out of control. It proves impossible to get his mother to attend clinic regularly – but when all seems lost and the Social Worker puts him on the 'at risk' register, his mother sees sense and allows him to attend Pollards Well daily. She loses her antipathy – born of fear – and cooperates from then on with his and her own rehabilitation through long term counselling with our Nursing Staff, but it's a long hard road for all concerned.

George is 9. He starts making funny noises and is suspended from school for cheek. The Educational Psychologist is unhappy about this and refers him. We agree and he is seen as an outpatient. Tourette's is diagnosed (tics, vocalisations and disturbed behaviour). He is put on the appropriate medication by the Paediatrician, then seen as an outpatient with long-term counselling for the family.

Lynette is 12 and suffers from cystic fibrosis, from which an older sister has died. She is refusing all medical help and her parents are desperate. It takes a long time for a Nurse, visiting every few days, to gain her trust, but she eventually shares her despairing conviction that her case is hopeless. Working at first separately with the parents and then gradually together, the Nurse helps them all to share their grief and anger and cope better with her condition. She puts them in touch with charitable organisations that can help.

John is 10. He is an odd boy, pedantic and stilted in speech and the butt of teasing in school, which results in violent attacks on other children. He is a loner and the headteacher fears he will not manage the transition to secondary school. Aspergers Syndrome (now

187

ASD) is diagnosed formally and a period of day treatment in Pollards Well reduces his anxiety and gives him time to learn limited but helpful social skills. An interagency conference decides on his next school placement well in advance and with a gradual introduction to sympathetic staff there. He returns to Pollards Well, our children's unit, daily for part of the school holidays for a couple of years to follow an individually designed scheme for learning social skills. He grows up as a delightful if still slightly eccentric young man, with a dry sense of humour and a very caring nature, looking out always to help others – even if he makes occasional mistakes in how best to do so.

Jane is 12 and out of the blue, it seems to the family, starts to have violent tantrums and extreme antagonistic behaviour (that's professional-speak for kicking your psychiatrist on the shins!). It emerges that her mother has recently been diagnosed with a life-threatening endocrine disorder and not surprisingly Jane has developed an anxiety state, which she cannot otherwise express. All pressures are taken off for both mother and daughter. Home tuition is arranged and a long-term course of outpatient therapy focuses on general anxiety reduction. The relationship with her mother restores itself as a result (the psychiatrist's shins recover even quicker).

Gareth is 14. His mother died of breast cancer 18 months previously. He has become extremely verbally violent and taken up with a gang who are stealing and vandalising cars. It's a serious downward trajectory. The police refer him and he is seen on a regular basis for bereavement counselling and to support his father, who is also put in touch with CRUSE. The father tries to readjust his work hours to allow him more time with his son at the weekend, but he can't. However, he arranges for an old friend to give Gareth a nominal 'job' on Saturdays in his garage. The old codgers working there won't stand any nonsense but they look after the lad, who blossoms in this masculine, grown-up atmosphere. Sadly, health and safety rules mean this would probably be impossible to arrange now.

Julie is 15. She is referred by the GP for difficult behaviour at home. That proves to be the tip of the iceberg in a very disturbed, completely dysfunctional family, with all of the children showing problems. It emerges that she has been horrifically sexually abused by her mother's boyfriend. He is prosecuted, unsuccessfully, because of a legal twist. Julie's mother breaks up with him and does her best to hold this very fragile family together. Julie herself develops symptoms of obsessive-compulsive disorder and later becomes anorexic. A plan is made for the Child Psychiatrist, the Community Psychiatric Nurse and the Educational Psychologist to work together, giving support to Julie herself, her mother and other family members who are – not surprisingly – showing emotional and behavioural disorders. In practice, it proves extremely difficult to get all these agencies to work together, however much the individuals try to do so. We manage to get her through some years of anorexic disturbance, but the family fragment even more and we lose touch. It is ethically very difficult to find out how someone is doing long-term, because they may definitely NOT want someone inquiring about their mental health years later, revealing what may be a secret.

I would like to note here that young girls with anorexia nervosa were a large part of our work. It is a very serious illness with a frightening mortality rate unless recognised, taken seriously and treated with great care and understanding. It occurs increasingly in boys too. Our team in this was led by our long-term Senior Sister, Joy Jones, who worked for many years to understand and treat the condition, becoming a recognised authority on it and passing on her knowledge.

May I be indulged if I end here by putting in a poem that I wrote as a sort of tribute to all these girls, struggling with eating disorders, particularly those we could not save?

Epitaph for an anorexic girl

This girl never blossomed, never bore fruit.
Her life was broken by secret battles
In a war no-one ever declared.
She fought determinedly through fat and thin,
No-one gave her an alternative.
There is no ceasefire.
No armistice.
No medal
No honourable discharge
No peace in our time
For this bone-thin army of girls,
To which she never knew she was conscripted.
This girl thought that she alone had heard
The call-up trumpet thrilling in her gut.
She wore the pared-down uniform with pride.
When at the end she found herself alone
In a muddy foxhole
In no-man's land
Blindfolded
Deafened
And gagged,
She fired randomly at friend and foe,
And rescue came too late.

Elinor Kapp, written 1999

Portraits of Eleanor Kapp

193

195

Family Photos

Elinor with baby Andrew on the beach in Sussex, 1965

My children, Amanda and Rupert

Elinor 1966, Andrew's birth in hospital

School photo of my son, Rupert

*My grandparents, Gordon and Ellen Wilkins,
with my mother's sisters, Joyce and Phyllis Wilkins*

*Ken Rawnsley, my second husband,
father of Rupert and Amanda*

My daughter, Amanda Foster [nee Rawnsley], in the snow with her husband, Jon Foster, and sons Freddy and Frankie

My father, Reginald Otto Kapp

My mother, Dorothy Wilkins, as a child

My Mother, Dorothy Wilkins,
graduating as a doctor in the 1920's

Elinor, one of a group dancing before the President of Austria,
at the opening of a ball in the Musikverein, Vienna, 1961

Elinor as a schoolgirl

My daughter, Amanda, with her great aunt Joyce Wilkins,
my mother's younger sister

Elinor with Aunty Mary Mildmay and her companion,
Auntie Doria, at the coming-of-age ball
for John Kapp, brother, 1957

Joyce Wilkins, Elinor's much-loved Aunt,
younger sister to Dorothy Wilkins

KENNETH RAWNSLEY C.B.
21.9.1926 — 1.4.1992

. . . Not fare well

Kenneth Rawnsley

Reggie [Reginald] Kapp, my father
on RHS Queen Elizabeth

48

A STORYTELLING APPROACH

I HAVE TRIED to tell some of the more upbeat stories, and indeed I know for certain that our service had many positive results. But I would not be honest if I didn't tell how often we despaired at the way it was impossible to get the recognition, funding and cooperation from above that we so desperately needed. It was always a dilemma whether to start, knowing you might do more harm than good if treatment was stopped abruptly and inexplicably for the child. It didn't even help if you went to all the case conferences and had a good relationship with the Social Worker – some of whom were excellent.

I have been at case conferences where we would solemnly work out a care plan, covering all eventualities and specifying the long-term treatment we were undertaking – only to find a couple of weeks later that the higher echelons of the Social Services Department had totally ignored it and sent the child somewhere faraway, impervious to my ranting and raving on the phone or even more measured letters of complaint.

I cannot get this across better than by this true story from my early days in child psychiatry – but these things never truly changed through all the years. A boy in care, let's call him Wayne, came several times to explore his aggressive behaviour. We worked well together, he was bright, and although inarticulate he showed by sand and water play what he had suffered and what he needed. His behaviour improved dramatically, but we still had far to go. I gathered things were also improving in the care home.

On what became his last attendance – though of course I did not know or intend that it would be – he cleared a great valley in the sand tray and put himself as a small toy animal in the centre. He surrounded this with larger animals, all looking over the rim from a distance: lions, tigers, cows, giraffes. He told me that these were his social workers and carers.

I asked if I was there. He shook his head and after a moment's thought, he added a small, frail-looking model gazelle on the slope, between him and the pack of animals. Sadly, his estimate of his situation and my inability to help him was confirmed. He was moved 'out of county' without explanation before his next appointment and I couldn't find out anything more about his fate!

This use of objects such as toys and a sand/water area was a luxury I didn't have in most clinics. So, I learnt to compromise by encouraging my own and the child's imaginations with storytelling. Although I regard my work with children as a branch of medicine, based as far as possible on medical principles and ethics, the actual practice, particularly with children and families can be very different. I learnt as much from good practices by teaching staff as by research and textbooks. So my 'taking a history' often involved getting children at any age to tell me a story – definitely that way round, not me telling them. Even very young children could be nudged into this and it opened up a dialogue telling me much of what I needed to know in order to help them.

As a broad generalisation, younger children would talk readily in fairy tale metaphors – stories which I have always adored and within much ancient wisdom is stored. Older teenagers were more likely to talk of action films, horror stories and soaps.

In fact, in all those years I never found a child who didn't watch *Neighbours*, the Australian soap! As it happened, I liked that soap and followed it every day for years with my daughter Amanda, a nice bonding thing for us after work and school. I grew to admire the way it was done. I noticed that episodes didn't end on a cliff-hanger, leaving children anxious overnight. The storylines too held a basic decency, alarmingly missing from many soaps and in stark contrast to EastEnders, which I hardly ever watched and detested when I had to because of its cynical world view. There has never been any character in it who isn't greedy, vindictive and corrupt, except the occasional religious ones who are just silly.

Neighbours was actually very much more subtle and indeed did well for one young teenager. He sat down in the chair in my clinic and opened with "can you hypnotise me so I can go out again and play cricket?" I enquired about this – very unusual – opening request. Apparently, a storyline in *Neighbours* that week, which I had missed, was about a boy who couldn't leave the house and so couldn't play cricket, but 'the doc' hypnotised him and he could go out and play again. The youngster revealed that he was housebound with classical features of a phobia. Me being therefore cast as 'the doc', I gravely suggested that hypnosis could be very helpful in these instances but we would need to talk to his father about this. Also, I said that though I was sure that I would be able to help with his fear of going out, I couldn't be certain that it would help him play cricket! His father was brought in, I discussed with them my practice in hypnotherapy, he gave consent and they returned weekly for a couple of months of tuition in hypnosis very successfully. In fact, he did take up cricket again!

I should say here that my practice with hypnotherapy was quite extensive but was always 'auto-hypnosis', in other words, teaching the recipients to put themselves into a light trance state and emphasising that they would not be under the power of myself or anyone else. Reputable practitioners will all tell you that all of us are regularly going into light trance states of our own accord – such as when concentrating on a book or the tv – so it is harnessing a useful normal characteristic, not trying to replicate a showman's dramas.

I learnt it first for my own benefit in childbirth, with good effect, and still use it almost daily for pain relief and relaxation, like mindfulness. In fact, a colleague with an interest in hypnosis taught me in the easiest possible way – by putting me in a trance state.

Later on, he taught me how to do it to myself, with obvious advantages. He then told me that I would be able to follow it up by helping others in the same way and I therefore found it came very readily. Hypnosis has been shown not only to facilitate pain relief in labour but to shorten the first stage and other benefits. It certainly helped me and I think the advantages of it in medicine should make it far more widely used. But it must be used very ethically and is far away from the 'magical tricks' attitude to it as a nightclub or theatrical presentation.

Anyone is welcome to ask me more about it. I always, of course, got parental permission for youngsters. It had quite dramatic effects with asthma sufferers, reducing hospital visits, even their steroid drug usage and improving school attendance. The paediatricians and I wanted to explore it further with controlled trials, but we never managed to make the time.

It will be evident that working with disturbed families, and the children and adolescents, is not always like a well-ordered hospital ward – nor should it be. Though I suppose the more lurid hospital soaps (not naming any) come near it! I would often have to visit a home that was really difficult to sit in for mess, hoarding, dog poo or other signs of disturbance. I only remember one in all that time where I literally could not bring myself to accept the usual cup of tea – I think better not to describe it!

After those early weeks, I got quite used to chatting to reluctant children in all sorts of places, tolerating interruptions and acting-out behaviour. Though one did tax me considerably – being called out in the early hours to drive from Cardiff to the unit, where an angry teenager had managed somehow to evade all the protective devices and climb onto the roof of Pollards Well. I'm not sure if it was me and the night nurses who talked him down, really. I think he just got bored and hungry. But it was long enough for all the potential lurid newspaper headlines to invade my head.

Only slightly less dramatic was the lad from a farming family who came to every outpatient session carrying a strong rope with a business-like noose on one end, refusing to discuss the obvious symbolism, though I wasn't sure if it was meant for him, me or someone else. He was a nervous, polite and very likeable youngster. It would be possible to dismiss such an obvious sign of his depression as histrionic, but unfortunately young people can miscalculate, as well as the doctor doing so. I never dismiss anything outright. The first time he came like this, I rang the GP afterwards to discuss it. This was a country practice in Gwent where the doctors are used to dealing with anything thrown at them. "Not to worry," he said, unfazed, "I've known him and his family for years. I'll keep an eye on him."

I think that if it had been a town case, it would have been much harder to deal with calmly like that. The lad did very well, longterm.

Going out at night was quite rare, though towards the end of my working life I had a call from a GP who had himself been phoned from the Brecon Beacons by a foster mother known to our service. I agreed to deal with it and drove straight up there, sometime after 11pm. It was summer and an eerie moonlit night. I was looking for a girl of colour, 16 years old and pregnant, who had only just been taken into care and had run away from her new home on the edge of the Beacons. She was being closely followed by the foster mother who luckily had her mobile phone with her and talked me in. This lady hopped into the car with me, explaining she had only received this new girl a few days previously from a terrible abusive situation and hadn't had time to build up trust.

We followed the girl, driving very slowly, through the countryside, giving her plenty of space for quite a while. Eventually she decided enough was enough and got into the car too, shivering and crying. She was hugged and comforted by the excellent foster mother whose response was clearly totally unexpected by this much-abused child. We all returned to the house for a cup of tea and I dozed until all was settled again. I visited a few days running, then handed over to a nursing team member and I don't remember learning the outcome.

So, I am telling stories, carefully anonymised for anyone who is interested. But let's not forget that we are all making up stories all the time – for what else is the narrative of our lives that we hold within ourselves and share at times with others?

I remember the very first, very early 'case' in which I consciously used this story-making approach. Jamie, a little 8-year-old boy, came in with a phobia of water. Washing him was a nightmare, rain panicked him and he obsessively followed the weather forecast, refusing to go to school if it might rain.

Asked about stories, he told me a scary one from the telly. It led fairly easily, however, to some nice things about water: his favourite drinks, cooling down on a hot day. I then facilitated a jointly imagined made-up tale of two boys who wanted to be friends, but lived on opposite sides of a river – he came up with several ingenious and fantasy ways they might meet without getting wet, ranging from flying on a bird to building a boat.

He enjoyed this and we followed a similar pattern in subsequent visits. He did extremely well, essentially devising his own 'treatment' by making up heroic stories in which he was clearly the protagonist. An early one was about a boy risking his own life rescuing a cat from a pond. In his last session, with his life returned to normal, was his story of a pair of big welly boots who learnt the fun of stamping in squishy muddy pools and took their owner into every puddle in the park. He enjoyed the power in this invention of his, and you can imagine the fun I had acting out the delight of the welly boots in my retelling back to him of his story!

I developed this approach in many cases. The important features were that the child did most of the invention, though often needing help and encouragement and we always had a little ritual at the last bit of the session in which I would say "that's a wonderful story you've made. Would you let me tell it back to you?" They always said yes and I would then tell them their own story in my best dramatic mode. I learned storytelling essentially from doing this!

Of course, my job overall, especially with the adults, involved a certain amount of sifting 'truth' from 'embellishment' and 'downright lies', and I could bore anyone for hours in discussing that, but it's not a major interest. One question I'm quite often asked is "but how do you know your patients are telling the truth?" Almost as if they expect the mentally ill to be automatic liars! My answer is, "the same way you or anyone else does." Apart from a rare subset of patients (often known as Munchausen Syndrome, better as 'Factitious Disorder') where this is the defining feature, it is very important to take – certainly initially – a warm accepting line to what the patient tells you, to allow people to talk freely. Forensic psychiatrists, dealing with potential criminals, obviously have to take a different line; they too want to encourage openness, but within an honest statement as to why they are there.

In addition, it is a well-recognised path in cognitive therapy to encourage people to 'rewrite' their inner story, the inner dialogue they have with themselves. For example, many of us have nagging inner voices, often from adult unkindness long ago, which say things like: '…you're fat, you're ugly, you're stupid, you'll never amount to anything.' These may be replaceable with positives: '…you're beautiful, you're kind, you're clever, you'll go far.'

Christine's Story

Let's give one of my lovely teenage patients her own words. She was a long-term patient, both as an outpatient – I visited her at home for a while – then she attended our Day Unit on and off for several years. My connection with her and the family was close, terminated only by my retirement.

Some of this was literally a present to me on my last day. I asked if she would allow me to tell her story and show it to other people. "Yes, but I don't think boys would like it," she said. I think anyone would like it! (I have of course changed all names). In this, she showed how she understood the purpose of the stories and other sessions. Christine needed extensive psychotherapy and social care, CBT and autohypnosis treatment for a clothing phobia, other phobic symptoms and behavioural problems over a long period.

The story she told for me is about a little girl called Alice, with blue eyes and blonde hair (Christine is a brown-eyed brunette). Alice wears dresses all the time, white with flowers on, and frilly short sleeves. "Alice is my second name," says Christine. She dictated parts to me very carefully; at other times she told me fast and at length and I've had to summarise it.

She starts slowly: "She went to the beach, and when she was digging she found a box. It was all rainbow colours, with flowers on it – wild flowers and roses and daffodils. Inside was a big huge rose that played music and sparkled… it was soft, slow music like opera."

She tells me that if Alice is naughty, the petals fall off, day by day, and the music stops. "She starts to be good because she knows the rose is special to her. She keeps it a secret no-one else knows about. She is good and she feels better."

When I retired, in 1997, Christine wrote this further little story herself, with another name, and included it in a farewell card (spelling and punctuation as in original):

"Once upon a time there was a little girl called April and she had big very big problems. She had so many problems you couldn't say them all. Her mum was very ill because of all the problems her daughter had until one day she met a lady called Dr. Kapp and she said she will help April get through these problems she had and by and by April was getting better and every day Dr. Kapp came to see April, April seemed to be getting better two weeks later Dr. Kapp saw that April's problems were gone away so Dr. Kapp didn't need to come anymore, three weeks later on Dr. Kapp had to retire so everyone done something nice for her retirement and it was the happiest day of her life. The End."

More casework

I should warn readers that it is possible that the topic covered here of abuse of children may be too distressing for some – and you are welcome to skip it, though I promise that I give no distressing details. It was a very large part of my work.

Hush, don't speak, don't tell, don't cry

When I was offered a post as a consultant alongside Dr Andy Wills and Dr Mike Morgan, my mentors, I became almost by default a specialist in child sexual abuse. Earlier in my career, we saw occasional cases in adult services, but later it became obvious that it was a far more common crime and often more horrible than had been realised. The great majority of the children, including boys, almost always preferred to talk to a woman, certainly at first. Indeed, many adults came forward in the families with whom we were involved, with stories of abuse often going back generations.

All this was well known in the 70s, let alone the 80s, but it is quite disturbing how many people and whole institutions turned their backs on it. So I have to say a little about it, not least because out of all the fine colleagues outside our own NHS service that I was blessed with, the most helpful and understanding were the police – more specifically the CID.

I partly put this down to the Head of the CID in Gwent at that time. It may be relevant that he had started work as a nurse and then transferred to the police. He was also Deputy Chief Constable. We worked closely together for several years and ran joint multidisciplinary conferences for three years running, from 1989, using the police headquarters – thereby I suspect generating much more interest and attendance than in a medical setting. He too passed away many years ago, but I have always been glad that I reciprocated his many kindnesses to me by writing to him and his wife with a full tribute before he died.

The regular police also got to know me and over the years would sometimes ask me to see adult women victims, though I prefer the title 'survivor'. These I saw in my own time and often continued with therapy (unpaid) provided their GP agreed to it, so I was covered. The GPs never refused, my colleagues also knew about it and so, of course, did my wonderful husband Ken, so I always had someone with whom I could discuss any confidential details within the medical profession and accept advice.

In these memoirs I want to share not so much the horror as a couple of stories that have given me insight into the goodness in the heart of so many people, even survivors of abuse, because their lives have taught me, upheld me and given me insight into this goodness. However, the accounts of the abuse they suffered are far too distressing to recount. One learns ways of coping with those, as a therapist, so that the many, tragic, nightmare things others have suffered do not prevent you from helping them to process the trauma. Now that I am getting old and my mind is slipping a bit, these memories are not so safely buried and I also – for my own protection – do not wish to dwell on them except when it is necessary. How many victims never make it as far as therapy? We can only guess, but the number must be very high.

One such woman, nearly 30 years ago, was talked down from suicide off the Newport transporter bridge, late one evening. The sympathetic policewoman rang me as she couldn't think of anything else to do. I ended up seeing this lady every week, then fortnightly, on my way home from work for three memorable years, as she was petrified of hospitals and almost house-bound. I learned such an incredible amount from her and other survivors, though these are the ones, I must admit, that come back to haunt me on bad nights.

This lady had severe Dissociative Disorder (previously known as Multiple Personality) with depression, phobias, auditory hallucinations and anorexia – all as a result of child sexual abuse. In addition to the damage done by the original abuse, she fell into the hands of a religious sect who 'treated' her for demonic possession (non-existent in her case), making her symptoms all much worse. In spite of that, she retained a marvellous sense of humour and a caring love for others. She is one of the bravest and loveliest people I have known in all my life.

These special people have reappeared in my life after many years in between medical care and friendship. So, I'll tell you about another such friend, who also gave me an account of her life's experiences over many years of therapy – another such brave and lovely woman. She too has had to have enormous courage just to keep going and now shows a caring heart and a great sense of humour, although her story could have ended very differently. It is inspirational so I have written it for sharing, more like a story, with her permission and minor changes to reduce identifying features.

I was a stranger and you took me in

A little girl is walking down a railway track in a Welsh mining valley. She is trying to help her younger sister along too. She stumbles and one of her older brothers turns and takes her hand for a moment, helping both girls along. Her mother looks back and sighs, but speaks kindly,

"We must get to the other side of this valley before this shift at the mine ends. It's our only chance of escape!" gesturing a little wildly behind her.

The four children follow obediently, speeding up. Their world has come to an end. Two days previously the boys, only 14 and 16 years old respectively, had turned on their father and hit him repeatedly to stop him beating their mother, a regular pastime on his part which had gone on unchecked by anyone for many years. Astonished and outraged, he stormed off, threatening Armageddon on his return.

Throughout her young life, the young girl had learned to listen out for the nightly return of her father from the pub and in fear had needed to gauge the intensity of his outpouring of threats and intimidation before allowing herself, reluctantly, to sleep.

Two days previously after the boys' retaliation, the mother grabbed the two girls, aged 6 and 12, from their beds, got all four children to pack a few essentials and hastened them out of the house. She knew that this could only end in murder and, at last, necessity gave her the courage to leave.

At first, they had gone to a relative in the next village, who she hoped could offer shelter. Her aunt fed them and arranged a temporary sleeping arrangement for the night, but the next morning her husband insisted they be sent away.

Now, the frightened little family was truly running away. The mother, despairing and with nowhere else to go, simply took the road down the hill, turned left at the railway track and they trudged along it for several miles. The older girl, walking in a daze but still trying to comfort her crying little sister, hardly knew what she felt. The thought of freedom from the terrifying secret home life should have been good, but it was equally terrifying to be unwanted and afraid of being caught again, by a father whose abuses of her in particular did not stop with the beatings and rages administered to the rest of the family.

They came near the next small town, all very hungry. The poor mother, still in turmoil with no idea of where she could go, took them into the local shop to get them something to eat. By a strange million-to-one chance, she ran into a lady who she had worked with for a while many years previously, not even in that particular town. "Hello Mary," she said tentatively – not even sure she would be recognised. Mary smiled with pleasure,

"My goodness!" she said, "So these are your children? How lovely to see you. What are you doing here?"

It was no use to try to keep up any sort of a façade. Mary quickly learned of their situation and registered the despair in the eyes of her one-time friend.

"But of course," she said, "You must come home with me."

Mary took them to her little house, where she and her husband lived with their own young sons and daughter. The husband, sitting by a warm fire, smiled broadly and welcomed everybody. Jane, the 14-year-old daughter, two years older than the girl, smiled at her, even when told she would be sharing her bed with her that night.

Mary bustled around, making them welcome. She too smiled at the 12-year-old and gave her a hot milky drink, Ovaltine, unknown to her before. The girl never forgot that new sensation of tastiness and warmth – for her it was a completely new experience of care and shelter. Ever afterwards, that moment and the drink remained as the signal of salvation from terror, the start of a new life of peace and love, so freely offered by Mary and her family.

They stayed with the family for six months, until the council found them accommodation. Looking back, the girl remembers that she used to wet the bed, but Jane never complained. If there were any tensions in this suddenly doubled household, the girl does not remember them. There were many problems for the grown-ups, as the outraged abuser tried to recapture his prey. Later still, when the girl grew up, there were many problems too with the post-traumatic stress disorder induced by the abuse and yet the girl grew up into a conscientious adult, with love in her heart to offer to those in need.

In the time of their greatest need, they were kept safe by the wonderful generosity of an ordinary church-going Welsh family, who understood the bible text: "I was a stranger and you took me in." Indeed, they did – without question and all summed up in a cup of hot, milky nectar, aka Ovaltine.

49

CLOSE ENCOUNTERS OF THE
THIRD AGE KIND

I **HAVE ALWAYS ENJOYED** sci-fi and was hooked on Isaac Asimov many years ago. I also loved a much more recent visit to the Space Museum, near Leicester, where you can have your tea under the looming bulk of a Russian rocket and pretend you are a spacewalker in a special suit. So, of course, I loved the 1977 Spielberg film *Close Encounters of the Third Kind.*

I'm also a devotee of really awful puns – like the ones you get in crackers. When I got nearer retirement it was therefore probably inevitable that I would start writing and collecting up a series of little vignettes under the generic title of 'Close Encounters of the Third Age Kind' (ouch!) Here's the first one:

Close Encounters of the Bird Kind

A great many years ago I had a sort of holiday epiphany or revelation. It came at a time when I was working extremely hard as a child psychiatric consultant and clinical director at St Cadoc's Hospital in Gwent, where I stayed for nearly 30 years. The pressure sometimes made me feel like some kind of desperate mountaineer, toiling up slopes to ever-receding summits. Holidays were incredibly precious, a gap in the unrelenting responsibility of clinical work. I would see myself as reaching a chasm of tiredness and hoping I could survive the leap to the sunny uplands of a week's holiday in order to keep going.

Something had to change. In this case, me. One day, walking in the grounds of the hospital, hurrying from one rush to another, I heard the cry of a lone seagull. Tossed and rolled on the winds from the river, the young bird swooped and squawked piercingly above me. We seemed to be in a dance together, his black and white plumage flashing, my hands up-flung. I was entranced. A Close Encounter of the Bird Kind!

Suddenly I was carried back, re-experiencing a moment on a long-ago holiday in Devon with my late husband and young children. I seemed to be listening to gulls fighting, looking at the water under the pier, hearing it gurgle and splash, tasting the salty, fishy air. "Oh My!" I thought, "I'm on holiday!"

It was over in an instant, but my thoughts went on. Sometimes, when we are asked if we enjoyed our holiday after our return, we may well say it was wonderful and mean it. We've been free and relaxed and had fun. But during the actual time away, most of us don't really think of that. Only in the briefest of moments do we consciously have that joyful, ecstatic knowledge, "I'm on holiday!" What if such a feeling could be bottled and sold? Is that what we are trying to do when we bring back broken seashells and drying seaweed or hideous souvenirs from tourist destinations?

Why should I not experience that at any moment I choose? I answered my own question by trying it out. At any pause in my day, or the connecting times between tasks and places, I would say to myself, "I'm on holiday!"

It would now be recognised as a form of mindfulness, of living in the moment, but even though I had spent time in meditation and on retreats, I didn't quite see that this was what I was doing or that it was one way to get into relishing the 'now'. I can recommend it though. I went on doing it pretty well every day, till retirement made them all holidays. My longest 'holiday' was twenty minutes in a bluebell wood. My shortest, twenty seconds by the side of the road.

Mostly I used this new practice as I walked across the grounds of the hospital. Designed and planted up when the place was home to many staff and patients, it had the layout of more spacious, gracious days. Interesting shrubs, placed carefully to allow views on rounding corners. An avenue of lime trees that were once threatened by 'progress', that is to say, being chopped down. I and the other staff swore we would chain ourselves to them if necessary – that would have been an interesting 'holiday' – but of course in the Alice in Wonderland world of hospital management, nobody ever actually did anything, so the threat passed.

Sometimes, as I walked the long corridors, my eyes half-closed, I would create a more exotic holiday for myself, footsteps deadened as I passed ancient tombs or smiling statues, all of them gone, *pfff*, in a breath of air if I opened my eyes properly again. I could conjure up a six-foot-tall dog-companion, look down vistas of sparkling ice, or vortices of strange galaxies, for the time it took to get from ward to office.

Some holidays were just ordinary. The taste of hospital curry could easily transport me to the orient, chips to Yorkshire, and the lights of Caerleon on a winter evening become the Blackpool illuminations. One sunny day, after finishing my Pontypool clinic, I bought an ice cream at the corner shop and ate it by the side of the road. "I'm on holiday," I thought, as I stared over the valley. Then I went on and up to a house visit on the Varteg, as refreshed as if I had been away for a week.

My longest holiday? The twenty-minute one? It was a spring day and I had just finished visiting a school. I had thirty minutes before my next appointment in the hospital, a five-minute drive away. I had a million and one things I should have been doing, but a row of trees and bushes edging the road intrigued me. I parked and walked in for a few yards. Magic! It was a strip of bluebell wood in the middle of nowhere. When I say strip, I mean it too. The flowers were concentrated in a long narrow ribbon so that only a few steps forward revealed the parallel road at the far side. But if you stayed quite still in the middle, you could believe you were in a forest, miles from any town. I sat there, breathing in the scent, watching the earwigs and spiders, and studying the many shades of the bluebells with attention and love. After twenty minutes of deep peace, I was happy to return to the car and my work. That was a really good, long holiday.

The twenty-second one? I wanted to cross the road and there was a car coming. I noticed in myself the irritation of my inner demigod who believes the world should always stop and give way for me, and can't bear to wait for anything. Pulled up short by the pettiness of my impatience, I said aloud, "I'm on holiday!" Peace flooded through me. As I stood on the edge of the pavement waiting for the car to pass I smelled a wonderful scent of lilacs. There was a bush right over me, in bloom. Unbelievable that my self-important impatience could block a scent so strong, but it had. I breathed it in deeply and stepped across after the car had gone, filled with contentment and flower breath.

50

MORE CLOSE ENCOUNTERS
OF THE THIRD AGE KIND

N **OW I WOULD LIKE** to fast forward again and look at some of the things that happened when I retired – sort of – in 1997 at the age of 60. By that time, five years into widowhood after the death of my husband Ken, my son Rupert was away at university studying Electronic Engineering, and my daughter Amanda was about to fly the nest too to go to East Fifteen Drama School.

I had more free time now than I really wanted in a way, but had taken up embroidery to City & Guilds level and found my feet as an avid – if amateur – storyteller. I was collecting ideas and talking to groups about textiles and words (eventually resulting in two books) and was on the lookout for new adventures – very much as I suspect I was at the age of 11. Though possibly with a little more common sense. Or possibly not!

I would like to have written about the six visits I paid to Armenia at around this time, assisting the charity CAFOD to start a child psychiatric service out there. [This follows later in Section 66: MY LINK WITH ARMENIA.] In those years I also went six times to India with one of my most close and wonderful friends – better even than a sister – Dr Lata Mauthur, who took me to join her family in Jaipur on many occasions. I should also have written something much earlier on, about my time in the 1960s as head of a doctor's trade union – the JHDA (Junior Hospital Doctors Association).

Well, maybe I will get round to all that one day, but for the time being let's explore the little pieces I wrote about some things to do with this 'third age': the time of retirement, the time when I first retired, aged 60, in 1997 and my second retirement just five years ago. A year after the first time, in '98, I was asked to come back and 'fill in' as a locum in my old job in Caerleon. As it was difficult to fill child psychiatric posts at that time, I did two and a half days a week, being offered free board on the St Cadocs site and with no admin duties, just the clinical work with my previous lovely team of nurses and other staff.

It was wonderful – far less stressful – and it all actually stretched into several years in which I did such locum work in various parts of mid-Wales and Cheltenham, after they managed to fill the original post in Caerleon. I finally came off the medical register completely and finally in 2015, by which time I had been on it for 50 years. Complete retirement, and no more responsibility, felt a little strange – almost as if I had stumbled into old age by accident (don't laugh – just ask any others over the age of, say, 65!).

Close Encounters of the Referred Kind

A few years ago in 2015, in my late 70s, I was referred for a follow-up appointment a few weeks after a nasty bout of diverticulitis, which had put me on a hospital trolley for 48 hours. The slow-motion life to be observed, both within and outside of oneself, on a hospital trolley for 48 hours in the corridor of a major hospital, is practically a full-size novel in itself – but I'll spare you that! I did recover, after all, which at the end of the day – or days – is all that really matters.

As I went into the consulting room, a very pleasant man with white hair shook my hand vigorously and said, "Hello, Dr Kapp. Or rather, hello again, Dr Kapp!"

At my look of surprise, he smiled and told me he had been called out of retirement and asked to do some of the follow-up clinics, and that we had met, many years before, in the Welsh National School of Medicine.

I expressed my appreciation but admitted I could not remember him. I was searching in my mind for senior colleagues who might have been mentoring me when I worked there. He then told me that I had been his teacher in psychiatry when he was a final year medical student and I was a lecturer in the department where Ken Rawnsley was a professor.

I recovered my usual poise and sangfroid and responded appropriately, while inwardly weeping because I had just had to face the knowledge that I was now senior even to 'senior-senior' retired colleagues with white hair. Such an idea was completely impossible to my inward self, with my endless supply of youth and bright purple hair. Any contemporary will smile ruefully at this point.

I pulled myself together, acknowledged the 10-year gap with a smile and had a delightful conversation with him about those days. He did his stuff on my recent illness and pronounced me fit in a professional and reassuring way.

As I left he said, with a slight twinkle, "Did you marry the professor then?" knowing full well that I had. I laughed, and we reminisced about how my running off with my boss was one of the better and more juicy scandals of that era, and how I and Ken had been featured daringly in that year's scurrilous medical students' pantomime, with (pregnant) me acted by a very pretty girl with a balloon up her skirt. I always felt it to be a great compliment if the medical students send you up and I had enjoyed the experience and the teasing. A few months later, the young lady who took me off was doing her psychiatric training and was under my teaching in the department, so I was able to talk to her. I think she may have felt a bit embarrassed by it all, though I was still delighted and told her so. So I came home, and a little later that day was telling this story to my son, Rupert, when a saucer-eyed Alex – my grandson, who was listening as well – suddenly realised that the balloon, in fact, represented his dad. What goes around comes around and his grandmother Mimi's little stories go on to another generation.

So, another little reflection on this experience…
Another five years have passed since then, and Alex – that same grandson – has now gone off to Oxford to study medicine and become a doctor himself. He has a special interest in psychiatry, neurology and genetics, in which it is my belief we have the best hopes of future discoveries, but the whole great area of medicine will be his to explore over many years.

I am thrilled that he is following a tradition started by his great grandmother, my mother Dorothy. Don't get me wrong – all children are uniquely themselves and can move into areas of interest and talent completely different from those of their parents and earlier forbears. Indeed, that is a very good thing. It is also often, though, nice to see how an interest jumps a generation. I don't recall any particular way I may have influenced him, but of course, I valued and loved my work and I hope some of that rubbed off on him too. Alex never met my own mother, his great grandmother, of whose pioneering medical qualification I am also so proud. Nor, sadly, did he know his paternal grandfather, Professor Ken Rawnsley CBE, Head of Psychiatry in Cardiff for many years, who died before he was born.

I think that in this case, the genes have played their part. So many of my own forebears went into engineering or the medical profession, represented in many cousins: first, second and third. I am always happy that my son Rupert, Alex's father, went in for electronic sciences and runs his own business. Add to that the particular talents and skills of his beautiful wife, my daughter-in-law Erika, of music, teaching, writing and homemaking, and I think Alex will do well.

I really enjoyed writing up little incidents like these, and under this basic title over several years. It seems good to share them, hopefully without anyone trying to work out if I've got the arithmetic right about when each one came about.

These two, each in a different way, are about the distant memories of healing methods that stick with us even into old age, sometimes filling in for the rational thought which so often escapes us at an older age. Therefore – I hope – cheering my contemporaries up as well as myself and offering hope to the young too! Also – poem alert – YES! Another poem will follow…

A Close Encounter of the Concerned Kind

Some years ago now, just after Christmas, I had occasion to go to my GP surgery yet again. As I came out, round the corner, an elderly man was coming towards me. I noticed his skin was greyish; he looked really ill. He was walking very slowly, indeed he came to a full stop, panting.

I said in concern, "Are you alright?"

"No," he answered. "I've been in bed all over Christmas. I'm trying to get to the surgery."

He obviously felt a little embarrassed at having to stop still – a brief encounter gave a suitable excuse. So we paused together and I chatted a little to him, requiring only a nod and a few words from him.

He said, a tad bitterly, "And I was in bed for my birthday too."

I commiserated with him, "Such bad luck! May I be a bit cheeky and ask which birthday it was?"

"My 60th," he replied.

"Oh my, you're much younger than me, I'm 77!" I said.

"You don't look it," was his gallant reply, his pale lips smiling almost imperceptibly. We turned to continue our separate ways, very slowly, befitting the aged who know that any quick movement brings vertigo. I found myself saying, completely without knowing I was going to do so, "Can I give you a kiss?"

Surprised, but evidently not displeased, he turned fractionally towards me, offering his cheek, and I leant in and kissed it. At that, the colour mounted in his face, a mottled flush of healthy pink. He turned his head too and kissed me on the other cheek.

Then we resumed our slow walk in opposite directions and I called, "Thank you. Bye!"

"Bye," he responded, and his voice and his step were perceptibly a little stronger. I watched and was relieved to see that he was safely swallowed up by the surgery doors.

So, what was that about? Thinking about it afterwards, I believe my impulse was not just because of my – somewhat excessively – affectionate and disinhibited nature. Somewhere, way beneath conscious thought, must have been my knowledge that to make a fuss of helping him, or even worse, bringing a nurse out to him, would embarrass and distress him, making bad worse. An unthreatening kiss on the cheek from a woman, irrespective of age, would cause a little dose of testosterone, dopamine and adrenaline to circulate in any normal man this side of the grave. Not enough to cause heart problems, but enough to restore a measure of health. A tiny pick-me-up to bring him safe to harbour with a warm feeling in his heart, and in mine. It's not the answer to NHS cuts, but I'm going to look out for opportunities to bring a blush to any nice old man I happen to meet who might need it.

A Close Encounter of the Absurd Kind

The house alarm was strident and annoying. It accompanied me down the road, with all the usual negative vibes of Irritation At People With Out Of Control House Alarms. Before I could wallow too much though, I was addressed by my gentle friend from a few doors up, and realised that it was her house that was irritating the road and that she was in obvious distress. "Please help me!" she said. "I can't stop it. I came home and I can't remember the code."

She is a young woman who suffered brain damage in a tragic accident years ago, childlike and kind, easily made anxious. I went into the hall with her but could see no way of helping. An enquiry as to whether the code was written anywhere, or with anyone who might know it, met a negative shake of the head. She was near to tears.

I thought quickly. First principles. "Could we have a cup of tea?" I asked, very calmly. Well, a cup of tea is, actually, always my default mode, but in this case it was the first element in A Strategy – even A Cunning Plan. "Don't worry about the number," I continued. "We'll sort it in a minute."

I led her into talking about her day, the shopping she had been out for and now began to put away, as she was too upset to manage the kettle. I asked for a pencil and paper, my tones soothing and quiet, and we kept to neutral topics for a few minutes. Then, in the same tone, I said, "Now, think of a number. Quickly. Any old number!" She mumbled something I couldn't quite hear. "Write it down!" I said and she obediently wrote something.

I led her back to the hall. "Try it in the alarm." She did so, and the alarm relapsed into blessed silence. Of course, it was absolutely right that it worked. Anxiety had made her forget the number, relieve the anxiety, then request an instant, staccato response – and hey presto!

All good scientific principles, but there was no one more astonished than me when it was proved to work. We had a big hug, and I went home for that cup of tea. I didn't want to push my luck and start walking on water.

* * *

I would like to add a poem here, written about the same time. It shows how the sort of small encounters with which I hope that I have helped others have also helped me at times of stress and unhappiness, whatever the cause. In this case a kind of 'revelation' as to the real nature of the Market Garden, which I happened on by chance.

Market Garden

Dry tears of leaving rutted down my face.
I stopped my car, not knowing where I was,
by a farm shop, one sunshine, leaf-drop day.
Three tiny dogs barked, wagging their tails,
eyes bright with love. Then they lay down.
I was accepted, silent tears and all.
A boy, sorting shallots, smiled, ducked his head.
The farmer briskly left off digging veg,
to make a cup of tea in the empty caff.
I bought leeks fresh with earth, potatoes,
jams, jars and jellies, the boy's shallots,
all ridiculously cheap; he gave the tea for free!
Air moved, sun shone, dogs slept, I left.
I fried the shallots, watching Coronation Street,
And ate the potatoes mashed, with milk and salt.
Their other name is 'Apples of the earth,'
And I recalled the triple-headed dog who guarded them.
A woman, in another Garden, scrumped one once,
but mine were fairly bought, and paid in tears
dropped from the heart, and copper cash –
although it was ridiculously cheap.
Earth apples bought by tears, or gold, or blood,
become the Golden Apples of the Sun.
I never tasted food so good before.
That Garden where I stopped – I know its name.
I know the Gardener who walked with me.
And the tea was given free.

51

A SERIES OF LITTLE ENCOUNTERS
OF THE TYRED KIND

I **THINK I HAD A SERIES** of angelic encounters a short while ago, starting at a motorway service station. Which is, if you think about it, the sort of place where angels would consider it very important to hang around, in order to look after careless and unthinking people like me, who don't always remember to get their tyres checked regularly.

On this occasion I was driving up to Oxford to the funeral of an old friend, leaving plenty of time to stop at the service station, which I duly did. As I came out again, a pleasant man in overalls was leaning against a wall near my car, drinking a cup of coffee. "Better get your tyre checked when you have a chance," said the man, indicating that the front nearside tyre looked a little flatter than it should be. I thanked him, making a mental note that it would be a priority as soon as the funeral was over.

But you know how it is? The angel's timely reminder was lost in the flurry of the day and finding my way to the friend who was putting me up and all the little things that a hapless fool like myself allows to take priority. Angels should be different, shouldn't they? Massively golden and oversized, carrying placards saying "Elinor! It is a command from the Deity that you get your tyres checked." You wouldn't forget something like that, would you?

So, I did nothing until the next morning, when preparing to go, I suddenly noticed the car tyre again and remarked on it. My friend

236

said, "There's a garage at the roundabout on the way to Woodstock." That was a second angelic intervention.

I looked out for the garage. There was one, on the other side of the main road, but it only appeared to be selling cars. I went another couple of miles. No other garage. Uneasiness made me turn back.

I called in and found an office where a young man – angelic intervention number three – gave me a string of complicated directions. I knew I hadn't the least chance of remembering any of them after the first one, except maybe the last, because I have a complex memory problem due to my heart surgery. I remember he said "Turn right at the next roundabout..." and ended with "...at the garage with Ford above it, ask for Gordon."

I set off somewhat gloomily, turning right as directed, then simply putting my mind in neutral and driving at random, without remembering anything, but not hesitating through some more turns and roundabouts, until I came to a little industrial estate. There it was, a big notice saying 'Ford' on a building.

I went in and said, "I was told to ask for – Oh! – Gordon," as I saw the name badge of a kindly grey-haired man at the desk.

Gordon – angel four – told me that they would look at my car almost at once, made me a cup of coffee himself, and was as good as his word. He and the mechanic drove the car in and called me to see that two of the tyres were actually below legal limits of wear. He told me the cost, complete with work and VAT, and I remembered it as a little less than the last tyres I had to replace, so I accepted at once.

He was pleased and surprised, saying that a lot of people tried to haggle. I said, "Why would I do that? It's my life at stake here." The replacement of the two tyres and all the transactions were done in just over half an hour.

Alright – not everyone would know there had been angelic intervention, would they? I can hear them sniffing, "Nothing but a few people noticing things or just doing their jobs. No golden lights or trumpet calls there." But some of us know better when we've been visited, don't we? Yes – that's all it takes – ordinary strangers doing their jobs, but doing them properly and with a heart of kindness.

I also have a new mantra for any situation of tension or uncertainty. I close my eyes and think, "Ask for Gordon." There is, after all, always an angel waiting around for you to give him a personal call, and Gordon is as good a name for him as any.

* * *

I have in my storyteller's sack some lovely real-life, uplifting stories of goodness and love. Some were from people who were originally patients, but most are not. I write them all as if they are fiction and leave out any identifying features – except where the friend has given me specific permission to tell their story – but all are true as told to me by the original teller. Here is just one of them:

Entertaining Angels Unawares

A close friend, now retired, recently told me a very moving story from her younger days. So as to keep her anonymity, I will not include individual details of herself or her life. Suffice to say that she was about 20 years old in the early 1960s, an era when we kept our innocence a lot longer than more sophisticated later times.
She was doing an extremely hard vocational job and was given far too much responsibility. One time, when she had been left in charge for too long and was quite exhausted, she experienced what in retrospect seems likely to have been a minor breakdown.

Sleepless one night, with no one in whom she could confide, she took to her only means of escape, her Honda 200T motorbike. Its cheerful yellow colour matched her yellow jacket, but not her despairing mood as she drove off impulsively into a large wooded area near her rented accommodation. As she went further and deeper into a darkness that was both within and around her, her thoughts were that she would go as far as possible, then curl up, hidden away from the path, and wait, hoping to die of exposure as it was a very cold night.

As she went, however, she suddenly saw in the distance a single bright light. As if mesmerised she drove towards it, hoping, somehow, that it was itself a sign of hope after all, even a sign of angelic intervention. Then, as she got a little nearer, she realised that it was, in reality, simply a pub, open in the small hours – probably illegally – and buzzing with light and music.

She went nearer, her mind being changed at that moment from deepest despair to a longing for warmth, light, companionship, and to seek sanctuary. It turned out to be a large all-male group of bikers. Hell's Angels, in fact, all kitted out in full gear, very merry, half drunk and very loud – just the people we would all tell a young girl in these circumstances to avoid.

They greeted her and bought her beer, pasties to eat, and included her in the merrymaking. When they eventually were turned out and found she had nowhere to sleep, they put her back on her bike and, surrounding her like a guard of honour, roared off with her to the nearby village. One biker took her to a bed and breakfast house, waking – and paying – the rather cross landlady, then zoomed off again.

In the morning he returned, led her to join the group for breakfast, and then the whole gang, having elicited from her where she was living, surrounded her once more with their bikes and escorted her back to her own village, leaving her there. Finally, they drove away with merry toots and shouts of good wishes.

Not one single man had said an untoward word nor laid a finger on her. She felt safe and restored to a much happier state of mind.

So - when and where will you find angels? Yes, certainly the answer is: anytime, anywhere, and often in the most unexpected places. Even perhaps Hell's Angels, just to show that the universe likes a joke too.

52

A LOST ROSARY & TWO ANGELS

I MAY SEEM TO HAVE a particular interest in angels, though I hadn't realised until I started to include them in my memoirs that this was so. I do not set out to offend anyone, so if my take on them, and indeed on all matters religious, is seemingly lighthearted to the point of irreverence, please forgive me. My Christian faith, as I have said before, is very dear to me, but it doesn't exclude a reverence and even love for other religions where they are based on love and acceptance – and that includes the atheist and humanist philosophies too.

This first story is true and refers to a fairly short relationship that I had after many years of widowhood and that finished a good many years ago. It is nice to record also that I wrote this up as it happened and that the gentleman in question made contact again soon after, so we were able to part in a very much better way, as friends, with no bitterness or regrets on either side in the end. I have followed it here with a much more recent poem.

* * *

One sunny August evening, the man I had loved for two years said he didn't want to go out with me anymore. No quarrel, no explanation, no discussion. It hurts just as much whether you are young or old. I'll tell you something you wouldn't want to learn from personal experience: it hurts a lot more than open-heart surgery.

When I had gone to see him the previous evening I had impulsively put my heart rosary in my bag, a sort of good luck charm, I suppose. Now it was gone. I looked everywhere, possible and impossible, on that sunny morning. I was drowning in misery and somehow it all crystallised into one single determination. I must have a rosary. Where could I get one? The little shop run by Barry's sister closed years ago. Why on earth should I want a rosary anyway? I'm not a Roman Catholic, I just like saying the rosary from time to time and holding it between my palms. I do without one for years, then buy one, then give it away and get another…

After a long time of nail-biting and mounting tension, puzzling vainly where I could get a rosary today, NOW, instantly, if you very kindly please, God, I decided to try the Cathedral, got in my car and drove through town.

It was traditionally cool and quiet, even though there were a few visitors around. Sure enough, the shop had cheap rosaries in little boxes and I chose pearls because they look like tears. I also bought a holding cross, chunky, smooth olive wood. Holding both in my pockets I wandered through the aisles and monuments, not really thinking of anything. Then, at last, I found a side chapel. Perfect.

I hadn't been able to bear the claustrophobic feeling of crying at home, where you somehow know you are polluting your living space. At home too you are alone, cut off from humankind. The Lady chapel felt perfectly private and open to God, yet also open to everyone and part of the greater world. I knelt and for the first time in 24 hours of pain, I could cry and cry and cry undisturbed for as long as I needed.

The next day I went back in the early evening, thinking I could attend Evensong in a secret sort of way. I love my own chapel life, but we nonconformists can't keep our buildings open on weekdays, nor are we either anonymous or liturgical, something I craved at that moment.

I've always liked the way you can go into any chapel and find yourself greeted in a highly personal hand-pumping way and offered tea as if you were the most welcome relative ever. But in a different mood, I've also liked slipping into a quiet Anglican service where no one attacks you with bonhomie and cake. The other worshippers pretend discreetly that you don't exist until you introduce yourself, so you can slip into a back row with the mice.

My attendance at Evensong that day, the first time I had done so in the Cathedral, was amazing. I crept in through the little door in the great heavy portal. It seemed to symbolise all I felt about being a tiny human in a big frowning castle of tradition and protector of the patriarchy; I was a mouse among some very big cheeses indeed.

Oh dear! It became apparent that there were some tourists wandering around, but Evensong was to be done by a few gentlemen sitting in the choir stalls who looked ecclesiastical. I couldn't possibly join the high-ups in the choir stalls! It seemed that I would be all on my own in the body of the Cathedral.

I was, of course, rescued by an angel. In fact, by two angels. The first of them welcomed me, called me up to the choir stalls and seated me next to him in a stall called Sanctae Crucis. The other one found my place in the prayer book, told me it was 'spoken Evensong', and what to do about the responses, especially that tricky pause in the middle of each verse of the psalms.

They both smiled at me and engaged me in polite, non-invasive conversation on our walk back up the hill to the car park. Because I have incompetent aortic valves and breathlessness, these spry oldsters had to moderate their pace to my infirmities. The angels, of course, were cleverly disguised as two retired clerics, one Anglican, one Roman Catholic. It is amazing how much spiritual direction and solace can be obtained in a slow walk up a hill. I knew that if I turned my head I would see their wings, but I kept looking straight ahead because it would have been too much for me.

After such a good experience, I began to attend almost every evening for the next few weeks. If I couldn't make it there, I would go to the short morning mass at the Catholic church, five minutes' walk from my home and get a blessing.

It was there that I later experienced a great healing of my relationship with my long-dead mother, which is, as they say, another story for another time.

Oh! By the way, the rosary with the heart-shaped beads that I had lost turned up on my bedside table three days later, having presumably done its work of getting me to the Cathedral. Which is, of course, known as the 'Mother Church'. Thanks be to God, Our Dear Mum who art in Heaven.

*   *   *

Simplicity

When I came home and parked the car today
God said to me, "Please come for a walk,
down by the river. Come with Me!"
I thought – I want my tea, a little sleep,
a mindless program on the telly. But God was
teasing me, as if I was a child. He said,
"I want to show you something. What if I say,
pretty please with a cherry on?" So I went.
We walked through the park and to the river,
in the teatime, glowtime, of the autumn sun.
There I saw the white dancer, the Birch Tree,
leaning breathless towards her Linden lover.
His trunk was mossed with green. Sunshine,
reflected from her leaves, transmuted all
to peacock and to gold. The trefoil ivy twined
to join them in a heart-to-heart embrace.
They demonstrate the Alchemist's retort
'Green is for Go, the way is clear!'
Heaven shines before me by the water.

I longed to share it. When a man passed by, I said,
"Look, isn't the river pretty in the autumn sun!"
He answered in a foreign accent, quite confused,
then laughed and smiled and thanked me nicely.
The next man, wheeling his bike,
Was typically embarrassed, didn't say a thing,
but as he moved away he called back to me,
"I love coming out this time of year, seeing
the sun on the leaves!" and I called "Thanks!"
We are three points on the ivy leaf, linked by water,
drawn up from the river, through the roots.
I am a birch leaf, I am the moss, the bank, the sky.
I am the passing strangers, and they my lovers.
I am Heaven itself, and Heaven is me,
here by the water, by the river, in the gold.
Then God said, "You can go home now."
So I went home to have my tea.
I slept on the sofa, while God watched my dreams.
He held my hand and said, "Thank you, my Beloved."

53

STORIES ABOUT HEAVEN AND HELL

IT HAS PROBABLY become evident that I love stories about Heaven and Hell and both collect them, and create my own, sometimes from a fragment of folklore or a line in a newspaper, or a story from a friend. Here are two more of them.

Trouble in Heaven

Many years ago there was trouble in Heaven, see, and it was all on account of the Welshmen. In earlier times there were never that many Welshmen in Heaven. Most of the women got to Heaven, but very few of the men on account of all the fighting and drinking. That all changed with the Great Chapel Revivals. The men didn't necessarily stop the fighting and drinking on the side, you understand, but they all went to Chapel and sang so many hymns, so loudly and beautifully, that they got into Heaven in spite of their behaviour. In fact, some of them probably got there all the quicker because of the fighting and drinking.

St Peter was finding it very hard to cope and he took his complaint directly to God.

"I can't be doing with these Welshmen, I just can't be doing with them at all! They spend almost all the time arguing and fighting!" he says.

"They sing beautifully. I love listening to them singing about Me," says God.

"That's all very well and good," says St Peter, "but what about all those songs about little saucepans and much, much worse things? I just can't control them when they get going on a Saturday night!"

"How about the women?" says God.

"The women are fine," St Peter replies. "Sure, they gossip a bit and they argue about who knitted the best socks for St Michael, but they're no trouble at all."

"I can't send the men away," says God. "That Evan Roberts the Revivalist will complain about the trouble he had getting them here in the first place and he'll come and preach a sermon at me. Goes on for eternity he does, arguing about the Bible. I sometimes wonder who invented Bible Study - him or Me?"

So, St Peter goes back and puts up with it, but after a while he's back, complaining to God again. "It's still those Welshmen!" he says. "Now they're arguing points of theology about something called the offside rule! I'm a simple fisherman from Galilee. How can I be expected to decide over it? It's doing my head in!"

"Don't worry," says God. "I've had an idea. Go outside the pearly gates and shout these words I'll teach you: '*Peint o gwrw a caws wedi pobi!*'"

"*Peint o gwrw a caws wedi pobi,*" St Peter repeats, carefully. "What language is that?"

"It's Welsh," says God. "I know it because it's the language of Heaven, see?"

So St Peter goes outside the pearly gates and shouts, very loudly: "*Peint o gwrw a caws wedi pobi!*"

At once all the Welshmen rush out of the gates. St Peter slips back in and locks them out. Of course, what '*Peint o gwrw a caws wedi pobi'* translates as, roughly, is 'A pint of beer and cheese on toast.' God sets up a pub outside, where the men can go and spend eternity arguing, drinking and eating cheese toasties. They go on believing they're in Heaven so they're perfectly happy.

The women are very pleased that the men don't come back drunk on Saturday nights, messing up their clean kitchens. By now they've probably knitted enough socks for St Michael and all the angels to last for eternity. And as St Michael is too kind to tell them that he really prefers his own brand (Marks and Spencers), they are perfectly happy too.

Sweet Fanny Adams

All was peaceful in Heaven, in the warm light of the early evening. The Archangel Raphael was enjoying an early evening snooze in a peaceful meadow when a beautiful little child in a white robe came up and said urgently, "Uncle Raphael, wake up. I want to tell you what I just seen!"

Behind him, panting a little to keep up, was another archangel. Raphael greeted him pleasantly,
"Hi, Gabriel. I thought you were babysitting this afternoon. What have you been up to?"

Before he could get his breath, the little boy said enthusiastically, "Oh yes, Uncle Gabriel was just ace! He showed me all sorts of things happening on Earth through a special glass."

The little boy appeared to be about six years old. He wore a long pearly white robe, and under an untidy mop of curly hair, his face glowed almost golden. Indeed, whenever he smiled, the air around danced with golden light. He laughed a lot and the two angelic beings couldn't help but smile at him adoringly.

"Sounds like you were breaking the rules, Gabby!" said Raphael quietly, out of the side of his mouth.

"You know how much he loves to see what's happening down there, Rapphy," said Gabriel in a similar fashion. "It's ever so hard to say no!" The archangels Gabriel and Raphael were on babysitting duty for the child.

"I don't know what time his mum's coming back. Leaves me to do the lot, bedtime stories, bathtime, entertainment… it's lovely, don't get me wrong, but it's hard work at my age, keeping up with the nipper. So what if I give him a portal down to Earth for a bit?" said Gabriel.

There was no stopping the child, who poured out what he had seen, delighted to have an audience. "I've seen a lady, I think she must have been a saint – Sweet Fanny Adams she was called. Well, I didn't exactly see her but these two men shouted out her name."

Resigned to hearing the whole, Raphael and a slightly guilty Gabriel sat down on the grass and paid him total attention.

"The name came to me in a flash," said the boy. "I mean it actually was a huge noisy flash. There were these two men, see, in a street, no other people and they were beside a great big metal chest with funny numbers and things on it. One of the men said, 'That's the one, the cash machine on the corner, as we were told.' Then they were playing games with things – you know – like on Saint Guy Fawkes night with all the lovely flashy lights?"

Gabriel thought of correcting him but sighed and refrained. Two millennia of Sunday schools had slightly dampened his ardour for religious, or any other education.

The child continued: "There was this wonderful terrific big flash and a huge BANG! Just like I was telling you! Both the men did the most beautiful somersaults backwards and landed on their faces. Then they got up all muddy and bloody and were saying all sorts of very religious words."

Raphael thought for a moment to ask exactly what words, but then quickly thought better of it and motioned the child to go on.

"Well, the front of the metal box was gone away in the bang, in all directions! The men went up to it and one of them said with really, really deep feeling: 'And after all that, what do we get? SWEET FANNY ADAMS – that's what we get!' Then they ran off very fast and I closed the portal 'cos the fun was over. I don't know what saint she was? Sweet Fanny Adams, but she must be nice to come with a bang and a flash, mustn't she? Most saints aren't nearly so exciting."

Gabriel looked at the boy. "You know," he said, "I have told you before, saints always, always have the letters 'St' before their names. Guy Fawkes didn't, so – honestly – he can't be a saint. Are you sure that Fanny Adams was either?"

Raphael also cut in, "Also, are you quite sure, dear child, that those two were good, religious, god-fearing men?"

The boy looked thoughtful, "Well…" he said, "They called on God a lot, very colourfully. They were in nice respectable clothes too, very covered up. Not like beach bums. Black all over with black hats and face masks. They had a big bag with the letters S W A G on it – perhaps the little 't' had fallen off and it belonged to St Wag?"

Gabriel signalled to Raphael, "I think perhaps these men were under St Reetwise and St Ealing," he whispered.

"Not to mention the utterly St Upid," replied his friend.

Gabriel turned back to the child who was still beaming with happiness at how enthralled his lovely uncles had been. "It's bedtime," he said, tucking a white cloud under the child's chin, "but how about I let you watch a really lovely grown-up Earth show as a treat because you've been so good?"

The child clapped his hands and shortly was watching a wonderful scene of gorgeously dressed dancing couples. They whirled and pirouetted, threw each other around the dance floor, all to the most amazing music, even to one accustomed to angelic singing. The child watched, entranced. "I want to do that too when I grow up!" he cried.

The archangels exchanged serious looks, then Raphael raised his eyebrows and said, quietly, "No harm in that – it's surely alright for us to give him the happiest possible childhood?"

Gabriel turned to the child and said, "That's fine. Whenever you want to join in with that dancing group, you just call for the saint in charge of them to come."

With a sheepish glance at Raphael, Gabriel continued: "Just call out 'St Rictly, come dancing!"

54

A WALK IN GOD'S GARDEN

A **GOOD MANY YEARS AGO** I was at a meditation conference and, as usual, browsing the bookstall. I picked up *The Gentle Art of Blessing* by Pierre Pradervand.

"Be careful if you're thinking of buying that book!" said a man beside me, similarly browsing. I looked up and smiled at him and he smiled back and continued, "It may change your life, you know!" before moving on.

Well, of course I bought it and if it didn't exactly change my life, it certainly enlarged my spirituality and is one of my best 'go-to' books. It is about blessing everyone and everything as a daily, constant practice. For me, it tackles the most difficult conundrum of the Christian way – the command of Jesus to love our enemies. Very briefly, among other things it shows that you don't need to start from the impossible thought of loving or even forgiving people. You are simply asking God to bless them, which you know He wants to do – even though sometimes you can't imagine why! By starting with blessing it takes 'you' out of the picture and lets you move on. The author has worked on the practice for many years and runs a retreat centre.

It certainly threw up questions for me. For instance, how had I found it in myself some years previously to forgive an unknown assailant who had struck me on the head with vicious intent in broad daylight, causing me to fall 10 feet down a muddy bank with serious, but luckily transient, injuries? He was never caught. And yet I had always found myself completely unable to forgive a friend of many years who had fooled and, I felt, used me. So, I still need and use the practices the book suggests and try to give silent blessings in all sorts of places and moments. There is much wisdom in the book, so here is a piece I wrote some years ago about this. Re-reading it in lockdown gives me a nostalgic feeling for a time when one could actually go for a bus ride or a long walk through Cardiff without thinking twice about it – and not wearing a mask!

A Walk in God's Garden

I set out at lunchtime to walk over from my home in the centre of Cardiff to collect my car from Penarth Road. The bus journey home after I had dropped it off had seemed so convoluted that I thought it would be easier to walk than try and decipher the tiny bus print on my map, not to mention better for me. Walking is too uncomfortable for me ever to find it a pleasure. My heart condition means I have to go slowly and it was very hot. The mile and a half took me well over an hour.

After I had left the pleasant leafy streets and the little shops of Riverside, my route took me for almost a mile along Clare Road, a concrete artery for the city, the traffic echoing noisily under the railway bridge. Not really a place for walking: dusty, fume-filled, graffiti on the walls, hard pavements. I became aware of God speaking to me. Not with words. He speaks always in thought forms that in memory can be readily clothed in words, often with subtle humour, always with gentleness and absolute approval, no matter what my response.

"Would you like to come for a walk with Me in My garden?"

My response was a simultaneous blend, in one brief instant, of pleasure ["yes please!"], flattery ["who, me?"] and surprise ["where is it?"].

Then I realised that we were already there. This was God's Garden. Clare Road. It was wonderful in its very ordinariness. It wasn't even some dramatic slum where people live colourful and exotic lives, but an ugly piece of unplanned urban neglect. I began, in God's company, to see it through His eyes. I became aware that it had once been an attractive, wide, residential road. Little houses still lined it, covered in dust, and many in poor repair. There were parking lots with the usual litter of used tyres and metal junk among the weeds and sinister and unidentifiable boarded-up shops.

I found myself using my new hobby of blessing everyone I passed, having read a delightful book outlining this method of constant prayer by Pierre Pradervand.[1] Only silently within my heart, of course, I didn't want to get arrested. The stream of passers-by created a rainbow collection of ages, races, colours. Blessing them each, in turn, was quite manageable, with time to look at them for a brief moment as we crossed paths.

According to Pierre, the words of your blessings are always positive, never aimed directly at changing others or yourself. If someone seems negative, maybe angry or sad, even acting badly, you bless them all the more for whatever they seem to be lacking at that moment, on the basis that it will be there, deep inside, in God's template for them. And of course, this includes how you bless yourself.

The Muslim men hurried past, careful not to catch my eye, so I blessed them in their friendliness and in the depth of their faith. The women with pushchairs and children looked tired and worn, so I blessed them in their freshness and beauty and for their loving hearts. It's very easy to bless young children. You just wish them well in their Divine Perfection and take a moment of pleasure in recognising that whatever happens, God will be holding their hands throughout life.

A few of the elderly people looked at me as we passed and we instinctively smiled at each other. I silently blessed them in the

---

[1] *The Gentle Art of Blessing.* Pierre Pradervand. Cygnus 2010.

Divine Perfection of their eternal youth, health and joy. Maybe older people recognise blessings more easily, having lived through curses and survived. Maybe they just have more time and less to lose by smiling at an eccentric stranger.

I began to see signs of human beauty in this concrete wasteland. A man was painting a house front. Here and there were signs of habitation as if a shy race of hobbits had moved in secretly. One window had creamy lace curtains and a china dog. Another allowed me a glimpse of a sofa and flickering TV, with a child's pram on the porch, a little treasure chest of plastic toys, bright as jewels. I blessed them all.

In one bare stretch, there was nothing but a couple of pigeons strutting and cooing on the pavement, so I blessed them in the Divine Perfection of their pigeon-ness and God was very pleased.

The whole earth is God's Garden and we walk in it with Him, knowingly or unknowingly, every moment of our lives. "The earth is the Lord's and the fullness thereof," says the psalmist.[2] Or more simply, "Then the Lord God planted a garden in Eden."[3]

I've added a short poem I wrote, also some years ago, as it references the natural landscape within us, as well as outside. It was written on one of the wonderful 'storytelling retreats' I used to go on annually in North Wales.

Landscape

There is a fruitful land wherein I dwell,
My home is here, within a garden fair.
The house is small, but suits me very well,
Come in, converse. I'll find fine fruit to share.
Come, taste my flowers, listen to my birds,
Enjoy my sunshine. Yours not to see the earth,

---

[2] Psalm 24, v 1
[3] Genesis, 2 v 8

The cesspit, hard-worked compost, dung and turds,
That bring my lavish roses into birth.
The night bird gives a tortured cry of warning,
As darkness over land and garden falls,
And trees grow to the light, to touch the morning.
This is the fruitful land which in me dwells.

Written by Elinor Kapp at Ty Newydd. October 2015

55

COMMUNICATION

S O MUCH OF MY LIFE, indeed of anyone's life, is concerned with communication. It's something, of course, which many of us have as the core of our work – from salesmanship, advertising, journalism, and the performance arts to my own specialty of psychiatry. Communication – or the lack of it – is particularly evident, of course, between the sexes. While I don't entirely go for that "Men are from Mars, Women are from Venus" idea, it has its merits!

So here's a little contribution – call it a pocketful – from some of this preoccupation. We start in the Elizabethan age with a poem I wrote in my years of total obsession with all things textiles (which continues to this day!):

Twenty-one Tudor Ladies

Twelve Tudor Ladies are Sipping Sirops on the Terrace.
Munching Morsels of Marchpane, they Sigh,
and Eye the Tudor Gallants
Parading in the Maze.
As they Gaze they long to be Pursued
and Persuaded to a Pavane
or to a Galliard, two by two.

Six Ladies, very neat, are Sewing Silently on the Lawn.
Garments gilded with Galloon are graced with Gillyflowers
–
Burlesqued Festoons, fooling the Bees,

who murmur their Summer Tunes
to Marigolds beside the Pool.
Ivory Oversleeves of softest Lawn
swirled by the Breeze
uncover curling Stems and Blackworked Leaves.
They Spangle and Speckle and Seed with Knots,
not sowing of Plots
but the Silken stuff where their Knot Garden is Sewn.

Here is shown the Pleasing prospect of an Arbour.
A Tranquil Harbour where three Ladies, all alone, partake
of Caraway Cake, Comfits and Candied Cherries.
Tendrils and Berries of the Trellised Vine
Quaintly combine with Peach,
each with each Plait, Pleach and Twine,
marvellously mimicking the Filigree Laces
framing their Faces.

Dulcimer, Flute, mellifluous Viola da Gamba are playing
Beautifully,
by Beckoning Beds, made up
with Sheets of Heartsease, sure to please,
Pillows of Pinks, covers of Chamomile,
and Damask Roses for Valance.

Those Ladies on the Terrace are Peeping Privily at the
Gallants,
Ogling and making Artful Designs on them.
But though the Ladies on the Lawn and under the Arbour
keep their Eyes down,
All Twentyone of them drown
in Desires for Amorous Dalliance.

Now follows a more up-to-date, if universal, poetic account of what
can change and go wrong over the years. I have only performed
this a few times, as it needs two voices, so I suggest reading it aloud
to yourself – unless that will make you sound weird to anyone who
happens to overhear you, even the cat.

Stalemate: A Prose Poem for Two Voices

SHE: Who are you? Are you my Persecutor?

HE: You know me. I'm your Protector.

SHE: I want to get out. Please, let me get out!

HE: You can't. You mustn't. You will be hurt. Don't you

Remember – we made a bargain?

SHE: No.

HE: You wanted my help. You were frightened and you asked

to stay in my cellar. You asked me to look after you.

SHE: I don't remember.

HE: I agreed to feed you, and look after you, and take out your

messages.

SHE: I spend my time turning the wheel that grinds wheat into

dust. I'm starving. I'm dying. My hair has gone grey.

HE: Why are you complaining? Don't I bring you three good

meals a day?

SHE: Why do you persecute me? I want to be out running like a

deer through the evening dew. I want to sing the moon out
of the sky and bite it till the silver juice runs down my
         chin.

HE: Your feet will get cold.

SHE: I want to pick the stars from the grass and put them in my

hair. I want to comb it till it shines like diamonds and
rubies and pearls.

HE: Your hair is a nest of snakes. You turn men to

stone.

SHE: You never told me that before.

HE: You have to wear a veil and go covered at all

         times, with

me for your mirror. You'll never find anyone else to protect
you from yourself.

SHE: Stop persecuting me. I want to find the den of the wolf
mother and suckle her cubs. I want to howl wolf flesh onto
my bones. I want to feel earth under my paw pads.

HE: You are dangerous!

SHE: I am howling in this prison.

HE: I know. The neighbours think you're mad. You're giving us
both a bad name.

SHE: I'm kept in prison, and I'm howling.
Aaoooohw…aaoooohw!

HE: It's very unfair. You pretend not to know me but we made a
bargain. You empowered me to act for you. Look – I have
the bond here.

SHE: I was young then. I didn't know what I was doing.

HE: They all say that.

SHE: I never said I would stay here forever. I never
promised that.

HE: I never asked you to.

SHE: What if I said I wanted you to release me from the bond?
What if I asked you to let me go?

HE: Why don't you try?

SHE: Please let me go.

HE: The door isn't locked. You can go anytime you
want to.

SHE: But if I go, what will happen to the mill? I have to make the
golden river that flows from your cellar door. What will
happen if I stop turning the wheel?

HE: If the wheel stops there will be no river of golden dust any
more.

SHE: Then the children will starve. How cruel you are!

HE: How can you say that?

SHE: You're sending me away. You would let the children starve.

That's cruel!

HE: You are old. Your hair is grey. You haven't ground

anything for years.

SHE: It's the thought that counts. I could grind all the wheat in the

world into gold if I wanted to.

HE: Why don't you do it then?

SHE: Because you said that my hair was a nest of snakes.

HE: I'm sorry.

SHE: Sorry isn't enough for what you did.

HE: What must I do?

SHE: You must stay by the door and act as my messenger. You

must keep carrying out the golden flour I grind. It's for the children.

HE: I can't! You don't grind wheat into gold anymore. There is

only the grey dust and the emptiness. I want to leave you.

SHE: You can't.

HE: Are you my Persecutor?

SHE: No. I'm your Protector. Don't you remember? You had no

fire, no breath, no life. I agreed to stay in your cellar and grind the harsh wheat into flour every day, to keep you and

the children alive.

HE: I want to ride a great horse through the wilderness carrying a

golden spear, shouting a challenge to the sun.

SHE: You'll fall off.

HE: I want to climb the ivory mountain and fly on the backs of

eagles to the end of the world. I want to discover their
        secret
nests and bring back wisdom in my saddlebags of red
        leather
set with silver clasps.
SHE: You have to stay by the door. Who else can carry
        messages
for me?
HE: Why do you persecute me? Why don't you come
        out and set
me free?
SHE: I choose to stay here.
HE: Let me go! I want to stride through seven seas
        carrying a
club made of an oak tree, blowing ships before me with
        my
breath.
SHE: We made a bargain.
HE: I was young then. I didn't know what I was doing.
SHE: They all say that.

*   *   *

And now a modern take on the same subject. How I have finally
realised a little personal wisdom – that there may be more
happiness in accepting defeat over this difference between the
sexes than in remaining at odds with the 'other'.

Don't Say a Word

How has this happened to me? No! I do not know.
I who so much love words and use them well
and longed to hear you speak them to my heart,
Have learnt the joy in your long speech of silence.
We both explored the ways that words will find escape -
we use emojis, stickers, innuendo, gifs on a phone.

Anything but words! Camouflage meaning, shifting, slipping into night,
painfully shared by fingers overlarge for such an instrument.
Yet we create a music for us both, find meaning from the air.
So, my best friend, you've found your refuge! all unknowing
– it is the sweet, quiet darkness in my silenced heart.
I meet you there! I put my finger on your lips, whispering "shssh."
I feel your lips move upwards in a smile, warm with the moment.
Your arms encircle, pull me close, silent and wordless.
Better so?

56

RESTORATIVE INTERLUDE
BY A STORYTELLER

I STARTED SENDING OUT these pieces of memoirs by beginning with the time I was in hospital in 2009, at a turning point in my life, having had to have life-saving surgery of the open heart. So, I think it would be nice to draw some of the stories together, returning to that time in the University Hospital of Wales when I was in the wonderful hands of doctors and nurses, and all the other staff. I was totally dependent on them for survival – and on the good wishes and prayers of my family and friends. This, epically, has already granted me another 11 years of life – and by no means over yet, during which I try to thank God and other people for such grace every day.

Since the word 'amateur' means someone who loves, I am happy to be an amateur storyteller, but of course as I have often said, we are all storytellers and we are telling – and asking for – stories all the time. … "So, how are you?" "What have you been doing?" "How did it go?" we ask. Or, "I must tell you what he/she/the dog has just done!" Sometimes a bit malicious: "That lady at number 7, you'll never guess what she's up to!" Or happy: "My sister/brother/friend/partner/myself has had such a piece of luck, you'll hardly believe it!"

In these exchanges, of course, we are telling true stories (probably!) but we tend to limit the term 'story' to untrue, made up, even lying accounts – or at least embellished ones. Perhaps that's a good thing – it adds a bit of spice to life. After all, our picture of a traditional storyteller, going back to earliest known times, is usually an enigmatic figure, male or female, wrapped in a dark cloak – but with a glimpse of a scarlet silk lining, a flash of mischief and fun and of lies, all in the darkness between dusk and dawn. That is why I adopted the words 'She Who Embroiders the Truth' as my own, with their ambivalent meaning.

So – here's a little, humorous account from the day I was told I had to stay in hospital and have major surgery, hardly an amusing matter!

When I had my heart surgery in May 2009, I was taken into hospital urgently and kept for nearly a fortnight of tests and preparation first, in which I was encouraged to walk around the corridors and wards on the cardiac surgery floor, so long as I didn't go out onto the stairs. I felt better than I had in a long time and it answered a vague question I had always wondered about: What would it be like to be in hospital for a while, but not (initially at least) feeling the least bit ill? I can tell you – it's rather nice. Like a holiday in an unassuming one-star holiday resort. Even the food tastes alright, if not inspiring. Boarding school food. And varied, unexpected, captive company, like when you're on a journey.

I was in a single-person side room, whether because of being medical or because my surgery was even more major than most of the other patients I don't know. I enjoyed the freedom to move around, to chat to medical students and to the other patients, keeping skilfully out of the way of the working teams. I learnt to use a new skill of texting on a mobile phone taught me by Amanda, but the only place on the ward with a signal was the landing – those far-gone days!

I quickly found some real kindred spirits in the bigger, five-bedder room next door, where five ladies quickly became my buddies. They all had different ages, backgrounds, conditions, and prospects and we bonded. I was careful not to reveal my job or medical connections, as I learnt something of this intriguing world. You learn about it quickly in these circumstances. It's a conspiratorial subculture, barely noticed by the nursing and medical world as it swirls past you.

265

A few days before my op was scheduled, I called into the five-bedder as usual just after supper and found four of the ladies in a very upset state. The fifth lady had collapsed and the emergency team had swooped in straight away and begun 'resuss', quickly moving her on to another ward somewhere. These ladies were all, of course, extremely shocked and distressed, crying and talking – emotionally going around in circles, without rest.

I was devastated. I knew instinctively that all my skills as a psychiatrist were useless in this crisis. Even to tell them that I was a doctor would reduce any help I could offer – I would no longer be 'one of them', but an outsider, however kind and well-meaning. It was a shocking moment for me! All those years! All those skills!

Without knowing in the least what I was going to say, I opened my mouth, "Would you like me to tell you a story?" I found myself saying.

A sense of shock. Then they all fell quiet and turned to me invitingly. The oldest patient, in her 80s, endearingly got into bed and sat with her arms around her arthritic knees as all children do when offered a bedtime story.

I told them a favourite of mine, *The Melon Princess*, an unusual and less well-known fairy-tale, which ends – appropriately – with an old lady who defeats a lion, a wolf, and a demon. I finished on the usual "And they all lived happily ever after" and "Sleep well!" All was silent. I slipped back to my room just as the night nurse team came into the ward.

Early next morning two of the night team came into my room to do my 'obs'. They were laughing and smiling.

"How on earth did you do that, last night?" one said. "When we went in earlier, they were all terribly upset and all their blood pressures were sky high – but when we came back after you'd been there, they were absolutely fine. Their blood pressures had come right down to normal!"

After that, I told my friends a story on each of the four evenings before my op. We discovered in a devious way that the fifth patient had survived and was now in the intensive care ward but doing well. After my op of course I was returned to the post-op ward, at the far end of the corridor, and I was very woozy for a few days. But they didn't forget me and one of them came down to tell me how happy they all were at my successful op and how much they missed me. I was only kept in for a short week, before discharge to convalesce at home, but I made sure to go and see them on my last morning before leaving, to tell them a final story.

* * *

Here is a summary of the story I told that night: the bare bones, as we say. Each storyteller enriches and individualises traditional stories in their own way. I'm very dramatic with a lot of gesturing and drawing the audience in, almost like stand-up comedy. I guess I revert to my great-grandma Luisa Cappiani, the Diva, at these times.

It starts with an old woman, living in a cottage with her old man. They have no children, but she still longs all the time for a baby. Eventually she shouts out, "I wouldn't care if the baby looked like a melon!"

The next morning, she goes to the door and finds a small green melon. She carries it in and it moves in her arms and wails, so she automatically joggles it and gives it milk – SLURP! It grows very fast, becomes large and yellow. She takes it out in her shawl, and at first is mocked, but she persists and so the children want to play with it. The melon can skip very well, if they turn the rope. She loves balls and bounces like them everywhere. She grows up so fast she tires her mother out, so is quickly sent to school, which she loves, growing ever faster.

One day, the prince who lives in a nearby palace is out, avoiding his tutor. He is intrigued to see the melon, rolling along, and follows her into a vineyard secretly. The melon splits open and out comes a very beautiful girl, who picks and eats some grapes. The next day, the prince hides and surprises her, begging her to marry him. Blushingly she agrees and he tries a ring on her fingers – they are so slender it only stays on her middle finger; then she gets back in the melon and rolls away.

The prince tells his parents he will only marry the girl the ring fits. Ladies-in-waiting are sent out, but have no luck in all the village. Eventually, they come to the cottage of her mother, the old woman, and the melon rolls in and puts out a delicate hand – middle finger first, as expected for the right girl. She comes out and is taken to the palace and marries the prince.

However, that is not the end of the story. The old woman is happy for her and visits the palace every day. However, not all is well in the kingdom due to evil forces: a Demon, a Wolf, and a Lion. One day, as the old woman walks along, the Lion leaps out and wants to eat her.

She persuades him to let her go, saying "you can eat me on the way back after I've feasted. I'll be fatter and more delicious then." The same thing happens with a huge grey Wolf and a hideous Demon.

Of course, all is well at the palace, but when she needs to go home to her old man, she doesn't know what to do. Her daughter puts her in the melon halves, to roll along, with holes for her eyes and mouth. The Demon and the Wolf are deceived and she even gets them to push her with a cloven hoof and a claw so she rolls merrily on each time. But the Lion, king of beasts, is offended by her ordering him around. He dashes the melon on a rock and it breaks.

The old lady comes out, raging at him so hard and furiously that he forgets about eating her and runs away. He passes first the wolf, who on seeing him running with the raging old lady behind, runs too. They pass the Demon, who is also terrified by her, and joins them.

"And for all I know, they are running still. I just need to warn you {spoken directly to the audience} of the serious consequences of annoying old women, whose anger, if roused, can overpower Demons, Wolves, and even Lions.... Sleep well!"

* * *

A further little observation about my time in the hospital I think is worth sharing, as it shows how intriguingly the brain continues to operate, sometimes successfully, under extraordinary stress.

My operation was a replacement of some heart valves and removal of part of the arch of the aorta. This was full-on open-heart surgery, which took about 8 hours overall and required the patient to be frozen and all blood circulated outside the body for a while. They could only stop the heart for about 20 to 30 minutes maximum – and hope that all systems would then return to normal. The highly skilled surgeons would be operating within millimetres of the arteries which serve the brain, so any slip ups would be catastrophic. I am meg-mega grateful to that incredible team of doctors, nurses and technicians!

The Anaesthetist talked to me some days afterwards and confirmed certain things. My aorta was already beginning the process of tearing, from the inside lining and would have burst within days, even hours, without intervention, hence the hospitalisation, the restriction on movement and the careful preparations. These included the freedom of movement around the ward, because otherwise blood clotting would be an even greater risk. Much later on, back in the ward the anaesthetist told me that after the surgeons had sewed my chest together again, he had brought me round, briefly, to check if I was reasonably whole mentally or in a vegetative state. They apparently had quite a problem during the operation in getting the 'acid/alkaline balance in my blood right. (No, I still don't quite know what that means!)

The anaesthetist, as normal practice, stayed with me in theatre to keep a check on me till I could be brought round again. He had also invited my son and daughter, Rupert and Amanda, who had been in the waiting room throughout, into the theatre, so that their familiar voices and faces would reassure me. I remember a sense of diving upwards and opening my eyes, seeing them dimly. I remember the anaesthetist's soft voice suggesting they talk to me and find out if I wished them to stay, or could leave me to sleep.

Amanda said, "Do you want us to stay, or go?" She told me later that she realised instantly how impossible it was for me to answer – I became aware that my head was tipped back and there was a great tube coming out my throat! I remember thinking, 'She taught me to text, so I'll text her.' My hand rose tremulously before my clever-stupid brain thought, 'But where's my phone?'

The clever part kicked in at that point and I wrote in the air with my thumb the single word 'GO' – but what was clever was that I actually registered that I must write it backwards so that Amanda could read it correctly. My children smiled at me and there was a burble of voices, receding, as the anaesthetist put me back into a mercifully painless oblivion. When I woke again, I was in the recovery ward and Rupert and Amanda were back looking much less anxious and suitably rested themselves, poor dears.

Enough about that tragi-comic time of illness and recuperation. The surgery was still relatively new in 2009 and I have never ceased, even in bad times, to remember that I am very lucky to be alive at all and reasonably intact. It is thanks, yet again, to the Kindness of Strangers.

I know I have always felt like this really, in my better moments, so it is relevant to go back in time and explore more of my attempts at the service of others, and how wonderfully rewarded I always am for even trying to do this.

57

THE ORIGINS OF CITY HOSPICE, CARDIFF

THIS RELATES TO the setting up of the palliative care service in Cardiff, in which I was involved from the beginning, and still am today. So, we are back in the late 1970s It would be rare if anyone could claim to be the sole generator of an idea or institution, and I make no such claim. However, I was fortunate enough to be present from the very early meetings, discussions, and working practises of the group that later became the George Thomas Trust for Palliative Care in 1984, and eventually, the City Hospice for Cardiff and the Vale.

Not all communication, even in words, comes from human sources – or even from this world. For me, it started in late 1979, with a strange experience. During one of my periodic attempts to practice contemplative care on a regular daily basis, I became aware of an interruption every time – a sad, sighing voice. At first I tried to block it, but it became more insistent, so I started to listen to it. A sighing female voice saying, "Oh, I wish we had a hospice in Cardiff!" "Why don't we have a hospice in Cardiff!?" "Oh, we should have a hospice in Cardiff!" Over and over again, with slight variations, but always this sad, soft, unearthly plea.

I knew little about hospices or indeed palliative care in those days. Of course, as a junior House Officer in A&E, I had seen much tragedy and trauma, as part of the job. Again, in Whitchurch Hospital I had done my share of prescribing for the dying elderly patients and then certifying death as the Responsible Medical Officer. I had also had my share of tragedy and death in my personal life, but never of Care for the dying themselves. In those early years (1968 on), palliative care, as we understand it now, did not exist.

So! I kept hearing this sad voice pleading, and I asked God out loud one evening for a more definite sign if I was meant to be doing anything about this. On that night I was on my own with my elderly Aunt Joyce in Sussex. I woke in the morning after saying this prayer and came down to breakfast.

The very first thing my aunt said to me was, "Oh, I've just heard such an interesting talk on the radio, by Cicely Saunders, about the hospice movement." There was no reason my aunt should have said this. She was not ill, nor indeed thinking about dying – nor knew of my repetitive thought. Nor had I heard of the program, though I knew about Cicely Saunders.

So I returned to Cardiff, very thoughtful, and that night had a minor blip – which I now see as very amusing. As I tried to sleep, I was thinking about the voice, which I felt was probably a telepathic experience of a real person somewhere, and what it meant. Almost certainly, I decided, in the usual self-important way we humans have, it meant that I must build a hospice. Not quite literally – I am not quite mad enough to enrol as a bricklayer – but by getting the money. So, through the early hours, I struggled with the idea of how to get money. Well – obviously – you go and ask a Very Rich Person!

The only local millionaire I had ever heard of was Julian Hodge, through the newspapers. I struggled with the apparent command that I must find a way of getting in to see Julian Hodge, in an office somewhere, to tell him to please "Give me a million pounds to build a hospice in Cardiff." What a crazy mindset one can get into when wakeful in the small hours! I really thought, for a short while, that this was what I had to do, and it terrified me. I'm not as insouciant as, in old age, I may appear. However, I eventually shouted aloud: "Yes! I'll do it!" into the void and slept peacefully till morning.

272

Of course, in the light of day, I laughed at the absurdity of that way of doing things. It was almost certain that other people were thinking about this too and I needed to find out what was already going on, then I could offer my help, not interfere in other people's plans by setting up a rival organisation.

As it happened, I had previously worked for six months in Velindre, so I still had some vague contacts there. And of course, my ever-supportive husband, Ken Rawnsley, as Professor of Psychiatry, was known to almost all the Cardiff GPs. So it wasn't difficult to find that a major cancer charity had a nursing home in Penarth, which was obviously helpful but covered only cancer care, not the whole range of terminal illnesses. There were other charities too, but none of them seemed to be particularly working in Cardiff.

It seemed there was no local group for me to join at that time. However, I quickly learnt that a Consultant at Velindre and a few General Practitioners had been working together previously on the need for a hospice in Cardiff, but had disbanded a year previously. I got in touch with them and we remade a small working group who were still interested, consisting at first, besides myself, of the Velindre doctor, whose name I'm afraid I can't remember, and a remarkable GP husband and wife couple, Dr Michael and Dr Margot Richards, living in Llandaff. We soon acquired a few more interested parties.

I remember well how kind Margot Richards was. Many of the meetings took place in her beautiful garden with tea and cakes. It stayed as an informal interest group for a long while, as we were all very busy, but we made new helpful contacts, notably Dr Ilora Finlay (now Baroness Finlay).

It became obvious that the real need was to find out what the public, the patients, wanted. Dame Cicely Saunders, that amazing pioneer, had transformed the whole attitude to terminal care. The movement had now advanced enough for many of the hospices to be suffering from an inevitable overload of cases and a depressing fight to keep afloat with buildings and beds in ever-increasing need. There was also talk around that time of services based on care at home, without the huge expense of beds and all that came with that.

With our little group, I arranged a day meeting, the venue and refreshments being provided free by my church, Llandaff Road Baptist Church. It was chaired by Ilora (now Baroness) Finlay. The public was welcomed and by word of mouth, many individuals and families with an interest were contacted to get at least a straw poll. This was done by questionnaire to ask what people felt was most necessary. I'm sorry I did not keep the results, but the result was an overwhelming wish by those attending, for themselves and their loved ones, to die at home and only in a hospice building or hospital if they absolutely had to. We had our answer.

Around this time, in 1980, Julian Hodge quite separately brought to Cardiff an order of Catholic nuns, The Little Company of Mary, whose calling is to nurse the dying. Being a very sensible woman, the Mother Superior of the order told him that her first task was to find who was already involved and she was quickly referred to our working group. So we were enriched to have on board Sister Kathleen Grew, Sister Kevin Murphy, and Sister Phyllis Burns.

We were delighted with this, of course, and we quickly became a more formal hospice care group, with Dr Nigel Stott as chairman, myself as secretary, and a very small committee to support the work of the LCM Sisters. Julian Hodge, assisted by his own sister, generously bought them a house in Ty Gwyn Road, Penylan, as a base, and our new-born charity operated from there.

Quite early on and before this more formal structuring, we had a less official meeting at which I met Julian Hodge for the first time. I remember that his sister, a very nice lady who helped us a lot, was present, plus three or four of our group. At this point – with an almost exquisite symmetry which seems unbelievable, but I promise it was true – I found myself in the exact opposite of my imagined interview in the night. I was being offered a million pounds to build a hospice – and I was refusing it!

Julian Hodge was trying to persuade us to accept a donation of one million pounds, but with the proviso that we used it to build an actual bedded hospice, for which we would become completely responsible. He had something of a record of one-off financing and donating wonderful buildings – but the charity then had to spend all its time and money on maintenance.

I have never, before or since, been in the position of being offered a million pounds – and certainly not of refusing it! But at that meeting, it became evident that I was the one who had to take him on, and it became a very polite duel between the two of us, in which I was – gently – having to refuse his offer!

I had learnt a lot since my innocent idea of what was wanted in that sleepless night, when I imagined my job was to ask someone for a million pounds to build a hospice. Now I fully understood how the purpose of the work must always come first, which takes time to evolve. Also, that one million in this context was a very paltry sum! So I begged him to let us have the money and trust us, describing exactly how we would use it to further a home care service, which he refused to do. In spite of that, I developed a great deal of liking for him and enjoyed the verbal, almost flirtatious, sparring over it.

The meeting ended in a polite stalemate, but with handshakes all round, and I was told by his sister, through other contacts, that he was well impressed by me. In fact, Sir Julian (as he later became), was one of our most generous and helpful patrons, since he took my refusal not as a defeat, but as a challenge.

He must have taken it all in too, because in effect, that was what he financed on a recurring basis, finding roundabout ways for him and his sister to fund us through his foundation; a great tradition continued by the family. We have had, through these offices and many other volunteers, far more money overall than I had innocently prayed for!

The Hodge Foundation bought another nearby house in Penylan, with a beautiful garden, from which the charity worked for several years until the present purpose-built Hospice Centre in Whitchurch, Cardiff, was opened formally by the Prince of Wales in 2005. At Sir Julian's request, it was named after George Thomas (later Lord Tonypandy) who became another great source of support as our patron.

The Sisters of the Little Company of Mary were expanded and continued to live in the first house that Sir Julian's foundation had bought. Sisters Kevin, Kathleen, Phyllis, Mary, Colette, Dorothy, and Margaret, could live comfortably, attend to their religious practice, and work with patients. There was no lack of these, referred by local GPs.

When the work of the budding service started, I much enjoyed the friendship that quickly developed, meeting with them at least fortnightly, to discuss their cases. This was not 'supervision', as I was not qualified for that, but a friendly meeting to support them and for myself to learn from them. I was often allowed to stay on for their evening prayers. On occasions, when I lacked care for my daughter, Amanda, she would come with me and be carried off to the kitchen to be amused by making gingerbread men with Sister Phyllis, and fed as necessary. These are among my happiest memories, and though sadly some of the Sisters are no longer with us, it was a joy to hear from Sister Margaret recently.

My diaries for 1980 to 1984 do mention some of the key early contributors, as there are occasional appointments and meetings regarding the hospice. Those early years, before it became an official charity in 1984, also note team meetings with the sisters of the Little Company of Mary, and individuals such as Dr Michael and Dr Margot Richards. There are meetings to enlist volunteers and run courses for them, and even informal meetings regarding bereavement counselling.

Sister Margaret Watson became the first full-time nurse manager from 1986 to 2001. May Foley, Anne Mark and Eileen Evans started up the shops, entirely with volunteers. The ever-popular Light Up a Life annual charity under Claire Bell came in in the late 1980s. There were, of course, many meetings with the health service and many official bodies. Our Chairman of Trustees was Prof Nigel Stott, Professor of General Practice, and many other valued volunteers became trustees over the years.

Margaret Pritchard became our first Chief Executive from 2000 to 2015, with a particular expertise in public relations, overseeing an expanding and vibrant charity, increasingly important to Cardiff and the surrounding area. She also masterminded the charity's move to the present purpose-built home in Whitchurch in 2005, and a grand opening with the Prince of Wales.

I remained as a trustee through all this until, for a few months between 1991 and early 1992, I stepped aside, when my beloved husband Ken was dying. I was able to be with him at home, thanks to the palliative care charity that I had taken part in building up – which had been long before he was even ill or I had any idea that we might need the service ourselves!

It was a humbling and rewarding experience. Ken was a model patient, resting patiently and accepting all that happened with Yorkshire stoicism. Towards the end, he had nursing care in daily visits from the district nurses under our excellent GP, but also weekend and many extra visits from the sisters of the Little Company of Mary, in what was by then the George Thomas Trust for Palliative Care. They phoned me frequently, and Sister Margaret or Sister Phyllis called in as friends at odd times in those last weeks. He had a lot of visitors and tributes to his international work and friendship, which were truly inspiring.

My old friend Dr Lata Mathur, also later a trustee, would call in unobtrusively every few days, staying for only a few minutes but leaving wonderful Indian food to feed us all. The children, Rupert and Amanda, were amazing – self-sufficient and caring beyond their years.

If ever 'casting your bread upon the waters' and getting far more back comes true, this is one such unexpected reward, which is why it seems good to write about it here, in the story of what is now the City Hospice.

* * *

So I feel that this prose poem is relevant as it was written while I sat with my late husband, Ken, in what turned out to be his last week in this life. Since that time, I have recited it on quite a number of public occasions, with a background of whale song playing on a CD, which makes it very atmospheric. I have not said anything on these occasions about where and when – and why – I wrote it. However, every single time that I have 'performed' it publicly in this way, a few people have come up to talk to me afterwards, often in tears, because it has moved them very much and always because it reminded them of the passing of a loved one. I then tell them the background – what it is 'really' about – that it was written in the last days of my husband's life, as I sat by him while he was dying.

It was the feeling of going with him as far as I could, understanding how I was privileged by being there with someone I loved so completely. It also expressed my very mixed feelings – a part of me wishing to go all the way, but risking not being able to get back from the underwater realm of Death.

I will just mention something else, in case it is helpful to others in this situation. While I sat with my husband and opened everything within my heart and soul to him for almost the whole time of his dying, it changed on the very last day when he seemed, on and off, mostly in a coma. I sat there beside him all day, speaking, but without touching him and without 'connecting' internally. I was detached, mindless, at a distance emotionally.

Afterwards I felt a little bad about it, though in a minor way, secretly wondering if I had 'let him down' at the end.

I think it might be helpful for others to know that sometime later, when I had learned more about palliative care, I regarded that last day very differently. I was grateful for some inner protective system that had not allowed me to be totally opened up inside at the very end, as there could be a real danger of actually not being able to 'come back'. The number of couples where one follows the other into death within a few days is well above chance (indeed it happened to my own parents) and I think some healthy life force within me drew me back from any risk.

* * *

The Conversation of Whales

The conversation of whales
Is slow and deep and strange.
Eerie blowholes of nouns, and
Mournful adjectives, spilling away
Endlessly through the oceans,
A haunting grammar of sounds,
Green silences, and punctuations
Of strange long beats. Glassy seas
And oceans rolling with tides,
Ship sounds, bell sounds,
Smack of waves and fins, go
Echoing over old hulls of hulks,
And through blue-patterned dunes,
Where whales sway and turn
Stirring the cumuli of sand.
Endless questioning spume-filled calls
Stretch through the sea miles
To interrogate the ocean.
If you want to follow the whales,
No – even more – to converse,
You must enter the sea. Dare
The treacherous waves pulling
You down. You must swim
Close to the whales, come to

That last terrified inch, where
The whale's skin takes you in
Its razor embrace, risking
The careless murder of the tail.
Close, closer still, meeting at last
The alien enquiry of the eye.
Even then, even more, you must
Submerge. Cease to breathe
Through natural orifices. Grow to be
Large as Leviathan. Every cell
Spaced out like a coral reef;
Thoughts deep as the tides
Slowly surging and receding.
Tide – race of juices, salty, strong,
Pour in torrents of blood
Into your cathedral heart,
Through great vessels, sounding
Organ notes. Booming tunes
Echo in your cave of ribs,
Where the bones are like ships.
Every pulse as long as a beach
And high as a curling wave.
Oh, but it would be worth it!
Worth risking the pull and suck
Of the sea as you returned –
But would you return; if so
Would you remember? Oh what if
Nothing could be recalled?
If you had nothing to share?
Mute as a mermaid! Even so,
Even so, it surely would be worth
Each stolen heartbeat,
To have shared for a while
In the long green life of the ocean tides,
And the conversation of whales.

Elinor Kapp. 1992

58

SPRING IN THE CIVIC CENTRE

THE FIRST DAY OF SPRING is traditionally the 20th of March. In 2021, putting together this 'patchwork' of memoirs, short stories and poetry, I often felt confused, bewildered and lonely, because of the Covid Lockdown. So here's something to lighten the mood briefly.

I wrote it some years ago, another time when I was in a rather bleak place emotionally. One day as I was walking through Cardiff Civic Centre, I suddenly noticed a municipal flowerbed of very bright varicoloured tulips. The beds all had a low decorative edging of iron work, most of them containing neat rows of small flowers – but these tulips were sprawling every which-way, for all the world as if they were trying to scramble out or attack the knees of passers-by. The flower heads were bending towards each other and peering over the fence and it looked to me as if they were chatting rowdily with each other.

The very idea of wild and dangerous tulips made me laugh aloud and as I walked on this poem formed itself inside my head, to be later written down and worked on.

Wild and Dangerous Tulips

The Mayor considered that the gardens ought
To have a share in Spring.
Tulips would be respectable, he thought,
Quiet, and quite the thing.

"Obedient tulips stand in rows," he said,
"And never make a mess,
But to make sure, we'll still fence off the bed."
The councillors said "Yes."

But oh, if they had only known the truth!
The Spring can't be confined.
Those wild and dangerous tulips, like our youth,
Subvert the civic mind.

The typists, all seduced from sober ways,
Remove their woolly vests,
While golden waves of flowers fall in spray
Around their naked breasts.

The treasurer cries "How erroneous!
The scheme has fallen flat.
Next year I say, stick to begonias,
And plastic ones at that!"

The stripy tulip tigers roar, and try
To reach with yellow paws
And swipe the ankles of the passers-by,
Gnashing their crimson jaws.

Pubescent schoolgirls walk in twosomes near,
Still thinking of their sums.
Those saucy orange tulips wink and leer,
And try to pinch their bums.

Tell all the filing clerks to stay away –
Some things cannot be filed.
With sex and aggro in the park today,
The Spring is really wild!

59

THE BOY AND THE
BEAUTIFUL BLANKET

HERE IS ANOTHER original fairy tale that I wrote. Once again, the inspiration was a brief mention in a folk tale, explaining why the sun sometimes sets with bright colours around it, which captured my imagination. Storytellers have a reputation for pinching and stealing threads and patches from other people's garments – or even the whole garment – and making it over to fit themselves. And why not? So, cosy up by the fire, hug a rug around you, and listen to my story of…

The Boy and the Beautiful Blanket

Once upon a time, there was a young man, hardly more than a boy, who lived with his grandmother in a hut at the edge of the forest. Until a few years earlier, his mother and father had been with them too. Although life was hard, the house then was full of love and laughter, with sunshine in summer and a warm fire in winter, and they had slept beside it on the hearth, where the boy was held closely by his parents against the cold.

Then, one bitterly cold winter's day, his mother and father had gone out to forage and had never returned. The boy and his grandmother were cold and hungry, but with a little help from the nearest village and his grandmother's skills, they got by. The boy remembered how his father had built up a warm fire and his grandmother taught him to make soup.

She began to weave a beautiful blanket to keep the boy warm. She used everything she could find, wool from the sheep, dyed in rainbow colours, feathers left by birds: robin redbreast, goldfinch, and blue jay. She wove in the colours of flowers and the magic of her love for her grandson. At last, it was finished and he wrapped it around himself, and at last he could sleep, warm and comforted.

So time went on and they did well, until one day, the unthinkable happened and grandmother went out into the forest and she also did not come back. The boy waited, one day, two days, and on the third day he knew she was not coming back and he must go and find her. All he could find to sustain him was the crust of the last loaf, the last berries from the tree, the last gourd of wine, and the blanket woven years before by his grandmother. It was now alas, old and dull in colour, worn threadbare, full of gaping tears and holes, so it barely protected him from the freezing wind and snow.

Soon he began to feel hungry and he was about to eat the berries when a robin redbreast fluttered down at his feet, exhausted, looking up at him beseechingly, unable even to chirrup. He could not help but feed the bird on half of the berries, but when those were gone it still looked at him so pleadingly that he gave it the rest and watched as the little bird flew unsteadily, but noticeably stronger, back into the trees.

He went a little further, then stopped, intending to eat the crust, but again he was interrupted by a little creature looking down at him beseechingly from a low branch. It was a red squirrel and he willingly gave it half of his crust. The squirrel too looked near to death, but began to recover, still looking so hungry that, with a sigh, he gave it the rest of his bread.

The snow had stopped and by now he was far, far into the forest, in a part he had never seen before, completely lost. He wondered if it might be best to drink from the gourd and perhaps lie down in the snow and sleep, even though he knew he would be unlikely to wake. As he sat down, wrapping his useless shawl more firmly around his shoulders and weighing the gourd in his hand, he became aware of a figure seated nearby, shrouded in a black cloak. He was startled and exclaimed in surprise, dropping then catching the gourd.

"Young man!" said a low, sweet voice and he realised that it was a woman.

As she slid back the edge of the cloak a little, he saw part of a face of startling beauty, radiating golden light and heat, so that the snow around him began to melt and he began to blink. At this, she closed the cloak a little but spoke again.

"I am the Sun," she said, "as you may have guessed! I am hiding from my evil cousin, the Moon, who forbids me from entering these woods by night, claiming them as her own. Don't be afraid, I will not open my cloak any further to harm you, only enough to prevent you from freezing to death."

The boy stammered his gratitude and she continued:

"I would dearly like a little of your wine, young man, if you so please?"

Mesmerised, he handed her the gourd and she drank a full half of it and sighed deeply as she handed it back. A shadow passed over them and they looked up. The silver Moon was peering down as she passed, riding a black cloud. The Sun shrank back into her cloak and covered her own face, just in time, as the round sneering face of the Moon passed overhead, looking down into every nook and cranny of the forest, but not seeing them.

The boy looked down at the gourd. There was hardly enough to slake his thirst or give him sleep now, anyway. He looked back at the Sun lady and held it out:

"Have what you want," he said simply. "I'm used to going hungry and thirsty, my lady, not like yourself."

The Sun thanked him and drank the rest. Then she said, "I owe you a good turn. What about your blanket? Is that all that you have to keep away the cold this snowy night?"

He laughed awkwardly. "It was once the most beautiful, warm blanket in the world, my lady, made by my grandmother, but now worn and torn and full of holes."

He handed it to her, and she held it up in her own light and said, "Then I must mend it for you!"

She gave a little call, like squirrels chatter, and suddenly the clearing was full of squirrels. The boy thought he could see they were being led by the one he had helped, but before he could be certain, the Sun had given her orders and they all whisked away returning with wonderful threads and furs of many different colours. Her hands came out of the cloak to give signs of what she wanted and as she made weaving motions the thread swiftly mended and remade the blanket without her touching it.

The boy noticed that each of the lady's fingers ended in a flame and he realised how skilfully she worked, so that she set nothing alight. She gave a chirruping call and suddenly the clearing was full of birds, each giving their brightest feathers to be woven in and add to the glory of the colour, the robin redbreast – who caressed his cheek in passing – the goldfinch, the blue jay, and many others. Then suddenly the work was done and the birds and animals vanished. He was aware that somehow the Sun was wrapping him in his beautiful renewed blanket without touching him and he felt very sleepy.

The Sun said, "I know where your parents and grandmother are. The Moon stole them and has them locked up in a place far, far from here, on the other side of the forest."

The boy struggled to stay awake long enough to look round the clearing and see that there were no paths nor anything to identify the way. Then he became aware of what the Sun was saying, as he sank into sleep: "Because you gave away everything you had in the whole world, without thought of yourself, you have nothing ever again to fear. Sleep now! And in the morning you will see what you will see."

The boy woke in the morning. He was still wrapped in the glorious rewoven blanket so he knew it was not a dream. The lady in the cloak had gone, but the Sun in the sky was beaming down over the forest, making the snow glitter and the Moon had set.

As he got to his feet, he saw that where there had been close clumped trees there was now a broad grassy path, straight and true, with the snow packed up the sides and the grass at the edges just a little charred. One way he could see almost far enough to know that it would take him home, but facing the other way – Ah! That was better than best! Along it, hand-in-hand were walking swiftly his mother and father, with his grandmother close behind. And what a meeting and greeting there was indeed!

They walked back to the cottage to make a feast – out of nothing! Then neighbours caught sight of them, having been looking out, running towards them with joyful shouts, bringing food and gifts. There was a great celebration.

As the Sun sank nearer the horizon, the boy took his blanket and slipped out to the edge of the forest. He remembered what the Sun had murmured to him as he slipped into sleep. Something about being where you had nothing and still gave away whatever you had. She had restored his beautiful blanket, so he had something after all. He raised his arms impulsively towards the sky and called out:

"I do have something now and you restored something even better as well. So this is for you, my lady!"

He threw the blanket up and a warm wind swirled around him, caressing his cheek and lifting his hair up, indeed singeing the tips very slightly as it passed. It carried the beautiful rainbow coloured blanket up, up into the sky, as the Sun accepted his gift.

So that is why, often at sunset and sunrise, when the Sun has escaped from the confines of the Moon's domain, she wraps herself in her glorious coloured blanket and dances and rolls around the sky till the whole horizon is covered in a blaze of glory. And in the forest, the small ones, the birds and squirrels, look up and wave and talk gratefully of anyone who helps them in bad times, so that everyone can live…

HAPPILY EVER AFTER!

60

THE MAN WHO CAME
TO ROB THE TEMPLE

A Traditional Story from Sri Lanka

HERE IS ANOTHER STORY with a lovely message, based on a traditional Buddhist tale. I have mentioned before now the lovely storytelling tradition, where people make one a 'gift' of a story from their own tradition, or even their own life, with permission to retell it. When I went to different hospitals to do locums in my retirement years, I would often find new acquaintances and watch TV and eat meals with them in the communal hospital accommodation. I learned to watch all the soaps as I was only there for a night or two a week and they were usually full residents for some months. There is an unspoken etiquette in these situations as to who holds the TV remote!

Often, when I mentioned storytelling as my hobby, they would ask me for a story – soaps eventually get boring! – and then would share one from their own culture. Stories told in these situations often include what is called the 'backstory' of how and when they heard it.

This story was told to me by a Sri Lankan woman doctor in 2008. I learned that when she was a child, she and her parents had escaped from their house only minutes before the Tamil Tigers came. Penniless, they fled to Canada and made a new life for themselves. She later came to England and got work where she could, as a locum, with a short spell in Wales. Her life story was enthralling and we talked all evening – the only time we met.

Because we had talked of storytelling, the next morning, over our hurried breakfast in the hospital residency, she announced, "I have a present for you" – and quickly told me the basic folk story, which I have worked up and carried on. We never met again and I can't even remember her name – but I have shared this wonderful story many, many times. Namaste, and thank you, my unknown friend.

The Man Who Came to Rob the Temple

Once there was a homeless young man living near a village in Sri Lanka. His parents had died when he was a child, barely able to fend for himself. He lived on what he could beg or steal and in the evenings he would edge in, near to the village fire, and listen to the men talking. Sometimes they would drive him away with curses, sometimes they let him stay. So in this way, he learned of the far-off town where people were so rich, they ate several times a day and were dressed in fine clothes. He also learned that there was a great temple nearby, full of chests of money and statues with gold chains around their necks.

"If I could get some of that gold," he reasoned, "I could go and live in the big town, in a house. I'd never be hungry again."

The young man found his way to the temple. For several days he kept at a distance, watching. He saw people going in and out. He saw the monks chanting and praying before statues with gold chains and jewels adorning them, though the monks wore plain, simple garments. He saw villagers coming in with money, which was put away in chests.

Then, with great difficulty, he worked his way round to the back of the temple, among roots in stagnant water, where snakes hissed and slid away. He found crumbling stones in the back wall and worked for days until he could prise one stone away and slip into a storeroom. He waited in the shadows at the back of the temple until he heard the monks chanting their evening prayers. They filed out

290

and away into silence as they went to their dormitory and only then was it safe to creep out.

In the light of the single candle, he could see the statues up close and he studied them all, marvelling at their splendour. He chose gold chains to put round his neck, then he opened the chests, which were full of coins and jewels. He found a white robe and belted it around himself, pouring coins in at the neck until his chest was like a sack of gold. So absorbed was he in this that he did not realise how time was passing. Suddenly, in the pale light of dawn, he heard the monks coming back, their chant growing louder. He tried to run, but he could hardly move and the clinking coins would give him away long before he could reach the hole.

He did the only thing possible: he sank down cross-legged, bowed his head, and pretended to pray. The monks came in and were amazed. The only door was locked and barred as they had left it.

"It's a miracle!" they cried, "A Holy man has come to us!"

They garlanded him with flowers and put candles around him, touching his feet with gentle reverence. Then they called in the local villagers. Through the day, streams of people from all around heard of the miracle and came to see the Holy man. They touched the ground before him with their foreheads. They brought children to him, begging his blessing.

A richly dressed woman whispered to him, "Pray for me, oh holy one. My husband beats me because I have no children. Pray that I may be blessed with a son."

A young man wept and said, "I cheated my brother; I will pay him back. Forgive me, oh holy one."

A man said, "Help my mother with your prayers, she is very sick." All day long, the stream of supplicants came.

In the evening, the monks bowed one last time, and then he heard their chant receding as they went away. Now! Now was his chance! He could get out through the hole, find the town, and make his fortune.

He sat still for a long time, tears rolling down his cheeks. In all his wretched life before this, nobody had ever touched his feet in a sign of respect. Nobody had asked him for his help or his prayers, or spoken of him as holy.

The young man put back all the chains and jewels. He returned the money to the chests. Wrapped in the white robe, he settled to sleep. He continued to live in the monastery, praying and listening to all who came. The monastery became famous for its Holy man and he made sure that nobody hung around the door afraid to come in. Beggars were fed, wrongs were righted. In time, the monks made him their Abbot and he stayed for the rest of his life.

When the man was very old, he called the brothers and said, "I am dying, but before I go I want to tell you how I came here. This is the story of the man who came to rob the temple and stayed to pray."

61

A CHRISTMAS STORY FOR ST FRANCIS

A **LITTLE PREAMBLE:** for those who may not know, we apparently owe the 'traditional' nativity scenes with the crib, holy family, stable and animals, to St Francis, that great saint of the 13th century. He believed that a tableau of the nativity story would come alive for ordinary people more easily than the normal church services and liturgy in Latin. It is said that he was helped by Messr Giovanni de Velluta, a rich landowner and supporter of the monks. The original ox, ass, and sheep were borrowed from a local farm, and a baby doll and 'treasures from the magi' were made from wood. St Francis always seems like one of the nicest and most approachable of the saints. Stories and legends about him, with many new miracles, continued to be told – and frequently invented – over many years. So I am sure he will forgive me for creating yet another of these stories for the enjoyment of young and old, whether it be Christmas or not!

The Robber Boy, The Donkey & The Ox

Once upon a time, there was a young boy living in a robber's den. His father was unknown, his mother had died the previous year. No-one cared about him. He grew tired of being with the band, preying on travellers: the knives, the shouting, the constant fear of death on the gallows. He grew tired of scavenging for scraps in the den. He grew tired of the constant beatings and passing kicks.

One day he ran away. He walked and he ran, hiding in farm carts, until he was many dozen miles away, in another part of the country altogether. He was free, but he was frozen with cold and starving. He saw above him on the hillside a small, soft glow of light and climbed towards it.

It was a marvellous open cave! There was nobody there, but a couple of soft lamps cast the glow he had seen. There was a donkey and an ox, both placidly munching hay. There was a sleepy lamb and a few sparrows pecking at the grains on the floor. In the manger, the boy could see a life-size wooden doll, like a baby. It was of no interest to him because it was only bound about with scraps of fabric, no better than his own rags.

What caused his breath to stop and his eyes to pop out were the rich gifts laid out around the manger: dishes of golden coins and jars and boxes encrusted with precious jewels! He was too dazzled to see that these were not treasures at all – only clumsily painted bits of wood and bits of metal and glass. He thought his fortune was made and he grabbed the nearest treasure.

At that moment two things happened. The donkey said, "You know, I really don't think you should do that," and the wooden doll burst into tears.

The ox started to argue with the donkey: "Look at the poor boy. He's cold and starving, why shouldn't he take anything he wants?"

The robber boy stared in astonishment. The baby was flesh and blood and bawling loudly. The animals were definitely speaking.

"There's no point in him taking those things, you clodhopper," said the donkey to the ox. "Those aren't valuable treasures; they're not worth anything. What he needs is food and clothing."

"I could warm his feet and give him some grass," said a little bleating voice, as the woolly lamb sat down on the boy's cold blue feet.

"I've got a carrot somewhere," said the ox. "I don't think boys eat grass."

The boy's baby brother had died along with his mother. Almost without thinking he picked up the crying baby and rocked him clumsily. The baby looked up at him, burped loudly, then smiled. Who can resist the smile of a baby? The robber boy smiled back as the little one reached out a pink fist trying to hit his face, chuckling loudly. They made silly noises at each other, both laughing.

Suddenly the donkey nudged him gently and whispered in his ear, "Don't let Brother Francis know that we can speak!" as a shadowy figure came in through the cave opening.

The boy held the baby closer to him protectively, until he saw it was a man in a brown robe, whose arms and hands were held open and wide in a gesture of peace. All the same, he kept up his guard, hunching over the baby to keep him safe, turning his shoulder in anticipation of a blow.

Brother Francis continued to smile at the boy, who said, defensively, "I didn't do nothing wrong!" He felt the baby tapping at his cheek again and rocked him until the little eyes closed in sleep, then laid him gently back in the manger and turned to face the man, raising his arm to shield himself from the expected blow. But Brother Francis was still smiling at him in a very kind way.

"Look, young man," he said, "the treasures you thought you found were worthless, but you can come with me to the priory if you like. There you'll be given food and shelter and the chance to earn an honest living. How about it?"

The robber boy didn't need to be asked twice.

As they left the cave, Brother Francis whispered to him, "The ox and the donkey will have a fine time chewing over tonight's adventures! Oh yes, of course I know about their little chats!"

The robber boy took a last look back at the ox and the donkey, snuffling around the manger. They were reassuringly warm and real, smelling of hay and dung. The lamb was asleep again and the sparrows were still pecking at the straw. The boxes of treasure were quite obviously nothing more than tinsel and paint; how could anyone have mistaken them for real? Nor was there any sign that a flesh and blood baby had ever been there. But the carved doll, wrapped in its swaddling rags, had a beautiful smile on its wooden face.

62

YOU SHALL HAVE A FISHIE
IN A LITTLE DISHIE...

IN RECENT YEARS, with all the problems of Brexit, there has been a renewed interest regarding fish and the sea. From the anxieties of fishing disputes to the spiritual significance of all that moves in the waters, the images of fish and sea creatures, as well as pure new springs and streams, seem to surround us. This story comes from one of the many traditional stories originally collected by the wonderful folklorist and storyteller, Duncan Williamson.

This version was rewritten on a course at Ty Newydd in North Wales by my friend, poet and storyteller Miriam Scott, and myself in June 2013.

The Wounded Seal

Seal of the swift sleek body
darting through the waters
your dark eyes are as deep as oceans
Morning and evening you sing,
basking on ancient rock
Seals, you Selkie people
draw near, join us
Listen to our story.

Once there was a hunter who lived in a small hut on an island, away from the village. He fished and collected seaweed for food, and he caught seals. He would skin the seals with his great hunting knife with the ivory handle, then stretch and cure them. These pelts would then be sold in the cities to make fur coats for the rich. In this way, the hunter earned a lot of money.

One day on the beach, he saw a group of seals basking in the sunshine on a rock. Among them was a great bull seal, the largest he had ever seen. Very carefully, he crept near. Silently, he raised himself up over the edge of the rock and inched nearer until he knew he could plunge the great knife down into the bull seal's heart. But as he raised it, the seal opened its eyes and turned; the knife entered its shoulder instead and man and seal wrestled furiously.

To and fro they rolled, the seal almost pulling him into the sea. Eventually, the hunter broke free and drew back as the seal, with his knife still in its shoulder, dived into the waves and was gone.

The hunter went back to his hut. That night, a stranger came and knocked on the door. He was muffled in a long coat, down to the ground. His hat was pulled right down over his ears, his collar turned up and a scarf was wrapped around the lower part of his face, so it could not be seen.

The stranger shuffled into the hut. "Have you seal skins for sale?" he said, "I want many skins."

"Yes, I have skins," replied the hunter.

"Come with me then to my master. He wants to meet with you and buy your skins," said the strange man. "My master waits at the top of the great cliff. Come."

The hunter was delighted to think he could sell many skins. Collecting a bundle, he followed his visitor, who led the way up to the top of the great cliff over the bay. "Stand near me," said the strange man, drawing him to the edge. The hunter looked straight into the man's face and saw a pair of large, sad, dark eyes under the hat brim in the moonlight. The man suddenly put his strong arms tightly around the hunter, blew a long, strong breath into his mouth, and jumped. Suddenly, the two of them were falling.

Down, down, down they went into the sea. The stranger pulled the hunter faster and faster through the dark waters and under the surface. At the bottom of the sea there was a door and beyond the door a mighty hall, all under the sea. The hall was full of Selkie people, young and old, male and female, weeping and keening in great sorrow.

"My father, the King Seal, is dying," said the stranger, who was now both man and seal. "Do you recognise that knife?"

At the end of the hall, on a stone dais, the hunter saw a great bull seal lying. His eyes were closed and he was near to death. In his shoulder was a great wound, and in it, the hunter recognised the ivory handle of his own knife.

Terrified, he said that indeed, he recognised the seal and his own weapon. "Are you going to kill me?" he asked the stranger.

"No," said the Seal Prince. "Our people are not like you. We do not get angry and vengeful or seek the destruction of others. We want you to draw out the weapon and heal my father, the King. Only the hand that gave the blow can heal the wound."

The hunter came near and, stretching out, he tried to draw out his knife. Twice, he failed; the third time he put out all his strength and the knife came out. The hunter threw it behind him, onto the floor. The wound gaped wide open, enormous. He drew the sides together with his hands and suddenly, the flesh grew together, and there was no more wound. The great King Seal opened his eyes and sat up. He looked like a seal, and he looked like an old man.

Again, the hunter asked in terror, "Are you going to kill me now?" and again the seal people shook their heads and the Seal Prince answered, "No, that is not our way. We bless you for your healing."

Then, the Seal Prince drew the hunter back into his arms, breathed a great breath into his mouth, and took him back, far and fast through the waters. When they reached the shore, the Seal Prince threw him high, high into the air. The hunter found himself on the top of the cliff.

He took the path down the hill, back into his hut, sank down by his fire and sat there a long time, leaving the door open. From then on, he never again killed seals, but lived sparingly on fish and seaweed, collecting shells and flotsam from the beaches to sell.

Many a time afterwards he would stand on the clifftop, looking out over the cold Northern waters, or sit by his fire. He wondered whether he would ever again hear a knock on the door and if so, would he dare go away again with the stranger?

Seal of the swift sleek body
darting through the waters
your dark eyes are as deep as oceans
Morning and evening you sing,
basking on ancient rock
Seals, you Selkie people
draw near, join us
Listen to our story.

63

WINDING DOWN

AT THIS POINT I felt I had written enough of my memoirs, and I thanked all who had helped me by giving me great encouragement for what initially was just to amuse my family and leave a legacy of my life thoughts. I just added a couple more stories.

I have always liked fairy tales where someone – commonly but not invariably a female – comes out of a magic mirror and sets the house to rights before vanishing again. Just what I need.

I idly reflected, one day that – apart from employing a cleaner – what would be the equivalent magic today, including of course the romantic fairy-tale ending? Well, the nearest magic item in most houses is a computer… so here is my contribution.

My thanks also go to my wonderful magical friend, and professional koto musician, Hiroko Edge. A koto, in case you don't know, is a table-sized Japanese harp and when played as exquisitely as she does, is truly magical.

This is not her story of course, but is my friendship offering to her, and to her husband Richard and their daughter Emily. I therefore set it, and told it, originally in various places in Cardiff. Anyway, I like modern fairy stories that also have a sense of place. Just remember it is a STORY and any resemblance to real individuals is a coincidence! Sumire is the Japanese name for Violet.

Sumire

Once upon a time and in a far-off land – like, a week ago last Tuesday in a flat in Victoria Park – a young man was sitting at his computer.

He sighed, and said to his only companion, his old dog Ned, "I wish I had a girlfriend I could love and take care of."

We shall call him Richard, as a nice name for anyone. Richard looked around his terrible untidy bachelor flat, thinking no girl could bear it, but he longed for love and companionship even more, as Ned wagged his tail sympathetically. For a moment he could have sworn that a hint of golden light swept over the keyboard with a faint ripple of electronic music, but after a moment nothing else happened, so he closed down the computer and went to bed.

In the morning, when Richard woke up, to his surprise his computer had turned on by itself, with a swirl of dots moving around the screen invitingly. He sat down and the dots turned into a pattern of violets and the word 'Sumire'.

Richard yawned and finished dressing, then saw the words, 'Invitation – Click Here.' Of course, he knew full well that nobody should ever do this, but somehow he couldn't help clicking on it. The computer then showed 'Access accepted' and closed down.

Shaking his head, Richard set off for his work as a design engineer on the other side of town. But let us stay in the flat and keep an eye on that computer! Sure enough, no sooner had Richard left than it switched itself on again and the screen glowed goldenly. A beautiful young woman in a Japanese kimono stepped out onto the table and scrambled to the floor. She was carrying a small koto and looking around in astonishment. Ned, the dog, came over sniffing suspiciously. This wasn't the old lady who came daily to let him out while Richard was at work; besides, it was far too early. But as he sniffed, his body language changed. Here was a Good person. A

Mega-Good person. A person he already loved and trusted. The girl smiled at him and stroked him behind the ears, looking round in wonderment at where she found herself.

After a little while, she looked at the mess around and started to tidy up. Ned helped her, nudging her to the little kitchen where there were cleaning things, so she started a good clean up too.

After a while she rested and played the little koto, making such beautiful music that the birds came to the window and the mice stirred in the wainscoting. At the sound of the door opening, however, the girl climbed hastily back into the computer, which turned off again.

Of course, Richard was surprised when he came home to find everything a lot tidier and cleaner, but assumed it was the old lady upstairs who kindly let Ned out each day and for whom he shopped and gardened in return. Every day after this, when he was at work, the computer would switch on and the girl with the koto would come out, clear up, play her music to Ned, cook a delicious little meal and vanish again into the screen. She always appeared with a swirling cloud of violets, so let's call her 'Sumire'. She also spent time looking at the photos on the mantelpiece and learned that the young man was called Richard and the dog called Ned.

Well, after a few days Richard spoke to the old lady upstairs about it. To his surprise, she denied having anything to do with it, apart from having noticed that the flat was much improved and Ned seemed happier. She also mentioned having sometimes thought she heard beautiful harp music coming up to her part of the house, but assumed it was the radio. So, a few days later, Richard took a day off work and hid in the communal hall of the house till he heard the sweetest music imaginable coming from his flat. He burst in and saw the beautiful girl in a kimono playing a koto, with Ned looking up at her adoringly. He cried out in astonishment and Sumire instantly jumped onto the table and vanished into the computer, which went dead. The koto was left on the table and he sat a long time, looking at it and stroking Ned.

Richard stayed awake all night, enchanted by what he had seen but desolated at having lost her so suddenly. He took time off work and for days searched for the lost beautiful girl all over town. Ever practical, he even advertised in the *Evening Echo*, the *Western Mail*, the *Barry Gazette*, the *Cardiff Freepost*, and the *Penarth Times* and searched every street around for miles.

Meanwhile, just across the other side of Victoria Park, a Japanese girl called – you've guessed it! Sumire – was living in a little bedsit and trying to make a living by waitressing most of the day and playing the koto till late every evening, wherever she could. She was so tired that she often slept in late till it was time to rush out to work. She had suddenly started to dream that she was in an unknown flat somewhere, cleaning, tidying and cooking, petting the dog, and falling in love with the photograph of the young man on the mantelpiece.

Richard had nearly given up one day, but Ned seemed to be insisting on a walk, unusually for him, so Richard sighed and took him over the road to the park. The dog picked up the koto and seemed to be nudging him with it, so Richard took it with them, even though he had all but given up on the search for its owner. He slumped down in the little pavilion by the lake.

Sumire had been searching too, but with no success, as of course she had never seen the outside of the mysterious flat. She had given up too, but as she approached the lake, she suddenly saw Ned. He saw her too and barking excitedly he ran to her, nuzzling her hands, while she cried out in joy. Hearing this, Richard came out from the pavilion and ran towards her holding out the koto.

They sat and talked for ages. They could not make any sense of what had happened, but they enjoyed talking and being together so much that they kept on meeting every day. The more they chatted and learned about each other, the closer they became and the less they remembered the mysteries of their first encounter. Sumire's career with the koto suddenly took off and Richard got promoted at work – everything was blossoming for the two young lovers. Finally, they decided to get married and arrangements were made with both families. Richard's parents came from England and Sumire arranged to bring hers over from Japan. It was a wonderful wedding for all to share!

Now, of course, there never are – nor are ever needed – explanations in a fairy tale. However, it may be interesting to note the following. Sumire's parents loved their only daughter, the koto player, so much that they unselfishly helped her to follow her dreams to Wales, even though they longed for her presence and missed her every day. Both of them worked in a computer factory, her mother supervising the robots that made the computers, her father packing and sending them out.

Thoughts are a form of electrical energy and love is the most powerful energy in the world. Might it not be possible that the generous love of two parents would be enough to trigger a strange fault in a computer one day, and also see that it somehow ended up in Wales, a land full of love and music? Only you can decide that one.

64

THE BLESSINGS OF
NON-COMMUNICATION

THROUGH THE HALF-OPEN DOOR of the front room, a little spatter of conversation flowed out to the old lady, tiptoeing past.

"Did you manage to…." "I said to her, pardon me but…."

The voices spilled out with the teatime sunshine. The old lady studied the patterns it created on the liver-coloured tiles by the front door. There would be no escape that way. She drew back, picking at her lips with a dry grey finger. Then she inched slowly back along the wall, her bedroom slippers shuffling along the floor. The voices stopped and the old lady froze, not breathing until they started again, covering the creak of the kitchen door.

Out at the back, round by the tradesman's, she reached the road under cover of the fig tree and paused, hidden from the house by the big board with its faded lettering – 'Honeysuckle Lodge. Rest Home for the Elderly.'

Freedom! The old lady moved off down the street, fear of capture forgotten, smile wrinkles showing her triumph. Several corners later and pleasantly lost, she looked up at a concrete block of flats. Flats were usually good, no one knew who you were or cared where you had come from. On the other hand, these looked like the sort that held harassed mothers and little children – no chance of a cup of tea there. Further down, the character of the street changed and there was a row of houses, some obviously with apartments or bedsits. If you struck lucky, there would be biscuits or even cake, but there was always the risk someone would mention the Welfare.

Greed, caution and curiosity rose, struggled, and reached a compromise. She crossed over and trod quietly up the pathway of the shabbiest house. Seen from close up, it was unattractive. The old lady tut-tutted behind her dentures and picked blisters of black paint from the door, too absorbed to notice a shadow falling across the peeling paint.

"You want someone?" a voice said, behind her.

The girl who had spoken dropped a blue laundry bag and a pile of shopping and fumbled for a key. Trickles of sweat ran down her skin, mingling with the clots of mascara and the magenta lipstick. She looked very young and very, very pregnant.

"Ground floor's at work. First floor does nights, he'll be sleeping. Collecting, are you?"

The old lady mumbled, smiled and shook her head. "Just a glass of water," she said pathetically.

The girl's hard expression softened as she found the key. "Come up if you can manage the stairs," she said, manoeuvring body and bags through the entrance.

Once up in the small stuffy room, the old lady sat unasked on the only easy chair. The girl threw the blue bag into a corner, filled a kettle at the washbasin, and put it on a gas ring in a frowsy alcove. The room smelt of food and dust and faintly of cat, but the girl was now smiling as she put out mugs and a milk bottle.

"Would you like a cup of tea? You're the only visitor I've had. Except my social worker and I don't count her. My name's Ceridwen."

There was a Welsh lilt in the confiding voice and she suddenly seemed much younger in spite of the bulging body and the overpainted face.

The old lady cleared her throat with a rustle no louder than a cockroach over linoleum. "That's right, dear," she said. "Milk and two sugars." Her watery eyes, dark as wet pebbles, flickered expertly from the wardrobe to the shelves under the gas ring and retired, disappointed. No sign of a biscuit tin.

"What's your name?" This time the girl expected an answer. Really waited for one.

"Florence... Florence... White. They call me Flossie, but I prefer Flo." The old lady smiled after a long moment of thought. Really, it was too bad to be expected to remember things like that. However, her hope of avoiding questions was realised, and her reward swift. Ceridwen had decided that this was a social call and she was brightening by the minute. She pulled a packet of biscuits from the shopping bag and a loaf and butter appeared from a cardboard box. She busied herself in a pleasant little clatter of preparations.

"My social worker's called Mrs Williams. She's a right cow. You'd think it would help, her being Welsh and all, but it doesn't. You can see I've been a naughty girl, can't you?"

The tone was saucy, but the girl looked up anxiously at her companion. At the mention of a social worker, Flo had put on one of her special expressions – the one reserved for contacts with 'the Welfare,' a mixture of imbecile blankness and guile. It apparently reassured the girl.
"I can see you're broadminded. Not like some. What I say is, why should you get married just because there's a little mistake on the way? The way some men talk you'd think that's all a girl should want."

Ceridwen made angry jabs at the kettle and mugs as she made the tea and then laughed. Flo cupped her hands around the mug and sighed into it, relishing the warm steam.

"Yes, some men fancy themselves no end they do. A girl's got to look after herself. It's all worked out, though. I'm going into a special home to have the baby. In a couple of weeks, that is. I'll be out of this crummy room anyway. Then afterwards, I'll have the baby adopted and... er... go back to work." Her voice faltered slightly.

"Mrs Williams been ever so helpful, I'll say that for her. She found me this place in the mother and baby home. Religious place it is I think – nuns or something. She did ask about my family, nosy old thing. It's not her business! – I'm overage. I wouldn't go back to that dreary little village no matter what. The idea! I can look after meself!"

She seemed to expect a response. Flo nodded her head up and down. The girl filled the mugs again and pushed over the biscuits. Flo took two and dipped them in her tea with anxious care, sighing deeply again.

"You're ever so nice to talk to," said the girl, wistfully. "A bit like me mam. I suppose I might go down and see her when... after it's all over. Just for a visit. It'd kill her to know about the baby – ever so strict me mam is. They said I was too far on for an abortion, so it's got to be adoption."

Flo furtively took the last two pieces of bread and butter. Her expression was one of absorbed attention. Contented wrinkles ran up to her eyes as she dipped the bread into her tea and sucked it through the gap in her ancient dentures.

Her ever-gnawing hunger for once appeased, she gazed around the room with a child's greedy interest. Her eyes absorbed, with minutest detail, the exact pattern of biscuit-coloured cracks on the surface of the basin, the pits like bullet holes in the lino, the coffee-coloured splash on the faded wallpaper. Then her eyes passed on and the images were immediately lost, unrecorded and unremembered. Confused inner memories took their place. Long forgotten vistas of dreary rooms like this one. Places of lost hope, of lost battles – against cockroaches, against marauding cats, against age, and against hope itself.

"Not very nice, is it?" said the girl, unwillingly following her gaze. "It was cheap, see? When I lost me job... well – not sacked; I wouldn't want you to think that, but it's not good standing too much. Me feet swelled and they said at the clinic 'better give it up' – it was the nurse that said that. Ever so nice she was. Well, they try to understand but it's hard to manage. I hadn't the stamps, see? But I always say I'll be alright afterwards. I'll get ever such a nice place when... when I go back to work... after the... when I go back..."

Her voice trailed away. It was as if great pits appeared in the air around her, gaping crevasses that should have been filled with quick comforting voices – 'You'll be alright. We'll find you a nice place to go. You can have the baby adopted. Don't worry. Give up work. Take these tablets. Sign these papers. It's all for the best. You'll be fine.'

A piece of biscuit was stuck behind Flo's dentures. She didn't like the feeling of the black pits either. The unpleasant sensation of them remained in a mind that had lost the knack of papering them over with easy phrases. She explored the piece of biscuit with a sore pink tongue. Of all things, people trying to make you remember the past were worst.

"Don't want to go back," she said eventually in a little croak.

The girl stared at her. The minutes lengthened the silence that became frightening in its emptiness, until the air, splintered, cracked in fissures of feeling around them.

"Go back! Go back! – I can't go back… You don't understand. Oh, I wish I could. Me mam would kill me. Oh God! I'd give anything to go home… Oh God, I wish I'd never been born."

The girl put her arms on the table. Suddenly defenceless, she was crying. The blobby makeup smeared on her plump arms, the great belly heaving with sobs and sympathetic blows from the protesting life within it.

"You don't know. Nobody knows. I told me mam I was getting married. I told her we couldn't come down because he was working long hours building up his own business. It was all lies. I couldn't tell her he walked out on me, leaving me like this. He never cared at all. He left me when I was five months g…gone!"

The girl was suddenly bellowing. Storms of tears were coursing down her cheeks, rivulets of tears squeezing out of fat eyelids, oceans of tears soaking the dirty blue smock and threatening to wash mugs, plates, rickety table, girl and old woman out, out, down a fresh dancing green river to the furthest valleys of Wales.

The old woman stayed put, like a bundle of twigs caught in the eddies. She worked her jaws once or twice. The biscuit crumb gone, the sore place seemed less tender and the emptiness in her belly was satisfied.

"Ah," she said. Ceridwen was snuffling now, collapsed on her knees by the table, the storm spent. "Oh God, if I could only go home. Oh, I know I said I want the baby adopted, but I don't. Oh, if only me mam would help me, she wouldn't let them take me baby away. I want me mam. I want to go home," she cried.

Now that she was more comfortable inside, Flo was paying attention again. Home? Time to go home. She wanted the toilet and she was suddenly, pathetically tired. She wanted to be back at Honeysuckle Lodge being scolded by Nurse Dobson and Matron. 'Naughty Flossie,' they would say, 'Naughty girl, no supper for such a naughty girl' and Nurse Brown would bring her hot milk and a sandwich and brush her hair.

"Time to go home," said Flo firmly and then repeated it even more loudly, rising tremulously to her feet, leaning over the kneeling girl and supporting herself on the table. "Time To Go Home!"

To the girl, looking up at her through tears and mascara, she loomed like an ancient prophetess. "You mean it?" she said. "Just like that? Just go home? It's too much. How could I face them all, I couldn't! Could I?" She wiped her face on her dirty smock, peering up at the sibylline figure, implacable, unmoving, who said no word more than those which rang in her mind. 'Go Home!' the oracle had said, 'Time to go Home!'

Having made her own decision to go, Flo's attention was no longer on the girl. A little stiff from sitting, she leant forward on the table for a few more moments, then straightened herself. The movement seemed to release Ceridwen into obedience.

"I must go home, mustn't I?" she said. "It's the only way? I don't care what they all think. I must go tonight, now, on the bus, before I get too scared to face me mam. Oh! I've been such a fool! Surely mam will understand? Oh! I want to go home SO much! Me mam'll kill me but it'll be worth it. How could I have been such a fool?"

Ceridwen was up and darting around the room with soft exclamations, finding her purse and a coach timetable, pulling out a little case and a few things, but when Flo started down the stairs she ran after her and helped her down. "Oh, I do love you. Thank you a million times! No one understood like you, or gave me such good advice, ever. I shall never forget all you've said to me, and I – we – will never forget you."

Flo walked back uncertainly in the early dusk. A car was coming slowly up the street. A panda car. Somehow, she was suddenly nearly in the gutter, a pathetic old lady collapsing onto the hard cruel kerbstones. In the car, she snuggled down pleasantly. The young policeman was talking into the car radio.

"By the way – we've found the old girl from the Care Home. Taking her straight back there as usual."

Then back at Honeysuckle Lodge. Familiar comforting scolding voices:

"There you are, Flossie!" "Hi Matron, Flossie's back! "Naughty girls don't get any supper!" "I'll help you to bed." "Naughty Flossie, what sort of sandwich would you like?"

Flo sighed gustily and surrendered herself up, deeply content. It had been a very good afternoon.

Elinor Kapp, 1984

65

THE OLD WOMAN WHO WAS LONELY

Let me share with you an uplifting original fairy story from my book, *Tales from Turnaround Cottage:*

* * *

ONCE, THERE WAS an old woman who was very lonely. "Oh, if only I had a husband who I could care for and who would care for me," she sighed every day. "I feel so alone!" Indeed there came a day when the loneliness swept over her so strongly that she cried out aloud: "I don't care who or what he might be; I would marry him, whoever asked me!"

Three nights later there was a knock on the door. A tall man stood there, face and body masked by swirling grey and white clothing, or was it mist?

"I am the husband you have asked for," he said. "Will you agree to a betrothal, a sure promise of marriage?"

She started to protest that she didn't know who he was, but he cut her short. "My name is Death," he said, "but you agreed to marry anyone who was sent to you, and I will take you with me to my castle for the wedding itself."

Well, the old woman was so lonely that she said she would marry him, but asked for more time. Death agreed and told her to be ready for his next visit. She looked around at the bareness of her cottage and started to make things for a dowry. She made clothes for herself, serviceable and plain. She made warm things for a husband who would never wear them and toys for children she would never have.

After a year and a day, there was a knock on the door, and there was Death again.

"I'm not ready," she protested. "Look at all the things that aren't finished!" So Death agreed and went away again.

After a year and a day, he was back, but once more she protested she was not ready and he went away again.

The third time, after a year and a day, she had finished all she could think of to make, and she was tired. She rested until the knock came on the door, and then let Death in. "What shall I do with all the things I've made?" she asked him. "Leave them," he said. "You won't be coming back here."

"What about locking the door?" she asked. Death shook his head and she wrote a little note and put it on the table, that anyone who came should take what they wanted. Leaving the door open, she went out with him to where a great grey horse waited.

Death swung her up before him and rode away so fast that in an instant, it seemed, they had left the familiar fields and farms behind and were riding deeper and deeper into a dark forest. Branches whipped her face and body. She cried out and tried to escape, but he held her fast. The twigs whipped her so hard she could feel the blood running down her face and body.

It seemed to go on forever, but suddenly, they were free of the forest and running across a dazzling desert. The sun shone on the white sand pitilessly, even though she tried to close her eyes against the light. Death suddenly swerved and bent her first one way and then the other. She cried out again, then realised that he was avoiding arrows, shot at them from every direction. She could hear them hissing like snakes, as they went past, occasionally grazing her, so that again she felt the blood running down her skin and soaking her clothes.

Suddenly the grey horse stopped and reared. They had come to the shore of a wide and restless sea, stretching to the horizon. Death held her closer and the horse waded in, deeper and deeper until it was swimming and she was almost submerged and drowning. The saltwater soaked her clothes and washed away the blood, but oh how it stung in her myriad cuts and bruises!

At last, she felt the horse climbing onto sure ground and opened her eyes. They were in front of a towering castle. She saw high walls, turrets and windows, gleaming in the morning sunlight as golden as the dawn itself.

"This is my home," said Death, lifting her off the grey horse, and leading her up a magnificent staircase into a great hall.

Ahead, the old woman saw a figure coming towards her as if to welcome her. It was a woman, young and beautiful, with skin as pearly as dew, clothed in rainbow colours of the finest fabric.
She stretched out her arms and smiled and so did the woman, but when she moved forward, her fingers met glass and she realised that it was a mirror.

"That can't be me!" cried the woman. "She is young and beautiful, not old and battered!"

She looked down at her arms and body, and touched her cheeks, for of course, we can never see our own faces. Sure enough, all the blood and signs of age had been washed away. She appeared to have soft young skin and was dressed in a rainbow of beautiful colours.

She looked up again, amazed, but now recognising her own reflection. The mirror dissolved away and she could see shallow steps leading to a great throne. So much golden light came from the figure on the throne, that she could not have described it in any way except that her heart was filled with awe and love.

"I am the High King of all the Universe," said the man on the throne. "I heard your plea, and I sent for you to be my Bride. You consented, but I need to hear it again from your own lips, my beloved one."

When she began to stammer in surprise and shock, the King spoke again. "A King cannot go out to fetch his bride; he has to send a proxy who will arrange the betrothal and bring her to him." He turned his golden look towards Death. "I sent you, my servant, to bring her to me," he said. "Surely you explained it all, and exactly who she was marrying?"

Death shuffled his feet and looked extremely sheepish. "Well… not exactly, Sire," he said. Then added defensively. "It's a bit of a boring job you know, riding around all the time, getting shot at and never having anyone of my own. Perhaps I wasn't quite as open about it all as I should have been!"

And the woman who had once been old, understood at last that she was the Bride of the Golden King, Chatelaine of the Castle and most of all, was totally loved and no longer lonely. Reaching up on tiptoes she pulled Death down to her and kissed his cheek. She said to him, "Indeed you told me everything I needed to know, and you brought me here safely, which is all that matters. Thank you!"

Death turned and stumped off down the steps. He rubbed his cheek thoughtfully for a moment, then went off to look after his horse, smiling to himself for once.

The woman turned back to the Golden King, who held out his arms to her, laughing. She ran up the steps to him and was enfolded in the golden mist, forever with her Beloved.

66

MY LINK WITH ARMENIA

"WOULD YOU LIKE TO GO TO ARMENIA** and help set up a children's mental health service?" said the unknown man on the telephone. "YES!" I yelped in astonishment. My goodness! I had developed a slightly vague idea of planning forward to retirement, a few years off, by visiting a country where I could get to know people, then be in a position to offer something helpful on stopping paid work. This all took place in 1993. As soon as I came off the phone I ran for the atlas, to find out where on earth Armenia was – knowing only vaguely that it was 'somewhere there', 'out east'. This was confirmed, with a somewhat more exact location. I always knew my indifference to geography classes could prove embarrassing one day!

I recalled the only other things I knew. Of course, I remembered about the catastrophic earthquake, five years earlier in December 1988, because like most people I contributed to the Armenian Aid appeal. I knew that they were a remarkable and ancient civilisation, rich in artistry, and were the first Christian State in the world, which had led, ultimately, to terrible genocide by the Ottomans during WW1, though denied by some to this day.

I found when I went there, that these small bits of knowledge were almost enough on their own, being the most important to the wonderfully hospitable and generous Armenians I was soon to meet. I am eternally grateful to them, to CAFOD, and to Patrick and Jerome – the 'team' mentioned, for a series of visits which were a very life-enhancing privilege over several years.

How did this come about? I had tried one or two big charities who had no interest in me, but one passed on the name of a small charity which existed in order to 'place' people like me. I had to go to London for an interview and they didn't seem to have anything to suggest, but they put me on their books and the outcome was this one call from Patrick. He went on to tell me that he was a Mental Health Nurse and was due to go out to Armenia soon as part of a very small team, tasked with providing a western style mental health facility for children and families, which was being funded by CAFOD. My excited response must have slightly startled him, but we seemed to get on well and he arranged to meet and confirm [or not] my membership of the team.

I must have passed, because the two CAFOD leaders, Jerome and Patrick, welcomed me and we went over for three hectic and amazing weeks, to discuss building, staffing and teaching a Child Psychiatric Service. I mention it here because we went back six times in all, over the next few years and I was also able to take a small team of a few of our Nurses, another Doctor and an Occupational Therapist. Our own clinical team, based in Caerleon, were fascinated and wanted to join in after my first visit. Our local Health Board were good enough to support this officially, so we could all take the visits out of our paid time, with a great deal of local interest and support in Gwent regarding this very different culture. There was virtually no specialisation for children's mental health problems in Armenia and the Russian-based service overall for mental health was very different from our own.

That first visit in particular was life changing in its insights to another way of life. Armenia was only recovering slowly after the earthquake and was still, of course, owned by Russia. We three foreigners were put up in a nice little flat but there was very seldom electricity or water. On the odd occasion that both came on at the same time for a few minutes, we did a sort of war dance round the flat and one lucky person got to have a bath in three inches of water. Just like my memories of wartime Britain!

On the other hand, food was not a problem. The Armenians are noted for their generous hospitality. Wherever we went – and however poor the locals were – we would be offered a meal, all the friends and neighbours excitedly joining us to provide a feast of special delicacies. I had to learn two lessons in manners though. It was not 'done' to clean your plate of all food – if you did so it was a signal you wanted more and had to accept another helping. It was a fine art to judge exactly how much to leave, after a childhood in which completely cleaning your plate was drummed into you.

Similarly, at home I would of course always note if someone could not reach a dish of food and helpfully pass it to them. I was fairly soon told by my shocked hostess that it was absolutely taboo for a woman to offer any food to a man – indeed tantamount to a proposal of marriage. I learned fairly quickly, but I daresay I'm still slightly engaged to a lot of Armenian men!

Of course our work was the important thing and we were made very welcome by the Professor of Psychiatry, Prof Danielian and his whole team, which included his son, Armen. We were able to bring the latter and a very good woman doctor over for a few months, to give them some extra training. We were also allowed, with translators of course, to interview a number of child patients and families. The normal interviews there were very formal and I remember that my first case, when I got down on the floor and played with a small child at his level, induced something of a sensation. "She sat on the floor and the children came to her!" said the astonished onlookers at my [routine] approach to a small, shy child.

We learnt a great deal too but since my heart operation I have some trouble remembering details. At present I do not think I could give justice to the rich and life-enhancing experience of those trips, but I had to include at least this mention – and my gratitude to CAFOD, to my colleagues and to the many friends I made in those years, now dispersed around the world.

67

A HOLIDAY IN FLORIDA
AND THE BAHAMAS

A TRUE STORY

O NE DAY, well into my retirement, I got one of those pop-
up birthday cards on the web trying to sell you something.
In this case a cheap holiday in Florida for up to 4 people at a
ridiculously low price. I will never again scorn those simple souls
who succumb to such things because I now understand that all of
us can be vulnerable to seduction in certain circumstances. If they
send out enough free email cards, millions say, they are sure to
get responses. I was vulnerable because I had been hoping to go
to a conference in Armenia in the autumn but hadn't been able to
book because of an NHS legal case for which I had been
subpoenaed. I didn't want the NHS to settle a most unreasonable
claim but I desperately wanted to be able to go and speak at the
conference and see all my old friends. It wasn't up to me to solve
the dilemma, fortunately, and the day of my birthday I heard the
unreasonable complaints had been withdrawn, so I was able to
rush out to book for Armenia – but that's another story.

So on that day when I came home, rejoicing I was a sucker for the
idea of a cheap holiday, for any time in the next year. It just
chimed in with my sense of adventure. I like traveling. I get very
excited at the thought of it and make plans and have ideas for way
ahead. The nearer the time gets the more my anxiety levels rise. I
remember that I hate travelling. I hate it more and more the nearer
the time gets. I know I will lose my tickets and my passport and
my sanity before I even get to the airport. The year I went to

Kashmir I completely forgot about getting a visa until 3 days before my travel date. I had to take a day off work, go to London and queue round the block for three hours to get it, back to Cardiff, pack and leave on the coach in the early hours of next morning. Still – I made it, and always had a wonderful time when I actually got away.

So – having spoken at length to a lovely person in the Florida agency on a free call I paid for the two-week holiday, with a week in Orlando, two nights in Fort Lauderdale and three days in the Bahamas.

I had plenty of time afterwards to rue the day and believe it was a scam, or at least something I could only regret having been fool enough to get drawn into. The thought at the back of my mind, of giving it as a present to Rupert or Amanda and their families, were quickly dashed. My friends were either unavailable or insolvent. I kept putting this embarrassing mistake to the back of my mind until I suddenly realised I would either have to go on my own or lose the money.

That really concentrates the mind. I am far too mean to waste so much cash. I decided that (a) I would go on my own and (b) I would really enjoy myself. These things are all in the mind. Rather to my surprise this attempt at positive thinking worked a treat. I had a very good time. As usual I took too much luggage but I managed to ditch quite a lot of it and fill up with lovely cheap children's clothes for my new grandson.

I had a really fun time in Florida – rather to my surprise. Sunny tropical beaches and theme parks aren't usually my scene, but I very much enjoyed seeing Sea World, MGM Studios, and Disney's Magic Kingdom and Epcot. I couldn't think of Orlando as a real place though – it's like a weird film, very plastic.

The accommodation was cheap, but very nice because it was time-share flats in lovely parkland. Of course, you had an obligatory hard-sell hour or two, but once that was over you could just enjoy it.

I couldn't take up the offer of a free hire car because no way could I face finding my way in a strange country, by myself, in the car, and driving on the wrong side of the road – I still get lost in Cardiff after over 30 years. The price of taxis was a real rip-off, and public buses were poor. However, I liked the way people were always so polite and friendly. I love being called 'Ma'am' – like the Queen – and wished a nice day! Also, everyone tidied up their litter and had real civic and national pride, most unlike home.

I loved the Bahamas too, though two days were probably enough. I got to be kissed by a dolphin, something I've always wanted [and I have the photo to prove it]. Also, a beach party with plenty of free rum punch and dancing.

I talked to lots of people and never felt lonely or lost, but I hardly had any deeper or more meaningful contacts with anyone. I probably wouldn't do anything quite like this again, but can see how I could construct really good holidays with solo travelling, particularly to parts of the world where I have friends, combined with organised tours of two or three days at a time when there to take advantage of cheap easy travel. I also loved the way, in America, I seemed to be treated better, not worse, as a single woman traveller – the opposite of what happens in Europe and the UK.

As a slight bonus, and in repentance for having thought it was a scam, I asked in Thomas Cook, when I was booking a different trip, how much my American holiday would have cost if I had booked it through them. It was considerably more than I had paid in all, even allowing for all the clothes I bought in America.

68

RESURRECTION EXPERIENCE

A PROSE POEM

THIS IS A SHORT but vivid piece I wrote some years ago. It is in one way specific to my experience, as a woman who lost a child, but that in itself is – sadly – not uncommon. It has helped me identify with a 'real' Mary, Mother of our Lord, in her anguish, not a sanitised and saccharine version.

This is the circumstance in which I experienced this vision – an experience of the whole body not just in the mind's eye. I was up in London years ago for some meeting, not very important. I stayed in a cheap hotel on my own. In the evening I sat and said some prayers and suddenly felt impelled – or perhaps very gently invited would be a better way of putting it – to stand up and spread my arms out like a crucifix.

As soon as I did so I experienced my arms being violently and cruelly wrenched back, even though I also knew and could see that they were in fact still spread out, untouched. Still, it was extremely painful and I cried out through clenched teeth as I experienced being pulled along, wrenching the arm sockets, a breaking of bones and tearing of ligaments, then thrown down and dragged further, before being forced upright again. Of course, although the pain was real and strong it was not anything like as much as in 'reality', as I would probably have become unconscious quickly.

It stopped as suddenly and I knew that my outspread arms were embracing the whole world and everything and everyone who was in it. Crucifixion, Resurrection and an outward Embracing of the world through love, all at the same time.

Released from the vision after a few more minutes I retired to bed to write down what had happened, as I felt somehow asked to do. I was also exhausted. I wrote the following words straight away that same evening, tucked up in bed high up in a strange little hotel room.

I changed very little even then, but put it away and am sharing it now, with this little background explanation, because it is the right time to do so. Incidentally, when on my own in prayer since then I quite often stretch out my arms in a crucifix gesture and remember – but not re-experience – that I am embracing the world.

I have changed nothing of the original piece, which I regard as a 'Prose Poem' if we need a genre for it:

We Start from the Resurrection
We start from the Resurrection. Every time.
Put the crucifixion behind you; it has gone.
The passions, the pains, the burnings, the angry crowds, the rapes, the murders.
Open or secret; the tortures and deaths of all the innocents and of all the guilty parties too.

The coarse world of matter has spited its worst. And lost.
Your arms are opened wide. Open to be tied, pierced, bent, wrenched, forced back, broken afresh,
– as you make of yourself a crossing place of choice for others.
You are there to protect the children; to hold back the surge of hatred that chooses to destroy.
You are there to welcome the younger child home, to offer the older son all that you have.
You are there to welcome your lover, your beloved, the apple of your eye and the joy of your life.
With your whole heart.

Maybe you will curve the whole world into your embrace;
the earth and all that in it lies.
You are given this Resurrection choice by free gift,
undeserved and yet deeply deserved
because you are one of the Blessed who mourn.
You too lost your son and it is given to you to understand,
for a moment, the grief of Mary and the Heart of God.

69

Memory of my dear husband
Professor Ken Rawnsley CBE

I COULD NOT FEEL IT RIGHT to end my memoirs without at least a little mention of Ken, but he was an intensely private man and therefore, even so many years after his death, it seemed better to stay with just a few words from others. Anyone interested can find an excellent article about Ken's life and work in Wikipedia. I add here a loving memorial address from our dear friend, the Rev Julie Hopkins.

His funeral took place at The City Church. Windsor Road, Cardiff, on 10th April, 1992. The church was packed to overflowing, as indeed was a Memorial Service held in London, six months later, by the Royal College of Psychiatrists.

FUNERAL ADDRESS for KEN RAWNSLEY C.B.E

By the Rev Dr Julie Hopkins, Theologian.
The Free University, Amsterdam.

The Address - Today we are here together as family, friends and colleagues to celebrate the life of Ken Rawnsley and to finally relinquish his presence with us into the unfathomable presence of God. We can no longer travel with him on the journey of life upon the earth, but we can remember and pray and hope – and these are not negligible aspects of our relationship with him. Memory and vision are essential and very practical dimensions of human consciousness and bondedness. So too, communication, love and the sacred spaces in the depths of our souls endure and these are far from fleeting phantasms, our lives are more than a stage for fools. Sometimes we feel that this is so and in our anger and despair shout defiance at the unfeeling gods on high. But in lucid moments of insight we touch a deeper bedrock of reality. If this is a cosmic dance, then it is indeed the dance of creation and connectedness, the pattern and forms, a sharing in the beauty and love of God in whom we live and move and have our being. And the power that we touch and is released between us as lovers, family, friends, doctor with patient is not purely an effort of our own will, its source is the same power that motors and sustains the living universe.

I have the privilege today of talking about Ken. Naturally I can only speak from my own experience of him as a friend over the last 15 years. It is hard for me to separate the man from my subjective experience of him because he deeply influenced my life and, indeed that is true for all of us here. So it is that individuals shape human history and the being of one touches the becoming of another in a never-ending spider's web of relationships that constitute and sustain human existence. My way of seeing Ken is influenced not only by my character and personal story but from my work as a pastor, minister and theologian. Therefore, in the context of this act of worship, in the presence of God, I will talk about Ken as a moral and religious man.

Ken Rawnsley, as we all proudly know, reached the pinnacles of his profession, influencing fundamentally the methodologies and practice of psychiatry, not only in Welsh hospitals, but through his work as Dean and later President of the Royal College of Psychiatrists; he exercised authority in the fields of national government policy and international research and standards of excellence.

The qualities of character usually associated in the public mind with such powerful and successful men are generally negative. It is generally assumed that they are motivated by aggressive ambition; their behaviour is dominating, even obsessional, intolerant, manipulative, dangerously charismatic and they have an

328

overweening sense of self pride, a self-righteous and intellectual bigotry. Ken had none of these negative qualities; in contrast he is one of the few men I have ever met who had no hang-ups about power and whose integrity was as clear as crystal.

He was simply himself, a careful and open-minded, empirically based scientist, intellectually motivated to understand the life of the mind but also committed to effective intervention of mental illness for the benefit of his patients. Systems, structures, institutions and commissions should be cherished and served to the extent that they could improve medical research and practice, nothing more and nothing less. So this professor and first-class administrator was first and foremost always available for his patients and students. He was a good listener, patient, reflective, wise, tough-minded but generous of spirit, a healer and a teacher. And above all he had a quite remarkable respect for others irrespective of social standing or mental state of health.

Ken has won the highest accolades, receiving the CBE from her Majesty the Queen, but I can assure you, for I have observed it many times, the attention and respect with which he would talk and listen with an unhappy black teenager, a demented old woman or a psychopath serving life imprisonment was not more or less than that which he exhibited at the Royal Garden party. Ken's power lay precisely in this fact, that he had no pretensions, he knew his own strengths and weaknesses, accepted them and accepted them in others. He was a true lover of humanity, even its shadow side. The native honesty, open-heartedness and wisdom of the man was his only power and people respected and loved him for it.

70

MY MOST RECENT VISION

RELATING AGAIN TO MY BELOVED LOST CHILD, ANDREW WALTER TUDWAY, ON JUNE 1ST 2020

WE WERE STILL in the pandemic lockdown and I had been troubled by deepening depression in a friend's texts and had been praying for him frequently, then enlarging it to all who are struggling in the present circumstances – praying for all in conflict or danger, and all sick people – including indeed myself.

I used a method I felt I had been 'taught' just the day before – to have soft, gentle music in the background precisely to distract my mind. That part of it which is already 'loose' to suffering and memories, fantasy and horror, needs to be occupied so that it cannot throw up distressing, even dangerous images for me. This has only become a problem in old age, when it feels that the protective barriers I once had are loosened. During this time, when I was deep in meditation, but completely aware of my surroundings and not dreaming, I suddenly found that I was in a field, in an unknown country, yet known to me. It was the field where I last saw the vision of my beautiful lost child, Andrew.

I stood looking up the hill and saw two people coming down together. As they came closer, I recognised my parents, as I had so often seen them, walking together as one, talking to each other. I saw that my father was carrying a toddler, held close in his arms. The child's face was buried in my father's neck but I knew instantly it was my Andrew, as the 20-month-old he had been when he died.

This could not be in any way a memory – Andrew as a toddler had never been with my parents. My father had only ever held him a few times in the first month after his birth in 1966, as he and my mother died just after that. In this wonderful inner vision, my father reached out to pass the child to me as I reached out my arms to him but – as children do – he clung on, staying where he was. My mother, laughing, gently detached him and passed him over to my waiting arms. As my mother turned Andrew around, he saw, heard, smelt me. A smile broke out and he clutched me so tightly I could hardly breathe, wrapping his arms and legs, tightly, tightly, round my body and snuggling deep into my neck. We stayed like that for a long moment, outside time. Then I was back, in my chair, as the music gently flowed to an end. I opened my eyes to the sitting room, filled with a deep, continuing happiness and peace.

* * *

These memories and poetic ways of expressing myself can maybe show how we can honour them and help ourselves by our resilience after the death of that particular loved one. It seems like a kind of resurrection for them, as well as for oneself if after a period of grief and mourning, one is able to live again and accept happiness and new relationships, of whatever kind. It is a recognition that the lost one's love has immeasurably enhanced and enriched our own capacity for love and for kindness to others. This should be seen as a compliment to the deceased, a good legacy and not in any way as a betrayal.

So, just as my life after Andrew's loss was immeasurably fulfilled by the marriage to Ken and to our wonderful children, Rupert and Amanda, I know that Ken would have wanted me to continue to be happy in life, how best I could, in his honour after his untimely death. Certainly, I could not be more proud of my children, who coped with the early loss of their beloved father. They have also been wonderfully supportive of what may sometimes seem to them to be their wayward and eccentric mother!

71

HELLO, GOODBYE!

I PUT OUT THESE MEMOIRS as a Blog, between September 2019 and February 2021 and then stopped, having added a lot of my poems and stories, but not really wanting to write more about my family and the many, many years of happy and productive life I have had – at least, not just at present.

My two children, Rupert and Amanda are the best children I could have wished for. Both approaching middle life now, I feel it would be to invade their privacy to write about them in detail – that is for them and their circle to do. I have put down a few affectionate memories, particularly for Amanda, who was only 14 when she lost her father, my wonderful husband, Ken Rawnsley. Although Rupert at 19 remembers more and was a true support to me at that sad time, has had to manage without a father since barely adulthood, with all that means.

I am sad to stop writing in many ways and I am grateful from the depth of my heart to all the lovely friends, and also strangers who have read and commented on them – after all, a stranger is only a friend you haven't met yet! There are, of course, lots of things I haven't included. I think I need to give it all a rest for a while.

* * *

It seems appropriate to end, for the moment anyway, with these notes about **STORYTELLING**.

I came to it as a defined hobby in the 1990s. I had to give a talk in Armenia about my work as a child psychiatrist, in which I described how I had developed my own therapeutic methods of using stories. At around the same time, I had discovered the friendship of a wonderful group of professional storytellers, notably Richard Berry, Cath Little, and the Cardiff Storytelling Circle.

The Wonderful Therapeutic Power of Storytelling

I will include in this fairy tales, myths, wonder tales, jokes, and many other narratives. They can be old and traditional or freshly minted and written down – but all must be TOLD in some way eventually. The story demands it – and you can't keep a good story down! You must realise that we are all 'telling stories' all the time, we just don't recognise it! We are telling others what we have been doing, incidents, ideas, and longings. When we structure the narratives and the chit-chat of our lives, it becomes a story, long or short, entertaining or boring, happy or sad. As with a 'traditional' story it can be true or completely made up!

So, when we turn to look more closely at the stories we tell others or are told, here's a thing to note. Even when they are about 'other people', the tale and the descriptions have come from our minds, so they are also 'us', whether we like to acknowledge them or not. Like dreams, all the characters in a story can be 'read' as aspects of one person. This applies to the place, atmosphere, animals, objects as well. This is very similar to dreams and cultural stories, which have been described sometimes as 'collective dreaming'. In the same way, all the characters can represent aspects of a whole society; stock types and stereotypical characters are common and this is not accidental.

Structured stories have certain characteristics, almost rules. For example, the 'happy ending', usually a wedding, so often present in fairy tales can stand for the integration of the divided personality, maturity, and individuation, and is a powerful symbol. Worries have been expressed that it 'gives children the wrong idea about marriage', but I think these are misplaced. I could have written much more about this, but others have already done so. Here are just a few – I hope helpful – notes breaking down the practical use of stories, especially traditional wisdom tales and fairy stories. These are some of the reasons why they can be so useful therapeutically, without the recipients even being aware of the medicine, so sweetly it slips down!

1. Making sense: links with cognitive therapy
a) Stories can be used by the listener to make sense of events, crises and emotions. They can create order in disorderly thoughts and messy or unacceptable emotions.
b) By exteriorising the inner life in telling, creating, or listening to a story, trauma and challenge can be more easily understood, digested, and coped with.
c) Order is imposed on disorder, often by an unexpected twist – lateral thinking and unusual solutions can be encouraged by example. It gives us ideas about looking afresh at mundane human problems.
d) General thinking ability is improved by practice, in a pleasurable way.

2. Problem solving
a) Some stories have a clear didactic or teaching role. This is rather frowned on now by some people, but children, and often adults, can find this reassuring, educative and fun, and such material has a useful place in therapy and education (see 9).
b) Encouragement of creativity – Abstract thinking – Lateral thinking – Organising inner material – Negotiating with others – Improving memory by learning to tell.
c) Alternative endings can be imagined and played with creatively.

3. Permitting
By this, I mean that subjects that are often taboo or disapproved of in a culture can be explored in metaphor by a story.

a) This can be enough in itself, or it can lead into actual therapy by someone trained, since forbidden and dark material is given safe, contained expression in an orderly framework.

b) Ambivalence is particularly hard for individuals to cope with. By dividing up the roles in a narrative, there is a timeframe to resolve them. Examples are the division of the good mother (often dead) and the evil stepmother. Feelings of mixed love and jealousy for siblings often find expression during the story by the differing fates of three brothers or sisters.

4. Anxiety management

a) Repetition can lead to desensitisation of painful material. Stories often include stock repetitions, often both by teller and audience.

b) Stories were often accompanied or took place during textile work – sewing, weaving, spinning. These may have had an effect similar to Eye Movement Desensitisation Therapy. This as a whole area in itself, which is very important. I have explored it elsewhere.

c) Some stories have a somewhat bleak, but often reassuring, subliminal message: "That's just the way it is." This can reduce the guilt of imagined responsibility often felt by the hearer about his/her own life. Mothers die. Ogres eat children. Life's like that. Shit happens.

5. Comfort and security

Similar to 4, but very much a function of bedtime stories: to soothe, reassure and induce a warm, safe feeling with which to go to sleep or to face a new situation.

6. Identification and role-playing

a) A very useful way for children to try out all sorts of different ways of being and thinking. A useful exercise is to act a brief traditional play several times with each role in turn, or to rewrite it from the point of view of a minor character or villain. This is especially useful when done as a joint enterprise with the Storyteller and a child, or group of children. It would be very useful with adults too, but it was not so easy to get them to work like this with me.

b) However, adults can certainly enjoy identifying with characters that represent suppressed or unacknowledged parts of themselves in a safely contained way, discussing, acting, or writing about them. Again, villainous and horrible people are necessary in stories, not just to shift the action along, but to explore the dark or shadow side of life.

7. Sharing and cooperating
a) Many stories depend on cooperation, kindness, and compassion for their safe resolution. This is sometimes an open message, sometimes concealed. Sharing and negotiating can be further encouraged by listening to and acting out traditional stories.
b) Those who feel most alienated and have most difficulty cooperating in society would be likely to be strongly affected by this message. They will have seen much – both in personal experience and popular culture – that runs directly counter to it. It could be a particularly useful element of stories on which to focus, indirectly leading to a discussion with adults or children.

8. Confidence building
a) Stories stretch the imagination and often have a message that success can come to the weakest and smallest member of society.
b) By learning to join in, firstly with repetitions, then encouragement to tell, the individual can develop confidence in their speaking out, their unique voice, and their ability to get others to listen. Again, equally important for adults and children.

9. Passing on the culture
a) This has always been an important part of storytelling in oral cultures. It still takes place, not least by the development of urban myths and reworkings of old tales to give them a modern twist.

10. Speaking to the heart
Above all, stories are used for:
Sheer entertainment, passing the time. Fun: sharing laughter and companionship, lightening life, nurturing and caring for others by telling and listening.

The power of stories – images, metaphors, pictures, and branching narratives – are created in the mind. They are part of the ordinary interchanges of everyday life; your story versus my story should result in a creative synthesis, but too often can become a power struggle.

When I used to speak to an audience of health professionals, I would emphasise the following: It is more important that you acknowledge in your hearts the power of stories and recognise that you are using them all the time than that you learn my way of using formal storytelling with patients. I want you to use the ordinary stories in your day to enrich and empower people. My clinical material can only faintly reflect what you can bring.

In the place between the storyteller and the listener, between the singer and the audience, is the 'sacred space'. It is given other names, but it is an essential part of attentive and creative interplay between people. This 'space' is also there between the therapist and the patient. The therapist's words and silences and the attentiveness or even the disinterest apparently shown by the patient, create something new, with much potential. The use of traditional story motifs is a valuable adjunct to cognitive models because the symbols pack a punch beyond their smooth-seeming surface. Jung has shown how a whole story (a narrative) can be condensed into a single scene or symbol, compressing and increasing its power.

So, we must be aware of what we are doing and its potential also for harm, but not be too alarmed by it. Cultures are awash with stories and healthy children pick and choose and are immunised by some exposures, warned by others, and enchanted by many. Those whose experiences in childhood are particularly brutal, in any sense of the word, may have difficulty disentangling themselves from their inner narrative or may use the powers it gives them in unhealthy and destructive ways on others. The use of stories gives them safe spaces in the mind and heart, where they can begin to heal at their own pace.

Finally, here are a few tips to help those who may be less used to telling stories to others, whether individuals or a group.

Firstly, it's FUN! Just do it!! Start with a simple story or something true that happened to you or your family. Don't ever be tempted to read your story out loud instead of telling it. If you are worried, have a few key words written on a little card to check, or do a small drawing, like a map, as a reminder before you start.

Take any opportunity to practice your story on anyone you can capture for a few minutes! If you forget where you are while you are telling the story, don't panic. Say you've got lost and ask the audience to remind you what it was you were just saying. Similarly, if you realise that you forgot to tell your audience some essential piece of information earlier, don't panic. Just say something like, "Oh, I forgot to tell you...." and put it in.

Some of these stories are very well known, but none the worse for that. If a child – or an adult come to that – calls out that they know it, don't worry, get the audience to help you tell it.

HAPPY STORYTELLING – AND LISTENING! We have two ears and one mouth – the proportion for stories is about right – but you will find it hard to stop me!

*   *   *

And we can't really call it THE END –
because how can a Memoir end during life?

Printed in Great Britain
by Amazon